BILLIONAIRE'S SECOND CHANCE

A COMPLETE COLLECTION OF BOOKS 1-3

MOLLY SLOAN

Copyright © 2019 by Molly Sloan

All rights reserved.

No part of this book may be reproduced in any form or by any electronic or mechanical means, including information storage and retrieval systems, without written permission from the author, except for the use of brief quotations in a book review.

ALSO BY MOLLY SLOAN

Free copy of Beholden to You: https://dl.bookfunnel.com/kq1zzfidj4

KEEP IN TOUCH WITH MOLLY SLOAN

GET THE SLOAN EXCLUSIVE
Like Molly
Follow Molly
Email Molly

CONTENTS

Also by Molly Sloan	1
Keep In Touch With Molly Sloan	3
Dedication	8
Acknowledgment	9

BELOVED BY YOU

Chapter One: Touchdown	13
Chapter Two: The Forgotten Goodbye	16
Chapter Three: Driven	22
Chapter Four: All Mines	27
Chapter Five: Digging up the Past	35
Chapter Six: Friends and Butterflies	40
Chapter Seven: Once Bitten, Twice Shy	48
Chapter Eight: That Girl	53
Chapter Nine: Seal the Deal	62
Chapter Ten: Deja Vu	66
Chapter Eleven: Betrayed	69
Chapter Twelve: Coming Together	73
Chapter Thirteen: The Call	79
Chapter Fourteen: X-Ray Vision	83
Chapter Fifteen: The BBC	87
Chapter Sixteen: Goodbyes	90
Chapter Seventeen: Released	94
Chapter Eighteen: City Lights	99
Chapter Nineteen: Collateral Damage	103
Chapter Twenty: Red on the Carpet	108
Chapter Twenty One: Graceful Exit	112
Chapter Twenty Two: Dropped	116
Chapter Twenty Three: The Eyes Have It	123
Epilogue	129

BEGUILED BY YOU

Chapter One: The Wake-Up Call	137
Chapter Two: Do Not Pass Go	140
Chapter Three: Doctor's Orders	144
Chapter Four: Rick-Rolled	148
Chapter Five: Deep in the Heart of Texas	153
Chapter Six: The Gift	158
Chapter Seven: Starting Time	161
Chapter Eight: Essere	167
Chapter Nine: Digging Out the Truth	171
Chapter Ten: Served	177
Chapter Eleven: Presence	180
Chapter Twelve: Dirty Hands	186
Chapter Thirteen: Bucket List	190
Chapter Fourteen: The BBC 2	194
Chapter Fifteen: Torn Between Two Covers	198
Chapter Sixteen: Puttin' on the Ritz	203
Chapter Seventeen: Fool's Gold	208
Chapter Eighteen: Day in Court	211
Chapter Nineteen: Plan B	216
Chapter Twenty: Good Knight	220
Chapter Twenty-One: One Thing I Know For Sure	226
Chapter Twenty-Two: So Close and Yet So Far	230
Chapter Twenty-Three: Hidden	235
Chapter Twenty-Four: Where There's Smoke, There's Fire	239
Chapter Twenty-Five: Revealing	245
Epilogue	252

BETROTHED TO YOU

Chapter One: Dreams	257
Chapter Two: The Best Laid Plans	261
Chapter Three: A Little Yelp from our Friends	265
Chapter Four: The Love of a Good Woman	269
Chapter Five: Players Gotta Play	272
Chapter Six: Small World	276

Chapter Seven: Girl Talk	282
Chapter Eight: Ancient History	286
Chapter Nine: Unforgettable	291
Chapter Ten: The Truth about Money	296
Chapter Eleven: Assumptions	302
Chapter Twelve: Clearing the Air	308
Chapter Thirteen: Hot Water	314
Chapter Fourteen: Photo Finish	320
Chapter Fifteen: Cherries Aren't The Only Things That Blossom In Japan	325
Chapter Sixteen: Kanpai	329
Chapter Seventeen: Mile High	335
Chapter Eighteen: Pun and Games	341
Chapter Nineteen: Surprise Party	344
Chapter Twenty: Sucker Punched	351
Chapter Twenty-One: A Keeper	355
Chapter Twenty-Two: Family Honor	359
Chapter Twenty-Three: The Family Tree	366
Chapter Twenty-Four: Turbulence	372
Epilogue	378
About the Author	385

DEDICATION

To my sweet RSL. Who encourages me everyday to be the change I want to see in the world.

ACKNOWLEDGMENT

To D.A.- You are my champion!

BELOVED BY YOU

CHAPTER ONE: TOUCHDOWN

"Aren't you that model?"

Andrew Atherton pulled off his expensive Hi-Fi headphones and asked, "What did you say?"

The woman seated next to him on the plane repeated herself. "Aren't you that model? The one that used to be on those diamond ads? 'The Face of Atherton' or something?"

He always hated this question. Yes, Andrew had done some modeling for his family's diamond empire when he was in college. His sister Claudia used to tease him and call him The Adonis of Atherton because, evidently, she thought he was good-looking. But, since then, he'd gone on to get his MBA from The London School of Business, and now headed the Acquisitions division of the family business. These days, the only thing Claudia teased him about was the fact that she was the CEO of the company and, technically, his boss.

But the fact was, they were both billionaires. Atherton Diamonds has been the leading diamond manufacturer in the world for more than two hundred years. And, Claudia and Andrew were the only heirs to the business.

Looking back at the woman seated next to him, Andrew

realized that he really didn't want to talk. They had a long thirteen-hour flight ahead of them before landing in Botswana. Andrew just smiled at her and shook his head and said nicely, "I'm sure you must be mistaken." Placing the headphones back over his ears, Andrew reclined his plush First Class seat back to the sleeping position, closed his eyes and began to dream…

"I'm blinded by your hair! All I can see is red!" Andrew laughed as Janet straddled him. Her full breasts were tantalizingly close to his mouth. Her body was lightly dusted with freckles, and it turned him on to think of licking each freckle one a time. "Mmmmmm…come here, you vixen."

The dream fast-forwarded. They were in a pub in London and Janet was angry with him about something. They were fighting.

"All the women keep hitting on you and you just sit there and smile. I think you like all the attention! That's why you became a model." Janet was both crying and angry — something Andrew never understood about women.

"I do not. I just think their come-on lines are funny. Really. Who says, 'Is it hot in here or is it just you?' Not even my roommate Cole says that." But Janet wasn't having it, and the next thing he knew, her red ponytail was swinging as she stormed out of the pub. "Come on, Red!"

The dream changed again. They were in bed in his flat. White sheets tangled around them as sweat ran down his back. Her legs were over his shoulders and they moved in unison. The only sounds were the moans of their lovemaking. Oh, how he loved making love with Janet.

His heart began to pound in his sleep as the dream became his nightmare. The day he came home to find the "Dear John" letter that she was leaving — going back to America. "Don't bother looking me up. I won't take your calls." Andrew had been devastated. Yes, they had problems.

But couples should be able to work through them. How could he live the rest of his life without Janet?

"Ladies and Gentlemen, we are beginning our initial descent into Sir Seretse Khama International Airport. Please place your seat backs and tray tables…"

Andrew awoke with a start. What a terrible dream! Except that it had been real. Gazing out the window as the city lights of Gaborone, Botswana came into view, Andrew reflected on the dark period in his life after Janet broke up with him. "I wonder what ever happened to her?"

"Did you say something?" The woman seated next to him looked overly eager to think Andrew's comments might have been directed at her. Andrew just smiled and shook his head "no" again.

CHAPTER TWO: THE FORGOTTEN
GOODBYE

Janet Girard hated hospitals. One would think that after spending so much time in them that she would have developed some sort of resistance to the feelings that the antiseptic smells, hushed voices, and stern faces in white coats stirred in her, but repeated exposure had only seemed to make her senses keener. The fine hairs on her body notice the shift of energy in the room. Noticed how the mouth of the last nurse that came in to check Gouta's vitals set in a grim line before she made a few notes in her chart and walked out. Noticed how, even as she cuddled her son in close to her side, Gouta struggled with each breath.

Her name meant gold in Setswana, and the day Janet met her, her dark skin had shone like a layer of gold was hidden just beneath the surface. With her bright smile and beaming optimism, no one would have even guessed that she was sick. And her little boy, Oba, wide-eyed and shy, who hid behind her leg when strangers spoke to him…that sweet face. It was almost inevitable that Janet would get attached. She tried so hard not to do that. There were so many kids at A Place of

Grace that she couldn't afford to give a piece of herself away to every child in her keep. Practically every child in the orphanage was there because his or her parents had died of AIDS.

Botswana had once had the unfortunate privilege of having the second-highest human immunodeficiency virus infection rate in the world, with one in three adults infected. This meant that A Place of Grace was filled to capacity and demand for beds was growing by the month.

Things had definitely improved in the fifteen years since she started her humanitarian work in this part of the world. Safe sex practice was taught and was now the norm so fewer new cases were being diagnosed, which gave Janet some hope that there would be fewer boys like Oba. But that really didn't help Oba, did it? Janet shook her head to fight off the tears that threatened to flow.

Her dear friend Gouta was dying. Probably today. And Oba—poor Oba. How does a five-year-old watch his mother die?

"Janet?" Gouta whispered, lifting her oxygen mask away from her face.

"Yes?" Janet stood and wiped her hands on her pant legs. Anxiety had clung to her all day. The end was so close that it felt like another presence in the room. And when she came to stand next to her friend's bed, she could tell that she knew it too.

"Our little king is sleepy, I think."

Janet looked at him and smiled. "I think you're right."

"I'm not tired," Oba said, but it was a half-hearted protest. His eyes drooped as he laid his head back down on the pillow that was propping his head up on the chair. "I am awake."

Janet walked around to the opposite side of the bed and picked up the five-year-old. He wrapped himself around her and nuzzled his head into the crook of her neck. Since Gouta had been sick, Janet spent more and more time with Oba. She was practically a second mother to him at this point.

"Hm. He is so long. Pretty soon he'll be too big to carry that way," Gouta said. Her smile was sad and her eyes went glassy with tears.

"We'll see you tomorrow, yeah?" Janet said, reaching for Gouta's hand and giving it a gentle squeeze.

"Tomorrow," she said, but there was no promise in the word.

Janet shifted the weight of the dozing child in her arms and left the hospital room, ignoring the chill that had passed through her as Gouta's fingers slipped from hers.

It wasn't right. It wasn't fair. Just eight months ago, Gouta had been a beautiful young woman, brimming with potential, and now she was wasting away in a hospital bed from a disease that still had no cure, but was so easily prevented. How many more children have to face this before something is done to stop the crisis? It was absolutely heartbreaking to see.

"Are you hungry?" Janet asked as they crossed the street, Oba's tiny hand in hers. "We can stop and get you something if you're hungry."

"I'm not hungry," Oba said. His voice was solemn. It was almost as if the same wariness clung to him that had bothered Janet when she was sitting next to Gouta's bed in the hospital. He was such a sweet, sensitive boy. He knew what was happening.

"How about some ice cream? I could go for a vanilla cone right now. What about you? Do you want to get—"

"I didn't kiss mama goodbye!" Oba's eyes grew wide in terror as he yanked Janet to a stop in the middle of the crowded sidewalk.

She stroked the back of his hand with her thumb. "It's all right," she said. "Just be sure to give her double the kisses tomorrow."

"No!" he said, snatching his hand free. "I want to go back and kiss mama goodbye!"

Janet squatted down to get at his eye level. "Oba, your mama was very tired and you're very tired. Let's just get back to the—"

"No! I want to kiss mama goodnight!" he shouted defiantly and before Janet could react, he squirmed out of her grasp and took off.

She always forgot how fast little kids were. Oba was small for his age. Janet had at least three feet on him and most of that was legs, but Oba evaded her grasp with frightening ease. With his little legs and arms pumping, he barrelled down the sidewalk, heading back the way they came, heading straight for the intersection.

"Oba!" she shrieked, shoving people out of the way now.

The light had changed and heavy traffic sped through the intersection. Oba stepped off the curb and Janet dove for him. Their bodies collided and she pulled him into her chest and rolled onto her side at the same time, hoping to take the full blow of the fall. With his tiny body tucked against her, momentum rolled them into the intersection. Janet screwed her eyes closed and prayed to a god that she didn't believe in. Brakes screeched all around them and her back was pelted with gravel.

Janet was terrified to open her eyes but she was sure that she felt the heat of an engine block on her shoulder. She just held her breath and crushed the boy against her while chanting. "We're okay, we're okay," into his ear.

"Miss?" A voice called out. "Miss, are you all right?"

Was she all right? Janet did a quick assessment. Her toes wiggled. Her knees still worked. Her right arm felt like it was on fire but that was understandable considering that she had slid on it across rough blacktop, but otherwise, she felt fine.

"Oba?" she said, holding the boy away from her so that she could see his face. There was a gash on his forehead and his eyes looked a bit unfocused. "Oba? Oba, speak to me. Are you okay?"

"My head hurts," he said finally then began to cry.

"Miss, pass me the boy. Let's get the two of you out from under there."

Under?

It was then that Janet looked up and realized that heat she felt on her shoulder was from an engine, they were under a large truck.

"Oh, my god!" She passed Oba to the man and slowly, gingerly, scooted out from underneath the truck. Once she was out, she tried to stand up her head swam and she faltered.

"Whoa! Miss, are you okay? Oh my god. The boy came out of nowhere—"

"I know. He was upset... he ran away from me..." The world started to dim around the edges, but slowly like some was closing heavy theater curtains.

"Miss!"

She was passing out. It wasn't an unfamiliar feeling, but it was a frustrating one. "Oba..." she slurred reaching for the boy. She needed to tell someone where to take him. She had to tell someone who to call. "Call Place of...Place of..."

"I got ya."

Strong arms scooped her up, cradling her against a broad chest. The voice was American and vaguely familiar. Janet looked up to see who had come to her rescue.

"Janet?" the deep, familiar voice with a thick New York accent said.

Her vision was blurry. She must have a head injury. She

blinked once...then twice. The man's face slowly came into view.

She must have a severe concussion because this was the face of a man that she hadn't seen or spoken to in nearly a decade. Yes, she had a severe brain injury. There was a big gash in her head, it was gushing blood. Maybe some of her brains had leaked out on the pavement. That had to be it.

"Janet, it's me."

She frowned. "No...it can't be you."

"Yes, Janet. It's Andrew. Andrew Atherton."

"You've got to be fucking kidding me," Janet said, then promptly passed out.

CHAPTER THREE: DRIVEN

"Where have you been?" Andrew was completely stunned to see Janet standing in front of him. He had just been dreaming about her on the plane!

He'd seen the woman dart out in front of the lead car, with her pale skin and red hair flying out behind her like a flag, and for a second he wondered if he were still dreaming. Of all the trucks to dive in front of, she chose the lead one in his caravan as they made their way through Francistown, heading back to the hotel after spending the day exploring a potential mine site. Part of him was ready to call this divine timing, as if the man upstairs finally decided to answer the pleas he sent up years ago, by throwing her right into his path.

Andrew had spent a lot of money and wasted a lot of time trying to find her when she ran off, seven years ago. It took him four of those years to get over her and then another two to finally admit that he never really would be over her. So, he'd thrown himself into work and a few meaningless romances here and there. But now, here she was. Running out into traffic, sacrificing her life to save a little boy. *Typical Janet*, he thought.

Janet was looking a little woozy and so Andrew decided to wait on the questions until after she was checked out at the local hospital. "Actually, let's get you and the boy to the hospital. Come, get in my car."

Dazed, Janet and the boy hobbled into the back seat of the limo. Andrew was half-expecting her to refuse and to insist on walking. She was stubborn like that.

As the doors closed, the partition that separated the back seat from the front rolled down. "Should I cancel the dinner reservation or do you think we'll make it in time?" Fiona asked.

Fiona Durant was his Personal Assistant—and former lover, but that was insignificant now. She ran his personal and private life like a well-oiled machine and their brief interlude didn't affect her ability to do her job. It's not like they ever loved each other… it was just a relationship of convenience that ended when it became inconvenient.

"Go ahead and cancel, Fi. I'm staying here until I can see Janet and make sure that she's all right."

She raised an inquisitive brow and pivoted away from him as she brought her phone to her ear.

"You do realize that you've done your part, right? You don't have to hang around to wait and see if she's okay. You got her to the hospital. That was chivalrous enough."

"Nah, I'm staying."

Winston Konteh was the head of the African division of Atherton Diamonds and was still in the limo. After Janet and Oba got in, Winston leaned over to Andrew and whispered, "Do you know her?"

"Yeah, that's Janet," Andrew whispered back. Janet and

Oba appeared to be dozing in their seats, so he continued in a low voice.

"Who?"

"Janet! You know—"

"The red-haired minx that ruined your life? That Janet?"

Andrew winced. "She didn't ruin my life exactly—"

"Those were your words, mate. Not mine."

He may have spent one too many nights deep in the bottle, trying to figure out where he had gone so wrong and how he would win her back.

"But what is she doing here anyway?"

"I don't know which is why I need to stay here until—"

"Well, I'm fine," said Janet who was most definitely not sleeping.

"Hey, Red," Andrew said sheepishly.

"Yeah. Not sleeping." She glared at him. "I have a cracking headache."

Damn. Even all scuffed up from the accident and pissed off at him, she was still gorgeous. Her auburn curls were wound into something that looked as if she would have a terrible time detangling. He'd always said she had Disney Princess hair and that hadn't changed. But the African sun had darkened her complexion from its usual New England pale to a peachy tan. It also made the freckles on her nose and cheeks darker and more plentiful. Someone probably got to have a hell of a time counting all of the new ones. *Someone...I wonder who is the lucky guy who gets to lick those freckles now...*

"Hello?" she asked, her tone icy. "After we get to the hospital, feel free to leave. Seems you were in a terrible hurry. Don't change your plans on my account." Fiona turned and nodded triumphantly from the front seat.

"No, I want to stay. Let me give you a ride back to your hotel."

"Oh, I don't need a ride. I'm going to stay at the hospital with Oba."

"Oba?"

"Yes, Oba." She pointed at the sleeping boy next to her.

"Oh! You know him?"

She pushed up her defiant, adorable little chin. "Yes. I know him. We just left this hospital a little over an hour ago after visiting with his very ill mother. She's dying, actually. That's why Oba ran into the street. He wanted to give her one last kiss."

Winston overheard and shook his head sadly as Andrew took a good look at Oba for the first time. The way he curled up so tightly next to Janet told him that they were very close. He could see that Janet was trying to be strong, but soon his façade began to crumble.

Tears filled her eyes as she whispered, "She knew she was dying and we didn't want Oba to witness it. Now we're back here and I have to tell him. I know he already knows, but I have to tell him."

"Oh, Janet..." He placed a hand on her back as she was getting out of the limo and into the wheelchair the nurse had at the curb. "I'm so sorry—"

Janet threw his hand off. "I'm fine." She swiped at tears on her cheeks. "*We* are going to be just fine. We don't need your pity."

"I'm sorry, Janet. If there's anything I can do—"

"Just get back in your SUV and drive out of my life. Let's start there."

As the door slammed shut, Winston clapped a supportive hand on Andrew's shoulder. "It's probably pointless to make a plea for you to keep your head on straight and stay focused on the business of acquiring this mine, right?"

Andrew gave his friend and colleague a stiff nod. As he watched the love of his life and that sweet little boy being wheeled into the hospital he knew one thing for sure. He would never be driven out of her life again.

CHAPTER FOUR: ALL MINES

Janet pulled the blankets up to Oba's chin and backed out of the room as quietly as she could. Ever since his mother's condition deteriorated, Oba had been staying at A Place for Grace. Gouta and Janet both agreed that it would make the inevitable transition much easier. Janet had given him a private room in the wing closest to her cottage. While she didn't want to seem to play favorites, she did tuck a few special things into his room, like a baseball lamp and a matching blanket. The boy loved to play ball.

It had taken hours to get him calmed down after they left the hospital. At five years old, Oba knew death. So many of his friends had lost their parents. Although Gouta had done her best to shield her son from the harsh realities of the HIV crisis, not one soul in Africa was untouched. But no matter how much you understand death, you can never be prepared to lose the comfort of your mother. Especially when you're just a small boy.

"Is he sleeping?" Elyse Green asked.

"Finally," Janet said as she collapsed on the couch,

grimacing when her arm banged against the cushion a little too hard.

Elyse was the youth counselor at A Place for Grace and she was probably the only person who got less sleep than Janet. Caring for the emotional and mental health of kids orphaned by HIV/AIDS was hard work, especially now that their occupancy had doubled due to the increase in children left orphaned.

"You should get some sleep, too," the older woman advised.

"Can't. I'm gonna crash here for a few hours, but I have to be at The Department of Mines at 9:30."

Elyse tsked. "Are they trying to expand the mines into the cemetery again?"

"Yes. There are diamonds out there. They'll eventually find someone with enough money to pay everyone off and proceed to desecrate those graves."

"But nothing has been done since that mine collapse two years ago."

"Of course not. They don't care about how it affects anyone. That's why I need to be there. No one ever talks about how The Department of Mines downplays the negative impact of the mining in Botswana. None of it makes the international news. The impact of mining on natural resources, vegetation, soil, bodies of water, and the human population aren't even recorded. If they did, the mining council would have to actually do something about it!" Janet felt herself getting angry again, and knew she wouldn't be able to sleep.

Janet knew the impact. She fed, clothed and wiped the tears of that very human impact every day.

BELOVED BY YOU

Elyse walked across the room to drape a throw blanket over her.

"You can't save all of Botswana, Red."

Janet grunted in response and threw an arm over her tired eyes.

I might not be able to save all of Botswana, but I'm sure as hell going to try.

At 9:30 am sharp, with little more than a buttered English muffin and strong coffee in her belly, Janet arrived at The Department of Mines, ready to do battle. She was meeting Radhika, A kindred spirit from Francistown who was determined to keep the cemetery intact. Some of Radhika's family members were buried there. She was a sort of community leader and mouthpiece for the indigenous people living in the area.

"Janet, it is so good to see you this morning. I heard about the accident. You are looking well."

Radhika's English was perfect as she strode across the lobby. Her style could best be described as Modern Traditional. Today she wore dark blue trousers with rust orange colored high-heeled boots under them. Because it was a business meeting, Janet supposed, Radhika's normally bold printed top was replaced with a more subdued turquoise blouse. The only compromise was a safari-inspired scarf wrapped around Radhika's long, elegant neck. Next to her, Janet felt frumpy, despite Elyse's assurance that she looked great today.

"I'm fine, Radhika. Come, sit here." The two of them had long since been banned from the inner offices, but they had no problem sitting quietly in the lobby to wait for Mykel Batou, Director of Banking and Economic Development to escort whatever CEO he was buttering up today. Today wasn't any different.

The women were catching up when Radhika's phone

rang. She whispered, "I need to take this," and Janet could hear the clicking of her boots echoing through the lobby as she walked to a private area to take the call.

Resting her eyes for a moment, and now that the adrenaline and fatigue had worn off from the the previous day, Janet couldn't help but think of Andrew Atherton. His was the last face she expected to see in Botswana.

Last she heard Andrew had become the face of Atherton Diamonds. He had dabbled in modeling in college - mostly holiday ads for his parents, but when they graduated, he started modeling full-time for Atherton. In those days, Janet couldn't walk two blocks without seeing his steel blue eyes staring out at her from the side of a bus, or in storefront windows. Then there were the fashion shows and industry parties, and suddenly he was a part of the crowd that they loathed. The rich, beautiful and unaffected. A crowd she was born into, but never seemed to fit in.

Andrew's and Janet's families had different missions in life. The Athertons were diamond miners — the very industry that was threatening the indigenous people Janet was here to protect. And Janet was the descendant of Stephen Girard, the wealthy philanthropist who'd donated his fortune to the education and welfare of orphans.

At first, Andrew and Janet's relationship was built on his rebellion from the family business. To him, modeling was a way to mock the family business. Yes, he would be a billionaire, but on his own terms.

But that started to change. The more Andrew rebelled, the harder his family clamped down. And dating a Girard was not part of their plan for him. The more they tightened their grip, the more he dived into the world of modeling and high fashion. Neither of those was Janet's scene, and that's why she left.

That glossy cover model was nothing like the boy she

fell in love with. But he also wasn't the handsome rescuer who had lifted her into his arms last night. With that thick black hair and stubbly rough cheeks, this Andrew looked like some dashing billionaire version of Indiana Jones. He was broader and maybe even a little bit taller than the Andrew she knew. And damn sexy. She knew this from experience.

With Radhika still on the phone, Janet's mind continued to wander. What purpose could Andrew possibly have in Botswana? He must be on holiday. Maybe he bought one of those safari vacation packages that they are always pushing at the airport and hotel. Or a big game hunt, or whatever the ridiculously rich did when they came to Africa.

Either way, it was none of her concern. If last night was any indication, she would stay out of his way.

Janet was startled out of her reverie when she heard, "Here they come!" Radhika was elbowing Janet to get her attention.

They both stood and rushed to the other side of the the marble-floored lobby.

"Dumela, Mykel!" Radhika called out loudly. "And good morning to you!"

Mykel Batou sucked his teeth as he muttered to the man walking with him. "Pay no mind to these women…"

"Is this the businessman who wants to buy the land near the cemetery?"

"Cemetery? What cemetery?" the tall dark-skinned man with Mykel asked.

"Oh, he didn't tell you?" Janet asked. "So you don't know that where you want to dig is protected ancestral land? Or that there are tributaries on that land that feed into the Tati River? Or that building a mine there would destroy local vegetation, poison a water source and displace the people and the animals-"

MOLLY SLOAN

"Is this true?" the man asked, looking at Mykel with a shocked expression on his face.

Janet squinted at him. He looked familiar. Where had she seen him before?

"Mr. Konteh, I assure you that The Department of Mines makes every effort to minimize exploitation-"

"Of the socio-economic and financial integrity during the the extraction and processing of precious minerals," Janet interrupted while rolling her eyes. "You're getting really good at that. Too bad you don't put some of that effort into safeguarding the health of your employees and minimizing the..."

Janet's words of protest died in her throat as another man strode up to the small group, piercing her with his steel blue eyes.

At the same time, each exclaimed, "Janet?" "Andrew?"

Andrew's brow furrowed and a nervous smile twitched at the corners of his mouth. "What are you doing here?"

"You know this woman?" Mykel asked.

Andrew's gaze traveled from her eyes and raked down the length of her body. Her eyes were blazing in anger, and her red curls looked like fire escaping from her head. He could almost feel the heat coming from her and was transfixed for a moment.

"Yeah," he said finally. "I know her."

"Well, maybe you can convince her to stop delaying or impeding progress on every mining permit that comes across my desk. You gentlemen have a great day. I'll be in touch." He strode away indignantly, leaving the rest of them staring at each other in the lobby.

"We have over fifteen hundred names on this petition!" Radhika shouted after him. "We will bring legal action if necessary!"

"Legal action" Andrew echoed, alarmed. 'What is all of this about, Red?"

"So that's why you're here? You're here to build a fucking mine?" Janet asked. "Are you here to dig up graves to get some damn diamonds?"

Andrew turned to his colleague, with his eyebrows raised, expecting an explanation.

Suddenly Janet recognized him. It was the man from the limo! Andrew's colleague.

"Don't look at me," the man said. "We were in the same meeting. I know as much as you do."

Andrew moved in close to Janet and dropped his voice. "If you know something, I need you to tell me, Red."

He was standing close enough for Janet to smell the hot cinnamon gum on his breath he liked to chew, and she could smell his sweat mingling with a clean, tangy citrus. It was a familiar scent that caused every nerve ending in her body to tingle. Oh, she remembered his spicy taste…

Janet clenched her teeth and attempted to steel herself before she looked up at him. "Where did he take you on your tour? To the gold mine? And then to some barren land full of scrub brush and told you that's where you're mine would be, right?"

"Are you implying that he showed us land that wasn't for sale?" Andrew's colleague asked.

"What's your name?"

"Winston Konteh," he said and his accent had a bit of Jamaican in it.

"Well, Mr. Konteh, that's exactly what I'm saying to you."

"How is that legal?" Winston was perplexed.

"It's not illegal. No money has been exchanged. At this point, it's all just talk." Janet could barely contain her anger.

Andrew turned and glared in the direction of Mykel Batou's office. Janet knew him well enough to know he was furious. No one tried to pull one over on Andrew Atherton. No one.

She could tell that he was debating whether he should stalk down the hall and give Mykel a beating. But instead, he looked at her and said, "Take me to the actual site for the new mine."

He then turned on his heels and strode past his waiting limo toward Janet's beat up old Land Rover.

CHAPTER FIVE: DIGGING UP THE PAST

Andrew seethed quietly as he rode in the passenger side of Janet's beat up old Land Cruiser to the real mining sites that he had flown halfway around the world to buy. He hated the fact that someone had attempted to con the big, dumb American for a fool. It was shit like this that made him reluctant to join the family business in the first place.

People had been surprised when his father named his sister Claudia as his successor. She wore the mantle of CEO and President of Atherton Diamonds well. It suited her, but the family business had never fit him. At least not until he was able to mold and carve his position into something he could stand doing every day. But that meant he had to try twice as hard to get everything right and this could have been a mistake that cost him billions of dollars.

That's billions with B.

The thought of it almost made him want to vomit.

"So this is what you're doing now? Prospecting for Atherton Diamonds?" Janet asked.

Andrew bristled. He wanted to have a serious conversation and he could sense that this could go sideways and he didn't want that to happen with Winston and Radhika in the backseat.

"Yeah," he answered finally. "When dad retired I had to step up and take a larger role. I couldn't stand the idea of being chained to a desk so I created a job that lets me work in the field."

She looked at him. Her light brown eyes caught the sunlight he was reminded of a weekend the spent at her family's home in the Hamptons. How he had spent the day kissing every inch of her on that private beach.

"What happened to the modeling?" she asked, a sardonic smile twitching at the corners of her mouth.

"I gave that up years ago. People didn't take me seriously. I got tired of being treated like an empty-headed pretty boy."

Janet scoffed. "Well, I'm glad that worked out for you," she said, though her tone said she was anything but.

"What about you? Have you been in Botswana all this time?"

She shifted her attention back to the road. "No. I spent some time in South America and Southeast Asia, but...Botswana has my heart. I volunteered here and decided that I wanted to open up orphanage here. Now I have three."

"Wow." There was really nothing more he could say about that. Janet had always been the nurturing type and had never met a worthy cause that she wouldn't get behind. "You really did it, huh?"

"Yeah, I really did."

They were outside of the city now and driving through one of the townships that skirted Francistown. The views were what one would expect to see in Africa with its sweeping landscapes and a sky so blue that it felt low enough that Andrew could reach up and touch it if he tried. In the distance, he could see a cemetery come into view. Janet pulled off the road and parked under the shade of some trees. The four of them got out, but Winston tapped him on the shoulder to get his attention.

"I want to go on record as saying that I'm not okay with desecrating graves. This kinda thing always comes back on you somehow."

"Comes back on you? What are you talking about? Karma?"

"Karma, payback, haunting, superstition, whatever you want to call it. I don't mess around with this kinda shit."

"Hm. I never took you for the superstitious type."

"Call me superstitious, but I don't mess around with shit like this," Winston repeated. "And you shouldn't either."

"Are you coming?" Janet called out from where she stood in the middle of the road. She looked adorable, like one of those girls that backpacked through Europe in her utilitarian pants, boots, and a t-shirt that looked soft and well worn. Radhika looked very out of place in this environment, but she was just as passionate as Janet about protecting the gravesite, so she kept up with Janet.

Winston tsked and fell in step alongside Andrew. Nodding his head toward Janet, Winston said, "Still say you need to keep away from that one, too, but you ain't listening."

"Nope. Not a chance."

They followed Janet through the cemetery skirting the graves. Andrew stayed close to and listened intently as she explained the customs of the Batswana people.

"Their an ancestral people meaning that the elderly and the deceased are revered. Most are Christian but still practice cultural rituals. they believe that the souls of the ancestors are close to them, close enough to hear their prayers and carry them to god."

"Modimo," Winston said, surprising Andrew.

"That's right," she said. "Modimo is a Supreme being. A

creator and a director but he's not the sort of god that has time to intervene in the lives of the people who worship him."

"How do they...interact with these ancestors? Is there some sort of ceremony involved?"

"Ritual ceremonies occur around all of the major milestones of life; birth, death, coming of age. But they are also part of their everyday life so they talk to them daily."

"Hm. I can see why desecrating a cemetery would be disrespectful. Not that there is ever a respectful way to desecrate human remains, but…"

They arrived at the edge of the cemetery. The stand of trees continued for a few yards, but soon they were in the relentless midday sun. Andrew looked over at her and instantly began to worry about her fair skin. He moved a bit closer to her, positioning himself so that he stood between her and the sun, allowing her to walk in his shadow. She looked up at him. A strange expression came over her face.

"So what about this legal action?"

Radhika answered quickly. "The Department of Mines has offered a payout for the families that agree to have their relatives exhumed. But they won't pay up until all three-hundred and fifty families who have relatives buried here agree to accept it."

"I can imagine that has caused some discord in the community and within families as well," Winston said.

"Yeah, it would be a hard sell to get everyone to agree to exhume an entire cemetery."

"It definitely has caused problems in the community. And the worst part is that they don't even need to do it" Janet said as she tipped her chin toward a plot of land about three hundred yards away that was marked off with orange flags. "There's the mining site."

"But there's nothing else out there. There are ways to approach this dig without touching this cemetery,"

"Precisely, right. But they want to to go through the cemetery because digging there would be easier and they wouldn't have to build any roads."

"Is that what it's all about? Roads."

"No, it's really about money. The Department of Mines will always take the highest bidder, but will cut corners and do it as cheaply as possible."

Andrew had a look of contempt on his face as he folded his arms over his chest. "So how do I make this work? How do I get this mine and escape this corruption."

She sighed. "That's going to take a while to explain."

Walking a few steps ahead of Winston and Radhika, Andrew replied. "Okay, let me take you out to dinner so that we can talk about it. There has to be a middle ground and you seem like you're the person I need to talk to in order to make that happen."

Janet looked up at him warily. She wasn't the naïve type. Andrew could tell that she knew that dinner to discuss the mine was just a pretext to get her alone. But he also knew that this issue was something she felt passionate about and hoped that it would override whatever wariness she felt about being alone with him.

After looking him up and down skeptically, Janet said, "Fine. I'll drop you back at your limo and you can meet me at Lila's Bistro at seven," she said then pivoted away from him to head back to the car. Andrew fell in step behind her unable to suppress his smile.

CHAPTER SIX: FRIENDS AND BUTTERFLIES

Stepping into the shower, Janet could hardly believe that she agreed to have dinner with Andrew. *What was I thinking? We could have discussed the mine on the phone. Or in my office at least. This is a very, very bad idea.*

Yet, the entire time she was in the shower, Janet wasn't thinking about work. No cemeteries, no corruption, not even the orphanage. The warm soapy water running over her body as she washed reminded her of Andrew's hands. Those big, strong hands running over every curve of her body... exploring her dark places... No, her excitement over dinner was not for business. It was purely for pleasure.

As she was getting dressed, she tried to shake some sense into herself. "No, it's a business dinner. That's all. I need to make sure he doesn't get caught up in the corruption. That's what any decent person would do for an old friend."

Andrew really was a good friend, too. She'd forgotten how much care and consideration he instinctively gave her-like walking next to her at just the right distance to keep the harsh, midday sun off of her face. Or how he listened intently to her thoughts and opinions and trusted them-trusted her. It had been a long time since she had a conversation with a man where she was treated with intelligence and respect instead of being treated like a meddling woman sent to inconvenience them.

In short, being around Andrew felt good and Janet denied herself of so many things that indulging in this one seemed harmless.

Grabbing her purse and keys, she stopped to kiss Oba goodnight. His little brown eyes were sleepy as he said, "You look pretty. Where are you going?"

"I'll be back soon, little king. I am just having dinner with a friend."

Lila's was within walking distance from Janet's place, and it was a lovely evening for a stroll, so she left the Land Cruiser at home. Janet had donned one of her three dresses - the one in forest green, and paired it with gold sandals, and some gold earrings she'd bought from a street vendor. Also, for the first time in a long time, she let her hair down. While her outfit wasn't 5th Avenue chic, she felt like she cleaned up nice, which was affirmed when she and Andrew locked eyes as she entered the bistro.

He stood to greet her, a slow appreciative smile spread across his lips. "Janet, you look great."

"Thank you…"

They fumbled through an awkward greeting-Andrew went in for a kiss and Janet thought they might hug which ended in a combination of both that made Andrew blush hard.

"Sorry, about that," he mumbled as he pulled out her chair.

"It's fine," she said tucking behind her ears, realizing that her face was probably beet red, too. She grinned and shook her head. "Why does this feel so awkward?"

"I ordered us a bottle of wine. Do you still drink chardonnay?"

Janet didn't want to let on that she hadn't been to dinner with a man in nearly three years, so she smiled and said, "Of course."

Andrew poured her a taste, and she nodded, and then he filled her glass before filling his own.

After a few minutes, the awkwardness subsided and they fell back into the comfortable repartee from years ago. They caught up while they drank the first glass and surveyed the menu. Janet told him about her time in Southeast Asia where she had lived for several years after she left New York.

"I just needed to get away, you know? Far away from anything that looked or felt familiar or reminded me of home and-" She stopped short of saying what she was really running away from.

"Anything that reminded you of me," Andrew finished for her.

Janet didn't answer, but she really didn't need to; they both knew that what he said was true. "Either way, I needed to get away. I found myself and my real purpose when I left New York. I don't think I would have if I had stayed."

"How ironic. You found yourself during those years and I lost myself in ways I would have never predicted."

"Are you talking about the modeling and working with Atherton Diamonds? It seemed like you liked it."

"Hm." He drained his glass and took a moment to gather his thoughts while refilling it and topping hers off. "To be honest, I don't know if I liked modeling all that much. I did like the attention that came with it," he said honestly.

Janet always knew that was true, but it felt good to have that affirmed.

"Red…" He reached across the table and cover her hand with his. She looked up at him; met his earnest eyes. "I didn't treat you right in those last few days. you were right to leave the way you did. I just wish..."

Janet flipped her hand palm side up and laced her fingers through his. "I know what you mean." She stroked her thumb along his, a small, sad smile graced her lips. "For months after I left, I hoped you would just show up, engagement ring in hand, and an apology on your lips."

Andrew frowned, confused. "But no one knew where you were-"

"I didn't say the daydream made any sense," she said with a laugh. I just always hoped that you would come find and me and rescue me from myself and then you show up here."

"To be clear, I didn't rescue you. If anything, you rescued me. I almost killed you and that boy."

"But you're here. Of all the diamond mining sites in all of the world, you end up in Francistown. It could have been anywhere, but you're here." She gave his hand an affectionate squeeze. "You're here."

It seemed improbable that years of hurt could be washed away with a simple exchange but Janet felt that some of it had.

They ate and drank another bottle of wine. As the evening progressed, their chairs moved closer and the smiles came easier until finally, it was time to pay the bill. Andrew paid the tab end offered to walk her home.

"So you live at the orphanage?" he asked.

They were on the sidewalk outside of the restaurant, Andrew maneuvered her to the inside, away from the street and tentatively took her hand.

"Yeah, I have a little cottage out back. It's cheaper and I'm still renovating and working out the particulars with this one. It presents a different range of problems. Sickness, war, displacement, all of that is at work here. It's a puzzle that is hard to solve, but I think that I'm getting close to a solution."

MOLLY SLOAN

"And mining plays a big part in that."

"It does." She nodded but was reluctant to dig deeper. The night was so good. she didn't want to darken it with all the negative bits she fought to overcome every day. But on the other hand, he did ask her to dinner under the pretense of learning the particulars about the mining site. "What we really need is a mining company that makes a true effort to integrate into the community. The Department of Mines is supposed to facilitate that, but as I've explained they aren't too keen on doing that. In a perfect world, a portion of your proceeds would be invested into hospitals, schools, and the like."

"Are you receiving any funding from the local mines?"

"We had a little something going for a year or so with the company that runs the gold mine, but that fell through."

"So, how are you funding everything?"

"The Girard Foundation carries most of the weight, but my mother is always finding ways and reasons to make that difficult. I have a few really phenomenal brand ambassadors that raise money and collect shoes and clothing. We do all right, but we could always use more funding. "

Janet and Andrew were nearing the orphanage, and she found herself instinctively slowing down. She wasn't ready for the night to end.

"The site by the cemetery...its part of a land parcel that they have been trying to acquire for years now. I've helped in the fight to keep them from acquiring via imminent domain, but it's a struggle when so many people would benefit from the payout. Not only that...there aren't any other cemeteries close to here. It would leave families without a place to lay their dead."

"Like that boy...the one you saved."

"Oba?"

"Yes, Oba. What's his story?"

"His mother's name was Gouta. We spent most of that day visiting his mother in the hospital. She's succumbing to the final stages and symptoms of AIDS. It's any day now, actually. Gouta came to us over a year ago. No family, no support system and a tiny boy to take care of. She signed over custody, but we allowed him to stay on with her while she was still well enough. She wanted him to have a home when she left this earth. Just recently, we moved him into A Place for Grace so that he wouldn't have to deal with the double trauma of losing his mother and his home."

"Wow," Andrew said simply. "I can't even imagine."

"Anyway. I have a soft spot for that kid. I try really hard not to get attached, but there's something about this little boy."

"He's pretty cute, so that's totally understandable. Will his mother be buried in that cemetery?"

Janet nodded. "More than likely, yes. We're gathering the funds to give her a proper burial now."

"I'd like to contribute," he said. "In any way I can. How is Oba doing?"

Janet shook her head. "Not great. But we're doing what we can to help him grieve. I know from experience that the funeral is going to be the hardest part for him."

He squeezed her hand. "He's lucky to have you to help him through this."

"I hope I'm enough," she said. "Sometimes I wonder if I'm doing the right thing with the little ones like Oba."

"Have you ever thought about adopting any of them?"

"I have, but not right now. Maybe when I'm a little older and a little more settled. I want to be able to give a kid a real family. Most of them have already gone through so much before they even get here, that I don't want to add more problems."

"I don't know, Red. You've always been a nurturing soul. I think you will make a great mother."

She looked up at him and smiled. "Thank you for saying that."

"It's the truth," he said with a shrug.

"Well, here we are," she said. Janet turned to face him at the foot of the orphanage's stairs and was surprised to find that she wasn't ready to say goodnight. "Do you want to come in for a cup of coffee or tea? The kids are probably getting ready for bed, but I could give you a tour."

"Can I take a raincheck?" he asked. "I want to get back to my hotel and talk to Claudia about all of this. She's establishing a relationship with a friend of ours that's an investor and I want to see how much of this we can make happen."

"Right. Of course," she said with a nod. "Actually...I have a new group of volunteers coming in tomorrow to help paint some newly renovated rooms and set up bunks and bureaus for the kids. One of them is actually an old friend of mine - a magazine publisher who is doing a write-up on A Place for Grace. Why don't you stop by then?"

"An old friend, huh? Do I need to bring my boxing gloves?" Andrew smiled.

"Hahaha, no, it's a woman. Nicole."

"Oh, okay then. I'll definitely be there. Is it alright if I bring Winston along?"

"Sure. We need all of the help we can get."

"Okay, then. It's a date." Andrew smiled at Janet. "We had a good time tonight," he said. It wasn't a question. It was a statement. A statement that she couldn't help but agree with.

"Yes, we did," she said with a smile.

"I don't want to fumble my way through a goodbye that will probably be as awkward as our hello so, I'll settle for this."

He brought the hand that he was holding to his lips and

gave each of her knuckles a sweet kiss. It shouldn't have affected her, but those sweet kisses sent a thrill through her as if he'd brushed his lips across her lips instead of the back of her hand.

"Goodnight, Janet."

"Goodnight, Andrew." With warm cheeks and belly full of butterflies, she went inside.

CHAPTER SEVEN: ONCE BITTEN, TWICE SHY

"So how are things going over there?" Claudia asked.

Andrew had spent several hours "working" (really daydreaming about his dinner with Janet) when he suddenly remembered that New York was seven hours behind Francistown. Luckily, it was early evening in New York and Andrew had caught his sister just as she came in from the office.

"Things are going pretty well. Winston and I toured a couple of mining sites in the area and we've narrowed it down to one of two." For some reason, Andrew didn't want to mention the issue with the Department of Mines just yet.

"Wow, that was fast. But that's good. Real good."

"How're things going with Cole?"

Cole had been Andrew's roommate in college and was actually Claudia's fiancé. But Andrew wasn't referring to their personal relationship. Cole was also deciding on whether or not to invest in Atherton Diamonds, and without the infusion of his capital, it would be very difficult for Atherton to purchase one mine, let alone buy the land around it. In other words, Cole's decision to invest in the company would make or break this deal.

"He's a bit..." Claudia paused for a moment. "Unconventional," she said finally. "But I guess things are going all right."

Andrew nodded. "Good, good. You know how you guys are. Just keep working on him." Then casually, ever so casually, Andrew mentioned, "Hey, you'll never guess who I ran into over here."

Claudia sounded confused and slightly suspicious of her brother's overly casual tone. "Ran into? It's Botswana. Who could you have possibly run into in Botswana?"

"Janet."

"Janet?" Claudia sounded shocked.

"Yep." Andrew could practically see the look on his sister's face right now.

"Janet Girard?"

"Yeah, she lives here in Botswana. She runs an orphanage out here."

Claudia groaned. "Of course she does. So did you let her have it? Did you demand to know why she disappeared without a word?" She sounded angry, but then again, she also watched her brother fall apart from the heartbreak.

"No, I didn't let her have it. But I did take her out to dinner and apologize for how I treated her."

"*You* apologized to *her*? What for? She left you! You were a wreck when she left. You got a DUI, you were splattered across all of the gossip blogs and tabloids-"

"Yes, I was a wreck, but she was right to leave. I turned into one of those rich dirtbags and I lost sight of the things that were important to me. Janet was one of those things."

"Sounds like a convenient excuse if you ask me. So, what

did you talk about? Are you going to adopt an orphan or something?" Claudia still had a tone, but it was softening.

"She actually knows a lot about how things work over here." He broke into an amused smile. "She actually showed up at the Department of Mines to confront the officials and revealed some unethical practices-"

"Wait. She's involved in this mining deal?"

"Only peripherally. The site we're most interested in is near a cemetery. Department of Mines wants to pay all of the families and exhume the bodies-"

"That's awful."

"Yeah, you have no idea. But I think that if we put our heads together, we can come up with a way for us to purchase the mining site, keep the cemetery intact, and make a positive impact on the surrounding provinces. But we're going to need a lot more money, so see if you can't patch things up with Cole along as quickly as possible."

Claudia rolled her eyes again. "You say that as if you think I'm hindering this process in some way."

"Well...I didn't mean it that way at all. Defensive much? "Andrew smiled because this was the way he and his sister talked. They were always honest with each other.

"He's just...unconventional, but I will try to move things along."

"Good. I'll send you the details as soon as we get it all down on paper."

"I'll keep an eye out for it. One other thing...Andrew?"

"Yeah, sis?"

"Just...be careful. It sounds like you and Janet have come to some sort of understanding, but be careful. Once bitten, twice shy and all of that."

"Okay, sis. I will."

The next morning during a long hard run on the treadmill in the hotel gym, Andrew considered the fact that both his sister and his good friend Winston had warned him against getting tangled up with Janet again. *Who knows? Maybe they are right. Maybe she'll run off again and break my heart.*

But Janet seemed different to that temperamental redhead he knew in college. She seemed centered and more mature. Andrew knew that he had matured a lot in the years they spent apart. He was ready to settle down and start a family.

Pulling on his jeans he couldn't help but laugh at that thought. "Who would have ever imagined me, Andrew Atherton, thinking of settling down and getting married…"

Walking into the hotel restaurant, Winston and Fiona were already at the table. They were having breakfast to go over the specifics for the mine purchase.

Moving the salt and pepper shakers aside, Winston unrolled a map. "I got this from the girl at the front desk. It's completely different than the one the official gave us yesterday."

"Wait…you've already been to the Department of Mines this morning?"

"No…" Winston said with a sly smile. "She delivered it yesterday evening."

"I see," Andrew said with a knowing raise of his brows.

"Anyway, can we get our minds back on our business?" Fiona complained.

"Right, so this is the parcel of land they want to sell us and here's the cemetery," Winston pointed out. "But there's also this adjacent parcel over here."

"Yeah, Janet mentioned that. She said that we would have to buy both in order to leave the cemetery untouched."

"And you think the Department of Mines would allow that?" Fiona asked. "They went out of their way to hide the fact that they planned to exhume those bodies and raze the cemetery."

"True," Winston agreed. 'And what about the families? The ones who want to exhume for the money? Are we going to pay them off?"

"No...that wouldn't make sense fiscally. Besides, isn't it their job to make sure they hire from within the community?" Andrew asked.

"I've looked into it, but I haven't been able to find any community initiatives," Fiona said after taking a sip of her coffee. "They only seem to hire unskilled workers locally and don't do much locally to get the people in the neighboring provinces more training."

"But can't we make that our focus? When we open the mine? Just because things have always been done this way doesn't mean it is the only way to get things done," Andrew said.

Winston nodded. "You're right."

Fiona gathered up her things. "I'll get started on the necessary paperwork," she said as she stood up. "Oh! I saw that you blocked out most of the morning with a visit to A Place for Grace. Do you need me for that or…?"

"No. I'm volunteering a few of hours to help Janet and her staff set up some bunks and stuff. I could use your help, Winston. If you don't have anything planned."

"You mean like manual labor?" Winston asked for clarification.

'Yeah. Have you suddenly became too precious to get your hands dirty?"

Winston scoffed. "What time are we leaving?"

CHAPTER EIGHT: THAT GIRL

Janet's morning started even earlier than usual. The delivery trucks were coming at 7:00 am to drop off boxes containing fifty new bunk beds and bureaus. And, before they could be assembled, there were three newly renovated rooms that needed a fresh coat of paint. Janet and Elyse had moved all of the furniture out of the rooms the day before, but there was still a lot to do before the trucks arrived. And the ten volunteers - twelve with Andrew and Winston - were due to arrive at 6:45 am.

She didn't run A Place for Grace like most of the orphanages she had volunteered at over the years; meaning she didn't have a constant stream of volunteers. While it was nice to have the help, her main goal was to maintain consistency and stability for the kids at Grace and that was hard to do with a constant stream of volunteers coming and going. However, it was difficult to get things done without the free and steady support - even with The Girard Foundation footing most of the bill. Her mother was constantly tightening those purse strings as if Janet's requests were frivolous.

That's why Janet's best friend from New York had flown

into volunteer. Not only was Nicole Burns Janet's oldest friend, she was also the head of Straw Barn Publishing. She was here to do a profile on A Place for Grace that would appear in several of Straw Barn's publications. There would be magazine and newspaper coverage, as well as a YouTube documentary. The idea was that generating publicity would help raise awareness - and funds. Plus, Janet and Nicole hadn't seen each other in a couple of years, and it was definitely time for a reunion. Even if it did mean assembling furniture as an excuse to get together.

The dining hall was packed with kids gobbling down their breakfasts before heading off to school. The clang of metal utensils and boisterous voices of the children were some of Janet's favorite sounds on the planet. Happy, normal children sounds.

Except there was one sad-looking little boy sitting alone at the end of a long wooden table. It was Oba, and he was pushing some scrambled eggs around on his plate with a fork. Janet grabbed a bowl of cornflakes and a banana. She took them and her coffee over to sit down beside him.

"Good morning, little king," she said cheerily as she peeled the banana and sliced half of it into her bowl before giving Oba the other half. He pushed his plate away and nibbled on it and at this point, seeing him eat half of a banana was almost as good as a smile.

"Do I have to go to school today?" he asked.

"Of course! All little kings need schooling so that they can become wise, big kings. What's wrong?"

"I miss mama." Oba's eyes brimmed with tears.

"Oh, honey. I know you do. But if you go to school you might just forget how much you miss her...just for a little while."

"Can't I stay with you? Just for today, I promise. I won't be in the way. Tomorrow I will go back to school and be happy. Just one day. Please?"

Janet couldn't resist his little face.

"I know you're sad, Oba, but going to school might be just the thing to not be sad for a little while."

"I know, but...can't I just stay here?" He put down the half-finished banana and leaned against her.

"Okay, Oba. You can stay today, but you're going to have to help me. I have lots of hard work to do."

"Don't worry, Oba," said a familiar deep voice. "We'll help you with some of that hard work."

Janet looked up to see Andrew standing over her. The smile that spread across her face was bright and involuntary.

"But you're gonna have to use your muscles," Winston said before flexing his biceps. "My mate Andrew and I don't hang around with slackers. You're gonna have to pull your weight. All right, Oba?"

Oba sat up straight and proud as if to show he were a man, too. He nodded. "Alright."

"I can't believe how good it is to see you again!" Janet hugged Nicole tightly.

Nicole's bouncy blond curls swung as she shook her head from side to side. "I can't believe you aren't aging. What is in this African water? And where can I get some?" Nicole laughed.

"I'm glad you brought your camera and notepad. I can't tell you how much I appreciate you being here to help. It's not really a big thing - just some furniture. But bringing attention to A Place for Grace will help shine a light on how many kids are in need over here."

"Well, I'm here to help, too. Don't be fooled by this dainty exterior. I'm like one of those mints in a can. I'm 'curiously strong'" Nicole flexed her non-existent biceps at that statement as Janet laughed.

Elyse and Janet conducted a brief orientation and they split up the group: some to paint the newly-renovated rooms and the rest to assemble the bunks and bureaus. Winston and Andrew ended up in Janet's group. Together they unloaded the truck full of flat-packed furniture. Oba helped them tear into the boxes and kept track of all of the screws, washers and lug nuts.

It was fun for Janet to work shoulder to shoulder with Andrew again. It reminded her of those summers when they volunteered for Habitat for Humanity.

By lunchtime, they had seventeen of the bunks assembled and just about the same amount of bureaus stood between them. Getting those put together was a little bit slower because it was a two-man job.

Janet invited Winston and Andrew back to the cottage for lunch. She'd invited Nicole, too, but she wanted to take some notes while the morning was still fresh in her mind. Winston begged off too - apparently, he had a lunch date. So it was Andrew, Oba, and Janet in the kitchen of her tiny, two bedroom cottage.

Andrew was sweaty. His dark curls clung to his forehead and the nape of his neck. Janet grabbed two bottles of water while she made the sandwiches, and gave them to Andrew and Oba.

"Thank you," he murmured before twisting off the top and drinking the whole bottle in one swig.

Oba's big brown eyes watched Andrew, and then he parroted, "Thank you," and opened the top of the bottle before trying to drink the whole thing like Andrew had.

Unfortunately, his five-year-old throat was too small, and Oba started coughing and sputtering water.

It went all over Andrew's white t-shirt, and Oba was terrified that Andrew would be angry. His eyes filled with tears. "I'm sorry I got your shirt wet. I didn't mean it."

"Slow down there, little man," Andrew said with a chuckle as he reached for a dry dish towel to clean off Oba's face and shirt. "It's not a big deal at all. Shirts can be replaced. People cannot."

With that, Andrew grabbed the bottom of his wet t-shirt and pulled it over his head, revealing the rippled muscles that Janet remembered so well.

Janet's cheeks flushed bright pink as he used the shirt to mop up a droplet of sweat making its way down the middle of his chest. The man hadn't gained an ounce of fat in a decade. He was as fit as ever.

His eyes met hers and it was clear that he had noticed her noticing. With a roll of her eyes and a slight smile, she took his shirt out onto the porch and left it to dry.

"How about we have a contest to see who can eat the most of their sandwich? But, it's not a race. We don't want any more choking, do we, Oba?"

Oba smiled and picked up one half of his sandwich. With a bite full, Oba said, "I'm going to win!"

Watching Andrew and Oba laughing and talking and eating around her kitchen table warmed Janet's heart. It felt like the most natural thing in the world. The boy she loved and the man she... What did she feel for Andrew? She couldn't help but wonder what it would be like if this were her family.

After their sandwiches of leftover roast beef and thick homemade bread, Oba was declared the winner of the contest.

Janet was secretly impressed that Andrew had gotten Oba to eat his whole sandwich. And her heart was warmed when she saw he'd left a little bite on the plate so that Oba could "win."

Setting a plate of chocolate chip cookies down on the table, Janet asked, "So did you get a chance to talk to your sister?"

"I did. She's on board with buying both parcels as long as I can get the community element without encountering a ton of red tape. Do you know who I contact about that? Any organizers who know exactly what the people need?"

"Of course! I'll get you a list of names."

"While on my run this morning, I thought of some ambassadors I can hook you up with back in London."

"That would be super helpful. Thanks for doing that."

"No need to thank me. You're helping me out so of course, I want to do what I can to help you, too."

Janet smiled at him and for a moment, she allowed herself to think of how it would be if they were truly partners, if they were still together and supporting each other in this way. She's been doing it alone for so long that the thought of having someone help her navigate all of this nearly brought her to tears.

Andrew reached out and touched her arm. "You got real quiet all of a sudden. Are you alright?"

She nodded. "It just feels good to have someone help me without all of the begging. Whenever I need money or funding for A Place for Grace it always requires some level of groveling, even when I go to my mother. It's just refreshing, that's all."

"I'm sorry that you feel so alone in all of this. I wish I could do more."

"You're doing more than enough. And I will thank you

properly with a drink of the alcoholic variety when we're done building all of these bureaus and bunks!"

It took much longer than anticipated to get all of the bunks and bureaus assembled. The kids were asleep and most of the volunteers agreed to head down to the local bar to drink away the aches and pains of the day. As expected, Nicole had some work to do at the hotel and couldn't join them. Janet and Andrew went and bought the first round.

With a few drinks in her and so many hours working closely with him, she felt brave enough to ask the question she'd been dying to ask.

Janet leaned her elbows on the table and looked him in the eye. "Tell me the truth. Were you ever really in love with me?"

His eyes widened with surprise. "What a question!" he said. "Do you really doubt that I did? When I told Claudia that I'd run into you - literally - she proceeded to remind me of the DUI and all the tabloid and gossip drama that I brought on myself in the months after you left."

"Oh, so...all of those drunken antics were because I left? Is that what you're saying? You didn't look all that lonely."

Andrew looked into his glass. "I was. There may have been women in my bed, but I was very lonely." He sighed and leaned his elbows on the table, bringing their faces within inches of each other. "Now, let me ask you the same question. You left without a goodbye or a forwarding address. Did you ever love me?"

"I loved you more than I loved myself. I saw that I was willing to change who I was. To make sacrifices that I would have never considered just to be near you."

"You saw yourself becoming your mother," he said.

"Right." Janet's mother Alexis had always been jealous of

her. Janet never really understood why. Alexis was gorgeous, smart, funny and married to a successful businessman. Why she felt the need to intrude on Janet's life at every turn, play power and guilt trips, and basically make Janet's life difficult was something beyond comprehension.

Alexis had sacrificed everything when she got unexpectedly pregnant and married Janet's father. She'd given up everything that mattered to her, and Janet felt the same thing happening during those years with Andrew. She never wanted to end up bitter and angry like her mother.

"Dad made her give up so many of her career goals. And she resents me for it," Janet said, sighing deeply.

"I would have never done that to you. Your dreams and goals are too important to you — and to the world. To ask you to give up your passion..." Andrew shook his head as if to drive away the thought.

"But..." The tears started to flow down Janet's freckled cheeks.

Andrew tenderly wiped them away, repeating, "I would have *never* done that to you, Red. And I would've never let you do that to yourself."

Ugh. She was that girl. That drunk girl at the bar, and crying while her boyfriend tried to console her. Except she wasn't a girl anymore. She was a grown woman almost in her thirties and he wasn't her boyfriend. *Just a good friend*, she thought, as she closed the distance between them giving him a shy, tentative kiss.

He didn't return the kiss at first. Maybe it was shock, or maybe he wasn't interested, but whatever it was, his hesitance stole her bravado.

"I'm sorry," she murmured as she pulled away. "I shouldn't have-"

"Don't you dare," Andrew all but growled then took her face in both of his hands and kissed her thoroughly.

Oh, god. Now she was that girl kissing her ex-boyfriend in a bar, but she was too electrified to care. Every place on her body that he had ever kissed or touched remembered the feel of his mouth and hands. It was all she could do to stay on her side of the table and not crawl into his lap.

"Damn, Red," he whispered. "We've been drinking. We should not be doing this, but god...I really don't want to stop kissing you." Andrew captured her mouth again. Tongue plunging into her mouth, hot and searching, making her forget that she ever had inhibitions.

"Mmm..." he moaned as he pulled away again. "We're both a little drunk. I should get you home. But I strongly suggest that we resume this again when we're both sober. Let me settle up this bill."

Janet watched him walk toward the bar. She respected the fact that he wanted to revisit this when they were sober and clear-headed. But part of her wished that he wasn't such a gentleman and would take her back to her cottage and make love to her.

CHAPTER NINE: SEAL THE DEAL

He was done for.

Andrew had been reliving that kiss in the bar all night after he dropped her off at the orphanage. He knew that he had done the good and noble thing by taking her home but his body didn't agree. He'd spent a considerable amount of time in the shower trying to alleviate the need that those kisses had inspired. After a hard run and a slow rub and tug, he came to one conclusion:

He was still in love with Janet.

And while that kiss in the bar, the one on the street corner while they waited for the light, and the ones on her doorstep were amazing, he didn't want to take this a step further until he knew they were on the same page.

Ding. It was a text message from Janet. "Good morning, handsome. You up?"

Laughing, he typed back. "Always."

"Last night was amazing. I can't stop smiling."

Andrew was delighted to see that she was happy about the kisses. He was afraid it would be a block of text detailing why it had been a mistake. Instead, here they were flirting.

BELOVED BY YOU

Ding. "I have what you need. You know, what I promised you last night?"

Oh, this was fun. "Is that so? When can I have it?"

He laughed when she texted back the names and contact information of the community leaders he could talk to. He forwarded that one part to Fiona. Carefully.

"Will I see you later, Red?"

"I hope so. Can you come by after your morning meeting?"

"I wouldn't miss it for the world."

Andrew, Winston, and Fiona had a meeting at the Department of Mines at 9:00 am. Fiona had the paperwork squared away and they were going over the documents before a 9:30 with Mykel Batou. He was still unsure about Cole and the financing, but he had to keep things moving forward.

In the car on the way there, Andrew's phone rang. It was Claudia's ringtone.

"Sis'? Is everything okay? It's late over there."

"Yes! Everything is okay. Better than okay." Claudia's normally composed demeanor was replaced with an almost giddy flush to her voice. "We have the financing. Cole signed the investment papers tonight!"

Andrew did a fist pump. "Yes! Way to go Claudia. He won't be sorry. This investment is going to pay off. Not only in terms of money, but in helping a community that really needs it. Thank you so much."

"Now, you go seal the deal at the Department of Mines."

Cole and Claudia had worked out the investment end of things in New York. All systems were a go. The meeting was just a formality.

Fiona was waiting in the lobby of The Department of Mines with the paperwork in-hand and a cup of coffee for Andrew.

"I heard you had quite the night. I figured that you may need this."

"Good news travels fast. Are these the documents?"

"Yup. You know the drill. Sign and initial next to the tabs."

"Gotcha." he took the pen from her and proceeded to apply his John Hancock where it was required. "Did you contact the list of community leaders I sent you?" he asked as he scribbled away.

"Yes. I'll call Janet and see if we can set up a meeting this evening."

"Good. That's great."

Fiona sipped at her coffee, then leaned in close to him. "Can I say something?"

Andrew cut his eyes at her. "You're asking to speak your mind? Since when is that a thing?"

"I have no problem talking to you about business related stuff, but…"

"This is about Janet," he finished for her.

"Yeah, you two have history."

"We do."

"I'm gonna say this and you can take it or leave it, but I think you need to be careful about involving an ex in your business dealings. Most exes are exes for a reason."

"Fiona, I really appreciate your concern, but…"

"Am I late?" Winston asked as he jogged up.

Fiona looked irritatedly at her phone as Andrew stood to greet his friend.

Winston looked at the cups in hers and Andrew's hands and said jokingly, "You didn't bring me a cup of coffee?"

"I'm his assistant. Not yours," she said with a shrug. "Besides. You're late."

. . .

"Mr. Atherton? Mr. Konteh?" the receptionist called out. "Mr. Batou is ready to see you now."

"Well," Andrew said. "Let's get this over with." Fiona stepped aside to make the call to Janet while Winston and Andrew went through the glass doors to the offices.

Mykel Batou was more pleasant and forthcoming than he had been at previous meetings. He was more than happy to facilitate the purchase of both mining sites and didn't even question what would happen to the cemetery or where Andrew got the information that they could buy both parcels from. He simply took their signed contracts, initiated the transfer of funds and shook their hands.

"It was a pleasure doing business with you," Mr. Batou said.

It was disturbingly easy, but Andrew didn't dwell on it because it meant that he could go to the orphanage for lunch.

"I guess he really only wanted the money," Winston commented as they walked out the front door of the building. "No concern for the people at all."

"I've always found that in business, compassion is more rare than diamonds, my friend."

CHAPTER TEN: DEJA VU

"Good morning, A Place for Grace. This is Janet."

"Janet, hi, it's Fiona. Andrew's assistant?" Her voice was artificially sweet.

"Oh hi. Nice to hear from you. What can I do for you?"

"This morning over coffee, Andrew showed me the text you sent with the names of the community leaders you wanted him to contact. We called them, and we were wondering if you could join us at our hotel for a meeting."

Our hotel? He showed her the text? The one she sent when he was in bed? What was Fiona doing in his bed? Visions of them in bed, drinking coffee and making those calls made her nauseous. Her head started to spin. He *was* a little drunk. Maybe all that kissing got him too turned on, and he knocked on Fiona's door at the hotel, and…

"Well?" Fiona sounded impatient.

"Why don't we all meet here. For dinner. At my cottage. 6:30." At least if she were going to see them together, she could do it on her own turf. Hitting the "end" button a little too hard, Janet struggled to focus on her work while her stomach churned.

Composing a text to Andrew, Janet wrote, "Too busy for lunch today. Don't come by. See you and Fiona at dinner." Tears in her eyes, the words blurred, as she hit "Send."

"Can I come to dinner and see Mr. Andrew too?" Oba looked up at Janet with those big, pleading eyes. "I won't spill anything."

"No, little king. This is a business meeting. Mr. Andrew will be leaving soon after he finishes his business here. But I'll come back and give you a kiss goodnight. Okay, Oba?"

Janet's heart was heavy. All of her fantasies about Andrew and getting back together were just that. Fantasy. He was the same playboy she knew from college.

"And so here is a list of things we intend to do for the community, now that we have the parcels that surround the cemetery." Fiona passed out a list to each of the leaders that sat around Janet's small table.

"I wanted to meet with you all at once so that we could decide together what is best for the community."

Andrew kept trying to catch Janet's eye with furtive glances and smiles, but she avoided his glance. *Just get through the dinner and he will leave and you'll never have to see him again. You can do this.*

Fiona was really putting on a show for Janet, too. Leaning over Andrew's shoulder as she pointed to something on the list. Refilling his iced tea whenever he took more than three sips. It was clear there was something going on between them, even though Andrew was pretending there wasn't.

"There are a lot of things that Atherton Diamonds can provide for the community on the land surrounding the mine — schools, hospitals with special accommodations for patients with HIV/AIDS where they can receive the best and latest treatment. We also want to build a place where families can be together during long hospital treatments."Andrew looked at Janet, as if for approval, but she just looked away.

He's just using his money to try and get me into bed. I'm not falling for it. I'm not that girl.

As the meeting drew to an end, and everyone was trickling out the door, Andrew caught Janet's arm. "Hey. I haven't talked to you all night. I missed you today."

"Did you?" Janet couldn't stop the tone from seeping into her voice. "I was busy today. Sorry."

"Are you upset with me, Red? Did I do something?" His face looked crestfallen.

He was so clueless.

"You could say that. Listen, I promised Oba I'd tuck him into bed. I need to go. Good luck at your final meeting with Mykel tomorrow."

Leaving him with a confused look on his face, Janet turned and walked out her own front door, swinging her red ponytail behind her.

CHAPTER ELEVEN: BETRAYED

"I do not understand women, Winston. At all." It was 11:00 pm and Andrew was running his frustration off at the hotel gym. Winston was seated near him, texting someone on the phone.

"They are mysterious creatures, mate. That's for sure."

"I mean, one minute Janet and I are flirting and making plans to see each other, and then the next minute she's ice cold to me." He turned the speed up on the treadmill. "I don't even know what I did!"

Just then, Andrew's phone began to ring. It was Claudia's tone. Andrew hit "stop" on the treadmill and answered the phone. "Claudia? It's the middle of the day there. Is something wrong?"

Her voice sounded stressed. "You could say that. It's this mining deal. It's falling apart."

"What do you mean? We signed the papers yesterday. Fiona wired the deposit this morning. I'm just going in in the morning to pick up the confirmed copies."

"That's what I thought too. I got a call this afternoon from a business friend of mine. That Mykel Batou? He's crooked.

Those papers you signed were fake. He took our money and still owns the land."

Andrew was blinded with rage. "What the hell?" He ended the call abruptly. "I'll get to the bottom of this and call you back."

Winston, who had only overheard Andrew's side of the conversation, looked up, shocked. "What is going on?"

At that moment, Winston's phone buzzed. "Yes? Wait, what? They're where? Oh my god. Thank you for calling. We'll be right there.

"Andrew. That was…a friend of mine. She called to tell me that there are bulldozers right now down at the cemetery. They are going to raze the grounds in the middle of the night! We need to get over there."

The lights could be seen from a mile away. The Department of Mines had set up huge focus lights that illuminated the entire cemetery. As Andrew sped down the winding roads that led there, his heart pounded with fury. "I can't believe he did this. He stole our money and is now going to desecrate graves that have been here for hundreds of years. Under the cover of darkness, no less. How can someone be that disgusting?"

Winston answered as he texted. "They'll get their karma. Don't you worry."

Andrew's hands gripped on the steering wheel as he replied, "It will be sooner rather than later if I have my way."

Dust flying in the dark, Andrew and Winston screeched up to the dirt lot next to the grave site. To his surprise, Janet's friend Radhika stepped out from the shadows and into the beam of light from the headlights, and headed toward them.

"This is your friend?" Andrew looked at Winston. "This is who you've been seeing in town?"

Winston grinned and looked down as he unbuckled his

seat belt. "We can talk about that later. We have some destruction to stop."

Radhika and Winston embraced briefly and then headed toward the cluster of lights and bulldozers. Andrew sat in shock for a moment before he heard his friend say, "Come on mate. We need to hurry."

Andrew was still wearing his athletic clothes, and so he took off in a sprint toward the site. As he got near, he saw what could best be described as a standoff. On one side of the graves were a group of a dozen or so construction workers, wearing hard hats and standing in front of looming bulldozers. Facing them in a human chain that made a perimeter around the entire cemetery was a huge group of, probably 10,000 locals. Nearly a tenth of Francistown's entire population had come out to protect the graves.

As he approached the group, he saw Mykel standing near one of the construction workers. He was still wearing a suit. *Who wears a suit at midnight?* Andrew couldn't help but wonder.

"What the hell is going on here?" Andrew stormed up to Mykel, whose eyes widened in fear.

"We are performing within our legal rights, Mr. Atherton. I'm afraid there was an error on the paperwork you signed, and we are still in ownership of this land. Please step aside, or I will have you arrested."

Eyes blazing in fury, Andrew grabbed Mykel by his collar. "You are right that there has been a mistake. But the mistake was you thinking that you could get away with this. You have NO idea who you are dealing with. Zero. My family has been in the mining business for more than two hundred years. Do you know what that means, MYKEL?" Andrew was so close to him that his name had come out like a bark.

Mykel, whose throat was still in Andrew's grip, tried to swallow as he shook his head.

"It means that we have a lot of friends. Friends in high places. And we also have friends in low places. Very low places. Do you know what I mean by that?" The last part of the sentence came out as a menacing whisper.

Mykel's forehead was beading with sweat.

"This is what is going to happen. Listen very closely to what I say, because I will not repeat myself. You are going to call off those bulldozers. They are NOT going to be tearing up the graves of these people. Not tonight. Not ever. You will not dishonor their ancestors like this. Do you understand so far?"

Mykel nodded yes.

"Then, I am going to arrive at your office at 9:00 sharp, and you will have legal versions of the paperwork I signed yesterday. If I find out that you pulled any more bullshit, you will be very, very sorry. Your career will be over, to say the least. Your government will face decades of legal battles. And, more importantly, you will never get a good night's sleep again because you will never know when one of my *friends* will come to your door in the middle of the night." He released Mykel's throat. "Got it?"

"Yes." Mykel was rubbing his neck where his shirt had been choking him from Andrew's grasp.

"Oh, and one other thing. The Department of Mines will pay for the headstones for every family who needs one for the next five years."

Before he could hear Mykel's response, Andrew turned and walked away. Passing Winston and Radhika, he simply said, "We're good here. See you in the morning."

CHAPTER TWELVE: COMING TOGETHER

Janet popped open the top of another beer and handed it to her friend David while he was regaling the group with the story of what had happened last night at the cemetery.

"There must have been fifty thousand people there!" David said, gesturing his hands wide.

Janet laughed as she sat down at her dining room table. "Really, David? We all know you have a tendency to exaggerate."

It had been a while since Janet had hosted a dinner with the women who had befriended her when she first moved to Botswana. Although David was not a woman, his flamboyant personality made him a welcome addition to the group.

They still met for the occasional beer and ranting session, but whenever they came together like this, around her kitchen table, Janet couldn't help but feel warm, fuzzy feelings of family that made her wonder why she didn't do it more often. *These are my real friends*, she thought as she looked around the table at Elyse, Radhika, David and Coral, a local teacher.

"Speaking of last night," David lowered his voice to a gossipy whisper, as he turned to Radhika, "are you going to tell them who I saw you kissing in the shadows last night, or shall I?" He had a mischievous smile on his face.

Radhika's ebony skin flushed a little as she grinned. "I think we have more important things to talk about. Like how Andrew saved the cemetery."

The deflection didn't work. David blurted out, "It was Winston! That is who Radhika has been sneaking off to see!"

The women's faces lit up with happy surprise. "Winston! Radhika, why didn't you say anything?" "Sister, he is seriously handsome." "And that accent!" They all chimed in.

Radhika commented softly. "I didn't say anything because I'm not sure if it's going anywhere. He doesn't live in Botswana, as you know. But, I do really like him..."

The other women and David just nodded and started talking about how Winston and Radhika could be together. But, Janet's mind started to wander as she thought of Andrew.

Radhika had told her how Andrew stormed down to the cemetery and confronted Mykel. They had been trying to get the upper hand on Mykel for months, and somehow Andrew accomplished it in a matter of minutes.

Janet's heart started sinking again. *He is so perfect in so many ways. If only he weren't such a playboy,* she thought. Taking a swig of her beer, she shook her head to clear the dark thoughts.

"Janet? Did you hear us? We were asking how long Andrew was planning on being in town?"

She forced a professional smile on her face and said, "Probably not much longer. His business here is done."

"Ummm...there's one little piece of business he hasn't finished yet...am I right?" David was looking at her pointedly. "Monkey business with you." Everyone but Janet laughed.

"Yeah, that's not going to happen."

Everyone looked shocked. Radhika was the first to ask, "Why not? You are both so perfect for each other!"

"Not if he's sleeping with his assistant. I don't exactly call that perfect." Janet looked down at the plate of chips in front of her.

All at once, the group burst out in Andrew's defense. "Fiona? No way." "You have to be kidding me." "She's not even pretty!" This last one came from David, who was looking rather agitated.

Radhika had been silent. "Janet. I can tell you with 100 percent certainty that Andrew is not sleeping with Fiona. Winston and I talked about it one night, and he told me that they'd had a fling shortly after you and Andrew broke up, but that was in the past. Janet. Andrew is in love with you."

Elyse confirmed. "She's right. That day when we were building the bunk beds, I overheard him asking Nicole if she knew your ring size and what color diamonds you prefer."

Janet's head started to swirl. *He's not sleeping with Fiona? He's in love with me? He was asking Nicole about a ring?*

It was almost too much to take in.

Coral stood up from the table. "I think it's time we call it a night, ladies. Looks like Janet has a phone call to make."

"I'm glad you called, Red. It feels like forever since we've been alone." Andrew stepped through Janet's front door with one hand behind his back. He presented her with a dozen ruby red roses, wrapped in newspaper. "A peace offering? Even though I'm not really sure what I did. But whatever it was, I'm sorry."

The look in his eyes was so intense that it made her heart stutter in her chest. "How did you get roses this late at night? Everything in town is closed!" Janet pushed her face into the fragrant bouquet and inhaled a deep breath. She was as much trying to calm her heart as she was trying to smell the roses.

"I have friends everywhere," he said, as he took the flowers from her and laid them on the counter. "But there is only one woman I love."

Andrew pulled Janet close, took her by the waist, and pulled her up against his strong, hard body.

"What?" she asked, looking into his eyes.

"I love you, Janet," he said softly. "Even though we've been apart for so long, I knew it the moment I saw you. I realized that I never stopped."

Janet pushed up onto her tiptoes and kissed him. "I never stopped loving you either," she whispered against his mouth. "I'm sorry for the-"

Before she could get the words out, Andrew covered her mouth with a deep kiss.

Janet took his hand and let him through the darkened living room to her bedroom. Before, their need for each other had been insistent, urgent and impatient. But now Andrew was so careful and almost reverent as he pulled her shirt over her head. He leaned in to kiss her again, his mouth hungry and questing as he undid the clasp on her bra, and pulled it off, revealing her breasts. His palms were hot and rough against her nipples. His gentle kneading sent zaps of pleasure to the place between her thighs.

"Andrew," she breathed. "I need you."

"I'm right here, Red. You have me."

He moved them toward the bed, lowering her down gently so that she lay on her back. Janet's fingers fumbled at the drawstring on her linen pants and he helped her pull them off, taking her panties with them.

Andrew leaned back and sighed while gazing down at her. "You're so beautiful," he whispered before covering her mouth with his again.

Janet reached for him, needily grabbing handfuls of his curls and pushing her hand under the t-shirt that she immediately yanked over his head. He caught her wrists, still trapped in the soft fabric, and pinned them over her head. She struggled against him for a moment, but he distracted her by making a trail of kisses from her mouth to her breasts.

When his mouth closed around one of her nipples, Janet moaned and arched off the bed. No man had been in her bed since they broke up. And Andrew's mouth sucking and nibbling at her sensitive nipples reminded her of why. Andrew was the first, and his hands and mouth reawakened that desire in a way no other man could. She writhed and twisted under his attentions and when his hand finally found its way between her thighs, she cried out.

"Please, Andrew. Please," she begged as his fingertips slipped over her tight bud.

"Shhh..." he quieted as he pulled away and stood at the edge of the bed to take off his pants. He made quick work of it, but her eyes still roamed every beautiful inch of his bared skin. Instead of climbing on top of her, he dropped to his knees and covered her achingly empty core with his mouth. His tongue lathed her clit and her opening with each broad lick and soon she was spiraling toward an intense orgasm.

Her hands, free from his makeshift manacles, grabbed two fistfuls of his hair and pulled him up to meet her. "Inside of me. I want you inside of me when I come."

"Do you have condoms?" he asked.

"No. But there has been no one else..." She hated to break the moment but had to ask. "Do you?"

"No. But I had a complete physical not too long ago. And it's been years for me too. We're good."

Relieved, Janet leaned back on the bed and smiled. "Then, get over here."

Andrew crawled across the bed and settled himself in the cradle of her thighs. She kissed him and tasting herself on his lips made her need spike. She rolled her hips against him until the tip of his cock was positioned at her entrance.

"Please, please, please," she begged again until he finally slid inside of her.

"Oh, god, Red," he murmured against her shoulder as he pressed into her slowly, gently, and carefully.

He moved with slow, shallow thrusts until she began to meet each thrust, seating him deeper. Then he stopped being careful and gentle. He hooked his hand under her knee and pushed her hips wider as he plunged deep, over and over again until she tightened around him, squeezing, triggering a release that made her slipperier and heightened all of the nerve endings inside of her.

"I'm coming..." she moaned but the words had barely left her mouth before it rolled through her, clamping down on his cock so hard that he gritted his teeth and growled.

Before she could catch her breath, he hooked her knees over his shoulders and pumped into her, hard and fast. Soon she felt the pleasure building again.

"Come with me," he whispered. "I want to feel you coming around me as I come."

His words worked like some kind of spell and with panting breaths and strangled moans Andrew chased her orgasm with his own.

CHAPTER THIRTEEN: THE CALL

For a moment, Andrew was confused. First, there were birds chirping outside. *Why are there birds in my hotel room?* Then, there was an incessant buzzing coming from across the room. *Is that my phone? Why isn't it on the nightstand?* And, last, it appeared from the feel of the sheets on his bare skin that he was naked. *Where are my clothes?*

But before he could open his eyes, the memory came to consciousness. Janet. They made love. Almost all night... The memories stirred in his mind. And soon, something else started to stir.

"Are you going to sleep all day?" Janet walked into her bedroom holding two steaming mugs of coffee.

Sitting up in bed, he answered, "If I can sleep with you, absolutely." Reaching out for the mug, he heard the buzzing of his phone again.

Janet was looking around for the source of the sound. "Where is it? Under my pants? Your t-shirt? I can't find it!"

Janet looked like a Disney princess the day after a night with her prince. Her red curls fell down over her face as she was bent over looking for his phone. Those delicious breasts were falling out of her robe as she leaned forward, moving pieces of clothes about.

"Leave it, Red. I have something else that's buzzing that needs your attention more…"

"Oh here it is. How did it get under the bed?" Janet handed him the phone, without looking at it.

Reluctantly, Andrew took the phone. "I'll just get rid of whoever it is… Cole? Hey, buddy. Why are you calling so late?" Although it was 9:30 am in Franciscown, it was 2:30 in the morning in New York.

"Sorry to call so early. I've been trying to get you all night. It's Ryan. There's been an accident."

Andrew sat up straight in bed. Ryan was Andrew's college friend. Cole and Andrew had been roommates, and across the hall were Ryan and Michael. Ryan was Ryan Cummings, and his family owned Cummings Construction, a large firm in California. Ryan had taken the first few commissions from his role as the lead architect and invested in tech stocks. A couple of good calls meant that he, too, was a billionaire.

Not that any of that mattered now. "How bad is it?"

"We don't know yet. Mike got the call last night and he called me from the plane. I'm headed to London in a couple of hours myself. It doesn't look good, Andrew."

Shit, shit, shit. They were too young to be dealing with this. "I'm on my way."

Janet had been standing nearby, watching, and said, "On your way where? What happened?"

"To London. Ryan has been in an accident."

"Ryan? Ryan Cummings? From college?" Janet looked pale. "Oh my god."

"I have to go." Embracing her, Andrew pleaded, "Will you come with me? Please?"

Janet took a step back. "I can't. I have to stay here. There's

Oba and A Place for Grace. And I have meetings with the community leaders. I just can't go."

Pulling on his jeans, and running a hand through his hair to straighten it, he said, "I understand. But I have to go. Ryan, Cole, Mike…we're like brothers. If I can help in any way, I have to be there."

They kissed, and held each other tightly, not wanting to let go. They had just found each other again. It just wasn't fair. "I'll call you when I land."

As the doors opened to Bart's, St. Bartholomew Hospital in London, Andrew recalled the last time he'd been in a hospital. It was the day his caravan had almost killed Janet. The day he met Oba. The thought of them so far away made his heart sink. But, they had walked out of the hospital with little more than a few scrapes. *Who knows? Maybe Ryan will get lucky, too.*

"Andrew! I'm glad you made it." It was Cole.

"I jumped on the first flight I could catch. I had to fly coach!"

Cole chuckled. "Such indignity! Did you at least have a pretty seatmate?"

"No, it was a very large Irishman named Fergus. Not a good way to spend seven hours, I'll tell you. How's Ryan?"

"Still unconscious. He hasn't woken up since they brought him in two days ago," Cole whispered.

"There he is!" Michael strode toward his two friends and embraced Andrew. "Usually when one of us is passed out for two days, it's you, man." Only a good friend could get away with a comment like that.

"What happened? Why is he in London?"

"Not sure. The last I heard was that Cummings Construction was in talks to build a hotel out here. Kind of a Hotel

California vibe. Maybe that's why he was here?" Michael didn't seem to know more than that.

"That's kind of random," Andrew said. "I wonder what the backstory is that led a California construction company to want to build a hotel in London."

Cole chimed in with more information. "Don't know. But they were on their way to tour a potential site when some car came into their lane and crashed head-on. Ryan lost control of the SUV and it rolled. Thank god he was wearing a seatbelt. It saved his life."

Michael added, "They had to cut him out from the car, though. Some kind of head injury. We're not sure."

Andrew looked at his friend, unconscious in a hospital room, far away from his family and felt a rush of emotion. *You have to make it, buddy. We need you. At the very least, I need you in my wedding...*

CHAPTER FOURTEEN: X-RAY VISION

"You hang up first." Janet was laying in bed, Facetiming Andrew. Since London was two hours behind Francistown, it was still dark where he was, but the sun was just coming up through Janet's window.

"I've told you a thousand times, I am not ever going to hang up on you." Andrew's deep voice stirred something primal in Janet.

"A thousand times? Really? Who are you, now? David?" Janet laughed. Andrew had been gone for a little more than three weeks, and they had managed to Facetime every morning since he left.

"How is Ryan's PT coming along?"

Ryan had awakened from his coma a few days after Andrew got to London. He'd had a concussion - a pretty bad one - and lost some function in his legs. He was doing physical therapy every day to regain his ability to walk normally.

"Pretty good. In fact, I need to get over there early this morning. Mike has to get back to the States, and we are meeting for breakfast before he leaves for Heathrow. What about you? What's my gorgeous girl doing today?"

For all her independence, Janet still swooned when Andrew called her "my girl."

"Just another meeting with the architect on the construction for Extended Grace."

"I love that name, by the way. It's like an African version of Ronald McDonald House, where families can stay together during medical treatment. You have the biggest heart of anyone I've ever met, Red. I love you."

"I love you too, Andrew. I can't wait to see you again."

Pulling on a pair of black slacks and a turquoise top, Janet headed out to kiss Oba in the dining room on her way to her office. *Things are going so well right now,* Janet thought. *A little too well, actually. What do you bet my mother calls today?*

"Mama look! I have a loose tooth!" Oba had just started calling Janet "Mama." At first, Janet felt a little uncomfortable. But Radhika had assured her that Gouta would have wanted her son to call Janet "Mama."

"Why yes, yes you do, little king. It's your first one! When I was a little girl, when I lost a tooth, I put it under my pillow and a fairy left me a dollar for the tooth."

Oba's eyes grew wide. "A fairy! Can I put my tooth under your pillow, too?"

Janet laughed and affectionately patted his head. "We shall see, little king. We shall see."

"I need to see the spreadsheets of the budget forecast for A Place for Grace." Alexis' voice was demanding and shrill as she didn't even bother with saying hello to Janet.

"Good morning to you, too, Mother." *I called it, didn't I?* Janet thought.

"It's not a good morning to me when I am expecting to see a report detailing how the foundation money is being spent and I'm not getting it. What are you doing out there, Janet? Do I need to come out there and see for myself?"

Rolling her eyes, Janet appeased her mother. "No, you

BELOVED BY YOU

don't need to come here. The reason the forecast is late is because I need to see how much we are going to need for Extended Grace. Those figures should be in later today, and I'll have the spreadsheet to you tomorrow."

Just then, there was a knock on Janet's door. "Come in." The door opened to reveal Elyse and Oba standing there. "Mother, I have to go."

Oba was standing with a huge smile on his face and a gap where his front tooth used to be. Extending his hand toward Janet, he proudly stated, "Look, Mama. My tooth is out! Can we put it under your pillow now?"

Walking over to the small boy, she kissed him on the top of the head and took the small pearl of a tooth cradled in his pink palm. "It's supposed to go under YOUR pillow, little king."

Elyse gave her a warning look. How would it look if one of the boys got a visit from the tooth fairy and didn't visit the rest?

"But, you know what? I bet the tooth fairy will think to look under my pillow, too. Let's go put it there for her to find."

"Has he ever had an X-ray of his teeth before?" The dentist was looking at Janet as Oba sat in the huge chair with a paper napkin tied around his little neck.

"No, this is his first time to the dentist. I just figured since he lost his first tooth this morning, we should have him looked at."

"That's fine. Let's go ahead and get a set of X-rays." Leaning over and whispering to her, the dentist added, "I find that the little ones get nervous. Can you stay with him during the X-rays?" Janet nodded as he handed Oba a lead blanket. "Just put this blanket on your lap."

Handing her a lead vest to wear herself, he asked Janet, "There's no chance you might be pregnant, is there? X-rays can damage a fetus."

Pregnant? Janet started doing mental calculations. Could she be pregnant? Andrew had been gone almost a month. When was her last cycle? Was it before…?

"Little king? Mama is going to step right outside while the nice dentist takes pictures of your teeth. You'll be fine."

Oba was looking at a book of stickers and said, "Okay, mama."

As she closed the door to the exam room, her heart was pounding. Could it be possible?

CHAPTER FIFTEEN: THE BBC

"Are you seriously going to eat all of that?" Cole laughed at Michael, as he sat down at the table in the hospital cafeteria with a heaping plate of scrambled eggs, bacon, sausage, potatoes, beans, tomatoes, fried bread, and for good measure, a slice of dark blood sausage.

"Hey. They don't have a full English fry-up in California. Who knows when I'll get to have this food again?"

Andrew came to the table with a bowl of porridge and steaming hot coffee, nodding at Michael's plate. "Going back to the land of tofu making you hungry? When's your flight, anyway?"

"Actually, it's whenever I want. I booked the jet. The pilot is waiting for me at the airport, in fact."

"Ah, the perks of being a billionaire." To that, all three men toasted with their orange juices and coffees.

Cole commented, "Sadly there are some things money can't buy."

Michael nodded. "I'm just glad Ryan is going to be okay. It was pretty sketchy there for a while."

"Me too," Cole added. Claudia has been bugging me to come home. Gotta keep the woman happy, you know?"

Looking at Andrew, Michael said, "Speaking of which… what's going on with Janet? And where's Winston?"

"Winston actually stayed in Botswana to help make sure that The Department of Mines was going to make good on their promise to the people of Francistown."

"Claudia told me what you did over there. Well done, bro." Cole playfully punched Andrew on the shoulder. "I wouldn't want to be on your bad side. That's for sure."

"Hahaha. Well. Thanks. It was just the right thing to do. I mean, what's the point of having all this money and power, if we aren't going to use it for good? I just wish I could do more."

Michael agreed. "When my investments took off and I made all that money, my dad sat me down and talked to me about the responsibility of wealth. He said, 'It's all well and good to have fun, son. But at the end of the day, you're going to be remembered for what you did with your money. Did you make the world a better place, or did you act like that Billionaire Boys' Club, and use your influence the wrong way?' His words always stuck with me."

Cole nodded. "Hey, we're all billionaires. You, me, Andrew, and Ryan in there. We use our money for good. We're The Billionaire Boys' Club 2.0!"

Andrew took a big gulp of his coffee and pushed his chair back."You know. That gives me an idea. Janet's friend Nicole e-mailed me that the YouTube documentary she did on A Place for Grace is done. Since you guys are heading back Stateside, maybe I can change the perception of the name of the Billionaire Boys' Club. Work with Nicole to bring awareness to the good that billionaires can do. Each one of us has given back in some way. Let's change what people think

BELOVED BY YOU

when they hear the name BBC. Not for ego, of course. But to spread the good word."

The men all stood, and Michael grabbed his laptop bag. "I like it. We can be the BBC 2."

Walking down the hallway to Ryan's room to say goodbye, they were all chuckling. "Leave it to us to come up with a stupid club name after all these years. You can take the boy out of college, but you can't take college out of the boy…"

"A charity gala?" Fiona sounded surprised. "You want me to plan a charity gala? For Janet?"

Fiona had flown back to New York at about the same time Andrew had come to London. They had been working with the time difference for almost a month now, with Fiona handling a lot of the business there.

She'd been asking Andrew when he was going to come home for weeks, but Andrew had been putting her off. If he was going to get on a plane, it was going to be to see Janet.

"No, I'm going to plan the gala. I just need you to handle a few details. And, it's not for Janet. It's for A Place for Grace. We'll have the world premiere of Nicole's documentary, and raise funds for the orphanage, so that innocent children with no family will have a home.."

"Does this mean you aren't coming home? Claudia said that Cole is arriving tomorrow." Fiona was practically whining.

"Is there a problem? If you don't want to do it, I am sure I can find someone else to…"

"No, no," Fiona interjected. "It's fine. You just caught me off-guard. Email me the list you have so far, and we'll get going."

CHAPTER SIXTEEN: GOODBYES

Janet had one black dress. It was a simple black sheath. Perfect for a funeral.

Gouta had no family, but everyone in the community had loved her. Janet had invited the teachers and staff from the school, and it was likely to be a large, traditional ceremony.

Standing sideways, Janet smoothed the dress down over her belly, peering to see if there were any change. Her abdomen was as flat as ever. *Not for long*, Janet thought.

It had been a few days since the fateful dentist appointment, and Janet's test confirmed the next morning that she was, indeed, pregnant. She was pregnant with Andrew's baby! Although the news had come as quite a shock, Janet was elated. She found herself daydreaming about what the baby would look like. Would he have her red hair? Would she have his piercing eyes?

But Janet hadn't told anyone yet because she wanted Andrew to be the first to know. Their daily Facetime chats had been canceled the last few days - largely because Janet wasn't feeling that well in the mornings anymore.

They would bury Gouta before noon, as was the tradition, so right after breakfast, the small group gathered in the courtyard to get ready to head to the cemetery. Oba looked solemn but strong in his tiny, dark suit. Gouta had been Christian, and the service would be a blend of tribal and Christian expressions.

"Is your man coming?" Elyse asked.

She shook her head but didn't say anything else. She was trying so hard not to let on about the pregnancy that she was afraid to even mention Andrew.

The gravesite was still being dug when they pulled up. Gouta's coffin rested on a wheeled cart under a green tarp. Seats positioned around it in preparation for the service. Oba was at her side, quiet and holding her hand.

"Is Mama in there?" he asked.

"Her body is in there, yes." Janet touched the centre of Oba's chest and said, "But your mama is in here. Always will be."

She'd been to so many of these, but her tears fell freely. Now that she was about to become a mother herself, she couldn't even imagine the pain of knowing you wouldn't see your child grow up.

Elyse and Coral walked around gathering stones to build a mountain on top of her resting place. Someone started singing and the service got underway.

As the final prayer was being sung, Janet looked over at Oba. His brave face had tears streaming down it. He sat tall in his chair, and he was gripping Janet's hand tightly, his lower lip quivering. He was trying so hard to be brave.

Suddenly, Janet knew. She knew without any reservation that Oba was her son now. That beautiful little boy came into her life for a reason. And that reason was for her to be his mother.

Leaning over to him, she whispered, "I love you, little king."

"I love you too, Mama."

The next day, the phone rang in Janet's office. It was Fiona calling from New York.

"Andrew has been trying to get hold of you." She sounded almost accusatory.

Janet looked at her cellphone and saw four missed calls from Andrew. "I guess I forgot to turn the sound back on after the funeral." Honestly, between the pregnancy fatigue and the emotions from burying a dear friend, all Janet could manage was to tuck Oba into bed and crawl under her own covers.

"Oh yeah. The funeral. Sorry for your loss." She paused long enough to be polite before moving the conversation forward. "Anyway, I guess I'll be the one to tell you. Andrew is planning a charity gala in two weeks to raise money for A Place of Grace."

"Two weeks! How can he plan an entire charity benefit in two weeks?" Janet was both stunned and impressed.

"Andrew has friends in every city, " she said tartly. "Anyway, I'm calling to fill you in on the details. Andrew wants to send the plane and fly you in the day before."

"Wow. I don't know what to say. This is all so sudden."

"Tell me about it." Fiona lowered her voice conspiratorially. "Frankly I was as surprised as you are, given how much he hates kids."

Confused, Janet repeated back, "He hates kids? No, he doesn't. He loves kids."

Fiona chortled. "He loves other people's kids. Sometimes. But we laugh all the time about the poor people who get trapped into having a family. Kind of cramps the billionaire lifestyle, know what I mean?"

Janet leaned back in her chair, in stunned silence. Janet's entire life was built around children. She was adopting Oba. She was PREGNANT! Pregnant by a man who didn't want to have any. What did this mean for them?

After the details of Janet's trip to London were worked out, she hung up the phone in a daze. All she could hear were Fiona's words echoing…"Trapped into having a family. Trapped…"

The last thing she wanted to do was trap Andrew Atherton into anything.

The two weeks had flown by. Janet had talked to Andrew a few times, but he was so busy planning the gala that the conversations had been really short. Which was just fine by Janet. If it were up to her, she wouldn't even go.

However, Nicole had been calling every day, completely excited about her movie premiere.

"I can't wait to see you. This is going to be so much fun. We'll have a red carpet, and we've invited Madonna and Angelina Jolie. They have a soft spot for African orphans, as you can imagine. It's so incredible that Andrew managed to convince them both to come on such short notice!"

Janet didn't really care which celebrities were coming, and she wasn't looking forward to the "fun." She just wanted to get it over with so that she could come home and get on with her life.

Laying in her cold bed alone, the night that Fiona had dropped the bombshell about Andrew's feelings toward having a family, Janet had tossed and turned. As the dawn crept through her window, Janet had come to a conclusion. She wasn't going to tell Andrew about the baby. No, after the gala, Janet was going to break things off with Andrew. This time, the goodbye would be for good.

CHAPTER SEVENTEEN: RELEASED

"Do you have everything?' Andrew carried Ryan's bag containing the few things he'd had brought over to the hospital during the six weeks he stayed there after the accident.

"Yeah, man. I'm good. I can't believe I'm finally getting out of this place. What's been going on in the real world? Did we colonize the moon yet?" Ryan was in good spirits as he was wheeled toward the elevator.

"Not yet, but when we do, I'm sure that your family will be the first to build a hotel there."

"You're funny." Ryan stood and embraced his friend as the driver opened the car door. "Thanks so much for everything, Andrew. I'm still blown away that you all just dropped your lives and came all the way over here for me like that."

Andrew patted his friend on the back. "Hey. We're the BBC 2 now. That's what we do. We're all about charity."

"Ha, the BBC 2. I wonder if that's really going to be a thing now." Sliding into the back seat of the limo, Ryan said, "Are you sure I can't drop you anywhere? Hard Rock? Buckingham Palace? It's the least I can do."

BELOVED BY YOU

"No, I'm good. I'm actually meeting Winston in Old Bond Street. We have an appointment at Atherton's, London."

"Finally tying the knot, are you two? I always did think you and Winston made a dashing couple…" With that, the door closed and the limo sped off.

"Mr. Atherton. It's an honor to have you here this morning. Here, let me take your coat." Giles Davis wore a stiff grey pinstripe three-piece suit and had a diamond pinky ring on his left hand. "Can I get you something to drink? Coffee, tea, perhaps a breakfast cocktail?" he lowered his voice discreetly.

"No thank you, Gilles. I am waiting on my associate. Bring him back when he arrives." Andrew had spent his life around diamonds and he knew just about everything there was to know about the rare gem. But this wasn't just any old diamond he was buying. This was an engagement ring. For Janet. The first time he'd proposed to her, it was so spur-of-the-moment that they didn't have time to get a ring. Ironic, huh? The heir to a diamond empire proposing without a ring?

Not this time. This time he was going to do it right. On bended knee and the whole thing. Starting with today, and buying the ring.

He surveyed the shiny stones in the glass case. First, he would choose the stone, and then he would choose the setting.

"Sir? Your associate is here."

Winston breezed through the door to the private back room. "Sorry I'm late. The plane was delayed." Winston winked at his old friend.

"You mean *you* were delayed, by Radhika."

"A gentleman never tells," he grinned. "What are we

looking at here? Did Nicole ever give you any information on what Janet likes?"

"Nope. Not a word. We are flying blind here, mate."

"Well, do you see anything that catches your eye?"

"Nothing as much as Janet. These are all gorgeous, of course. They're ours. But, I want something a little more…"

"Personal?" Winston added.

"Yes. Something that reflects our history. Something that shows that she is joining our family heritage. WAIT. Winston. You're a genius. I've got it."

Smiling, but a little confused, Winston replied, "If you say so…"

The sun was shining brightly on this crisp London afternoon as Andrew finally stepped out onto Old High Street. Winston and Andrew parted ways, as Andrew had several meetings planned to finalize the details for the gala. There was a lot to do in two days, and Fiona was still in New York. It was up to Andrew to handle the last minute "boots on the ground" details.

As he was walking, enjoying the fresh air, his phone buzzed. He didn't recognize the number, but he answered it anyway.

"Andrew Atherton."

"Andrew. It's Nicole." She sounded breathless.

"Nicole! I didn't recognize your number. How are things going with the documentary?"

"I'm calling from a different phone. My iPhone got stolen!"

"Oh no, I'm sorry." Andrew shook his head.

"That's not even the worst of it. Whoever stole my phone actually hacked into it, and sent a message to everyone in my phone. All of my media contacts. Celebrities. Even my mother."

"I didn't get a message." Andrew looked at his phone. "Oh

wait, yes I did. Since it's a hacker, I'm not going to open it. What did it say?"

"The theft wasn't random, Andrew. The person who stole my phone said that they are going to release a YouTube video at the same time as the premiere."

"So, what does it have to do with us? YouTube is a huge platform. What do we care about some other documentary?"

"The video is about you."

"Me? What about me?" Andrew was confused.

"It's an exposé on you and your friends. The Billionaire Boys' Club Two."

"What? No. No one can have anything bad on any of us. This has to be some kind of hoax."

"It's not. Come to my office and I'll show you the video. Andrew, this could ruin the gala. And my career!"

Standing behind Nicole, looking over her shoulder at the computer monitor, Andrew was sickened at what he was seeing. It was dark video footage of himself and Mykel Batou that night at the cemetery. Andrew's hands were at Mykel's throat and it looked like he was assaulting a government official.

"Who took this?" Andrew demanded.

"I don't know. It could be anyone. Everyone has cell phones these days."

"Well, this isn't enough to make a movie with. It's just a clip."

"Watch this." Nicole fast-forwarded to the next video clip.

"Is that Ryan's accident?" Andrew saw a black SUV flipping and crashing.

"Yes. The narrator said that he was driving recklessly."

"He was swerving to avoid the other car! This is crazy."

"There's more, Andrew. The whole movie is clips of the four of you, taken out of context. It's pieced together to make you guys all look like rich, spoiled brats who pretend to do philanthropy but really just use it as an excuse to do whatever you want."

Andrew slumped down in the chair next to Nicole's desk. He didn't even notice the expansive view of London out of her top, corner office window. This would taint A Place for Grace. If it got out. "What do they want? What can we do to stop the release?"

"I don't know yet. I'll let you know when I hear from whoever is doing this." Nicole put her head in her hands. "I'm meeting Janet at the airport tomorrow and we're going to do some shopping after she gets settled at the Ritz...I don't know if she knows anything, but I don't want to be the one to tell her that her charity gala is in jeopardy."

"Don't. Don't say a word. I'll handle this. I'll find a way to stop this piece of shit from being released."

CHAPTER EIGHTEEN: CITY LIGHTS

Looking out the window of the private jet, Janet tried to remember the last time she had been in a city as large as London. She'd been living in Botswana for several years now, and the simpler life had become the norm.

Yet, here she was, on a Gulfstream IV, indulging in Godiva chocolates and non-alcoholic apple cider. The flight attendant had offered champagne but fortunately didn't ask any questions when Janet turned it down.

"You better enjoy it while you can, little princess. This is the last time we'll be enjoying your daddy's money."

Janet didn't know if the baby was a girl, of course. It was too soon. But she secretly hoped to have a daughter with dark black curls, like Andrew.

Tears threatened to sting her eyes, and so she forced herself to think of other things. "It will be great to see your Aunt Nicole again," Janet told the baby. "Even if I can't tell her about you."

It was strange to not have a cellphone with her on a trip like this. But they didn't exactly have an Apple Store in Francistown, and her phone wasn't working after Oba accidentally dropped it in a puddle. "I'm sorry, Mama. I was trying to take a picture of the tadpoles." She was hoping Nicole would take her to one in London so she could be connected to the world again.

Fortunately, the flight went quickly, as there were several in-flight videos to choose from. The excitement of the trip, plus the fatigue that comes from growing a baby helped Janet to drift off to sleep.

"Miss. Miss? We are about to land."

Janet had been dreaming of Andrew. Again. It seemed that every night she dreamed of them in some romantic destination. Paris. Rome. The Empire State Building. In the dream, they were always kissing, as a gentle rain fell down on them, by the light of a full moon.

"Maybe these are experiences you will have, little princess. Maybe my dreams are for you."

"Private jets definitely agree with you! You're positively glowing!" Nicole rushed to hug her friend.

"You're too kind. I'm not nearly as glamorous as you are, my dear. But I am starving. Where can we get a big, juicy hamburger?"

"Ha! It's 9:00 am!"

"That's lunchtime at home. Get me some fries in my belly!" The women linked arms and laughed as they walked to Nicole's Jaguar.

After stuffing their faces at The Diner Soho, they headed out for an afternoon of shopping. "I need to get a new phone. Oba dropped mine in a puddle and it hasn't worked for days."

Nicole made a strange face at that, and said, "Oh! I was wondering why I hadn't gotten any calls from you. But I figured it was because my phone was stolen."

"Your phone was stolen? Well, then let's both stop by the Apple Store."

Nicole hesitated. "Uh, well. Maybe later. We have a lot to do before the gala tomorrow."

"Okay, just so long as I get one before I go back to Botswana. The one in Gaborone is too far out of the way."

Four hours later, and laden with shopping bags, Janet was exhausted. She and Nicole had hit almost every high-end boutique in London. Plus, she'd had her hair cut, they'd gotten facials, and manicures. The last stop was to get some new earrings to compliment her gown.

Frankly, Janet didn't want to shop anymore. The idea of a warm bath and a comfortable bed was calling to her. But Nicole's pleading won her over.

"Please. Atherton London is right here. Then I'll take you to your hotel. I promise."

Walking in the doors, and seeing diamonds everywhere, Janet's heart went to her throat. The first time Andrew had proposed, he'd said he would bring her to his company's New York store to get her engagement ring. But one thing led to another, and it never happened.

Placing her hand protectively over her belly, Janet thought, *And now it never will happen.*

Fortunately, The Ritz London was only a five-minute drive from Atherton London. "You sure you don't want me to help you up with your things?" Nicole had pulled her black Jag up to the valet. "I don't mind…"

"No, I'm fine. The porter can get my bags." It hadn't been so long that Janet forgot what it was like to stay at an expensive hotel. After all, she was raised a Girard.

"Alright, then. I'll see you tomorrow at the gala!" Janet watched as Nicole sped off.

"We have you in the Penthouse Suite, Ms. Girard. Mick here will bring up your things. Will there be anyone joining you that might need a key?" The man at the front desk lowered his voice slightly as he said the last part.

"No, it's just me."

Janet had to admit it felt very strange to be in such a luxurious setting after living in a cottage at an orphanage for so long.

Waiting for the elevator to take her to the penthouse, Janet could smell something delicious coming from Berners Tavern. The scent caused her stomach to growl and she realized that she was hungry again. "Little princess, I might have to rename you large queen. You've given me quite an appetite!"

Janet's room was breathtaking. She never would have chosen the Penthouse Suite for herself. It was bigger than her cottage! She wasn't sure which to do first, sit out on one of the three outdoor terraces and take in the London view, or strip off her traveling clothes and stand under the rainforest shower.

What Janet really wanted to do was check her messages. Without a phone for two days, she had no idea what was going on with Andrew. Plus, she wanted to call Oba and say goodnight. But, they hadn't gotten to the Apple Store today, so she would have to use the phone in her room. Expensive, yes. But what about this weekend wasn't?

Opening the fridge in the kitchen, Janet marveled at the selection of treats. She chose a sparkling water and went to go explore the rest of the suite.

In the master bedroom, on top of the plush king-sized bed, was a small envelope. Picking it up, she recognized the handwriting and her name on the outside. Inside, was a card that simply said, "You are my beloved. Andrew."

Tossing herself onto the bed, Janet began to cry. "It's not fair, little princess. But you deserve to be wanted and loved. And I will give you that life if it's the last thing I do." The tears subsided only as Janet drifted off to sleep, with the city lights of London reflecting in the mirror.

CHAPTER NINETEEN: COLLATERAL DAMAGE

Andrew was feeling a little better. He was in the middle of his five-mile run on the Ritz Carlton's treadmill and he was thinking about Janet. Just knowing that he was on the same property as Janet made him feel closer to her. But, he wanted to wait until the gala to see her. He didn't want to risk her finding out anything about the exposé. Or the engagement ring. She always did have a way of getting secrets out of him…and they had a lifetime to share together. Just one more day, and then Janet Girard would be his fiancée again.

He knew he was taking a bit of a risk booking her in the Penthouse Suite, just a few doors down from his own seventh-floor loft. But he wanted only the best for her from now on.

The treadmill beeped that his workout was over. Taking a swig from his water bottle, Andrew checked his phone for messages. There was one from Winston, another from Fiona, but nothing from Nicole about the video.

Wiping the sweat from his brow, the phone in his hand started to ring. It was Claudia.

"Hey, sis'."

"How's my favorite employee?" Claudia loved to tease her brother.

"Hard at work. I deserve a raise, don't you think?"

"Very funny. The check is in the mail. How's everything coming along for the gala tonight? I'm sorry I can't be there. We have way too much going on here in New York to get away."

"No worries, sis. This isn't an official Atherton Diamonds event anyway. Things are looking good. Fiona got into town yesterday, and we're meeting this morning to go over the timeline."

Andrew hadn't mentioned anything to Claudia or Cole about the exposé. Since she and Nicole weren't really friends, the hacker hadn't sent them the message about the video. Andrew also hadn't mentioned the proposal. Better to keep everything quiet so there was less chance of Janet finding out.

At least Claudia's attitude toward Janet had changed. His heart warmed to think of her. Janet had a captivating effect on everyone - his sister included.

"I'm about to get into the elevator. I'll call you tomorrow."

"Okay, so the celebrities are going to start walking up the red carpet at 6:00." Fiona and Andrew sat at a nearby Starbucks. While Fiona was pointing to the timeline, Andrew kept looking at the door every time it opened.

"Hello? Earth to Andrew. Are you even listening?"

"Oh, yeah. I'm sorry."

"Are you waiting for someone? Or avoiding someone?" Fiona leaned in close to Andrew. "Did you and Janet have a fight?"

Still looking at the door, he shook his head. "No. No fight. I just don't want to run into anyone this morning. Too much to do."

"Exactly, which is why we need to go over this timeline. So, red carpet at 6:00. The photographers will get there at 5:30. I think you and I should get there about halfway through the red carpet event. We don't want to be first, but we don't want to be so late that the photographers have left."

"Wait... we?"

"Yes. We. You and me."

"Why would I be walking the red carpet with you? Aren't you bringing a date?"

"Andrew. Why would I bring a date? This is a work event. For both of us. I just assumed we would be going together. We always go to these kinds of events together."

"Fiona this is different. Tonight is about Janet. I'm bringing her. She is the star tonight. It's her efforts that have saved so many children from homelessness. She's the one who founded A Place for Grace. This isn't just some business function. I thought you understood."

For a moment, Fiona looked crestfallen. But, she regained her composure and said, "Got it, Boss. I'll ride with Winston and Radhika. Okay, so after the red carpet is the champagne reception, sponsored by Dom Perignon..."

They'd spent about an hour going over the final details of the gala before Fiona left to go get ready. Andrew never understood why it took women so long to get ready for these things. Especially when they were naturally beautiful, like Janet. *I guess some women just need more work than others*, he thought.

Reaching down to get his laptop bag, Andrew saw something on the floor under the seat where Fiona had been sitting. Reaching down to grab it, he saw that it was a flash drive. Fiona must have dropped it when she pulled her notebook out of her bag.

It wasn't like him to snoop, but he also needed to check if the flash drive belonged to Atherton. It could contain sensitive company information, so just to be safe, Andrew pulled out his MacBook and plugged the drive in.

As it was loading, Andrew's phone rang. "Mike. I'm glad you called back. I need a favor."

Andrew detailed what was going on. Nicole's phone getting stolen and hacked. The message that went out to her entire contact list. The video that made all four of the men look like spoiled rich jerks instead of philanthropists.

"What did they think they have on me?" Michael was concerned. He didn't want his parents to see some movie filled with lies about him.

"I couldn't stomach watching the whole thing. After they tried to make Ryan's accident look like reckless driving, I turned it off. But the message said that the video would be posted on YouTube at the same time our documentary was going to premiere. So, that's 8:00."

"How can I help?"

"Well, since 8:00 in London is noon in California, what I need from you will be in the middle of the day tomorrow for you."

"Not a problem. What do you need?"

"Are your parents still couple friends with Susan Wojcicki and her husband?"

"The head of YouTube? Yeah. We saw them at Christmas last year." Michael's parents were early investors in Google, and Michael even did an internship there one summer when they were in college. He'd known Susan and Dennis practically his whole life.

"Can you make a few calls for me?"

"If it means that my parents won't see that video, I'm in."

Setting the phone down, Andrew grabbed another cup of coffee and opened the file on the flash drive. As the images popped up on the screen, Andrew couldn't believe what he was seeing. The drive did belong to Fiona. And, along with all of the spreadsheets and company information was a video file. It was simply called YouTube.

No. It can't be...

Andrew clicked on the video, and it began to play. The narrator's voice was female, but it was altered with a voice changer so he couldn't recognize it. "What you are about to see is the REAL story behind The BBC 2. These four college friends, Andrew Atherton, Cole Bennett, Ryan Cummings, and Michael Davis, are all billionaires. Their image is that of philanthropy...but the real story is one of rich men who think they are above the law..."

Why would Fiona have that video on her flash drive? There was only one explanation. She was the only person to have access to the footage. She was in Botswana when Andrew had his confrontation. He'd sent her footage of Ryan's car accident. She worked with Claudia to get Cole to invest in the mine. Lord only knows what she twisted around to use against him - and Mike. She must have arranged for someone to steal Nicole's phone, too.

There was only one reason he could think of that Fiona would do such a thing. To hurt Janet by discrediting him. Janet was Fiona's target, and Andrew and the rest of the BBC 2 were just collateral damage.

Andrew felt sick. Slamming his full coffee into the trash, he grabbed his computer and stormed out of Starbucks. Whatever Fiona thought she was going to do, she had another thing coming.

CHAPTER TWENTY: RED ON THE CARPET

Janet took one last look at her reflection in the mirror before heading downstairs. "Little princess, I think your Aunt Nicole is right. Being pregnant with you does agree with me."

She was wearing a floor-length silver satin evening gown. The bias cut clung to her curves, and the plunging neckline hugged her growing breasts. Janet could see a slight curve in her belly where a baby bump was beginning to emerge. But, if you didn't know about the pregnancy, it just looked like a pretty rounded belly.

Janet's red hair was pulled back into an elegant side ponytail, and her new emerald earrings sparkled, drawing attention to her long neck. Cherry red lipstick adorned her full lips, and a light touch of eye makeup complemented the look.

Twirling in the mirror, Janet loved the way the dress moved with her. *Oh, little princess. I hope you are a girl and get to feel this way. Even just for one night.*

Slipping on the clear high heels, Janet grabbed her bag and looked around for her phone before remembering she didn't have one and headed downstairs.

BELOVED BY YOU

The classical music in the elevator didn't have its intended effect of being soothing. Janet's stomach was in knots. She hadn't seen Andrew in more than a month. So much had happened since that night of passion. She couldn't let herself think that this would be the last night they would be together…

As the elevator doors opened and Janet crossed the lobby, heels clicking on the marble floors, she could feel the heads turning to stare at her.

Janet did feel like a celebrity tonight. London was a far cry from Francistown. And while she missed Oba terribly, she was determined to enjoy this night.

Suddenly, on the other side of the glass doors, she saw him. He was looking down at his phone and hadn't seen her yet. *My god, he is beautiful.*

Wearing a black tuxedo, the form-fitting shirt clung to that chest. Janet's heart pounded remembering every inch of his body. The tailored pants highlighted his long legs. The jacket strained at his broad shoulders. But the thing that got her the most was that hair. Those curls that were perfect for grabbing in the heat of passion.

Stop. Don't think that, Janet. Don't remember those things. Just focus on the gala.

～

Andrew stood outside the doors of the Ritz Carlton. Although it was a little silly to stand outside the hotel he'd been living at for the last several weeks, he felt it was necessary. Just a few more hours and he could tell Janet everything.

Before he saw her, his phone dinged. It was Mike. One simple text message. "Called Susan. She was pissed. She's on board. As soon as the video is posted, Susan will pull it.."

MOLLY SLOAN

Andrew smiled. Looks like he isn't the only ones with friends in high places.

Looking up, through the glass doors, Andrew saw her. For a moment, he thought he was dreaming. *That can't be her. She looks like a movie star.*

Their eyes met. The glass doors of the hotel opened, and Janet approached Andrew. Time stopped for a moment as they just gazed at each other. Neither one wanted to break the spell.

"Excuse me. Miss?" A little girl with dark curly hair and piercing blue eyes was standing next to them, looking at Janet.

"Yes, sweetheart?" Janet bent down to the girl's eye level.

"Are you a princess?" The little girl looked away shyly.

Andrew answered her. "Yes, young lady. She is."

⁓

The flashing lights of the cameras sounded like popcorn as Janet stepped out of the limo. "Ms. Girard! Over here!" Andrew's arm felt steady and strong as Janet fought to savor the moment. It was a little overwhelming!

The gala was being held at the Andaz London, one of the most popular spots for movie premiers. The hotel had been built at the turn of the century and was finished in 1901. But it wasn't until the late 1990s that a secret space was discovered behind a fake wall. It had been built in 1912 and was a grand, opulent room made with twelve different kinds of Italian marble on the floor, walls and columns, mahogany panels, an organ, candelabras and a blue and gold domed ceiling decorated with zodiac signs. It was unlike anything Janet had ever seen in her life.

Walking over to the bar area, they saw that Winston and

Radhika were already there. As soon as Radhika saw Janet, she practically sprinted over to her.

"Janet! Can you believe this place? A far cry from the lobby at the Department of Mines, isn't it?"

Janet embraced her friend. "It's magnificent."

"Look. Over there. Angelina Jolie is here with all of her kids. They are talking with Oprah and Stedman. I can't believe I am here."

Janet was glad for her friend that she was able to share in this glamorous event.

"Can I get you a drink?" Andrew asked as he leaned down to Janet's ear.

Radhika interjected before Janet could answer. "Actually, I want to steal her away to the little girl's room first."

"Sounds good. I have to go check on some things, anyway. Meet you back here in a few."

As Radhika and Janet made their way across the crowded room, she whispered into Janet's ear, "Does Andrew know yet?"

Janet stopped and looked at her friend. "Know what?"

"About the baby."

"Wait, how did you..."

Radhika just smiled and kept walking. "That glow on your skin isn't just from love, my friend."

CHAPTER TWENTY ONE: GRACEFUL EXIT

"How are we doing?" Andrew looked at the clock on the wall and it said 7:05. He was in a back office of the Andaz, with a security team of people and a bank of computers monitoring YouTube.

"Nothing yet, boss. Looks like he's waiting until 8 as promised."

Or SHE is, Andrew thought bitterly.

"Sounds good. Keep me posted. I need to get back down there so no one gets suspicious."

Slipping out the door, Andrew ran into Nicole in the hallway. She looked beautiful in a floor-length black gown, but Andrew didn't even notice. His mind was on getting back to Janet.

"What's going on? Are we still okay?" Nicole looked worried.

"We're good. Mike is at the YouTube headquarters in California right now, with the head of the company. She is couple friends with his parents."

"Wow."

"Anyway, as soon as the video posts, Susan is going to pull it."

"Why do we need all these guys on this end, then?"

"Because I'm not about to take a chance on our reputation. Mistakes happen. I don't want ANYONE seeing that video. It would ruin lives. It would ruin Janet's reputation if investors - and her mother - thought that someone disreputable had donated the land. I won't risk it. If for some reason, the video plays, the security team here will kill the Internet at the hotel. That would buy us time to get it pulled in California."

"I, for one, am glad. Let's head back down before anyone notices that we're missing."

Dinner had already started when Nicole and Andrew walked up to their table.

"Where have you two been?" Ryan was seated opposite from Winston and Radhika, and there were two empty spaces in between him and Janet.

"Oh, just attending to last-minute gala stuff," Andrew said as he pulled out Nicole's chair, seating him next to Ryan. "Have you two met?"

"No, I haven't had the pleasure." Ryan tried to stand and shake Nicole's hand, but he winced in pain and had to sit back down. "I'm Ryan. The brains behind the BBC 2."

Nicole laughed as she sat down next to him. "I see. The brains, huh? Then what is Andrew?"

"Andrew? Oh, he's the brawn. If we ever need heavy stuff lifted, or someone to sprint really fast across a parking lot, he's the one we call."

They were both chuckling. Nicole extended her hand, and said, "Well, I'm Nicole. It's nice to meet you, Ryan. I'm neither the brains nor the brawn around here…"

Ryan quipped, "Well, then you must be the beauty."

Nicole blushed as she leaned over and said softly, "I was really sorry to hear about your accident. You're really fortunate to have such loyal and amazing friends. It speaks well of your character."

Just then, a woman came up to Nicole and whispered in her ear. Nicole stood up, and said to the group, "If you'll excuse me, it's almost time to premiere the documentary, "Amazing Grace."

~

Radhika leaned across the table and whispered to Janet. "Where's Fiona? I haven't seen her tonight."

Janet realized that she hadn't either. She was about to ask Andrew when she heard his name being announced on stage.

"And now, ladies and gentlemen," Nicole said to the well-dressed crowd, "let's have a round of applause for the man who has made this night possible. Andrew Atherton."

He stood and made his way up to the stage. Standing in front of a large movie screen, he looked poised as he spoke to the crowd.

"A few months ago, I was in Botswana on a business deal, when I met a group of people who would change my life."

The crowd gave Andrew their rapt attention, as he continued. " It's been almost thirty-five years since the Live Aid concert that benefited the people of Africa. And, while massive strides have been made, there is still a crisis there. The AIDS epidemic has affected, probably, every person in this room in one way or another. But we are the lucky few. The chosen ones, if you will, with the resources to afford this thousand-dollars-a-plate dinner. Right now, in another part of the world, there are hundreds of families who can't afford basic medical treatment. Families whose loved ones are dying, leaving children orphaned. But there is a group of people - tireless workers - dedicated to helping ease the crisis. And, tonight, I want to introduce you to one of them. Ladies and Gentlemen, I want to introduce the woman who is the real reason we are here tonight. Ms. Janet Girard."

Andrew stepped down from the stage and gave Janet a polite kiss as she made her way past him. He wanted more, but not with a thousand watching eyes from the audience.

The bright lights blinded Janet as she took the mic. "Thank you so much, Andrew, for the kind words. But I'm not the real reason we are here tonight. The real reason we are here is because of the kids. And my dear friend Nicole was kind enough to create this documentary that shows what my organization, A Place of Grace, is all about. I know we're all excited to see the movie, but let me just take a couple of minutes to give you the backstory of how A Place of Grace came to be."

As Andrew headed back to the table, he placed another sealed note on Janet's chair. He then patted Winston on the back, and made a graceful exit out a side door, unnoticed by Janet. He heard the sound of applause as he headed back up to the offices.

CHAPTER TWENTY TWO: DROPPED

Andrew made his way down the hallway to the back offices of the Andaz Hotel. Behind him, he could hear the laughter and applause of the audience as Janet and Nicole were hosting the gala. A quick glance at his watch told him he'd better hurry. It was almost 8:00.

Turning around a corner in the brightly lit hallway, Andrew literally crashed into someone going the opposite way.

"Andrew! I didn't expect to see you here...why aren't you out at the gala?" It was Fiona.

Seething, Andrew put on his best poker face and smiled. "Fiona! I was looking for you! No one had seen you at the gala, and we wondered where you might be. I opened this door, and it led me down this hallway. What a coincidence that you're here. Let me just text the others and let them know I found you."

Looking down at his phone and texting, Andrew thought, *I should have been an actor. Looks like she bought it.* The text was really to Winston. "Call the police. Have them meet me in the back office at the Andaz."

"I think we need to go this way," Andrew said, as he took Fiona's arm and led her toward the offices. Glancing at his watch again, he picked up the pace a little. It was 7:54 pm.

∼

"Who are you texting, Winston?" Radhika whispered. "The movie is about to start."

"I'll explain later," he whispered back. It was six minutes until the movie was to be released on YouTube, and six minutes until every person in this room would receive an email, text, or push notification that the expose telling the "real story" had been dropped at the same time. Reputations and careers were on the line.

Winston kissed Radhika on the cheek as he stepped out of the room for a moment to call the police. From the other room, he heard Nicole on stage, talking.

"So when Janet invited me to A Place for Grace to volunteer, of course I said yes. What you are about to see is the footage from that day. It captures the life and feel of the orphanage. The heartbreaking story of a little boy who was losing his mother. And the courageous woman who fought to build a home for the hundreds of children displaced…"

∼

As Nicole was introducing the film, Janet ducked her head and headed back to her seat at the table. Instantly, she noticed that Andrew was not there. Where was he? The movie is about to start.

It was then that she saw the note at her seat. It was the same size and handwriting as the one that was on her bed. *Andrew.*

Quietly tearing open the envelope, she held the notecard

below the edge of the table so that no one could see that she was reading. The note said:

Something has come up and I need to go. Meet me at the base of the London Eye at midnight. We need to talk.

Janet's heart sunk. Did he know about the baby? Is that why he left? She knew that she had planned to end things with him tonight, anyway. But, she'd hoped that they would have at least one evening together before it happened.

Oh well, little princess. Fairy tales don't always come true, do they?

Janet's thoughts were interrupted by Nicole's voice from the stage. "And now, the moment we have all been waiting for. I present to you, Straw Barn Publishing's first-ever documentary, "Amazing Grace."

The crowd applauded. The lights dimmed. The screen lit up.

∽

It was go-time. 7:59 pm. Andrew had Fiona by the arm as he was hustling down the hall to the office. He wanted her to see that her plan wasn't going to work. And he wanted to see her face when she realized it.

"Andrew! You're hurting my arm! Why are we walking so fast? I think this is the wrong direction!" Fiona was struggling to keep up with Andrew's pace.

"No, Fiona. This is exactly right where you need to be."

Andrew opened the doors to the office and could see YouTube up on several screens.

"Hey, boss. Nothing yet. We have several channels on screen, from a bunch of different influencers. If something goes wrong, this is gonna drop worldwide. In about sixty seconds."

BELOVED BY YOU

Fiona looked completely confused. "Where are we? Who are these people?" She turned to Andrew and demanded, "What is going on?"

Finally, Andrew let his anger show. "Why don't you tell me?"

"I don't know what you mean?" Fiona looked at him innocently.

"Don't bullshit me. You have been planning this behind my back for weeks. You got footage from A Place for Grace, footage of me at the cemetery, images of Ryan's accident…" He was getting so mad that he was afraid he might lose it.

Taking a deep breath, he calmed and continued. "You sent that stuff to a producer and had a video made. You had Nicole's phone stolen, and then had a hacker send a message to everyone in her contact list. And you did ALL of it, while looking me straight in the eye and pretending to be a loyal employee."

Fiona just looked down at the ground. Tears filled her eyes as she looked up at him.

"Do you know why I did it, Andrew? Do you know why?"

"No, and I don't care."

"I did it because I love you. I have always loved you. From the time we were together until now, I knew that I was the right one for you. But, you had to go and run into Janet again. Fall in love with her. I knew that if I could get her out of the picture, you'd come back to me."

"That makes no sense. You hurt me and my friends so that I would fall in love with you?" Andrew stared at Fiona in disbelief. "Are you really that demented?"

Bitterness swept across Fiona's face. "You don't get it, do you? You and your friends are BILLIONAIRES. You have everything. You always land on your feet. My stupid documentary might dent your image for a few weeks. But, you'll always still be rich. You'll always still have the power to get what you want. That's what money does."

"Guys. Look." One of the security team pointed to the computer monitor. Music began to play, and some video footage from a drone started. "What you are about to see is the REAL story behind The BBC 2. These four college friends, Andrew Atherton, Cole Bennett, Ryan Cummings, and Michael Davis, are all billionaires. Their image is that of philanthropy... but the real story is one of rich men who think they are above the law..."

⁓

Janet wished that Andrew were here to see this. The documentary was magnificent. Images of Andrew and Oba, working together to build the bunk beds. Wide, expansive scenes of A Place for Grace. Elyse in her office. Radhika and Winston, laughing. Coral having a pillow fight with one of the kids. Even Janet, in her cottage. Although it was strange to see herself up on a movie screen, she knew it was for a good cause. But, it really did make her miss home...

I'll be home soon, little king, Janet thought. *And we can start our life as a family...*

Looking around the room, everyone else seemed to be riveted to the screen. Janet could see Angelina and her kids, Oprah and Stedman, and on the other side, Madonna and her kids, with an entourage of admirers. The room was filled with government officials, dignitaries, celebrities, humanitarians, and other people of influence. Five hundred people who could all make a difference in the lives of the African people. Not to mention five hundred people who paid one thousand dollars a plate to be here. That money meant that Janet wouldn't need the Girard Foundation money for a very long time.

How had Andrew managed to pull this off in two weeks? And, where was he? He should be here to see the fruits of his labor.

∼

Andrew sent Winston a text. "What's going on? Are people's phones going off?" Andrew could imagine five hundred phones buzzing and beeping at the same time, as the hacker sent out an alert that the exposé had dropped. While not everyone would stop and watch it right then, enough of them would. *Even if one person does, it will spread like wildfire...*

The security room was silent as the images on the screen continued. Were Mike and Susan going to pull the video in time? Onscreen, Andrew saw his face, and photos of Michael, Ryan, and Cole. Closed captioning had their names right there, in print.

Andrew looked at Fiona, who was watching the monitors with a smug grin.

Come on, Mike. This is going to destroy us.

All at once, the room let out a sigh of relief. The images of the movie were replaced with a black screen that said, "This video is no longer available on YouTube."

Fiona became indignant. "Wait? What? How did you..." Just then, the doors burst open. "Fiona Durant. You are under arrest."

"On what charges?" she demanded. "It's not illegal to release a YouTube video?"

"No, but defamation of character is. And slander, libel, and arranging for theft and phone hacking."

"But the video was pulled before it aired."

"Enough of it ran, and we have evidence that at least a few people saw it. I'd get yourself a good barrister, Ms. Durant. Now, please, come with us."

Fiona turned and glared at Andrew as she was being escorted out the door. "See what I mean? You rich folks always land on your feet."

Andrew just smiled at her and said, "Fiona. You're fired."

CHAPTER TWENTY THREE: THE EYES HAVE IT

The line of cars outside the Andaz was impressive - not only for how many cars there were, but for the opulence. Rolls Royces jockeyed for position with Porsches, Lamborghinis, Maseratis, and of course hundreds of limos. There were headlights and tail lights as far as the eye could see. A light mist was falling, and everything glistened in the light of the full moon.

It would have been a perfect night for romance, except…

Janet stood next to Nicole, Winston, and Radhika watching as the crowd trickled out into the street, looking for their cars and drivers. They could overhear comments about the evening, as the guests passed by.

"I was crying at the end! It was so beautiful."

"I just hope I can make a difference in the world like that."

"That little boy Oba is so cute. I want him!"

"That Andrew Atherton is sure easy on the eyes…"

Andrew. Somehow Janet needed to get to the London Eye by midnight. It was less than three miles away, but with this traffic, she had no idea how she would ever make it.

"Miss Girard?" Janet turned to see a man wearing a chauffeur's uniform standing behind her.

"Yes?"

"Mr. Atherton asked that you come this way."

The others in her small group had overheard, and all smiled, hugging her goodbye. "Have fun!" "You deserve it!"

But Radhika leaned over, and as she kissed Janet's cheek, whispered. "Listen to the man. Listen to what he tells you. Look in his eyes and you will see the truth."

Janet nodded weakly. *I already know the truth. I have to tell him goodbye.*

Winding down a maze of brightly-lit hallways and what appeared to be secret doors, Janet was sure they were going the wrong way.

"Just a few more minutes, Madam. I assure you. This is the fastest route."

"Where are we going?"

"This door will take us to Alderman's Walk. It's a passageway that leads to the large house and gardens of Sir Francis Dashwood."

"I have somewhere to be. I need to get to..."

"I know, Madam. Just trust me. You'll see."

A few minutes later, Janet was surprised to see a sleek black helicopter waiting on the lawn. "A helicopter? You expect me to get into that?"

"Mr. Atherton sent it for you. It's the fastest transportation at the moment."

Unsure, as she ducked her head under the spinning blades of the copter, she got inside. It was deafeningly loud. The pilot handed her some headphones and shouted, "Here, put these on."

As Janet placed them over her cold ears, the helicopter

started to rise. She could see the London Wall below her, as the body of the copter tipped and flew off. The city lights of London floated below her like fireflies. The River Thames glittered under the full moon.

Janet's stomach started fluttering. *Is that you, little princess? I can't wait to show you the world...*

Coming into view was the London Eye. Currently, Europe's tallest Ferris Wheel. It was incredible to think that it was below her. And even more incredible to think that Andrew was down there, somewhere, waiting for her.

Touchdown was much smoother than in an airplane. It was more like a bird landing on a branch. Taking the headphones off, Janet thanked the pilot and was helped out of the helicopter.

Sure glad I'm wearing a gown and high heels, she thought sarcastically. *It's a great night for a hike.*

Looking around, slightly disoriented, Janet didn't see him at first. But the din of the helicopter quieted as it sped away, and Janet heard her name.

"Janet. I'm here."

Walking toward her was the man she loved. The man whose baby she carried. And the man she needed to leave. It was almost too much to bear.

Pushing the thoughts out of her mind for a moment, Janet chattered about the documentary. She told him how the audience loved it, and how everyone laughed when Oba said he wanted to grow up to be a "dock worker" instead of a doctor.

All the while, Andrew was quiet. Janet suspected that he'd found out about the baby somehow and was going to tell her it was over. She needed to break it off with him first.

"Andrew, look. There is something I need to tell you…"

"Janet. Please. Let me go first."

They were standing in front of the London Eye. It was lit

up, but there was no one on it. Andrew opened the door to one of the passenger capsules, and said, "Here. Let's talk in here."

"This night has sure had a lot of ups and downs already," Janet quipped. "What's one more?" Secretly, she was glad to get inside and out of the cold. *Satin isn't exactly the warmest fabric.*

As the Ferris Wheel began to move, Janet got another perspective. What had seemed so far away in the helicopter was so much closer now.

As they reached the apex of the wheel, the movement stopped. It was just like one of Janet's dreams. A full moon...a gentle rain...

"Janet, I have loved you since the day we met. As you know, I was a complete workaholic. But you inspired me to see the world. You've inspired me to be a better person. Because of you, I want to make the world a better place. YOU did that. You are the most amazing, generous, compassionate woman I have ever met."

Andrew stood, pulled something out of his pocket, and got down on one knee in front of Janet. "Janet Girard. I would be the luckiest man on the planet if you would agree to be my wife."

Janet was stunned. Before her was the most magnificent diamond ring she had ever seen. Its sparkle beckoned her in the light of the moon.

"It was my grandmother's. Five carats. She wore it for sixty years. Claudia sent it to me this week when I told her I was going to ask you to marry me. She even hired a bodyguard to fly over with it to make sure it got here safely."

Janet wanted nothing more than to wear that ring for another sixty years. But, with tears in her eyes, she looked at her beloved, and simply said, "No."

Time stopped for a moment as the look on Andrew's face morphed from one of love to one of confusion. "No?"

"Andrew. I can't."

Shaking his head a little to make sure he was hearing correctly, Andrew repeated, "You can't? Why not?"

Janet had promised herself that she wasn't going to say anything. She planned to simply say that she didn't love him and that she wanted to end things.

But her mouth couldn't form the lies. Instead, it all came rushing out, in tears.

"Andrew. I'm pregnant. I'm pregnant and I don't want to burden you. I don't want to be one of those people you and Fiona laugh at…"

"Fiona!" Andrew stood up. "What did she tell you?"

Sobbing now, Janet said, "About how you don't like kids. You never want to be tied down with a family."

"Oh my god. Janet…" Andrew took her face in his hands. "She was lying. It was all lies."

Unsure, Janet looked up at Andrew. *Could he be telling the truth?* Those blue eyes were intense as they stared back at her. She remembered how great he was with Oba…how kind he was with that little girl earlier this evening. His eyes told her what she needed to know. Fiona had been lying to her.

Then, what she had said seemed to register on his face. "Wait. You're pregnant? Right now?"

Janet smiled and nodded. "Yes! I found out a few weeks ago."

Andrew dropped back down to his knees and pressed his face up against Janet's satin dress. "Hello… hello. It's me. Your daddy. I can't wait to meet you. Your mama and brother and I are going to give you the best life. We will be a family. Forever."

Janet could hardly believe it. She and Andrew would raise the baby and Oba… they would be a family.

And with that, Andrew stood and pulled Janet to her feet. At the top of the London Eye, with the full moon lighting the raindrops, and the lights of London illuminated like a Monet painting, Andrew slipped the diamond ring on Janet's finger, looked into her eyes and before he kissed her, said, "You are beloved."

EPILOGUE

"Mama, do I have to growl when I walk down the aisle?" Oba looked so handsome in his suit. He was fidgeting with the white flower pinned to his jacket.

"What do you mean, little king?

"If I am the ring bear, don't I need to growl?"

The women all laughed, and Janet kissed the top of her son's head affectionately. "No, my love. You just be you."

It was one year to the day after that fateful night. The documentary.. the Ferris Wheel… the night spent in her Penthouse Suite after she'd agreed to become his wife. The happy and proud day in court when Oba became their son...They all seemed like distant, yet cherished memories.

Today was the day Andrew would make good on his promise to marry her. This was their wedding day.

Oba had gone into the "Man room" to be with Andrew and his best men. When he'd told the other members of the BBC 2 that he and Janet were finally getting married, they started arguing over who should be best man.

"I was his roommate." "Yeah, but I introduced him to Janet." "Yeah, but I look better in a tux."

In the end, it was Winston who suggested, "Why is it the custom to only have one best man? Why not have all three?" And so he did.

For Janet, the choice was clear. Nicole was the only one who could be her maid of honor. Not only did they go back the farthest, but if it weren't for her, none of this would have happened.

Putting the final touches on her makeup, Janet reflected on the year. When they had gotten back to Francistown (after stopping off at the Apple Store in London to get a new phone), Janet and Andrew threw themselves into their projects.

For Andrew, the diamond mine he purchased turned out to be the most profitable one to date. And with the new sustainable mining methods, he felt comfortable that it was ethical as well as profitable.

The adjacent plots had been developed with the help of Ryan and his family's construction company. Cole infused some additional capital into the project, and now every one of Francistown's 100,000 residents had updated water, electrical, and HVAC systems.

Plus, they had conspired on one other project, dubbed The Hidden Gem. For months, the men would take day trips to who knows where and come back all dusty and sweaty.

For Janet, the infusion of cash from the gala meant that she could update and renovate A Place for Grace. Plus, they had finished construction on Extended Grace, and there were several families already living there. It was still heartbreaking to see, but at least Janet could keep them together as they faced the crisis as a family.

The additional resources, plus the donations and material support that came from the documentary, Amazing Grace, meant that Janet could expand the orphanage, and was able to make it into a self-sustaining charity. Janet no longer needed to take money from the Girard Foundation.

"You look like you're ready for a glass of champagne." Coral handed her a flute and toasted. "I am so happy for you, friend."

Looking around at the wedding preparations, Janet thought, *What an incredible day. Everything is perfect. Wait...you know what that means...*

Sure enough, there was a knock on the door. Without waiting for an answer, Alexis Girard breezed in. "Ladies. May I have the room?"

Grinning, Nicole, Elyse, Radhika, and Coral all filed out.

"Mother. I thought you were with Daddy in the waiting area."

"I was, but I wanted a moment alone with you. It's not every day that your only daughter gets married."

"True, but the ceremony is about to start."

With an expansive sweep of her hand, Alexis said, "Darling. It's not like they can start without you."

Janet laughed and took another sip of champagne. "Okay. Fine. Out with it. What are the pearls of wisdom you have for me?"

Alexis got strangely quiet. "They aren't pearls of wisdom. It's an apology. I haven't been a very good mother to you. I realized on the flight over here that I was jealous of you."

Janet sat back in shock.

"You are so beautiful and strong. You forged a life for yourself that is full of depth and meaning. When I got pregnant with you, I did the opposite. I folded my life into your father's. I gave up my dreams to become a mother. And I resented you for it."

"Mom…"

"No, wait. I have to finish or I won't be able to get it out. My wish for you, Janet, is that you know the joy in your husband and children that I never had. Not that it wasn't there, but I didn't look for it. I was looking for a life that didn't exist, when I had everything I needed right here. With you."

Crying, the mother and daughter embraced for several minutes. "Oh, now look. We've messed up our makeup. Let's get someone in here to fix it…"

Standing outside the door that led into the chapel, Janet heard her father's voice. "Are you ready?" Squeezing his hand, she nodded. *I've never been more ready for anything in my life.*

The organ music began, and Coral walked down the aisle, holding baby Gouta. Janet was so happy that Andrew had agreed to name their daughter after Oba's birth mother. The baby's dark ringlets bounced as her godmother Coral carried her and gave her flower petals to drop. Watching the petals float to the ground was a wonderful game to Gouta, and she giggled all the way down the aisle.

Next was Oba. Six years old and standing tall, he was so serious about balancing the rings on the pillow he carried. It was an important task, they'd told him. And he took it to heart.

Their friends were next, walking down the aisle arm in arm. First, Michael and Elyse. Then, Cole and Radhika. Finally, Nicole and Ryan walked together. Ryan still had a slight limp from the accident, and Nicole's arm was steadying as he held it. Was it Janet's imagination, or was there some chemistry there?

Before she had a chance to contemplate that further, the music changed. Everyone stood to face her. The bridal march commenced, and Janet and her father slowly made their way around the aisle. Janet was blown away as she looked around. The entire church was filled to standing room capacity with members of the community. The children from A Place for Grace had formed a choir and would sing the recessional hymn. Claudia was there, next to Winston and David. Everyone that she knew and loved was in one place...

As Janet's father passed her hand from his to Andrew's, her heart swelled. This was what life was all about. Love and family. Serving others. Making life better, every day.

Hand in hand, eye to eye, together, Janet and Andrew said, "I do."

"I am going to fall. I can't see where I'm walking!" Janet was gripping Andrew's arm. Blindfolded, he had whisked her away after the wedding reception.

"Do you want to see The Hidden Gem or not? We can turn around if you want?" Andrew was being playful.

"No, no. I have been dying to see this mysterious project of yours for months. Every time I ask anyone in town, they just look away and change the subject. It's a conspiracy!"

"Okay, then. Are you ready?"

"Am I ever!"

Andrew removed Janet's blindfold and caught her as she went weak in the knees.

"Oh my god. Andrew. Is this…?"

"Yes, Red. It's our home. The one we dreamed about that weekend in the Hamptons."

"How did you? I mean, this is Africa…" Janet was agape at the huge white house that stood before her. It was an exact replica of the house they had dreamed of building so many years ago."

"I told you. I have friends everywhere." He grinned, as he lifted her up to carry her over the threshold.

"It's so beautiful."

"No…our family is beautiful." Andrew carried his wife into their home, where Oba and Gouta waited. As they closed the door, Janet noticed a sign over the fireplace that said, "You are Beloved."

BEGUILED BY YOU

CHAPTER ONE: THE WAKE-UP CALL

You have to be kidding me, thought Nicole Burns, as her mind surfaced to consciousness. *Again? What time is it now?*

She reached over and grabbed her phone that was charging on the nightstand. Even before she opened her eyes, Nicole knew what it would say: 2:35 am. She had awakened at this same time for the past five nights in a row. Practically slamming the phone back down in frustration, she rolled back over angrily. *I do not need this insomnia thing again. What I need is a good night's sleep!*

A lot had happened in Nicole's life since her documentary chronicling the plight of AIDS orphans in Botswana came out last year. First, there was the Academy Award nomination, which had come as a complete shock to Nicole. As the head of Straw Barn Publishing, the world of movies was not one she had been familiar with. She'd produced the documentary mostly as a favor to her best friend Janet Girard - now Atherton - to raise money for Janet's orphanage A Place for Grace. They'd had a premiere in London, and then distributed the movie on YouTube, to worldwide critical acclaim.

But despite being her first effort, the movie, *Amazing Grace*, had garnered a lot of attention from celebrities and powerful Hollywood producers. Nicole found herself being interviewed on talk shows, flying around the world, and even giving a TED talk! It had been a whirlwind!

Although they didn't win the Oscar, the publicity helped Straw Barn get a ton of new projects. In fact, Nicole had to make some tough decisions and let a few publications go, as they didn't fit the new brand image of the company. In the past year, Nicole and her team had revamped the publishing company to focus on social causes and activism. The new tagline was "Do. Good." But the transition didn't come without a lot of stress and sleepless nights.

I don't think I've slept through the night since I got back to New York, Nicole thought, as she threw her covers off and sat up in bed. Leaning back on the down-filled pillow, she gazed out the window of her Upper East Side apartment. The city lights were twinkling and she could see the moonlight reflecting on the water. She wondered how many other people were sitting awake, too, in "the city that never sleeps."

Giving up on her quest for rest, Nicole put on her white cotton robe and padded into the kitchen to make a cup of tea. *There is something about being alone in the middle of the night that makes one ponder their life choices.* She thought of Janet, happily married to her soul mate Andrew. She'd adopted Oba, the young son of a woman who Janet had befriended before she passed away from complications of AIDS. She and Andrew now had the perfect life, with baby Gouta (named after Oba's birth mother) completing the family. Would Nicole ever find her soul mate and start a family? Or, would she always be so focused on her career that there would be no time for a real relationship?

Maybe I just need to have a baby... she thought. That made her laugh out loud, as she took her tea to the living room. *Right. I couldn't even handle having a cat at this point.*

Sinking into her white couch, and flipping on the television, Nicole began mindlessly surfing the channels. An infomercial for a new kitchen gadget... an old rerun of *I Love Lucy*... A Clint Eastwood movie dubbed in Spanish... Nicole was about to give up and turn the television off when she landed on the public broadcasting channel and a medical doctor talking about the devastating effects of stress in women.

"Do you find yourself waking up at night, sweating and worrying about your life?" *Yes,* Nicole thought.

"Have you felt your heart racing to the point where you felt like you couldn't catch your breath?" *Yes...*

"Do you suffer from intrusive thoughts that keep you from concentrating on the things you need to focus on? And, then overreact to small frustrations?" *YES!* Nicole sat forward, leaning into the TV. *That's me!*

"You might be suffering from Generalized Anxiety Disorder. Of course, only your physician can diagnose this, but there is help out there..."

That's ridiculous, Nicole thought. *I don't have a mental health problem. I have a stressful job. Nothing I can't handle.* And with that, she clicked the remote, turned the TV off, and headed back to try and sleep. *I'll call my primary care doctor tomorrow and get a prescription for sleeping pills. I just need to catch up on my sleep. That's all...*

CHAPTER TWO: DO NOT PASS GO

Ryan Cummings hated being left on hold. Especially when the receptionist didn't even ask him if it was okay. She'd just said, "Please hold" and the next thing he knew he was listening to Michael Bublé singing *Save the Last Dance for Me*. When was the last time he'd even danced, he wondered? Maybe Andrew and Janet's wedding? Unaware he was doing it, Ryan softly started singing along

"You alright, man? John Fisch grinned as he stuck his head in Ryan's office door. "You know, if the whole family business thing doesn't work out, you might try out for *The Voice*."

Pushing the button to hang up the phone, Ryan shook his head. "Very funny. Come in, sit down!"

Like Ryan, John was an Executive Vice President at Cummings Construction, the international consulting and construction company. But, unlike John, Ryan was the son of the company's founder. He'd risen to the top, first as an architect, all the way to become the head of the company's worldwide hotel and leisure division. John was the head of the gaming division and supervised the design and construction of casinos around the world. Needless to say, they often worked together on combination hotel/casino construction projects.

"You didn't have to hang up. I could have come back." John pulled out the thick leather chair that sat opposite Ryan's glass and steel desk and sank down into it. "I know how you hate being on hold."

"No, I was just trying again to reach Rick. I swear, I think he's avoiding me." Ryan swiveled his chair around to gaze at the San Francisco skyline out his top floor corner office window. The fog was now starting to roll in. Ryan ran his hand through his thick, chocolate colored hair.

Rick Tomson had become something of a nemesis to Ryan. He was Ryan's corporate equivalent at Cummings Construction's biggest competitor, The Eden Group. Both men often battled over the same property where they each wanted to build hotels or luxury resorts.

Now, they were both going after the same land in Texas. Ryan had plans to build a boutique hotel on some land near the new Dallas Cowboys training facility. Rick wanted to build a mammoth 1000-room hotel in the same area. Ryan had been trying to phone Rick to work out a deal, but the other man wouldn't take his calls.

"He probably is avoiding you. Remember how hard you guys clashed over the Prima deal?"

"How could I forget? That's what I was doing in London when I had the accident." The year prior, Ryan had been in London trying to secure a land deal to build a couples' retreat near the Thames river when he'd been in a devastating car accident. Three days in a coma were followed by three months in a hospital, relearning how to walk. Although his best friends had flown to his bedside, it was a dark, lonely time in Ryan's life.

Ryan paused to reflect for a moment and then shook his head as if to forget the painful memory.

John leaned forward empathetically. "We were all really worried about you."

Trying to lighten the mood, Ryan quipped, "Hey. I'm part of the BBC 2. Just another selfish, entitled billionaire, if you ask some people."

Ryan was referring to an incident that happened right after he'd been released from the hospital. A spurned lover of one of his best friends, Andrew Atherton, had recorded an exposé called *The Real Story of the BBC 2.* It was filled with lies and had been intended to ruin the reputation of Ryan and his three best friends from college, Andrew, Cole Bennett, and Michael Davis.

The four men had formed a club called The BBC 2 - a riff on the infamous Billionaire Boys Club from the 1980s. While the original BBC had used their money and power to bilk innocent people out of their retirement money, Ryan and his friends wanted to find a way to use their money and power for good. So, each of the billionaire friends spent quite a bit of time involved in charity work around the world. Fortunately, the men were able to stop the video from being released, and their reputations remained intact.

"Some people just want to believe the worst," John commented. "I, for one, know the kinds of humanitarian projects you guys do. Doesn't your friend Andrew run an orphanage?"

"His wife Janet does. But he lives in Africa full-time now, so you're close enough. He's there practically every day."

Standing to leave, John grinned. "I want to know how I can join this Billionaire Boys Club Two. What do I have to do, fall off a horse or something?"

"No, but if you win a billion dollars at the races, let's talk." Ryan teased as he picked his phone up.

Closing the door behind him, John said, "Let me know when you finally get hold of Rick. I have a feeling he is going to fight you on this Texas deal."

Ryan frowned as he held the phone to his ear. "Rick Tomson's office," the voice on the phone said. "Please hold."

CHAPTER THREE: DOCTOR'S ORDERS

"I can't give you a prescription for sleeping pills, Nicole." Dr. Aldi put her file down on the counter in the exam room.

"I don't understand. I can't sleep. Isn't that what sleeping pills are for? To help you sleep?" Nicole knew she was being a little testy with the doctor, but tiredness can do that.

Dr. Aldi sat down on the little swivel stool near his computer monitor and turned it so that she could see it from the exam table. "You're right that prescription sleep medications can help patients improve the quality of their sleep. However, you have more going on here than just insomnia. Look."

Pointing to the dizzying array of graphs and numbers, he continued. "Your heart rate is elevated. Your blood pressure is on the border of diagnosable hypertension. You've lost weight, despite you telling the nurse that you haven't been dieting or increased your exercise. This indicates to me that you aren't eating well. Your blood markers show an elevated level of cortisol, and your liver enzymes are a bit high. Have you been drinking a lot of coffee or alcohol?"

Nicole sat there for a moment, blinking. "Uh, well, yeah? I mean, I drink a fair amount of coffee because I'm not sleeping. And, there is usually a bottle of wine at my business dinners a couple of days a week." She didn't mention the nightly glass of red wine she had in order to get sleepy enough for bed.

Dr. Aldi turned to face her. "Nicole, I have been your doctor for many years now. Your life has been incredibly stressful lately. I don't only want to treat the symptoms I am seeing here. Your blood pressure... your insomnia... overusing caffeine and alcohol... those are just the symptoms of something deeper."

Nicole knew in her heart that what he was saying was true. Her eyes filled with tears as she nodded yes and asked, "But, what can I do? I don't know how to stop it."

"When was the last time you took some time off?"

"Last year I did some volunteer work at an orphanage in Africa. But that was a work thing."

"Let me put it to you as directly as I can. You really need to take some time away. I'm not talking a weekend or even a regular two-week vacation. You need some extensive time to recover your health. Right now, nothing irreversible has happened. But it is my professional medical opinion that if you don't find a way to reduce your stress level, your health is going to be in serious jeopardy. I've seen women have heart attacks, develop cancer, or ruin their endocrine systems from this kind of prolonged stress."

He put his hand on her arm. and looked empathetically in her eyes. "I care about you, Nicole. I really do. Please, take my advice."

"Hey, Janet. Is it too early to call?" Nicole was sitting in bed. It was 2:30 am again, and she couldn't sleep. But this time her mind was reeling with what Dr. Aldi had told her.

She waited until a respectable 7:30 am in Botswana to call her friend.

"No, not at all. Andrew and I are just sitting in bed having our morning coffee before Gouta wakes up. But it's the middle of the night in New York. Is everything okay?"

Nicole related everything the doctor told her. After she finished, Janet agreed. "I have been telling you this for months, Nic. It's been too much for you. I am not surprised at all that your health is starting to suffer. I mean, how many projects can one woman juggle? I know you're Superwoman and all, but everyone has their limits."

In tears, Nicole lamented, "I don't know what to do. I can't just take off work for weeks at a time. Plus, I don't even know where I would go."

Nicole could hear Andrew's voice murmuring in the background. Janet relayed his comments. "Andrew just had an idea. Remember his friend Ryan Cummings? From the wedding? Ryan's uncle Cal has a ranch in Texas. He's always looking for summer ranch help."

Nicole started laughing through her tears. "Are you kidding? Me? On a dude ranch? That is the funniest thing I've heard all day."

"Why not? It could be fun. It's certainly different than what you're doing now."

Nicole remembered her childhood summers in upstate New York. Her family would take holidays to Saratoga Springs, and she'd always wanted to learn to ride horses. Her mother thought it was too dangerous, though, and so she'd never been allowed near the majestic beasts. Something in Nicole's heart began to stir.

"But, there's no way I could get away. Certainly not for the whole summer." Although her words were protesting, Nicole's mind was working to find ways that this idea might be possible.

"Didn't you tell me you just promoted Christina? Surely a woman with an undergraduate degree in Communication from Princeton and double Master's Degrees in Journalism and Business from Yale is qualified to handle a few projects over the summer…"

"True…" Nicole's head was swimming. She did just promote Christina and trusted her completely. *It wouldn't be that hard to get her up to speed on things.* "But, what about this Cal guy? He's not going to want some city girl who knows nothing about animals to come work on his ranch."

"Andrew and Ryan actually spent a lot of time there when they were in college, and his Aunt Cathy always had a "bunch of city slickers", as she called them. They really like teaching people how to care for and connect with animals. Plus, it's free help."

With her last possible excuse extinguished, Nicole was silent.

"Do it, Nic. You need this. What do you have to lose?"

Imagining herself falling off a horse, being trampled by a steer, and then being pecked to death by chickens, Nicole quipped sarcastically, "I can't think of a thing…"

CHAPTER FOUR: RICK-ROLLED

"Does he know you're coming?" Ryan was talking to John through the Bluetooth speakers in the Cadillac Escalade. A switch from the white Porsche he drove in San Francisco, Ryan noted that it's true that 'everything is bigger in Texas;' including rental cars.

"No. He's still not taking my calls." Ryan was cruising up the Dallas North Tollway on his way to surprise Rick Tomson at his Highland Park home. He'd stopped by Rick's office as soon as his jet had landed, but the receptionist told him that Rick was working from home today.

"You know where that is, right?" she'd said, not even bothering to stop chewing her gum. Not wanting to tip Rick off that he was coming, and knowing that Google makes it easy to find anyone, he'd said yes and got out of there.

"I'm a little curious about something," John said. "You and Rick have had quite a contentious relationship over the years. What makes you think he's going to want to let you have any piece of this deal?"

"I don't know. Optimism, I guess? I always kind of hope that people will be generous and do the right thing. In this case, that land is plenty big enough for us to share, and I figure it doesn't hurt to ask."

"Well, just be careful. I hear he has a temper. And they like their guns in Texas." John chuckled.

"Not like us California pacifists, right?" Hitting "end" on the call, Ryan began to take notice of his surroundings. The first time he'd come to Dallas, years ago, Ryan expected to see open plains and flat land, just like on TV. However, much of Dallas was suburban and green. Highland Park was one of the wealthiest areas in town and Ryan was looking forward to seeing what Rick's house looked like. As an architect by trade, Ryan could always tell a lot about a person by the kind of house they chose to build.

As the road curved past the Texas Scottish Rite Hospital for Children, Ryan felt his heart tug. Ever since he'd attended the premiere of that documentary *Amazing Grace,* Ryan had developed a deep compassion for children in need. Ryan's own childhood had been wonderful, and he couldn't imagine how hard it must be as a child to lose your parents or to face a debilitating illness. Feeling a lump rising in his throat, he shook it off. *Stay focused, man. You're here to talk to Rick.*

Veering around Jourdan Way, Ryan was impressed by the massive mansions with their stately lawns and circular driveways. It wasn't the money, of course, that impressed Ryan. He was a billionaire himself, and could easily afford any one of these homes. It was the image of power and influence conveyed by the architecture. These were the movers and shakers of Dallas, Texas.

As his GPS voice announced "Arrived," Ryan had to laugh. *I should have known,* he thought, pulling in through the open gates of Rick's house. *Of course his house would look like this.*

Set among the elegant, beautiful homes was one that was so garish and, dare he say, tacky, that it could only belong to Rick Tomson. Huge stone gargoyles lined the driveway, emitting some kind of smoke from their mouths. It was like a scene out of Indiana Jones. The house itself was a strange conglomeration of different architectural styles. Classical columns lined the front steps, competing for attention with the church-like steeples of the Gothic Revival-styled roof. On the lawn was some odd modern sculpture shaped like a giant egg cracking open, and to the left, near the lake, was a Japanese tea house complete with blue tiles on the roof. Ryan literally laughed out loud as live peacocks strolled the grounds. *It's like he went to a buffet and brought back a little bit of everything,* Ryan thought. *But I'm the one getting indigestion.*

Leaving the huge white Escalade in the driveway, Ryan climbed the massive set of stairs that led to the front door. A huge metal knocker that was the diameter of a car tire adorned the gold and red flecked door. Spying a doorbell, Ryan pressed the button. From inside the house, he could hear what sounded like organ music. *That's his doorbell? It's as loud as he is.*

Ryan stood there for a good three minutes, waiting. He assumed that whoever was responsible for answering the door was checking him out on the video security camera, so he smiled and waved at the not-very-well-disguised lens. The Cadillac parked behind him would tell them that he wasn't there as a door-to-door salesman.

Finally, the massive door creaked open. Facing him was a tiny Hispanic woman in a traditional black and white maid's outfit, complete with a little white hat that sat atop her ebony bun. "Can I help you?"

"Yes, I'm here to see Rick Tomson."

"Is he expecting you?"

"No, I'm afraid not. We're old business associates and I was just in the neighborhood and thought I'd stop by."

Eyeing him up and down, the woman finally asked, "And what is your name?"

"Ryan Cummings."

"Please wait here." The solid door echoed through the house as the woman closed it behind her, leaving Ryan standing on the porch. He could hear the squeaking of her rubber soles fade away as she went into the bowels of the home.

Checking his text messages and e-mails while he waited, he was half-tempted to take a picture of this ridiculous house and send it to John. It looked like it belonged in one of his Vegas casinos. Before he could, though, he heard the squeaking shoes approach, followed by the clomping of what sounded like cowboy boots.

"Ryan Cummings. What the hell are you doing here?" Rick was smiling, as he extended a handshake to Ryan. "Come on in." He patted Ryan on the back, just a little too hard, as he escorted him through the mammoth door. "You want somethin' to drink? Lupita, get Mr. Cummings a beer." Turning to Ryan, "You like beer, right? What kind do you want?"

Imperceptibly shaking his head at the false hospitality, Ryan smiled at Lupita, and said, "Sure. Whatever you have…"

Following Rick across the foyer and into a massive wood-paneled office, lined with animal heads mounted on plaques, Ryan spoke. "I've been trying to call you for a couple of weeks about this Frisco land deal."

"Oh, yeah. That must be my new secretary's fault. She's kind of an idiot. But, she has other talents, if you know what I mean." Rick winked and laughed boorishly at his own joke.

Ryan knew full well that it wasn't the secretary's fault. Taking the beer from Lupita, he nodded thanks and then set the drink down on the coaster that was set atop the solid oak conference table. "I was hoping we might find some kind of compromise. I know that you want to develop the majority of the land and put up a large hotel. My plans are to build a small, boutique place, that accommodates maybe 50 people. It's targeting a completely different demographic than your hotel will. I suggest that we parcel the land, and Cummings can buy 20% of it for our project, leaving you with 80% for yours."

The veneer of hospitality faded from Rick's eyes, as he took a step backward. "Well, you see here Ryan, I'm afraid that's just not possible."

"Why not? It would save us from having to go to court. We approach the seller and get him to sell us separate parcels of land... What's the problem?"

"The problem, Mr. Cummings, is that I don't like to share. And I sure as hell ain't sharing with the guy who stole the Byrne property out from under me." Rick's face was getting red.

"Are you still on that?' Ryan was incredulous. "That was, like, ten years ago! And I didn't steal it. The seller chose my offer. That's the business. You know that." Taking a deep, calming breath, he took a swig of his beer. "Rick, listen. I respect that you've been in this business for years. Heck, I've even stayed in some of your properties. You do good work. There has to be some way we can both get what we want here. I'm open to suggestions from you as to how we can both win, and stay out of court. No one has to lose."

Rick wasn't budging. "Son. You got one thing right. I don't like to lose. And I sure as hell don't like to lose to you..." He stomped to the door of his office, yanked it open, and barked, "There will be no compromise. Lupita can show you out, and I'll see your ass in court!"

CHAPTER FIVE: DEEP IN THE HEART OF TEXAS

"Come on in, sugar." Cathy Cummings waved Nicole in through the front door of her home. "No one uses the front door around here. We're kitchen door folks."

Nicole was admittedly nervous as she crossed the threshold with her well-used Louis Vuitton luggage set wheeling behind her. She felt out of place, wearing her New York traveling clothes.

"Did you find Steve okay? I know DFW is a huge airport."

"Yes, thank you. He was waiting at the bottom of the escalator as I came off. The sign with my name on it was a nice touch."

Cathy laughed at that. "Steve has been our ranch manager for probably twenty years. He doesn't usually do our guest pickups, but Cal had to go into the office today. I'm glad he made that silly sign if it got you here faster. You want somethin' to drink? Maybe some sweet tea?"

Nicole set her luggage aside next to a large, curved stairway with a simple wood banister. She wasn't sure what she had been expecting, but the ranch felt so much more homely than she had anticipated. "That would be nice, thank you."

Following Cathy, Nicole walked into the large eat-in kitchen. White wood cabinets with open glass fronts lined the walls. Against the wall was a restored classic O'Keefe & Merritt antique stove. A wide, scrubbed pine table was nestled against the window, and French doors led out to a covered patio. "Let's have our tea outside, shall we? I can't wait to learn more about you and that publishin' business you run."

Cathy was charming and looked every bit the wealthy Texas socialite. Nicole imagined that she had once been a Miss Texas or a Dallas Cowboys Cheerleader. But now, in her fifties, Cathy Cummings was an elegant woman. Her styled blonde curls bounced as she walked, and her flat-soled Ferragamo shoes barely made a sound as she crossed the tile floor. Her look was completed with khaki pants, and a turquoise silk blouse, with simple pearls as an accent.

Taking a sip of the blessedly cool tea, Nicole carefully sat on one of the plush patio chairs. "This is delicious."

"Thank you, sugar. It's my mama's famous peach sweet tea. We live by it here in the summer."

Cathy lowered her voice discreetly. "I understand you haven't been feelin' very well. I am quite sure that spendin' the summer in the fresh air will cure everything that's ailing you." She winked and leaned back. "Now, tell me. What was it like goin' to the Academy Awards?"

As she sat on the patio, taking in the view, Nicole could hear Cathy's voice from the kitchen. She'd been called to the phone a few minutes before, giving Nicole a welcome opportunity to just sit and relax for a moment.

The whirlwind of the past week since the doctor's appointment and her decision to follow his advice hadn't done much to calm Nicole's stress level. When she'd called the staff meeting to announce that she would be taking the summer off to spend it on a dude ranch in Texas, the shocked look on everyone's faces had transformed into relief and support. "We are so glad, Nicole." "We've all been so worried about you." *Had it been that obvious to everyone?*

But now, as she sat in the warm summer Texas breeze, Nicole's mind started to calm down a little. She felt terribly out of place in this setting, of course. Her world was filled with honking taxis and Ubers, well-dressed business people hustling down the streets, and dark shadows cast from skyscrapers. This world was quiet. You could hear the leaves rustling in the wind, the moo of a distant cow, and birds softly chirping. And the sky! Nicole had traveled the world, but she couldn't remember ever having seen such a brilliant blue, wide-open sky. Only a couple of cotton ball clouds broke the vista.

"I'm so sorry, Nicole. This is takin' longer than I thought it would," Cathy whispered to her from the doorway. "Why don't you go get settled and join us for dinner at five." With that, she retreated in the house with a "Bless her heart…" to whoever was on the other end of the line.

When Nicole went back to the staircase for her things, they were gone. She assumed that someone had taken them up to wherever her room was going to be. Not wanting to wander around inside a strange house, she decided to go for a walk. *Time for some of that fresh air everyone has been telling me to get.*

She went through another set of French doors that led to the patio and walked past the neatly trimmed hedges that surrounded a sparkling blue swimming pool. Seeing it, she was glad that she'd dug her old swimsuit out of storage and packed it, and she headed down a gravel path next to a fenced-in pasture.

Off to the left of the pasture was a classic red barn. As she got closer, she could hear whinnying from inside. Horses! Curious as to how many there were, she went to the side of the barn and peered in the window. It was dark inside, but she could make out the shapes of two or three horses.

I don't even know what kind they are, she thought. *I am going to make a fine fool of myself this summer.* But something in her heart called to her, and she tiptoed over to the barn door and stuck her head inside. The scent of fresh hay hit her nose, along with a faint manure smell. The walls were lined with shovels and rakes and other tools, and there was a huge stack of hay along the back wall.

Drawn inside, Nicole walked over to a narrow workbench. Imagining she was a cowgirl working on horseshoes, she felt as if she were in some kind of Western novel. But she was still wearing her expensive New York traveling clothes, not blue jeans.

As her hand traced the leather saddle that sat on a stand, she practically jumped out of her skin when she heard a loud snort. It had come from one of the stalls.

Walking into the shadow, the image of a horse came into view. He was several feet taller than her (at least she assumed it was a he), and his long black mane looked as if it belonged in a shampoo commercial. His coat looked so soft - as if it were made of mink.

He seemed curious as to who this stranger was, and nickered a friendly greeting.

"Hi! Hello there." Nicole was mesmerized by those dark chocolate eyes. "Can I pet you? Your hair looks so soft..."

Slowly approaching his stall, Nicole leaned on the gate to reach out and touch the side of the horse's face.

But, instead of supporting her weight, the gate swung open, and Nicole fell face first into the stall!

The horse was spooked and retreated to the far side of the stall. Nicole was as frightened as he was! Rolling over onto her back, she smelled it before she saw it. She'd fallen straight into a large pile of manure! She was covered in horse poop! It was on her pants, the front of her shirt, on her face, and even in her hair!

Brushing as much off as possible, Nicole ran back out of the stall. *I'm an idiot! How am I going to walk back in that house looking like this? I don't even know where my clothes are!*

Nicole latched the gate to the stall and started to run back to the main house, mortified. *I never should have left New York. I am not cut out for this at all.*

CHAPTER SIX: THE GIFT

"I really appreciate this, Uncle Cal." Ryan was headed north on the 75 in the Escalade. "I was planning on flying back to San Francisco tonight, but things didn't go very well in my meeting."

I guess John was right about Rick, Ryan thought. *I had no idea he was still holding on to that Byrne deal. The man can hold a grudge!*

"Not to worry, Ryan. We have more than enough room. Stay as long as you need to." The older man's deep, slow drawl brought Ryan back to the summers he'd spent on the ranch as a child.

"I should be there in time for dinner. Five, sharp, right?"

Cal chuckled. "Got that right. You know your Aunt Cathy is a stickler for on-time family dinners."

Passing Plano, on his way to Parker, Ryan felt the tension dissipate as the landscape changed into ranch country. *I can't believe Rick still thinks I stole that deal from him. Oh, well. Like the old saying goes, "We don't see things as they are, we see them as WE are."*

Ryan's eye spotted a gift shop off the highway, and he

decided to take a few minutes and get a "thank you" gift for his Aunt Cathy. After all, he might be staying on the ranch for a while, since he was evidently going to have to go to court to fight over the Frisco land.

The gravel crunched under his tires as he pulled into the Gifts 'n Treasures gift shop. Chuckling at the name he thought, *Not just gifts, not just treasures, but gifts AND treasures...*

The girl behind the counter greeted him with a hearty, "Well hello there!" She wore a blue checkered top, some jeans, a silver metal belt, and had the requisite "Texas hair" that so many females in this part of the world wore. He wondered how much hairspray it took to get a woman's hair that big.

Rushing over to him, she said, "My name's Denise. Are you looking for something in particular?" *Is she batting her eyes?*

"Hi, Denise. Yeah, I'm looking for a house gift for my aunt. I'm going to be staying in Parker for a while on business and want to say thank you."

Denise unconsciously touched her hair, as she smiled and said, "Oh, you're from out of town, are you? Well, a big ole' Texas welcome to ya!" Her attempt at a flirtatious giggle fell flat.

Walking over to a glass case, she pointed to some ceramic cowboy hats and other touristy items. "What kinds of things does she like? We have these salt and pepper shakers…"

"No, I'm looking for something a little more… elegant."

"Ohhh! How about this?" Denise gestured to a case with a silver bracelet that had two "Cs" interlocking. It was perfect! Cathy Cummings!

"I'll take it." As he made his way to the register, something else caught his eye. It was a small pendant, with a black horse that had a long mane. It reminded him of the horse he used to ride as a teenager on Uncle Cal's ranch. *It's probably made of onyx*, he thought. At the top of the pendant was a diamond-encrusted horseshoe. It was a stunning piece, one that he'd be more likely to find in Atherton Diamonds than in a tiny gift shop. *Gifts AND treasures*, he chuckled again.

Not really knowing why, Ryan decided to get the pendant. *Maybe I'll give it to my mom for Christmas or something. It's just too pretty to pass up.* Pointing to the case, Ryan told Denise, "I'll take this one, too."

Denise's eyes and smile were almost as big as her hair when Ryan pulled out his American Express Centurian card to pay for his purchases. "Is there anything else I can get you, Mr. Cummings?" Leaning in to show her cleavage, she repeated, "Anything at all?"

"No, ma'am. You've been most helpful," he said, and the bells on the front door jingled as he opened them. "Have a nice evening."

Reminded of the time, he glanced at his Apple Watch and cursed under his breath. "Dammit! I'm going to be late for dinner!"

CHAPTER SEVEN: STARTING TIME

Nicole was practically running back to the main house. Covered in muck and feeling panicked, she was thinking of simply finding her suitcases, leaving the ranch, and going back home. *I can just send them a text message from the airport.*

As the white main house drew close, Nicole slowed to a power walk. The last thing she wanted was for Cathy to see her looking like this. *If I sneak in the door off the great room, I can tiptoe up the stairs and find my room. Then, I'll figure out what to do from there,* she thought.

In the distance, Nicole spied a large white car pull in the side driveway, and some kind of dog running to it, barking. *Great! A diversion! Maybe everyone will go talk to that person and not notice me coming in.*

Crouching down behind the tall hedges, Nicole felt like one of Charlie's Angels as she made her way up to the French doors that led into the great room. *Please don't let them be locked,* she prayed silently.

Pausing for a moment at the end of the hedge, all she had to do was make it across the deck of the pool, and into the doors. The man in the white car was talking to someone, and the dog was running circles around him, as they all went in the kitchen door. *Bless, you, dog,* she thought.

One…two…three…GO! Nicole took off running, still crouched, toward the doors. She reached out to turn the handle on the door, and… yes! It opened! Nicole quietly slipped inside the room.

Stopping for a moment to let her eyes adjust to the indoor lighting, she surveyed the room for the best path to the stairs. *The last thing I need to do right now is bump into anything and make a noise.* She could hear voices and laughter coming from the kitchen. "Good girl, Ellie!" she heard a man's voice say.

That's right, Ellie. You just keep distracting them. Nicole figured out that if she went around the back of the couch, in between it and the bookshelf, she could avoid the opening to the kitchen. She could then do a quick U-turn and run up the stairs without being detected.

Okay. Let's do this. Nicole scurried around the couch, and was about to make the U-turn when she stepped on something that went SQUEAK! She froze and looked down to see what it was. A dog toy! Deciding not to stop, she kept looking down as she approached the stairway, as to not step on any more noisy toys. She was almost home free.

Just as she was making the turn to climb the first step, Nicole ran smack into someone! Losing her balance for the second time that day, Nicole fell to the ground with a thud.

"Oh my God, are you okay?"

From the ground, Nicole spied a pair of brown cowboy boots, attached to a pair of long, masculine legs clad in blue jeans. "Yeah, I'm okay. I was just…"

As her eyes made their way up to the face of the man extending his hand out to help her stand up, she was confused. The face was familiar. She knew him. *Where do I know him from?*

"Nicole?" The man's face was as incredulous as she imagined her own was. "What are you doing here?"

It was Ryan Cummings. Of course he could be here. This was his uncle's ranch.

Taking his hand as he pulled her off the ground, she tried to maintain composure. "Oh, they didn't tell you? I came to spend the summer. To help with the animals. I was just.."

Suddenly, Nicole remembered. She was covered in manure! *Her clothes... was it still on her face? Oh my God. How embarrassing.*

"What happened to you? You're a mess!" Ryan chuckled, and his eyes twinkled with amusement. "Were you trying to get the scoop on one of the horses?"

Ignoring his publishing pun, she looked down at the ground, wishing it would swallow her up. "It was, yeah, something like that. Look, I need to find my things and get changed. I don't know what room they're in."

Ryan took her arm and headed her up the stairs. "Looks like you've had a rough day, Nicole. Let's go see if we can find your bags. I'll tell Aunt Cathy that you'll be a few minutes late for dinner.

Climbing the stairs ahead of him, painfully aware that he could see her disheveled clothes and hair, she thought, *so much for escaping undetected.*

Coming back down the stairs after a quick shower and change of clothes, Nicole glanced at the grandfather clock next to the doorway to the formal dining room. It said 5:15. She could hear various voices and dishes clinking. *Great. I'm late for dinner on the first night.* She hadn't taken the time to dry her hair, and so she felt like a wet dog as she approached the room. Lying next to the door, patiently was Ellie. "I hope they don't make me eat out here with you, girl," she whispered, patting the dog's head.

Nicole took a deep breath and went into the room. "Hey everyone, sorry I'm late." Nodding to Cathy, she said, "I know you said it was a five o'clock starting time."

Pretending to be serious, Ryan said, "That's okay, Nicole. There's a plate set up for you in the kitchen. That's where I had to eat if I was ever late to dinner. Right, Aunt Cathy?"

Momentarily stricken, Nicole looked at Cathy.

"Now, Ryan Cummings, that's not nice." She smiled warmly at Nicole and gestured to an open chair directly across from Ryan. "Welcome to our table, dear."

Before she was even seated, a woman was setting a salad plate down at the open spot.

"You must be famished," Cathy said, taking a sip of her sweet tea. "We were all just trying to remember the last time we saw Ryan. I believe it was when you and Leah came out for Christmas."

Cal took a swig of his beer. "That's right. Leah. Nice girl. How is she?"

Nicole nibbled on her salad as she took a good look at Ryan. The first time she'd met him was when he was seated next to her at the charity gala in London. She'd spent most of the time on stage, however, as she was the emcee of the event. She never really got a good look at him.

The only other time Nicole had met Ryan was at Janet's wedding. But, she had been the maid of honor and spent most of the wedding and reception making sure that everything ran smoothly for her best friend. Chatting up a handsome best man wasn't exactly on her radar.

But now, as they sat across the table from each other, she had a chance to get a good look at him. Those baby blue eyes that had twinkled in amusement earlier were looking at Cal and Cathy intently. He had hair the color of a mocha cappuccino, with one strand that kept falling over his forehead as he glanced down at his salad plate. Cathy said something funny, and when he laughed, it was a deep resonant sound that stirred something in Nicole that she hadn't felt in a very long time. When he took a sip of his beer, she saw the strong, masculine hands that had helped her up earlier.

"What do you think, Nicole?" She was startled back to reality by Cal's voice, asking her a question.

"Uh, I'm sorry. What was the question?" Nicole couldn't shake feeling so out of place.

As the woman from the kitchen was clearing the salads and replacing them with plates piled high with tacos and beans and rice, Cal repeated himself.

"We were just talking about the property deal that Ryan is in town working on. He's gonna put up a smaller, high-end boutique hotel right next to where the Dallas Cowboys training facility is. This other fella wants the land to build some huge hotel. Seeing as you're kind of a world traveler, I was asking if you thought that bigger hotels are still popular. It seems to me that folks these days want a more personalized experience. I mean, I'm just an old rancher and don't know much about the hotel business, but I do know that you gotta treat folks special or they won't remember who y'are."

Taking a sip of ice water, Nicole answered, "I agree, Cal. In New York, real estate is at a premium, of course. So, hotels and B&Bs have to find some kind of niche. You can't just have a nice room and some mints on the pillow anymore to stay competitive. Our travel magazine, The Wanderer is always profiling unique places like that. A trip to a farmhouse in Tuscany that includes a cooking lesson in authentic cuisine... a bungalow on the beach in Hawaii that comes with private surfing lessons." Turning to Ryan, and feeling more confident now that she was talking about work, she added, "I think your idea is spot on. That other guy seems to be stuck in the last decade. If you're going to build a huge hotel, put it near a stadium where you'll need to house a thousand guests. That's what makes sense to me."

Ryan smiled gratefully. "Thank you! That's exactly what our research shows. Unfortunately, Rick has made this into a personal grudge."

Wiping her mouth delicately at the sides with her cloth napkin, Cathy asked Ryan, "Well, sugar, if you're going to be here for a while, can we expect to see that girlfriend of yours? There is plenty of room in the ranch bungalow you're staying in near the back lot." She winked at him.

"Uh, well. I..."

Cal interjected. "Cathy, don't be puttin' your nose in other people's business. If the man wants to have his lady friend out there, he don't need to talk to us about it."

Nicole suddenly lost her appetite. *A girlfriend*, she thought. *Of course he'd have a girlfriend. Which is just as well,* she rationalized. *I'm not here for romance. I'm here to work and clear my head.*

As her dinner plate was being cleared, Nicole heard Cathy's voice say, "All right, all right. You win. Who wants to have dessert in the kitchen? Selina made a fresh peach pie that smells divine."

CHAPTER EIGHT: ESSERE

The sky was just beginning to streak pink and indigo as Ryan rolled out of bed and into his jeans. Raking his hand through his hair, he then pulled on a white t-shirt. Even though the sun wasn't up yet, summers in Dallas had moderate temperatures overnight. *Unlike San Francisco, where I'd freeze my ass off going out before dawn.*

Ryan was feeling frustrated at this property deal, and the best way he knew to blow off some steam was to go for a nice, hard ride before work. Ryan had spent several summers on the ranch as a child and teenager and loved riding. Today, he was looking forward to seeing his favorite mare, Essere. She was a Friesian, with a gorgeous black mane and a silken coat. Graceful and strong, she was exactly the right horse to help him clear his head. Her name meant, "Be" in Italian, and that's exactly what he needed to do. Just be.

Grabbing two apples on his way out the door, Ryan crossed the path from the ranch cottage he was staying in over to the barn. Normally, the horses were kept in the stables, but Cal had said that they were upgrading the facility, and so Essere was staying in the barn.

The light was coming up over the horizon as Ryan approached the red barn. The air was cool as his boots crunched the gravel. *What a beautiful place this is*, Ryan mused. *Someday, I'd love to live where the sky is this beautiful.*

Opening the barn door and flipping on the light, Ryan could hear the sounds of animals stirring. Slight crunching, a rustling of hay, and a gentle snort were already calming his nerves. As Ryan walked over to her stall, Essere immediately recognized her old friend. "Hey, girl. I brought us some breakfast!" Slicing part of the apple and giving it to the horse, Ryan ate a slice himself.

Peering inside the stall, he saw a mess with manure and what appeared to be footprints. Small, female footprints. Ryan grinned as he realized that this was probably what happened to Nicole yesterday. She came in the barn and somehow ended up face down in the stall. How a woman could look so beautiful covered in manure was beyond him. But, she did. She was gorgeous, no matter what condition she was in. Essere shook her head and swished her tail.

"Yes, you're gorgeous too. Whaddya say we go for a ride this morning?"

From behind him, a masculine voice replied, "Okay, but you'll have to get the saddle on me first."

Ryan turned and saw Steve, the ranch manager. Bursting into hearty laughter, the two men embraced. "Hell no," Ryan said. "I've seen you giving piggyback rides to your nephews! I'll stick with Essere, thank you."

"How ya been?" Steve and Ryan walked over to get Essere saddled up. "It's been since, what, Christmas?"

"About that, yeah." Ryan gave Essere another bite of apple.

"How is the recovery going from the accident?" Steve had a genuine look of concern. "You still had a pretty bad limp the last time I saw you."

"Actually, I'm almost back to 100%. I ended up spending a

few weeks at an equine therapy facility in Ferndale, California."

"Equine therapy. I've heard of that. And it helped?" Steve asked.

"It did. As you know, I'd broken my back in the accident and had to relearn to walk. But I also had trauma from the accident and was having nightmares and other symptoms. So, equine therapy both strengthened my back muscles and helped me regain my confidence. It was a great experience." Ryan effortlessly mounted Essere. "Have you ever thought about it for Andi?" Steve's daughter Andrea had been paralyzed in a car accident years before.

"Actually, no. It wasn't really on our radar. Something to consider, though.

Steve followed Ryan and Essere out and closed the barn door behind them. Changing the subject, he said, "Well, I'm sure your girlfriend, what was her name, Leah? I'm sure she was glad you got yourself completely healed."

"Yeah, Leah didn't make the cut. She got weird after the accident and said she didn't want to be anyone's nurse, and she bailed."

A flash of anger shadowed Steve's face as he shook his head and said, "Good riddance, then. People like that get what they deserve. Have a good ride, my friend. I'll talk to you later."

Ryan felt the cool wind in his hair as he and Essere sped across the ranch. In the distance, he could see the cattle grazing. C and C Ranch spanned about 20,000 acres and had about a thousand head of cattle.

Slowing down to a walk, Ryan and Essere went over to a stream, so that she could have a cooling drink. Sitting atop her, Ryan's mind began to wander to Nicole. Smiling and shaking his head at how cute she was when she'd run into him yesterday, he started to wonder why she kept showing up in his life. First, in London, then in Botswana and now here in Texas.

"Maybe it's fate," he wondered aloud. She was certainly the real deal. Beautiful, educated, intelligent, and very successful in her own right. Plus, she was funny. And humble. With a heart of gold, considering her charitable work. Nicole Burns was a completely different class of woman than Leah or any of the other women who'd tried to win his affection.

Heading back to the barn to put away Essere and head into the office to start his work day, Ryan said, "You know, Essere, I think I'd like to get to know her better. A lot better..."

CHAPTER NINE: DIGGING OUT THE TRUTH

"Mornin' Nicole." Cathy was already sipping coffee at the patio table when Nicole came through the French doors. "Wait 'til you taste Selina's coffee. I swear, I don't know what she puts in it, but it's the best darn coffee this side of the Mississippi."

Does this woman ever sleep? Nicole wasn't quite awake yet, and she certainly wasn't a morning person like Cathy seemed to be. "Thank you," she said, pouring herself a steaming cup of black coffee.

Spying the parking spot where the white SUV had been parked yesterday, Nicole assumed that Ryan had already gone into Dallas for work.

"There's also some scrambled eggs, bacon, and other fixin's in the kitchen if you're hungry. You might want to fill up, I know you've got a busy day ahead." Cathy winked at Nicole, as she took her own plate into the kitchen.

Looking out at the rolling hills of the ranch land, Nicole wasn't exactly sure what Steve had in store for her today. It was her first day "working the ranch," but what did that mean? Visions of herding cattle came to mind, but she'd never even been on a horse, let alone ridden one. *That's way outside my pay grade,* she thought.

Speaking of pay grade, Nicole hadn't checked her work e-mails since last night. Even though she trusted Christina implicitly, it was still her business and she needed to stay on top of things, even if from afar.

Grabbing a small plate full of scrambled eggs and toast, Nicole got out her phone to check messages while she ate. At the top of the list was a message from Christina, title "FYI."

Hey Nicole,

Just FYI, Bruce quit today. He didn't even bother to give notice, either. He just sent everyone a group text. Very unprofessional, if you ask me. Anyway, no need to reply. I'm on top of it. Already have two interviews scheduled for tomorrow to fill the vacancy. I'll let you know before we hire someone, obviously.

Hope your vacation is going great! We miss you.

Christina

Bruce was Straw Barn Publishing's Sales Director. Although Nicole hadn't exactly expected him to quit so suddenly, she wasn't really surprised. He was kind of a temperamental guy. It was certainly in character for him to do something like this. And she was confident Christina should have no problem finding a suitable replacement, as they were always getting resumés from people wanting to work there. Nicole had built an amazing workplace. She was surprised, however, not to have been included in the group message. *Talk about out of sight, out of mind. I've been gone three days.*

"Hey, girl. You ready for your first day on the dude ranch?" Steve crossed the patio to fill up his Thermos with coffee.

"Oh hey, Steve." Nicole put her phone down and smiled a little more brightly than she felt. "I sure am."

Walking into the barn, Steve asked, "How much weight can you carry?" Nicole had been paying $125 a month for a membership at the Madison Square Club, but was sad to say that she barely used it. Life as the head of a publishing house was just too hectic to get to the gym on a regular basis.

"I don't know. Maybe 25 or 30 pounds?"

"Okay, so we won't start you moving bales of hay. How about you muck the stalls while I stack the bales against the back wall to make room for the new ones coming in next week? We're making the first cut of hay then, and want to be sure to use up the old hay before the new stuff, so it doesn't spoil." Handing her a shovel, Steve smiled at her and said, "I heard you already know where the stalls are, but today you might want to use this."

Blushing at the memory of falling into manure, Nicole took the shovel and headed over to the stall where she'd seen the black horse yesterday.

Over his shoulder, as he was headed to the haystacks, Steve said, "First, put on some gloves and take all the hay out. Let me know when you're done and I'll tell you what to do next.

Pulling on the elbow-length rubber gloves and grabbing her first handful of hay, Nicole was glad she was wearing a pair of old blue jeans and some tennis shoes. Plus, having her hair in a ponytail helped keep her blonde locks away from her face as she bent over scooping up hay. *This is sure different than my life in New York...*

A couple of hours later, Nicole's back and legs were killing her, but she took pride in the beautifully cleaned stalls. *How these ranchers do this, plus all of the other work it takes to keep a ranch of this size running is beyond me.*

She was stretching her arms over her head when a woman walked in the barn. She was tiny, maybe five feet tall at most. Like most of the women Nicole had met here, she had perfect hair. Long, blonde, and straight down her back. She was holding a tray of what appeared to be sandwiches, and Nicole's stomach grumbled at the sight of them.

"Nicole? Hi, I'm Lucy, Steve's wife." She set the tray down on the workbench and extended her hand.

Taking off her gloves, Nicole shook the woman's hand. "Nice to meet you."

"I can't believe Steve has you mucking out the stalls on your first day. Surely he could have found a job that was a little less... earthy?" Lucy laughed and shook her head affectionately. "Men, right?"

"It's no problem, actually. I wanted to jump right into the middle of things."

"Well, you got your wish! Say, I brought some lunch, if you're hungry. There's a sink around that corner; you can wash your hands if you want."

After giving her sore, red hands a good washing, Nicole returned to the workbench to find that Lucy had set out a blue and white tablecloth, with two plates, and some clear plastic cups.

"You don't mind if I join you, I hope? It's not that often we get women volunteers around here. Most often, it's just Cathy and me and all these menfolk."

"No, not at all. I'd love the company." Nicole looked around for Steve.

"Steve had to drive out to the back fence. I guess one of the posts was coming loose, and the ranch hands were handling some other crisis. If it's not one thing, it's another around here." She laid out a sandwich, a bag of chips, a pickle, and some fruit salad on each plate. Pouring some sweet tea in the cups, she continued. "I'm just as glad. I was looking forward to getting to know you."

The women spent the next half an hour eating and chatting about their lives. Lucy mentioned that she and Steve had a ten-year-old daughter who had been paralyzed when the family car was hit by a drunk driver. Andrea, or Andi as she liked to be called, was only 7 at the time. It had been a tough time for everyone, but Andi had gotten used to life in a wheelchair. She still suffered from debilitating anxiety and nightmares, though. Lucy and Steve were just grateful that they hadn't lost their daughter.

Nicole shared a bit about her time volunteering at the orphanage in Botswana. Although the circumstances were different, of course, many of the kids still woke up at night calling for their parents. Trauma is trauma, they agreed.

"Let's talk about somethin' happier, now." Lucy leaned in conspiratorially. "I understand you've met our resident hunk Ryan?"

Nicole blushed at the sudden change of conversation. "Uh, yeah. We met a couple of times before, but he was at dinner last night, yes."

"Well, I'm a happily married woman, mind you. But I have eyes in my head, and if I were single I can tell you I'd be all over that like sauce on barbecue." Lucy fanned herself a little with her hands.

Nicole smiled politely, but said, "He is very handsome, but I imagine his girlfriend wouldn't take kindly to that."

"Oh, you mean that Leah woman? No, Steve told me this morning that she's gone. She had the nerve to dump him when he was in the hospital after his accident! Can you imagine? I never much liked her anyway. She wore too much perfume."

Wait. Leah broke up with Ryan? He's single? Nicole's mind was reeling. *Yeah, well. That doesn't mean anything anyway. I'm just here for the summer, and I'm here to work. No time for romance with the - what did Lucy call him - 'resident hunk.'*

Taking the last sip of her tea, Nicole put the cup and her napkin down. "Can I help you with these dishes? It's the least I can do after this delicious lunch."

CHAPTER TEN: SERVED

"Thank you so much for accommodating me." Ryan set his leather satchel next to the desk. "You didn't have to give me the biggest office, though. Just a cubicle would have been fine."

"It's been such a long time since we've had you in the office," the woman said, as she moved some files off the large mahogany desk. "And Tim is abroad at the moment, so it's no problem at all. Just let me know if you need anything."

Ryan sat down in the plush leather chair. She was right. It had been a long time since Ryan had worked in the Dallas office of Cummings Construction. Probably not since before he'd had the last conflict with Rick Tomson.

"Thank you, Nina. Can I have the wifi password for my tablet?"

"Absolutely. It's HomeCummings." Nina smiled.

"Cute."

An hour later, Ryan had pulled up all the information he could find about the land he was trying to buy. He'd searched the owner's property record to see what kind of other properties he had. Took a look at the comps in the area. Then he put a call into his corporate attorney, Jill Katz, to alert her that Rick was threatening to take them to court. "What is the basis of the suit," she asked? "It's not illegal to put an offer in on undeveloped land."

"I have no idea. My guess is that it's a BS lawsuit to scare me off. I guess we'll find out when we get served the papers."

"Yeah, this guy sounds like a real piece of work," she said.

"You have no idea…"

A while later, Nina poked her head in Ryan's office. "There's someone out here to see you."

Getting up and stretching his long legs, Ryan headed for the door. "It's probably the lunch I ordered from Emerald Garden. I got enough egg rolls for the office."

Shaking her head, she said, "I don't think so. He doesn't look like a delivery person."

Walking across the open office into the glass and chrome waiting room, Ryan saw a man impatiently looking at the framed photos of some of Cummings' famous construction sites around the world. Seeing Ryan, the man approached him and asked, "Are you Ryan Cummings?"

"Yes."

Handing him a manila envelope, the man simply said, "You've been served."

"So, what does it say?" Jill sounded skeptical.

"Well, it looks like Rick found some obscure law on the Texas books that says you can't own more than a certain percentage of your corporate assets in the state unless the corporate headquarters is in that state."

"What? Can you scan me the papers? I've never heard of such a thing. Let me get my team on it. When's the court date?"

"He must have pulled some strings, or greased some palms because it's in about a month."

"No problem. Get those papers to me, and we'll get on it."

The eggrolls had been eaten, and everyone was ripping into their fortune cookies as Ryan headed out the front doors of the office. "Don't you want to know your fortune?" they asked.

"Actually, I do. So, I'm headed out to the property to see if it's really worth fighting this hard for. I need another look at it to know for sure. I'll see you ladies tomorrow."

Half an hour later, Ryan's Escalade pulled up to what would soon be a parking lot on the east side of the property. Opening the glove compartment to get his digital camera, Ryan spied the box containing the jeweled pendant he got that day. *I think I know who I bought that for...* he thought.

Taking some photos of the land, Ryan tried to envision the plans that he'd drawn up and where the building would go. "We'll put in a row of trees over here..." he said aloud.

Just then, through the zoom lens of the camera, Ryan saw a truck on the far end of the property. Two people were outside the truck, a man and a woman, and they appeared to be arguing pretty passionately. *This doesn't look right,* he thought, as he jumped back into his car.

Texas dust flew behind the wheels of the Escalade like water spraying from a jet ski as Ryan raced to the truck. As soon as he got close enough, he was able to recognize the driver. Rick. And he was having a screaming argument with the woman, who was crying.

The woman saw Ryan's car speeding toward them and she jumped in her modest sedan and sped off. Rick merely shook his head, got in the truck, and sped off in the other direction.

What on earth was that, he wondered? *Whatever it is, it serves Rick right...*

CHAPTER ELEVEN: PRESENCE

"That is the craziest damn thing I have ever heard." Cal was genuinely angry when Ryan told him about Rick's lawsuit.

Nicole was glad that she had been on time to dinner this evening. A long soak in a hot tub was just what she'd needed after her first day working on the ranch. *I am going to be in great shape at the end of the summer, from all this physical labor,* she thought.

Joining them for dinner this evening were Steve and Lucy. It was a lovely summer evening, and so they'd all gathered on the patio for some barbecued chicken and ribs, mashed potatoes, and corn on the cob. The lights reflected from the pool and Nicole could see a full moon cresting over the horizon. For the first time in a long time, Nicole felt happy.

"Well, that's just the thing. I'm starting to wonder if the whole deal is even worth it. Dragging through court, incurring legal expenses… we have other properties to develop. This isn't a big project for us. Maybe I should just scrap it, and move on to the next one." Ryan took a bite of chicken.

"Aunt Cathy, this is amazing."

"Don't thank me, that's all your Uncle Cal."

"I think you should fight it." This was Lucy, and she had a fierce expression. "Guys like this Rick are building these giant hotels all over Dallas and it's ruining the character of the town. I grew up here. When I go into town for anything, there are so many tourists everywhere, I can't even find parking. Lines in the stores, traffic on the roads. It's a mess. We don't need more people coming to Dallas."

It was Cathy's turn to chime in. "Not to mention, they're always saying that these hotels bring in jobs. But, what kind of jobs? Minimum wage, that's what kind of jobs. People work in these hotels and don't even make enough money to support their families. I know *we Cummings* always pay a fair wage to our employees. Whether it's here at the ranch or in Cal's brother, your daddy's construction business." Cathy nodded to Ryan. "We take care of our family."

Nicole admired the passion of the people around the table. These were folks who cared deeply about right and wrong, and about taking care of others. It was so different from the "profit above all else" folks she knew in New York.

"Well, I have some thinking to do, that's for sure." Ryan stood up and pulled something out of his pocket, and handed it to Cathy. "Speaking of taking care of family, this is just a little gift I got to say thank you for taking care of me while I'm here. I appreciate your hospitality."

Cathy's face lit up as she opened a small box with a silver bracelet that had two interlocking Cs. "Oh my lord, what did you do, Ryan?" She was clearly delighted. "C C. Like the ranch, and my initials!" She handed it to Cal to clasp on her.

"Don't forget Cal and Cathy, darlin'," Cal said as his rough hands closed the delicate chain around her wrist. "This is mighty nice of you, son. Somebody raised you right."

Nicole felt teary-eyed, watching the scene. As Lucy

peered over to get a good look at the bracelet, Nicole stole a glance at Ryan. *What a man,* she thought. *Handsome. Smart. Strong. And a really good person. I wonder what it would be like to kiss those lips... Nicole! Stop that. You are not here for kissing. Or making love. What? Making love? How did you even go there? Seriously. Stop it...*

Feeling flustered, Nicole pushed her chair back. "Pardon me, I need to use the ladies' room."

Headed back to the patio, after a few calming breaths and some cold water on her face, Nicole was feeling stronger. Her attraction to Ryan was just a summer crush. No need to act on it, when she would be going back to New York and he would be going back to San Francisco. *Sure, a girl can fantasize, but that's all that would ever be between Ryan Cummings and me. A fantasy.*

"Hey. You took off pretty fast. Not a fan of barbecue chicken?" It was Ryan, and he was standing dangerously close to her in the hallway. She could smell a mixture of sweet smoke from the fire and something spicy. Maybe aftershave.

He was looking down at her, and she had to take a deep breath before she could answer him. "No, I just had a couple of glasses of wine with dinner and just had to go…"

"You look beautiful tonight." His voice was husky and deep. "The fresh air agrees with you."

Nicole felt a rush through her entire body. "Thank you," she said softly.

He leaned in and whispered. "Let's get out of here. Go for a walk by the lake."

"But, Cal and Cathy. Dessert." Nicole wasn't even able to form complete sentences at this point.

"Here's your dessert." With that, he kissed her. Gently at first, but soon he pressed her body up against the wall of the hallway.

Nicole returned the kiss with the passion she'd been fighting since they both arrived. He tasted sweet and spicy, just like he smelled.

Arching her back into him, he pressed the entire length of his body into hers. It was as if every part of their bodies were kissing.

"Oh! I'm sorry... I didn't... Oh gosh.." It was Lucy. "I'll just use the other bathroom. Carry on. Forget I was ever here." She scurried away before either Ryan or Nicole could protest.

Ryan grinned sheepishly. "My guess is that the whole table already knows about this. How about we slip out the side door, and head for the lake?" He grabbed her hand and led the way.

Nicole was grateful for the quiet night as she and Ryan walked hand-in-hand toward the lake. She needed a few moments to compose herself after Lucy had walked in on them kissing. *What does this mean?* She wondered. Looking up at the stars and the full moon reflecting on the lake, she thought, *Don't overthink this. Just enjoy the night.*

They came upon a wrought iron bench in the grass next to the lake. Ducks were paddling along, gently quacking. Ryan and Nicole talked as if they'd known each other forever. They discovered that they shared a passion for Kung Pao Chicken (Nicole liked hers with brown rice), and the Beatles (Ryan argued that Pete Best was a better drummer than Ringo Starr), and that they both once lived on the same block in New York. He'd been in college, and one of his roommates had dated the woman that ended up becoming Nicole's best friend, Janet. What a small world, they both mused.

"Hey, I just realized something," Nicole said. "At Janet's wedding, when you were the best man and I was the maid of honor, you had a slight limp still, from the accident. It's gone now."

Ryan nodded. "Yes. I had some equine therapy that strengthened my back. Plus, it helped me get over the emotional trauma of the accident."

"Equine therapy?"

"Yeah, it's kind of like what you're doing here on the ranch, but more structured. There's a lot of research that shows that working with horses is good for the body and mind. It's used a lot with disabled children to give them confidence and positive body experiences."

"That sounds amazing, Ryan. I can attest to the fact that being around the animals, especially the horses, is really helping me feel calmer." *Not just at this moment,* Nicole thought, *with you sitting so close to me...*

"It's true," Ryan added. "There's something about being around animals and their calming presence that helps you to just... be."

Nicole yawned, and Ryan put his arm around her on the bench. "We better get you back. It was a long day for you..."

She nodded in agreement.

"Before we go, though, I want to show you something." He turned to face her, and once again Nicole could smell that sweet spicy scent that was uniquely his.

"I was in that gift shop buying the bracelet for Cathy when a piece caught my eye. At the time I didn't know why, but I knew I had to buy it. Since you came here to the ranch, I realized... I bought it for you."

He pulled out a small box containing a pendant. It was a little hard to see in the dark, but from the light of the moon, it appeared to be an onyx and diamond horse that looked just like the one from the barn. On top was a diamond-encrusted horseshoe.

"Oh, Ryan. It's so beautiful. But, I can't accept it..."

"Why not? It's Essere, my favorite mare here on the ranch. And, the horseshoe is good luck. I want you to have all the good fortune you deserve. You are an amazing woman, Nicole."

Speechless, she took the pendant in her hand. *I am going to need all the luck I can get,* she thought, as he kissed her again.

CHAPTER TWELVE: DIRTY HANDS

"How are things in Texas?" John and Ryan were having a quick call to go over the status of a few projects.

"Slow. I need to stick around until the court date… unless I decide to blow the whole project off."

"Are you seriously considering dropping the project?" John was a little surprised. Ryan had been very excited about this hotel at one point. He'd invested quite a bit of time drawing up the architectural plans.

"I am. The money we're investing in legal and court fees is growing every day. It's going to take years to recoup the expense. Plus, I really have no desire to battle Rick over this. He's made it a personal vendetta."

"I'm sorry you're having such a rough time of it out there."

Ryan smiled and thought of Nicole. *It's not all bad. That's for sure.*

Nina stuck her head in the office, gesturing something.

"John, let me call you back." Ryan quickly ended the call.

"I'm sorry to bother you, but there's a woman here to see

you. Says it's personal. Won't give me her name or why she wants to talk to you. You want me to get rid of her?"

"No, no. I'll come out." Ryan followed Nina into the waiting room. The slight-framed woman had her back to him. Her body showed nervousness as she looked at the wall of photographs.

"Hi, I'm Ryan. How can I help you?"

When the woman turned around, Ryan immediately recognized her. It was the woman from the property! The one who had been arguing with Rick!

"Hi. I'm sorry to bother you like this. My name is Melissa Tomson. I'm Rick Tomson's ex-wife."

All kinds of possibilities as to why she would be standing in his office came to mind. None of them made any sense.

"Oh, wow." Then, realizing she was looking at him plaintively, he recovered. "Come on in my office. We can talk there."

All of the eyes in the office followed them as Ryan opened the door and led Melissa in. Closing the door behind them, Ryan nodded to Nina to indicate that it was fine. No need for concern.

Gesturing to the chair opposite his desk, Ryan said, "Take a seat." She did.

Fidgeting with her hands, and smoothing down her pants, Melissa seemed to take a confidence-building breath and said, "I'm sorry to bother you at work. I saw you the other day at the property. When I called Rick later that night to remind him that our daughter's birthday is coming up, he mentioned that he was going to be in court on that day and was going to be too busy to see Jenny. He is such a jerk."

Ryan could see Melissa fighting off tears.

"Anyway, I have a friend who works for the court, and she was able to look up the court docket for that day, and I found your name and tracked you down."

"Okay..." Ryan was still confused. *What does she want with me?*

"I'm not really sure the nature of the lawsuit, but given the kind of man Rick is, I'm betting that you're in the right and he's in the wrong."

"Well, it's not really a matter of right and wrong in this case. We both just want the same thing. It's a piece of land." Ryan smiled sardonically. "He doesn't seem much for sharing."

"No kidding. He left me for one of his secretaries when Jenny was only three. She's autistic, and I guess he couldn't deal with it. So he bailed. He never comes to see her, and only sends presents through Amazon." Shaking her head sadly and looking out the window, she continued, "I don't know why I keep trying to force a relationship. Jenny is ten years old now, and barely knows her father."

Ryan sat and let a moment of silence transpire before he said, gently, "I'm sorry for what you're going through. I've known him for years, professionally, and can't say I'm surprised. But, how can I help you?"

Melissa focused back on Ryan. "It's not how you can help me. It's how I can help you. I have quite a bit of proof of some of Rick's underhanded business dealings. Paper trails on bribes to judges and stuff like that. It's really incriminating evidence. I'm just so sick of Rick getting away with it all. I can give it to you if you think it will help you win your case."

Ryan leaned back in his chair stunned. He knew Rick was a jerk, but he had no idea he was involved in criminal activity.

"Wow, that's really generous of you. I'm honestly not sure what to say. Let me process what you've told me and I'll call you in a day or two. May I have your number?"

Melissa wrote down her name and number on a slip of

paper on the desk and slid it over to Ryan. "I feel a little bad about doing this. After all, he is Jenny's dad. But, it just feels like the right thing to do."

Standing to walk her to the door, he said, "Melissa, there is a huge difference between being a father and being a dad. He may be her father, but Rick Tomson is no dad. I'm sure Jenny will have a wonderful birthday because she clearly has a loving mom."

As she walked through the glass doors to the waiting room, Ryan realized the value of what just happened. He now had dirt on Rick that would allow him to get what he wanted out of the deal. But, is that how he wanted to win? His Uncle Cal had always said that when you play dirty, you get dirt on your hands, too.

CHAPTER THIRTEEN: BUCKET LIST

Nicole stood just outside of the barn, looking up into the charcoal black eyes of the horse. She was staring back at Nicole, and Nicole wondered if she knew the importance of what was about to happen.

"You ready Nicole?" Steve had put a saddle on Essere and had a hand extended to help her mount the horse.

Nicole had been waiting for this day since she was a child. She'd grown up in a fairly wealthy family, and although they'd spent almost every summer in Saratoga Springs - famous for horse racing - she'd never been allowed to ride a horse. "Please, Mom. I'll be careful" Nicole had begged and pleaded. "Daddy. Everyone rides. Tell Mom it's not too dangerous." Her pleas had gone unanswered until she finally stopped hoping it would ever happen.

Until today.

"I am so ready." Nicole smiled.

"Okay. You put your left foot right here," Steve said, as he helped her. "Then, you step up on the stirrup like you're climbing over a fence. Swing your other leg high and wide over the horse... yeah just like that, and THERE. You're on. Now, let's get you adjusted on the saddle."

Nicole felt exhilarated and a little scared, too. She could feel the horse moving between her legs and the ground seemed quite a ways down. She was glad she was wearing a helmet.

Steve effortlessly mounted his horse, and they walked up next to her. "Grab the reins, keep your heels down and just relax into it. Essere knows to follow me." He and his horse walked ahead of Nicole, and sure enough, Essere followed.

At first, all Nicole could focus on was balancing on the horse. As they walked past the gate to the barn and beyond the fence into the pasture, Steve was doing a good job of taking it slow. "You're doing great, Nicole. You want to go a bit faster?"

Unsure, but also feeling a little brave, she nodded yes.

Steve and his horse started a slow trot, and Essere followed. This was a bit more bouncy than the walk, and Nicole found she had to balance her back and legs a bit more. But within a few minutes, she got the hang of it, and was able to relax into it. *I'm riding a horse!*

Nicole and Essere caught up to Steve and they slowed to a walk again. He pointed out some of the features of the ranch and told her the backstory of how Cal had come to buy the land. As she listened, Nicole realized that had never felt more alive in her life than she did riding on the back of Essere. The cornflower blue sky stretched on for miles. The smell of the earth mingled with the sweet smell of hay. All she could hear was the gentle thudding of hooves, a slight breeze, and Steve's accented voice as he told her interesting things about the places they passed. *This is where I am meant to be,* she thought. *How can I ever go back to that claustrophobic town with the tall buildings and the noise?*

But as soon as she thought it, other anxious and intrusive

thoughts came up. *What are you thinking, Nicole? This is a summer vacation. Your life and your business are in New York. That's where you live. Ryan lives in San Francisco and you live in New York. This is a just a diversion from your real life so you can stop stressing out.*

Startling her out of her reverie, Nicole heard Steve's voice. "Hey. Did I lose you? I was asking if you wanted to head back."

"So, Nicole, Steve tells me that you learned to ride Essere today. How was that for ya?" Cal had a twinkle in his eyes as he bit down on a juicy hamburger.

"It was amazing, " Nicole replied honestly. "I've never felt anything like it in my life.

Cal and Cathy smiled knowingly. "Yeah. Once you're bit by the riding bug," Cal said, "you're hooked."

Tonight's dinner only included Cal, Cathy, and Nicole. Ryan "wasn't able to join us, this evenin', according to Cathy. It was just as well. Nicole was feeling pretty awkward about the whole thing ever since Lucy walked in on them kissing last night. Nicole guessed that Lucy and Cathy had talked and that everyone probably knew about it by this point. The last thing Nicole wanted was meaningful glances at the dinner table.

She did wonder, though, where things stood with Ryan. He'd given her that beautiful pendant, and they'd shared a few tender kisses. But, maybe he understood that it was just a summer thing, too. *In fact, he could be on a date with another woman right now.*

That thought hit Nicole in the stomach, and she set her burger down and took a huge gulp of ice water.

Dipping a French fry in catsup, Cathy said, "There's been something I've been wanting to talk to you about, Nicole."

Uh oh. Is this about Ryan?

"Sure. What's up?" Nicole forced a smile that belied the sense of dread.

"I'm not sure if you know, but every summer we host a huge Labor Day barbecue here at the ranch. It's kind of a way for us to give back to the community, to reward our employees and their families, and to have some good old fashioned Texas fun."

Relieved that Cathy wasn't talking about Ryan, Nicole brightened. "Oh, wow. No, I hadn't heard, but that sounds like so much fun!"

Cal nodded to Cathy, "You should see the shindig this one puts on every year. Pretty much every big name in town comes, as well as everyone from the ranch. I don't much care for parties, but I'll admit, even I enjoy myself at this one."

Cathy patted her husband's hand and turned to Nicole. " I'm not sure how long you were planning on staying or when you need to head home, but I was hoping you might stick around long enough to help me out with it. Usually, it's just Lucy and me planning the whole thing. But Ryan told us that you threw a huge charity gala in London last year. We could sure use your help!"

A big Texas barbecue? Working on that sounded much better to Nicole than mucking out stalls all summer. She smiled and said, "Count me in." The barbecue would be a great end to the summer before she headed back to her job in New York.

CHAPTER FOURTEEN: THE BBC 2

"Nina, is anyone planning on using the conference room in about ten minutes? I've got a Google Hangout planned with three other people, and want to use the big monitor in there."

"No problem, boss," Nina said, walking down the hallway to the conference room. I'll get everything set up for you."

Ryan was looking forward to talking with the guys. The four of them had been best friends since college. Andrew Atherton was the Vice President of Atherton Diamonds, one of the largest manufacturers, distributors and retail sellers of diamonds and other gems in the world. Cole Bennett was an investor in Atherton, as well as in tech stocks. Michael Davis was also in tech, having founded a software company in Silicon Valley that he then sold for 1.2 billion dollars to Microsoft.

After Ryan's accident last year, the four billionaires started calling themselves the BBC 2; first as kind of a joke, but then the nickname stuck. Now, the BBC 2 had monthly video conference calls so that no matter where they were in the world, the men could stay caught up with each other's personal and professional lives. Andrew was currently living in Africa, Cole was in New York, and although Michael usually lived in Northern California like Ryan, he was in Tokyo at the moment on business.

Fortunately, the men had found a time that was during waking hours for all of them. It was just about 4:00 pm in Texas, which translated to 7:00 am in Tokyo, 5:00 pm in New York, and midnight in Botswana.

Grabbing an iced tea from the fridge in the kitchen on his way to the conference room, Ryan decided that he wasn't ready to share anything about his feelings for Nicole just yet. She was Andrew's wife Janet's best friend and it was too premature to really "go there" with everyone. *I'll just talk about the lawsuit. See what they think about dropping the project or moving forward with it.*

"Hey, Andrew. What is that on your face?" Ryan squinted into the camera. "Did they run out of shaving cream in Botswana." He laughed.

"Very funny, man. It's called a beard. Real men can grow them." Andrew stroked the new addition to his face. "Maybe when you grow up, you can have one, too."

"Where's Cole?" Michael was sitting on a tatami mat in a very traditional Japanese looking room." I didn't get up this early for nothing."

"He texted that he's running a couple minutes late. Are you drinking tea?" Ryan smiled and shook his head. "What happened to Mr. Espresso?"

"Haha. Yes, this is tea. When in Tokyo, do as the Eddoku do." With that, he took a sip.

"Sorry, I'm late," Cole said. "You know what rush hour is like in New York."

Andrew chimed in. "Rush hour here is about ten cars and a long red light."

"I can beat that. Rush hour here is three cows and a

Golden Retriever." Ryan leaned back in his chair with his arms behind his head. "It's great to see you guys."

The men chatted for fifteen minutes or so, each talking about the work he was doing and the various charitable activities they were each engaged in. It was very important to them all to find ways to give back. They were fully aware of how rare it is for all four of them to have become billionaires, and how fortunate they were to be in a position of influence. The BBC 2 was about using their money and power as a force for good in the world.

"You've been pretty quiet, there, Ryan, about this land deal. What's the hold-up?" Cole took a sip of his ever-present coffee.

"Actually, I wanted to talk to you guys about it. I'm not sure if I should cut my losses and pull out of the project." He went on to describe what had happened with Rick Tomson and the lawsuit. He also told them about his visit with Melissa Tomson and the incriminating information she'd offered to give him on Rick. "I'm just not sure I want this deal so bad that I'd do anything underhanded like that.."

It was Andrew who spoke first. "Ryan. It's not you who is doing anything underhanded. It's Rick. If he's paying off judges and inspectors and shit, and you know about it, you have a moral obligation to get involved. If you look the other way, you're complicit."

Michael agreed. "Think about it from this perspective. How many people have been hurt by his shady dealings? How many more people are going to be hurt if he continues? Lots of people think that white collar crime is no big deal because no one really gets hurt. But, when people commit business crimes, a lot of other folks lose their jobs and their ability to support their families. It's not a victimless crime at all."

"Besides," Cole added, "the guy seems like a real asshole.

Abandoning his autistic daughter? Just meet with the woman and take the information from her. This way you'll have it if you need it."

"I like that idea," Ryan said. "I just wish there were some way I could help Melissa and her daughter."

"What about equine therapy? That really helped you after your accident." Andrew's wife Janet had come into the room to kiss him goodnight and made the suggestion.

"Oh hey, Janet," they all said.

"You mean pay for the therapy or something? Maybe. That's not a bad idea…" Ryan nodded. "I'll talk to Melissa when I meet her to get the evidence."

The men wrapped up the conversation, and before the call ended, Andrew said, "Don't forget, Ryan, Janet and I are coming to town on a layover next week before we head to Hawaii. We're staying at the Ritz for one night. Maybe you and I could grab a beer?"

"That would be great, man. I haven't seen you in person since your wedding. I'll bring you a present."

"You don't have to do that…" Andrew fell right into it.

"It a razor." Ryan grinned and the other men all laughed and groaned.

"You're an asshole, you know that?" Andrew laughed. "I'll see you next week, and you guys next month…"

They all hit the End button on the call, and Ryan headed back to his office to find that slip of paper with Melissa's number on it.

CHAPTER FIFTEEN: TORN BETWEEN TWO COVERS

It was becoming a delightful routine. Nicole would wake up shortly after sunrise, wash her face and put on some work clothes and her new boots, and go down to the kitchen for coffee. Selina always had a huge spread set out in the main dining room for the ranch hands, but Nicole usually just grabbed some toast and juice before heading out to the barn. There, she fed the horses, gathered the eggs from the coop, and snuck Ellie a treat.

After her morning chores, Nicole would head back up to the main house and go into Cathy's office to work on the barbecue. The rest of the morning was spent calling vendors, confirming the guest list, and responding to e-mails.

At lunch, Selina put out a platter of sandwiches and fruit, along with the ever-present sweet tea. Nicole would grab a plate and go into the library. She'd started reading a book on caring for horses, and was surprised to learn how many different kinds of horseshoes there are. There are special shoes for racing, shoes that correct imbalances, and shoes made of many different kinds of materials. *It's just like human shoes,* she thought.

After lunch was Nicole's favorite time of day. She'd go out to the barn, saddle Essere up, and practice her riding skills. Steve had been a patient and effective teacher, and although Nicole was very much still a beginner, she was able to do a lot on her own.

Riding Essere around the ranch was therapeutic for Nicole. She had time to really think about her life. She was ready for more than the life she'd created back home. It was time to find a mate, settle down, and start a family. *I have no idea how I'll manage it all with my busy career, but millions of other women do it. I can too.*

Those thoughts inevitably led to thoughts of Ryan. There was something about being astride a horse, with the rocking motions, thinking of how spicy sweet he smelled, and remembering his body pressed against hers… Yes, this ranch was bringing her back to life in many ways.

Nicole would put the horse away, giving her water and cleaning the tack. Grooming her, and picking the dirt out of her shoes, Nicole felt a special bond with Essere. Everything about that horse was calming and filled Nicole with a sense of presence.

Today, as she walked back in the kitchen, Selina said, "Miss Nicole, your cell phone has been ringing all afternoon. I didn't know where you were, so I just left it."

"Thank you for letting me know, Selina." She smiled and touched the woman's arm as she walked into the office where she'd left her phone.

Seven missed calls from Christina! Quickly hitting the button to call her back, Nicole started to worry. What happened? Did someone else quit?

"Hey, Nic." Christina sounded fine… "Sorry to bother you by calling so many times."

"No bother at all. What's up?"

"Well, today is the deadline for approval on the cover for

Calm and Collected. I know you said you always wanted the final decision between the two covers. I sent them over by e-mail yesterday, and when I didn't hear back…"

Oh my gosh. Of course. It's the 10th of the month! How could I forget?

"Christina, I am so sorry. I totally forgot to check my e-mails. Hang on, I'll check them now."

"Oh… well. The thing is, I had to get them into production. So, when I didn't hear from you, I just chose one. I'm really sorry."

"No, no. Of course. You made the right call. We can't risk production delays. They're expensive and, in this case, unnecessary."

Christina sounded relieved. "I'm so glad you feel that way. I didn't know what to do so I made an executive decision. I was hoping you wouldn't mind."

"Christina, you made an executive decision because you're an executive! You are running a major publishing company in my absence and are doing an incredible job. I'm proud of you."

Hanging up the phone, Nicole sat there shocked for a moment. *I can't believe I did that. I never miss deadlines. But it looks like things are running just fine without me.*

Nicole went up to her room to grab a quick shower before dinner. Before she had a chance to start the water, her phone rang. "Janet! How are you?"

"I'm great, my friend. Missing you, though."

"I miss you too. It seems like forever since we've caught up. But, it's midnight where you are. Is everything okay?

Janet answered, "Oh yes. Everything is fine. Andrew and I were out at a dinner thing and just got back so I figured this was a good time to call."

"It's perfect." Nicole flopped down on her bed,

"Before I forget, Andrew and I are headed to Hawaii next

week, but we are doing a layover in Dallas. One night at the Ritz. I was hoping we could have lunch."

"That would be amazing! Oh I can't wait to see you." Nicole smiled at the thought of an unexpected visit with her best friend. "Will Andrew be joining us?"

"No, actually he and Ryan are going to go out for a beer or something. Guy time. You know how it is."

Nicole laughed. It had been so long since she'd been in a relationship, she really didn't remember.

"Speaking of which," Janet said as she lowered her voice, "how are things with Ryan there at the ranch. You guys had some amazing chemistry in London and at my wedding. Are you two tangling the sheets yet?"

"Janet!" Nicole laughed but also felt a blush creep up on her face. "No, we are not 'tangling the sheets' or the covers or anything."

"Well, it's just a matter of time, then. You two are perfect for each other."

Nicole felt a warmth spread from her solar plexus up to her heart. "I don't know about that, Janet."

"You like him, right?"

This felt so high school. "Yes."

"Has he kissed you yet?"

"Mmmm hmmm." Nicole was a little uncomfortable, but also grateful to be able to tell someone about her feelings. It all came rushing out. "Oh, Janet, he is amazing. Handsome and sexy and an amazing kisser. He's also smart and such a good person. Even Ellie the dog loves him!"

Nicole could practically hear Janet smiling over the phone. "So, what's the holdup?"

"I live in New York. He lives in San Francisco. We both have busy lives. It could never work."

"Nic. The man is a *billionaire*. He has a plane. He has the money to make this happen. That's not an excuse. What's the real excuse?"

Spoken like a true best friend. "I don't know. I've been focusing on my career so long that I don't even know how to take care of myself anymore, let alone take care of a relationship. I'm scared I'll mess it up."

Janet took a deep breath and said, "Nicole, don't overthink this. Just relax and let yourself fall in love with him. Like the song says, 'Let it be.'"

Nicole couldn't help but wonder. Was it really that easy?

CHAPTER SIXTEEN: PUTTIN' ON THE RITZ

"I'm glad you called." Melissa Tomson stood to shake Ryan's hand as he walked into the Lobby Lounge of the Ritz Carlton Dallas. "It was a good call to meet here. Rick would never come to a hotel like this unless he were trying to impress a potential client. Despite outward appearances, the man is incredibly cheap."

Ryan sat down and ordered a beer for himself, and Melissa asked for a glass of chardonnay. "Are you staying here?" she asked.

"No, I have an uncle who has a ranch in Parker and I've been staying there for a few weeks until the court date. I'm meeting an old friend who is staying here on a layover."

"Ah, that sounds great. I love this hotel. We stayed here when Rick and I were dating. I guess I was the "client" he was trying to win." She smiled. "I moved to Highland Park when I married Rick. He got a really good lawyer that made sure he got the house when we divorced. Jenny and I have a modest house on the outskirts of Highland Park. They have great schools there."

After a momentary lull in the conversation, it was time to

get down to business. Melissa pulled out a thick manila envelope stuffed with papers. Setting it on the dark wood table, she placed both hands on top, protectively. Then, pushing it across the table toward Ryan, she said, "Here you go. This is a ton of stuff that documents Rick's activity. I had him followed by a private investigator for a while, and you'll see photos of him paying off judges, giving bribes to property developers, receiving kickbacks from vendors, and other shady dealings."

Ryan looked at the contents and took a deep breath. "This is quite a file, Melissa. Are you sure you want me to have it? This isn't a very big land deal we're fighting over."

Melissa nodded. "Yes. I'm not sure why, but something tells me that you are the right person to have this information now. I'm ready to move on from it, I think. Jenny deserves better."

"Well, thank you." Taking the file from her, and putting it in the leather satchel, he grasped her hands. "I promise you I will take good care of this stuff and use it as you would want it used."

With tears in her eyes, Melissa nodded yes and softly said, "Thank you."

"I'd like to repay you," Ryan said. As Melissa began to protest, he said, "Not in the way you might think. Have you ever considered equine therapy for Jenny?"

"Equine therapy?"

"Yes. I was injured in an accident last year and received equine therapy for my back and the emotional trauma after the accident. They had a program for autistic kids, and it really seemed to help them. I'd love to pay for Jenny to attend one. If you agree, of course."

"I'm not sure…"

"It's great. It helps children with autism create emotional bonds with the horses, which you know can be challenging when you're on the spectrum. Plus, there are sensory benefits, cognitive and language development benefits... plus it's fun!"

Melissa sat back in her chair considering what he'd said. "It sounds expensive."

"It can be, yes. I paid about five thousand dollars for my therapy. That's why I'd love to offer it to you as my gift. I just know how much it helped me. You're doing the right thing by giving me this information, Melissa. I want to do the right thing back..."

Ryan could see that she was conflicted. She had been the sole caregiver for so long, it was probably hard for her to accept a gift like this. He leaned in so that she could see the sincerity in his eyes and said, "I hope you'll say yes."

Melissa smiled, and said, "I might be interested in something like that. Let me do some research, and I'll give you a call. Thank you so much, Ryan. I appreciate it, and feel really good that you're the right kind of person to help stop Rick and his selfish behavior."

Rick stood and walked her to the door of the hotel. "I'll be in touch with more information on the therapy program," he said.

As he turned around to head back to the lounge to wait for Andrew, Ryan thought he spied a familiar figure headed toward the elevator. *Is that Nicole? Maybe... she could be having lunch with Janet while Andrew and I are out catching up.*

Before he had a chance to call out her name, he felt a tap on his shoulder. "What's a guy like you doing in a place like this?"

Turning around, he saw a smiling, bearded face. "Andrew! So good to see you."

As the men walked toward the doors to the hotel, Ryan quipped, "Hey. How about instead of going for a beer, we stop at a barber and get that thing shaved off your face."

As she pulled Cathy's red convertible Mercedes into the valet parking at the Ritz, Nicole was happy. She was so looking forward to seeing Janet and telling her more about her summer on the ranch. Plus, she wanted to hear all about Janet's children Oba and Gouta, and how things were going with the orphanage A Place for Grace.

Handing the valet her keys, she walked through the glass door entrance to the hotel. Not exactly sure where the elevators were, Nicole stopped to look around for a moment to get her bearings.

To the left, Nicole saw a little lounge area, with tables and chairs. *This is a nice hotel,* she thought. *Very different from the one in London.*

Just then, she spotted a familiar figure. Long blue-jean-clad legs. A pale blue short-sleeved collared shirt. That dark brown hair with the one lock that keeps falling in his face. It was Ryan! But, her heart froze when she saw what he was doing. He wasn't there with Andrew. He was there with a woman. He was leaning in to face her, holding her hands across the table, and gazing intently into her eyes as he spoke softly. The romantic scene was complete with his beer, and her glass of wine.

Oh my god. I am such a stupid fool.

Feeling the need to escape, Nicole practically ran to the bank of elevators. Pressing the elevator call button repeatedly, Nicole muttered under her breath, "Come on, dammit. Hurry up!" It was all she could do to keep it together until she reached the solitude of an empty elevator. *I need to get in the elevator before I cry. Hang on, Nic.. hang on...*

Thankfully, she heard the elevator go *Ding,* and the doors to the elevator started to slide open. Just as Nicole was about to make her escape to privacy, two people slipped in before her.

"Marvin, can you push the hold button? I need to grab Mitzy." A large man and woman with a small white dog lumbered into the plush elevator.

The man looked at Nicole and said, "Well? Are ya comin' or not?"

Glancing back to the Lobby Bar, not wanting to see Ryan and the woman go up to her room, Nicole nodded her head. Holding in her tears for a few more minutes, she entered the elevator. "Floor Eight, please."

As the elevator ascended, Nicole's mood plummeted. *I saw him holding hands with her. In a hotel lobby bar. His kisses and that pendant obviously meant nothing. He was clearly on a date with another woman. You are such a fool, Nicole. Just focus on getting back to New York, and you'll never have to see him again.*

CHAPTER SEVENTEEN: FOOL'S GOLD

The elevator door opened on the fifth floor, and those irritating people and their dog finally got out. Nicole only had about two minutes of peace before the doors opened to the 8th floor where Janet and Andrew's suite was.

"I need a minute," Nicole thought desperately. She walked the opposite direction from the suite so she could process what she just saw. Tears threatened to sting her eyes as she padded along the plush carpeted hallway. Windows looked out over the city, giving Nicole a sense of perspective.

She gave herself a pep talk. "Nic, look. This is actually a good thing. It makes things easier. You did say that you were in Texas to work on yourself, not fall in love."

Some people approached her in the hallway, so she put her cell phone to her ear and pretended she was talking to a friend. *Sometimes you have to be your own best friend, right, Nic?*

"Ryan Cummings is a player, and that's his business. What you're learning from this experience is that you are ready for a relationship. It won't be with him..." That thought felt horrible. She'd really started to hope for a future with him… "But, like that Adele song goes, 'I'll find someone like you…'"

Feeling emotionally stable enough to go have lunch with Janet, Nicole turned around and walked back to the suite.

"Nicole!" Janet looked as gorgeous as always, as she opened the door. Her red hair was tied back in a ponytail, and she was wearing blue jeans and a white linen collared shirt. Leather boots completed her look. "It is so great to see…" The smile on Janet's face immediately dropped. "What's wrong?"

"Nothing. Nothing's wrong?" Nicole tried to lie. "It's great to see you, too."

"Bullshit. I can see on your face that something happened. What happened?"

Nicole tried for another moment to keep up the facade. "I'm fine, really."

Janet took Nicole by the arm and sat her down on the couch in the suite's living room. "Nicole Burns, I know you well enough to know that something happened. I am going to go pour you a glass of wine and we are going to sit here until you tell me what it is."

Nicole could hear her friend in the kitchen, pulling the cork and pouring two glasses of wine. She returned, handed Nicole one of the crystal goblets, and sat down on the couch next to her.

Clinking their glasses in a toast, Janet said, "Here's to best friends, who tell each other *everything*."

They each took a sip and put their glasses down on the mahogany coffee table. "Spill it. Well, not the wine," Janet said with a reassuring smile. "But, talk."

"I just saw Ryan downstairs." Nicole could barely get the words out.

"I know. He was meeting Andrew for a couple of beers."

"No, he wasn't with Andrew. He was with… a woman."

Blinking in confusion, Janet shook her head slightly. "A woman? What kind of a woman?"

"A date."

"Honey, whatever she was, I can guarantee you it wasn't a date. What were they doing?"

"They were drinking and holding hands and gazing into each other's eyes!" Nicole burst into tears. "I was so stupid to think…"

Janet handed her a tissue from the box that was on the end table. "Nic.. it can't have been what you saw. There has to be a misunderstanding."

"It wasn't! I saw them gazing into each others' eyes."

"Nicole, Ryan is the nicest guy I know. Including my own brother. I'm telling you. I don't know what you saw, but I do know what you didn't see."

Nicole wanted so badly to believe Janet.

"I tell you what. Let's skip the Cheesecake Factory, and stay here in this incredible suite, and drink too much wine and order too much fattening food from room service, and then get a couple of in-room massages." Janet was smiling at her friend. "Trust me. This is all going to get straightened out, and you'll wish you'd said yes to spending an amazing day getting pampered in a suite."

Laughing through her tears, Nicole nodded. "Okay, Janet. I bet you haven't had a good Texas steak in a while. Let's take a look at the menu."

As she browsed through the decadent treats, Nicole kept hearing Janet's words repeat in her head. *I don't know what you saw, but I do know what you didn't see...*

CHAPTER EIGHTEEN: DAY IN COURT

Ryan pulled the Escalade into a space right in front of the Starbucks near the courthouse. He was meeting his attorney Jill to go over the documents she'd prepared before their 8:00 am court appointment.

She was already sitting at a table, hunched over a brown file folder, reading something through the turquoise glasses perched at the end of her nose. Taking a sip of her large coffee, she spied Ryan and stood to greet him. "Ryan, good to see you again."

Shaking her hand and then bringing her in for a professional hug, he patted her on the back and said, "You too, Jill. Thanks for flying out."

"Well, we're just lucky that I'm still licensed to practice law in Texas." She sat back down.

"We are lucky, indeed."

"Are you going to get coffee? I'm sorry I couldn't wait. I have to get my caffeine level up to a minimum threshold by 9:00 am or I have a headache the rest of the day." She took a huge swig from her cup as if to prove the point.

"No, I'm good. I had some before I left the ranch. So, what did you find?" He sat down in the chair next to her.

"Well, as you know, the basis of the suit is that Rick's attorney found some obscure law on the books that says that a company can't own more than a certain percentage of its assets in Texas unless the company is based here."

"Right."

"So, he's suing to try and block you from buying the land." She opened the folder. "I ran the history on our corporate assets with the CFO. I don't know if you knew this, but your dad is actually listed as a part owner on C & C Ranch."

Ryan shook his head. "I had no idea. I knew we had other properties in Texas, but I had no idea about the ranch. We always just thought it was Cal and Cathy's."

"For all intents and purposes, it is. But, back in the day, when Cal wanted to buy the land, he went to your dad for a loan. Cummings Construction was already doing really well by then. Your dad understood how tricky things can get when you lend money to family, so they set up a corporate trust."

"Wait. So technically Cummings Construction owns the ranch?" Ryan was shocked.

"Correct. But, the way the trust was set up, your parents, Cal, and Cathy are equal owners. And the corporate headquarters of Cummings Construction is listed as the ranch. They did it for tax benefits, as Texas is a more business-friendly state than California."

"So, does that mean..."

"Yes. It means that you are free to buy the land if you want."

"Wait. I'm confused..."

"The basis of the lawsuit is that a corporation can only hold so much Texas property in assets unless it is a Texas-based company. Since Rick thought that Cummings

Construction was based in California, buying the land near the Cowboys training facility would have put the company over the ownership percentage limit. But, now that we know it's actually a *Texas-based* company, that statute does not apply. Cummings Construction isn't legally barred from buying the land since its corporate headquarters is listed as Dallas."

Ryan sat back in his chair, stunned. He had no idea that his parents had set up a trust, or that Cal and Cathy were part owners in Cummings Construction, or that the ranch was part of the corporate assets. *I wonder when they were going to tell me*, he mused.

"What this means is that today should go fairly smoothly." Jill closed the folder. "We'll explain everything to the judge. I've already submitted copies of these documents as discovery, and Rick's lawyer has likely seen them. The case will be dismissed, and you can move ahead with your offer on the land."

Ryan sighed relief. "That is great news, Jill. I really appreciate your hard work." *And I didn't even have to use the information Melissa gave me*, he thought, as they headed out to their cars.

"All rise." The small group stood as the judge entered the courtroom.

Rick and his attorney were seated at a long wooden table adjacent to Jill and Ryan. Rick looked like the epitome of a "fat cat," with his expensive, overly formal suit, and his hair slicked back. His jowly neck looked like it was being choked by the bolero tie he was wearing. Leaning forward to glance at Ryan, Rick bared his veneered teeth in a fake smile.

Ryan ignored him and made sure his cell phone was turned off.

The judge's voice echoed in the small courtroom. "I understand that we have a dispute over some property that y'all both want to buy. Is that correct?" Both attorneys chimed, "Yes, Your Honor."

"What seems to be the issue?"

Rick's attorney stood, but did not approach the bench. Citing the old statute, he explained their side of the case. The judge listened, nodded, and then turned to Jill.

"Sounds pretty straightforward to me. What do you have to say Ms. Katz? It's pretty clear that Cummings Construction, is it, is a California corporation. They already have several other properties in Texas. This one would push the asset value over the limit."

"Actually, your honor, our research found that the corporate headquarters for Cummings Construction is legally located in Parker, Texas. On a ranch that belongs to Cal Cummings, part owner of the corporation."

There were a few moments of silence in the courtroom as the judge shuffled through the papers on his bench. Rick had the nerve to lean over and grin at Ryan again.

How odd. He is still gloating. It's as if he thinks he is going to win, even though we just gave evidence to the contrary...

The judge cleared his throat and spoke. "Well, h. Here's what it looks like to me. Although the headquarters are legally in Texas, there has never been a board meeting here, nor any business conducted from the ranch. The headquarters are, de facto, in California."

Jill leaned over and whispered to Ryan, "That means that even though the headquarters are legally in Dallas, they are really located in San Francisco."

The judge continued. "My interest in this case is not about the letter of the law, but the spirit of the law. The law was written to prevent out of towners from comin' in and makin' money and takin' it back out of Texas. It seems to me that Mr. Tomson will provide a greater revenue and tax base to this great state than will Mr. Cummings. So, unless you boys want to hash it out in mediation, I'm gonna say that Cummings Construction is barred from purchasin' the land unless y'all sell off some other assets. Mr. Harland, Ms. Katz, do your clients want to pursue mediation?"

Rick Tomson's voice boomed, "Hell, no."

"All right then." The judge banged his gavel. "Court is adjourned for a short break."

CHAPTER NINETEEN: PLAN B

"Where's Nicole?" Cal asked as he walked outside to the patio with his dinner plate. "And what's this rabbit food I'm eatin' here? Where's the meat?"

Answering his second question first, Cathy replied, "They're called vegetables, Cal. Selina saw some documentary about plant-based eating and how it's healthy for us, so she asked if we would give it a try."

"Hell, I'd rather die young than eat this stuff for the rest of my life." Cal frowned as he sat down and took a bite of his mixed greens salad.

"Sugar, you dyin' young is a train that left the station a long time ago." Cathy teased him as she sat down in between him and Ryan. Answering his other question, "Nicole wasn't feelin' too well this evening and she went for a walk down by the barn. I think she had a little too much fun with her friend Janet the other day, and she's still recovering."

Avoiding the sliced beets on his plate, Cal turned to Ryan and said, "You're real quiet tonight. Cat got your tongue? Or are you just dreamin' of the pizza we'll be ordering after this so-called dinner." He laughed heartily at his own joke.

Ryan cleared his throat and answered. "No, actually. I am just still really shocked about today. We lost in court."

Cathy put down her fork. "What? That's crazy! I thought your lawyer had a good case." Cal sent her a warning glance. "I mean, I was sure she would, seeing as she's a good attorney and all."

Cal cleared his throat. "That's a real shame, son. I thought it would go the other way."

Ryan nodded and said, "I did, too. Rick acted really weird in court. Like he knew he was going to win."

Cal furrowed his brow. "Who was the judge?"

"Delgadillo." Ryan took a big bite of his salad. "This is good," he said to Cathy. "Tell Selina that the dressing is fantastic."

Cal shook his head. "I'm not surprised. That guy has had a reputation for years."

"What kind of a reputation?" Ryan knew the answer before he asked it.

"For having a greasy palm. Some of my buddies said he was the cheapest way out of a lawsuit."

Ryan sighed. "Well, that's the thing. Tomson's ex-wife, Melissa Tomson gave me a bunch of papers that show that Rick is involved in some shady dealings himself. I didn't want to have to use them. But it does look like he might have gotten to the judge."

Cathy nodded. "A judge is supposed to uphold the law. And, legally, you have the right to buy that land."

"That reminds me..." Ryan took a sip of his tea and then set it down. "I learned something this morning that was pretty surprising."

Cal and Cathy gave each other a meaningful look.

"Now, before you go on, son, let me tell you. We never meant to make a secret of this thing." Cal looked serious.

Cathy added, "He's right. We plumb forgot about the paperwork and who owned what. We've had this ranch for thirty years, and never gave it a thought. Your daddy ran Cummings Construction and we run the ranch. To all of us, it was just a paperwork thing."

Ryan shook his head. "It's not that. I don't mind that you guys never said anything. I am surprised that my folks never did, though. It seems like the kind of thing you tell your only son."

"It does. We never had kids, as you know, and so it was never a decision we had to make." Cal took a swig of his beer and pushed the plate of offending vegetables aside. "But your daddy and I had planned to separate out the ranch and the business years ago. But one thing led to another and, well, it just never happened. I'm sorry, son."

"I understand, Uncle Cal. I really do. It's just all a lot to take in. This news, and then losing in court."

Cathy gently asked, "So, what are you going to do next? You could win on appeal."

Cal jumped in, "I have half a mind to give that paper trail of yours to some friends of mine. Get that judge kicked off the bench."

"I don't know, Uncle Cal. I think I'm just going to drop the whole thing and go back to San Francisco. There are other properties to build with that money."

"I have an idea," Cathy said, her face brightening.

Cal chuckled. "This should be good."

"Oh you, shush. Since you're technically going to inherit your daddy's part of the ranch, that makes you part-owner, in a way, right?"

Ryan furrowed his brow. "I hadn't thought about it, but I guess so."

"Well, why don't you take the money you were going to spend on the land and build that hotel here, on our land. Out on the back property."

"I appreciate the idea, Aunt Cathy, but I don't think folks are gonna come all the way out to Parker to stay in a hotel. It's not the right demographic. The only folks who are going to want to come out here are horse people…" Ryan's eyes lit up. "Wait. I just had an idea."

Cal cautiously stuck his hand under the table in an attempt to feed some squash to Ellie, and said, "All right. Let's hear it, then…"

CHAPTER TWENTY: GOOD KNIGHT

The sun had just set on the ranch as Nicole walked up the pathway to the barn. Her boots crunched the gravel and the pockets of her cotton hoodie were filled with carrots to give Essere.

It had been two days since her lunch at the Ritz with Janet. Although a lot of what Janet said made sense, Nicole still had a lot of questions. *If it wasn't a date, then who was the woman in the bar? Why were they holding hands?*

She really wanted to find out what happened with Ryan in court today, but she also knew that she wouldn't have been able to face him and pretend she wasn't having so many mixed feelings.

"That's why I needed to see you, Essere. You always make me feel better." She patted the horse on the head as she fed the carrots.

I need to clear my head, she thought. "How about we go for a ride?" Nicole had never ridden at night. *But it can't be that much different than riding in the day, right?* By now sShe had spent countless hours riding Essere all over the ranch.

After saddling her up, Nicole effortlessly mounted Essere

BEGUILED BY YOU

and they trotted off to her favorite part of the ranch - the stream.

"I can't believe the summer is going by so quickly," she said aloud to the horse. "In about six weeks, we'll be having the barbecue, and then I'll be heading back to New York." She leaned forward and patted the horse's jet black mane. "I am definitely going to miss you the most."

Nicole felt for the pendant Ryan gave her. Despite her concerns about Ryan and the relationship, Nicole hadn't taken it off since the day he'd given it to her. The necklace reminded Nicole of Essere and this special time at the ranch. In the few weeks she'd been here, Nicole felt she'd gotten to know herself as a person again.

Lost in thought, she reflected on the times she'd spent with Ryan. He was often there at breakfast, with an interesting story or suggestion for the barbecue. They'd had a few picnics here and there. Plus, the "five o'clock sharp" family dinners. Nicole really loved these people. They were good folks.

Essere and Nicole approached the part of the stream where Essere usually stopped to get a drink. Despite the warm Texas weather, the water in the stream was practically ice cold, as it came from a spring that ran under the land.

About fifty feet wide and fifteen feet deep in the middle, the cold water trickled and bubbled around the rocks that were staggered down the center of the stream.

Nicole looked up at the sky, marveling at how many stars were out. *It sure got dark fast,* Nicole thought.

Suddenly, there was a crunching sound behind them. It sounded like footsteps!

Essere heard it too and raised her head from the stream. Her tall black ears twitched to hear the sounds. The crunching was getting closer.

The horse nickered and Nicole started to feel unsafe.

"We're pretty far out from the barn, Essere. We better head back." It was so dark, it could have been anyone walking out there, and she wouldn't be able to see them. She clicked her tongue. "Let's go."

Before the horse could turn around, an owl swooped down right over their heads, and gave a loud "HOO HOO!" Startled, Essere jerked up, and Nicole lost her balance. She went flying off the saddle, and straight into the stream!

The ice-cold water seeped into her jeans and rushed over the front of her hoodie as she lay back down on a rock that had been sticking out of the water.

Dazed a bit, she took a mental inventory of her body. *My arm. I think my arm might be broken. Ouch. I need to get up and out of this water. Ohh.. this hurts.*

The next thing Nicole knew, a pair of strong arms were lifting her out of the water. She couldn't see a thing in the jet black darkness, other than a few reflections off the running water. But she would recognize that scent anywhere. Sweet. Spicy. "Ryan? Is that you?"

Carrying her back to the bank of the creek, and gently setting her down, he answered. "Yes, it's me."

Crying from relief, Nicole sobbed, "I am so glad you're here. The horse, she got startled and then…"

"Shhhh… it's okay. Let's get you back and see if anything is hurt. My cottage is closest. Do you mind if we go there?"

"No, that's fine. My arm.. I don't know if it's broken or not." Nicole was sopping wet and starting to shiver.

Putting his jacket around her, and lifting her up onto his horse, Ryan answered, "What they taught me in physical therapy is that if you're not sure, then it's probably not broken. But let's take a look at it to be sure."

Sitting atop Ryan's horse as he led the caravan back to his cottage, she thought, *He really is a knight on a white horse, isn't he?*

About an hour later, Nicole was sitting on a leather loveseat, wearing a thick blue bathrobe, drinking a hot toddy. After all the wine the other day, she wasn't sure she would touch alcohol again for a long time, but Ryan had convinced her she needed to warm up from the inside. The combination of the hot water, lemon, honey and whiskey did the trick.

"I'm glad your arm is feeling better. Can you move it fully yet?"

She flexed her arm to show she could. "Almost as good as new." She giggled. The whiskey was going to her head a bit.

"I see you're wearing the pendant." Ryan walked over to her and lifted the small onyx horse off her neck.

"I never take it off." He was so close to her, it was more intoxicating than the whiskey.

I should ask him about that woman, she thought woozily.

His hand went from her neck to her chin. Touching it gently, he whispered. "You are so beautiful, Nicole."

All thoughts of other people left their minds. Tonight, in this room, there was no Rick or Melissa. No Cal or Cathy. No lawsuits or publishing problems.

"Nicole, I think I am falling in love with you. From the first time I saw you in London, to the first time we touched walking down the aisle at Andrew and Janet's wedding, until our first kiss... I knew there was something special here. *We are special.*"

He kissed her. Gently at first. But, then, his kiss grew deeper. His tongue plunged into her mouth and she could taste the spicy sweetness she'd been smelling on him since they met. Her mouth responded to his, greedily.

He pulled back, and Nicole could see his eyes. Waiting. Wondering. It was up to her to continue or to pull away.

She didn't want to stop. She never wanted this to end. So she leaned in and kissed him back.

Their lips never parted, as his hands made their way down the front of the robe. Tugging it open, he cupped her breast, rubbing her nipple between his fingers.

An electric wave of pleasure shot through her, and she arched her back and moaned. *Ryan...*

Ryan lowered his mouth to her breasts. Waves of pleasure crashed around her as his warm lips encircled one nipple, and then the other, fluttering his tongue over them. *If this is what he can do with his tongue...* Nicole felt a raging fire begin to build from between her legs.

He stood before her and pulled his shirt over his head. Standing there, with tight muscles rippling over his frame, wearing nothing but a pair of jeans, he looked like the cover of one of those romance novels she used to read. *God, he is beautiful.*

Her eyes wandered down the length of his jeans, and she could see his need for her. Reaching out, she tugged open the button on his jeans and pulled them down.

Now freed from the confinement of clothing, Nicole looked at his erection and wondered how anyone could be more perfect.

She was not an ingénue. She knew what to do, and as she reached out to stroke his length, he closed his eyes and moaned. Yes, she wanted to make him feel the way she was feeling.

He pulled her to her feet, slipped off the robe, picked her up, and carried her to his bed.

Ryan laid Nicole gently down, and his hands began to explore every inch of her body. First, he caressed her face and kissed her. Wrapping her arms around his broad shoulders, she grabbed fistfuls of that chocolate colored hair and pulled him closer.

Without pulling back, he reached his hand down between

her legs and as he dipped into the warm, wet place between her legs, she instinctively opened for him.

Ryan moved atop her and looked at Nicole with such a warm, loving gaze that any reserve she might have had just melted away. "Are you sure?" he said.

Her passion was so intense, she could barely speak. "Yes," she whispered, and with one simple move, he became part of her. Moving back and forth, together, their rhythm increased. What started as slow, gentle lovemaking became fervent and passionate. Gentle waves of pleasure became pounding surf. As they reached their climax, Nicole heard him calling her name. "Oh, Nicole… I love you."

CHAPTER TWENTY-ONE: ONE THING I KNOW FOR SURE

How could anyone be so beautiful when they are asleep? It was barely dawn, and Nicole was curled up under Ryan's covers. He hadn't slept a wink all night. They'd made love and laughed and talked all night long, and she had just dozed off a few hours prior. Now, he sat gazing at her, as her body softly rose and sank with her quiet breaths. *I would do anything for her,* he thought.

Slipping silently out of bed, he tiptoed over to the small kitchen and turned on the instant kettle. Making sure to turn it off before the whistle sounded, he made himself a cup of instant Starbucks coffee. Taking it to the leather chair by the window, he varied his gaze between sleeping Nicole and the stirring ranch.

How can I pull this off? Ryan thought about the idea he'd had while talking with Cal and Cathy yesterday. He'd actually gone for a walk after dinner to think about it when he'd noticed Essere was not in her stall. Worried, he took the other horse out to find Essere, and that's when he'd come upon Nicole and the stream. *I'm definitely glad I found her when I did,* he thought.

What Ryan had decided to do was give Cal the information he'd been given by Melissa and let him deal with Rick and that judge. Ryan was going to drop the idea of the hotel near the Cowboys training facility. It really wasn't worth the hassle.

Instead, he was going to take that capital, and build an equine therapy facility right there on the ranch. And he was going to talk to his parents about moving his office permanently to Dallas.

The last piece of the puzzle was that beautiful woman sleeping in his bed. He'd need to convince her to leave her life in New York and move to Parker, Texas and take on some role in the equine therapy business. *Would she be willing to leave New York? Would she give up publishing? Does she even feel the same way about me that I do her?*

There were so many questions and not very many answers at this point. The one thing Ryan did know is that he'd need to go back to San Francisco to wrap things up there.

He wanted to keep the equine therapy place a secret from Nicole until it was constructed, so he could surprise her with it. Once she actually saw how beautiful it would be, she would better be able to envision what she was giving up her New York life for. Much better than some architectural sketches and photos.

It would take a lot of effort to keep such a huge secret - especially considering the fact that he'd have to hide out here on the ranch for a few weeks while construction was happening. But, with a lot of workers, they should be able to get the whole thing built in a few weeks. Good thing they already owned the land..

Ryan was startled out of his thoughts by Nicole's voice. "Starting without me, I see?" She had a mischievous smile on her face and she nodded her head to his coffee cup.

"I can make you a cup if you're ready…"

"Oh, I'm ready. But I've got something else for you to fill before my coffee cup." She leaned back on the pillow seductively, with her blonde hair spread out like a golden fan.

"Oh, you do, do you?" Ryan shed his robe as he walked over to the bed. "Well, as you can see, I'm ready for you, too."

An hour later, they both sat out on the porch, sipping coffee in companionable silence. It just felt so right between them.

"How's your arm today?"

"Good as new," Nicole replied, rotating her arm fully. "You know, if the whole construction thing doesn't work out, you might think about becoming a doctor. Your hands are pure magic."

Ryan laughed. "My hands are only for you, my dear."

"Mmmm… yeah. That's much better." Nicole sighed and stretched her long, muscular legs in front of her.

He considered walking over there and stroking those legs again but decided to stay focused on the topic he had to bring up. He hated to break the mood, but it had to be said.

"Speaking of work, now that the property deal is off, I have to head back to San Francisco pretty soon."

There was a moment of sad silence as they both gazed out at the ranch.

Nicole broke the silence with a sigh. "Yeah. I figured so. And, I'll be heading back to New York after the barbecue."

Not if I have anything to do with it, Ryan thought.

"I'll come back to the ranch as often as possible before the barbecue," Ryan suggested.

"And we can Facetime, too."

"Yes. Every morning and evening." Ryan's mind started wandering to how he could Facetime without letting on that he was there on the ranch too.

"And, I guess we'll just figure the rest of it out later." Nicole looked so sad that it almost broke Ryan's heart.

He crossed the porch, pulled her to her feet, and into his arms. "Don't worry about a thing, Nicole. It's all going to work out. That's one thing I know for sure."

CHAPTER TWENTY-TWO: SO CLOSE AND YET SO FAR

Nicole's mind woke up before her body did. It was still dark, judging from the lack of light coming in through her eyelids as she lay in her comfortable bed. *I wake up earlier now than I did when I had to be at work by 7:00 am,* she thought. But, for some reason or the other, she found herself waking naturally at 5:30 am. *Rancher's hours...*

The summer was drawing to a close. Ryan had been back in San Francisco for three weeks, and while she missed him, Nicole also knew that her emotional and physical recovery needed to be done alone. Spending these past few weeks working with the ranch hands, planning the barbecue, doing errands in the city with Lucy... these all had given Nicole the break her mind and body needed to re-evaluate her life.

Rolling over to grab her phone and check e-mails, she thought, *things will definitely be different when I get back to New York. No more booze-fueled business dinners or working ten days straight.* Nicole was ready for some serious life changes, including looking for some horse property in Saratoga Springs. Life on the ranch had permeated her soul, and she never wanted to go back to living in the city full-time.

Scrolling through her work e-mails, Nicole was impressed at how consistently Christina had handled every crisis that had come up over the summer. From key employees quitting to mechanical crises, and even a threatened lawsuit, Christina maintained the delicate balance of running things on her own and keeping Nicole in the loop. And, best of all, the younger woman seemed to thrive on the chaos. *Much like I used to in the beginning*, she thought, as she quickly checked her social media accounts.

Nicole's "On This Day" on Facebook was an enlightening trip down memory lane. One year ago she was at a publishing conference in Boston, hobnobbing with the heads of Martha Stewart Omnimedia and O Magazine. The weekend that followed on Martha's Vineyard was incredible.

Two years ago, Nicole was volunteering at A Place for Grace, and filming the footage that would eventually become the documentary that would change her life. *And, introduce me to Ryan...* she thought.

Putting her phone down, Nicole rolled over to gaze out the bedroom window. The first hint of light was coming up over the ranch, and she could see the velvet sapphire sky dotted with the last few stars of the night. Morning birds were starting to chirp, and from afar, Nicole could hear Chuck the Rooster beginning his morning song. It was funny to her that despite having traveled the world, mingling with celebrities and powerful people, this simple ranch life brought her more joy than anything else. *I need to find a way to keep this feeling of peace. I just do.*

"Mornin' sugar." Cathy looked particularly fresh, as she took her coffee mug and sat down next to Cal at the breakfast table on the patio. Kissing him on the cheek, she smiled at Nicole. "How's our favorite houseguest this morning?"

Pouring her juice and coffee, and grabbing a piece of toast, Nicole went to sit next to them. "I feel great today. I'm meeting with the caterer this morning for a final review of the menu for next weekend."

"Make sure they don't serve that dried out brisket we had at the Andersons' barbecue on the Fourth of July. That stuff was a disgrace to Texas," Cal said as he tore a bite from his maple applewood bacon.

Cathy playfully punched Cal. "We aren't usin' the same caterer, Cal. I've told you that a thousand times."

He winked at her and said, "Woman, you talk so much I can't hear half o' what you say."

Nicole wiped the toast crumbs from the corners of her mouth and took a sip of juice. "The guys we are using haves 250 five star reviews on Yelp. They'll be coming out the day before and setting up a smoker and will have someone actually tending the meat all night long. They have a little RV they bring, and they've got a guy that gets up all through the night to add wood to the smoker."

"That must cost a pretty penny," Cal said.

Cathy interjected, "It does, Cal, but this is our annual event. We don't want folks talking about our dried out brisket, do we?"

"No, I guess not. More importantly, I don't want to eat the damn stuff."

"There will definitely be plenty to eat," Nicole said. "Brisket, pulled pork, chicken with an apricot brandy glaze, macaroni and cheese, potato salad, corn on the cob, buttermilk biscuits with honey butter… what am I forgetting?"

"Praise the Lord that Selina's vegetable phase is over," Cal chuckled.

"Oh yeah! Also, green salad, creamed spinach, and coleslaw."

Cathy added, "Don't forget the peach pie and chocolate cake."

"You ladies are makin' me hungry. I'm gonna head out to the back lot to check on the..." Cal stopped speaking suddenly as Cathy kicked his shin under the table. "Fence," he added hastily.

Cathy quickly rescued him. "Yes. That fence has been giving us trouble for a while."

Pushing her chair back, Nicole offered, "Do you want me to take Essere out there and help? I have some time before my meeting, and I really miss riding her since she moved back out to the stable."

Simultaneously, Cal and Cathy both practically shouted, "No!" "No, darlin', you just focus on the barbecue," Cal said with a smile. "That's where we need ya' the most."

"How did your meeting with the caterer go?" Ryan's face was very close to his camera phone as he and Nicole were Facetiming.

"It went well. I sure hope they live up to their reputation. I would hate for Cal and Cathy to be the laughing stock of Dallas because the food was bad." Nicole was in the library, doing her daily reading on equine care and ranch management. "Where are you, anyway? You look like a hostage with that flag in the background."

Ryan laughed and turned around, to see the giant California flag that was the backdrop of his call. "Oh yeah, Nina went a little crazy in the conference room. Proud to be a Californian, I guess."

"Well, I know that you are two hours behind me, and it's still the middle of your workday, so I'll let you get back to it. I'm looking forward to seeing you here at the barbecue next week."

Ryan smiled tenderly and replied, "I am looking forward to seeing you, too."

"Do you need me to pick you up from the airport?"

Ryan grinned. "No, you'll have a lot going on that day. I'll get Steve or Lucy to pick me up."

"Okay. Well, I can't wait."

"Me neither, Nicole. It feels like you're so close, and yet so far away…"

CHAPTER TWENTY-THREE: HIDDEN

Ryan reached over to his phone and hit the "End" button on the Facetime call. It was getting harder and harder to keep his presence on the ranch a secret from Nicole. Hanging that giant California flag over the window in his cottage was Lucy's genius idea. It looked ridiculously out of place but did the trick of making it seem like he was in San Francisco. *Only one more week until I can stop this charade,* he thought. Cal, Cathy, Steve, and Lucy had all been instrumental in helping keep the secret. Cathy kept Nicole busy with the barbecue plans, Lucy kept her busy with shopping and lunch dates in the city. Steve had moved Essere out to the newly renovated stables, so that Nicole couldn't go off and explore the ranch on her own, potentially coming upon the construction site. And Cal was just Cal, running everything and making life seem normal.

Speaking of Cal, they had a meeting scheduled at the site this morning, and Ryan realized he'd better get going or he was going to be late. Stepping into his boots and heading out the door, he was happy with the progress on the equine therapy facility. *It's amazing what you can accomplish quickly when you throw enough money at a project,* he chuckled. Construction had been going 24/7 since they broke ground three weeks ago. It looked a lot like that old show Extreme Makeover, Home Edition, with different crews coming in one after the other to get the job done.

Early into the project, Lucy had the idea of hiring a videographer to record the construction so that Nicole could see the progression, once she saw the finished facility. Ryan loved the idea and suggested to Lucy that she ask around for a good videographer.

Turns out, Lucy already knew one - none other than Melissa Tomson! "I had no idea that she was that Rick Tomson's ex-wife," Lucy had said. "There couldn't be two more different people in the world." The women had met at a fundraiser for disabled children. Lucy's daughter Andi had a physical disability from when she was hit by a drunk driver, and Melissa's daughter Jenny was autistic.

The Beyond Foundation was dedicated to helping children with developmental and physical disabilities grow beyond their limitations. When Lucy approached Melissa about video recording the construction of the equine therapy facility, they had a good laugh when they realized they both knew Ryan and that Melissa's daughter Jenny would be attending therapy there once it was built. "What a small world Dallas is," the women mused.

"I would *love* to repay Ryan for all he's done for Jenny and me," she'd said. And, Melissa had been at the ranch every day since, recording footage of the construction of the cutting-edge facility.

Pulling his truck up to the site, Ryan saw Cal's truck already there. They were just putting the last touches on the office building and the final inspection was scheduled for Friday. The dream was about to be realized!

"How're ya likin' that new truck, Ryan?" Cal asked as he approached the new vehicle.

Patting the hood of his brand new silver Ford F-450, Ryan answered. "I love it. I didn't think my Porsche would fit in too well around here, so I gave it to Nina so that she could surprise her dad with it for his 60th birthday."

"That's some bonus. I bet she was mighty happy."

"She was. Say, listen, I got a call from Jill Katz yesterday. My attorney? She said that Judge Delgadillo was indicted on four counts of bribery. Our case is one of them."

"Good, good!" The older man smiled and patted Ryan on the back. "I gave that information you gave me to a buddy of mine. Looks like it made it into the right hands."

Walking over to the construction site, Ryan was pleased. "I'm really glad that such a crooked judge is off the bench. Who knows how much damage he did?"

"Damn straight," the older man nodded.

"Have you seen Melissa this morning?" Ryan wanted to check on her since Jill had also mentioned that Rick Tomson had been arrested for his criminal activity.

"Yeah, I think I saw her out by the riding arena. You go find her, and I'll go talk to the foreman and see if they fixed the filtration system yet. Meet you in the office in a few."

Approaching the newly built riding arena, Ryan saw Melissa with her video camera, recording one of the horses galloping riderless around the arena. She was down on one knee, filming the black and white spotted horse, with its mane flying behind. The sense of freedom and power was palpable.

When Melissa saw Ryan approaching, she put the camera down and headed his way.

"Mornin' Boss."

"Hey, Melissa. I wanted to check in with you this morning. I just heard the news about Rick."

Melissa sighed deeply. "Yeah, Rick's mother called me last night and read me the riot act. 'I just know you did this somehow. You were set and determined to ruin my son's life, and now you've gone and done it. I hope you rot in hell,' she said to me." Melissa smiled and spread her arms, gesturing at the ranch. "Honey, if this is hell, I am happy to rot here any day."

She and Ryan laughed, and he said, "Good. I am glad you are okay with it."

"I'm better than okay. I am finally free. Free to move on with my life. Free from feeling bad that my daughter doesn't have a dad. Maybe even free to fall in love again. Who knows? For now, I am just focusing on taking the final video footage of the facility and then working with my editor to piece it together into something really special for the grand opening."

Nodding his head, he said, "Good, I'm glad. I can't wait to see what you've come up with! I need to head over to the office to meet with Cal. I'll see you and Jenny at the barbecue, right?"

"We wouldn't miss it for the world!"

CHAPTER TWENTY-FOUR: WHERE THERE'S SMOKE, THERE'S FIRE

Ellie would not stop barking. The smells from the ranch were so enticing that not one nose for miles could avoid the tantalizing scent of barbecuing meat. The hungry pup kept running back and forth between the kitchen, where the smells of macaroni and cheese were coming, and the smoker. It was a dream come true for the Golden Retriever.

The caterer had arrived yesterday morning, in an RV that was towing a giant smoker the size of a small van. As promised, he'd spent the past 24 hours adding different kinds of wood to the fire so that the meats would be infused with maximum flavor.

In fact, Selina hadn't even bothered with her daily buffet of bacon and eggs. She knew everyone would want to save their appetite for today's feast. Instead, she'd set out a platter of freshly baked blueberry muffins and fruit for everyone to enjoy.

The ranch was abuzz with activity in preparation for the festivities. The driveway was a veritable traffic jam with cars and trucks coming and going. Delivery trucks, furniture rentals, even a petting zoo for the kids. It was quite a sight to see llamas and goats being herded past the pool out to the side lawn. *It's true that everything is bigger in Texas,* Nicole thought. *Even parties.*

"Darlin' there's a fella out front who wants to know where you want the stage set up." Cal was talking to Cathy, who was on the phone with the florist.

"So you're sayin' that every bluebonnet in the state of Texas is wilted? I have a lot of trouble believin' that, honey. Look harder and call me back." She hit "end" with a frown on her face and a sigh. "The bluebonnet is our state flower. I can't imagine there aren't any good ones to be found."

Nicole stood up from the table where she'd been nibbling on her muffin and going over the timeline and said to Cathy, "I'll talk to the furniture guy about the stage. You grab some food. It's going to be a long day!" The two women embraced as they passed.

"Honey, you're a lifesaver. This is the biggest guest list we have ever had, and with Lucy busy with..." she caught herself "her other projects, there's no way I could have done all this without you." Nicole gave her another quick hug before heading to the front door.

Six hours later, guests were starting to trickle in. There was a huge white tent set up out by the lake, filled with dozens of tables and chairs. The color theme for the party was blue and yellow, and there were clusters of bluebonnets and sunflowers atop crisp white linen tablecloths. (Turns out Cathy managed to find some, after all.) Fairy lights were strung across the top of the tent, and there was a small dance floor up by the stage. A local country band was playing, and a few folks were already dancing.

On the other side of the main house was a secondary stage. This one was much larger and had a full light and sound system set up, as there was a short concert scheduled for after sunset. The performer was a secret from everyone but Cal, Cathy, and Nicole. She couldn't wait to see the look on Lucy's face when the star came out, as it was her favorite performer.

The pool was decked out with balls and pool noodles and other toys for the kids. Cal insisted on hiring a lifeguard to watch over the pool so that all of the parents could relax and enjoy themselves, knowing their kids were safe. Several kids were already doing cannonballs into the fresh water, and playing the time-honored game of "Marco Polo." The handsome lifeguard had a gaggle of teenage girls flirting with him, as he blew his whistle now and then to stop the younger kids from running by the pool.

Some kids could be seen in the petting zoo, with nervous mamas following them around with hand sanitizer. "Johnny, come here, you're gonna be eatin' with those hands…"

The booming sounds of skeet shooting could be heard from out in the pasture. Steve had made sure to put the animals away, so they wouldn't be spooked by the noise. It was an honored Texas tradition and Nicole was hoping to try her hand at it later, after dinner.

Despite the perfection of the day, with the sounds of country music and laughing children in the pool, the smells of barbecue wafting through the air, and a gentle Texas breeze to cool her skin, something was missing. Ryan. Nicole kept looking toward the main house to see if he'd arrived yet. The party was in full swing, and she hadn't seen him all afternoon. *Where are you, Ryan?*

∼

In the distance, Ryan could hear the faint sounds of country music and the cracking of skeet guns. The barbecue smelled amazing, but Ryan knew he would be too excited to eat much. *Thank goodness for leftovers,* he thought. Taking one last look around at the equine therapy center, Ryan was momentarily brought to tears. So many children were going to be helped here. He was so grateful for everything that had happened. *Losing that lawsuit was one of the best things that ever happened to me,* he thought. *You never really know what path life will take, do you?*

Now, it was up to Nicole. Would all this be enough to convince her to leave her job in New York? He knew how much she loved her work. And she was damn good at it, too. There was a distinct possibility that she might say no, and choose to stay in New York. He had a backup plan for someone to run the center just in case. But he was sure hoping once she saw his vision for their future, she would agree to stay.

It wouldn't be the end of the world, of course, if they had to be a long distance couple. Now that he'd moved his office to Dallas, it was only a short flight to New York in the jet. But it wouldn't be the same as having her in his bed every morning. *Mmmm... I could get used to that...*

It was time to head over to the main house and get set up for the big reveal. Feeling around in his pocket for the velvet jewelry bag, and confirming it was there, he jumped in one of the golf carts to head over to the house. Valet parking was going to be a nightmare and he'd be better off leaving his truck at the cottage.

With a trail of dust flying behind him, Ryan said to himself, aloud, "Okay Cummings. Time to go get the girl."

∽

"Testing, 1, 2, 3." Cathy tapped the microphone as she spoke into it. "Sugar, is this thing on?" The crowd erupted in cheers and "We can hear you!"

"Okay everyone. Gather 'round. Grab your beers and whatever else Marcus is fixin' y'all, and head on over here. It's time for the main event."

Guests started making their way over to the large stage. "There's chairs for the adults and bales of hay for the kids to sit on," Cathy continued.

"Now, before I introduce our special guests... yes, that's a clue, there are two of 'em... I want to take a moment to thank y'all for comin' out tonight."

Cathy looked so comfortable up on the stage. She was wearing a blue and yellow sundress, to match the theme of the party. Her cowgirl boots were accented with the same colors, and her blonde locks were curled in a messy bun on top of her head.

"Cal and I... Cal, where are ya honey?" She put her hand over her eyes to scan the crowd. From the back, by the bar, she heard, "Right here, Darlin'." The crowd cheered.

"Cal and I want to thank y'all so much for bein' here. Most of y'all work here on the ranch every day, and this place really wouldn't have the heart and soul it has if it wasn't for y'all. I hope all a' y'all got lots to eat, and saved room for dessert. We'll be setting it up in the tent after the show. I also want to take a moment to introduce some special friends of ours..."

As Cathy was introducing the dignitaries and celebrities in the audience, Nicole kept scanning the crowd. She still hadn't seen Ryan, and she was getting worried. She's spied Steve and Lucy, and their daughter Andi. Someone was supposed to have gotten Ryan from the airport. But, where was he?

Slipping past the crowd, she heard Cathy on the loudspeaker. "We are so honored to have former First Daughter and Granddaughter Jenna Bush Hager here with us tonight." The crowd clapped.

Walking toward the barn, hoping maybe Ryan was in there, Nicole thought she heard voices coming from inside. The barn was empty, as Steve had put the animals in the stable to keep them calm during the party. Who could be in there?

Peering through the door, Nicole's heart stopped. It was Ryan. He was talking with that same woman he was with at the Ritz! They were huddled together looking at something on her phone.

What the hell is she doing here? What's going on?

Confused and needing a moment to decide what to do, Nicole ran back to the main house. *I can't believe it. I was such a fool to believe them when they said it wasn't what it looked like when I saw the two of them at the Ritz.*

Passing the stage, she barely heard Cathy announcing the special guest performers.

"Ladies and gentlemen. It's time for our special guests. You all know this first singer, probably for his Christmas tunes and crooner songs. He's not a Texan but is a Canadian. His singin' partner tonight isn't from Texas either, but he got famous from a song called Austin, so we'll give him a pass. Put your hands together for a big Dallas welcome for music superstars Michael Bublé and Blake Shelton!"

Nicole hoped that Lucy was one of the joyful screams she heard as she rounded the pool and into the library.

The house was empty, of course, as everyone was listening to Michael and Blake sing a duet of "Home." Nicole took a deep breath, and with tears stinging her eyes, thought, *Well, this is a fine end to the summer. I need to get out of here and go home. I'm just going to go up and pack my things, and see if I can get a redeye back to New York.*

Breathing in to muster her resolve, Nicole could barely see where she was going as she turned the corner to head up the stairs.

CHAPTER TWENTY-FIVE: REVEALING

"Have you seen Nicole?" Ryan asked Selina who was in the kitchen with the caterers discussing when to serve dessert. There were racks and racks of peach pie and chocolate cakes. Stopping to smell the pies, Ryan's stomach grumbled. He hadn't eaten a bite! But he didn't have time to stop and eat. He needed to find Nicole!

"No, Mr. Ryan. I haven't seen her. Maybe check in the library?"

Looking at his phone to see if she had texted him, he thought *This whole plan will fall flat if I don't find her soon.*

Walking through the door from the kitchen toward the staircase, Ryan had his head down as Nicole came flying around the corner. They bumped into each other, and Nicole fell flat on her back, just as she did the day they met on the ranch.

"Oh my God, Nicole!" Once again, she was splayed out on the ground, her blonde locks covering her face.

"Ryan! I was looking for you all night!" Her face lit up at the sight of him but immediately formed a frown. "You really should watch where you're going."

Trying to be playful, Ryan quipped, "We ought to stop meeting like this…"

Instantly, though, he knew something was wrong. "What's the matter?" Her eyes were teary and she was clearly upset.

"I don't want to talk about it, Ryan. I need to go upstairs and start packing for home."

"Packing? Now? Right in the middle of the barbecue?" Ryan was confused.

"Yes. It's been a wonderful summer and I accomplished my goals. I had… fun… with you." She had tears in her eyes again. "But it's over and it's time for me to go home."

"Fun?" He took a step toward her. "We were more than just fun. You know that."

"Do I? Were we?" Her eyes were blazing angrily. "I don't know any such thing. Several months ago I saw you at the Ritz with some woman. You were holding hands and gazing into each other's eyes. I listened to everyone telling me,' no no, he's not that kind of guy. You must not have seen what you thought you saw.' So, I dropped it."

Ryan's mind went scanning back in time. *A woman? Holding hands? The Ritz? Oh my God, she's talking about Melissa.* Opening his mouth to explain, she didn't let him speak.

"Now, tonight, after I've been looking forward to seeing you for weeks, I look all over the ranch, and where do I find you? In the barn. With *her*. You brought *her* here? Obviously, I was completely mistaken about you." Nicole tried to go up the stairs, but Ryan stopped her by gently grabbing her arm.

"You *are* mistaken. Nicole, listen to me."

Nicole wasn't listening. She was struggling to get free, so he let go of her arm and followed her up the stairs. She went into her room and dragged out the huge Louis Vuitton suitcase and started shoving clothes in it, all the while crying.

"Nicole. Listen. Melissa is just a friend."

Nicole scoffed. "A friend you have cocktails with and meet in barns?"

Ryan couldn't help but chuckle. "No, we don't meet in barns."

"You think this is funny?"

"Honey, if you just stop and listen to me for two minutes. Please."

"Fine." She stopped packing and stared at him defiantly.

"Her name is Melissa Tomson." Nicole blinked in recognition of the last name.

"Tomson? As in Rick Tomson?"

"Yes. She is his ex-wife."

"I don't understand. What do you have to do with Rick Tomson's ex-wife?" Nicole sat down on the edge of the bed.

"Shortly before court, she came to me and gave me a bunch of evidence that proved that Rick was engaged in illegal activity."

"I read he got arrested." Nicole was listening and thinking about what Ryan was telling her. "Okay, but why is she here?"

"I hired her to do some work on the ranch."

Nicole blinked her eyes in confusion. "But, you've been in San Francisco. Why would you hire Rick Tomson's ex-wife to work on the ranch? And why haven't I seen her here?"

It seemed to be too much for her to take in at once. So, Ryan added, "Nicole. I know it looks bad. But, I promise you, there's nothing going on. I need to you trust me. Can you do that?"

"I don't understand."

"You will. Will you come with me for a little bit? Please? It will explain everything."

She seemed unsure for a moment, as she pondered what

she'd learned. Then, Nicole visibly softened and said "Okay. I trust you." Ryan took her hand and led her back down the stairs, and out the French doors, back to the party.

∼

As Ryan took Nicole's hand and led her by the pool, strewn with toys and wet towels, across the lawn by the stage, where the guests were dancing and singing along with the concert, Nicole's mind was reeling. *Should I believe him that Melissa Tomson is just a friend?*

They crossed behind the crowd, and Nicole spied Cal and Cathy. They were dancing, off to the side, and Cathy twirled around, landing in Cal's arms as they laughed and kissed each other. *I want what they have,* she thought.

But, how do you get a relationship like that? Does it come effortlessly? Or does it come from trusting your heart, even when your head might tell you otherwise?

Ryan was quiet, deep in thought. As their shoes crunched the gravel path that led to the lake, she looked at him. *What is my heart telling me about Ryan?* Touching the pendant on her neck, the one he bought because his heart told him to, she listened to the answer her heart had been whispering. *Trust him, Nicole.*

As they approached the lake, Nicole stopped in awe. The lake was lit up with luminarias, and there were candles floating across the water. The moon reflected off the water, and the warm, clear night showed off a million diamonds in the sky. Off to the side, was Essere, standing regally, and behind her was a carriage. A horse-drawn carriage.

"Ryan! What is this?" she marveled.

Helping her in, and then sliding in next to her, he told Essere to go. Wordlessly, the carriage wandered a path around the ranch. By the main house, where the people she had come to love were all celebrating... by the barn where she'd achieved a lifelong dream of learning to ride... by the stream where Nicole and Essere had spent so many hours. The carriage passed by Ryan's cottage, she remembered making love and, yes, falling in love there.

Nicole was confused when she saw the California flag hanging by the window. "Wait, you've been here the whole time?" The suspense was killing her. Ryan just smiled mysteriously.

Off in the distance was a building Nicole didn't recognize. "What's that?" she asked.

"You'll see."

As the carriage approached, Nicole gasped. It was a two-story building with the same design style as the main house. White, with a wraparound porch, and balconies from each door on the upper floor. It looked more like a home than anything else. It was lit up, and Nicole could hear whinnying from some horses. "What is this?" she asked, incredulously.

Essere turned around the corner to the main entrance and then stopped. Nicole could see a sign over the front door. It said "Essere Equine Therapy Center".

"What? I don't understand." Nicole's eyes widened in surprise. "You built an equine therapy center on the ranch?"

Ryan grinned."I did."

Nicole could hardly believe it. This whole time she thought he was in San Francisco, he was here on the ranch, building this center. "But, why?"

"For you. For us, actually."

"For us?"

"Yes. For us. I want you to run the Essere Equine Therapy Center, and we'll fill it with kids who need our help. Melissa Tomson has an autistic daughter. Lucy and Steve's daughter

Andi. Plus hundreds of other kids who can benefit from the bond between a horse and a human. Look at what Essere did for you. And equine therapy did for me? We can pay it back by helping change these kids' lives… We can make it affordable for more kids to get this kind of therapy."

Nicole looked around. She knew then that she didn't want to go back to New York. Christina could take over the business easily. She could live here in town, or maybe even on the ranch.

"But you live in San Francisco."

"I moved my work here. Dallas is a booming development area right now. There are more than enough projects to keep me busy. I've already given up my car and my condo. I live here now."

"I can't believe you did all of this." Nicole was stunned.

Ryan continued, "Nic, I have fallen so deeply in love with you. Your heart, your compassion… you are beautiful and sexy, and intelligent."

She smiled, "Go on…"

He laughed. "I know that your home is in New York, but I was hoping that maybe, just maybe, you'd give it up and marry me."

He pulled the velvet pouch out of his pocket and removed a diamond and onyx ring. He'd had it custom designed by Atherton Diamonds. Ryan kneeled down on one knee and extended the ring to her.

"Nicole Burns. Will you marry me?"

Before she could answer, Essere whinnied.

Laughing through her tears, Nicole said, "I guess that's my answer… Yes. Yes, Ryan Cummings. I will marry you."

Just then, as they kissed, they heard the sounds of Michael Bublé singing.

"Do you think they'll be disappointed if we don't go back

to the party?" she asked, looking at the ring on her finger, as he took her in his arms to dance.

"In the words of Cathy Cummings, 'Sugar, I think they'll be disappointed if we *do* go back to the party." He kissed her deeply, and then crooned in her ear, softly the words to *Save The Last Dance For Me.*

EPILOGUE

"Mama, look, I'm riding a horse!" Andi's face was beaming with joy as she sat atop one of the equine therapy horses.

Lucy had tears streaming down her face as she said, "Yes, baby. You are!" For the first time since the accident so many years ago, Andi didn't need legs or a wheelchair to get around. Riding a horse put her on equal footing, so to speak, with kids her age who could walk. It was freeing to see her feel "normal" for the first time in her life.

It had been three months since the Essere Equine Therapy Center had opened. In that time, they'd signed on several kids, with different disabilities. Melissa's daughter Jenny was one of them, and she was thriving. The beauty of equine therapy is that it can be tailored to benefit so many different kinds of issues.

"It's something, isn't it?" Melissa walked up next to Lucy, sipping on a diet soda. Nodding to the other side of the arena, where Jenny and a therapist were feeding a horse a carrot, she said, "We are already seeing so many positive changes in Jenny. On the way home from therapy, Jenny tells me how she feels about 'her horsey.' It's truly a miracle."

"What's a miracle? That we got Steve to pop for a new pair of jeans?" Nicole teased, as she walked up to her friends.

Lucy laughed and said, "Oh, honey, that wasn't him. I just finally threw the old ones out and put new ones in their place. Typical Steve, never said a word. Just put them on."

The women laughed companionably, as they watched the kids and trainers working with the horses.

Every couple of weeks, Nicole, Cathy, Lucy, and Melissa would go into town and have lunch, just the girls. Nicole had actually hired Melissa to work as the official photographer on the ranch, after seeing the amazing footage she took during construction. They were planning an official Grand Opening event in another month or so and were going to show the video at the event.

Nicole was loving her new role as the Director. While it wasn't the same as running a publishing company, many of the skills were the same. Instead of dealing with advertisers who acted like children, she was now dealing with actual children. Instead of riding in an Uber to work, she rode a horse to work. Managing the staff of therapists and trainers and other employees was far easier than her work in New York. She'd given up her apartment, sold the business to Christina, stuck everything in a moving van and became a Texan.

"Isn't that your phone ringing?" Lucy heard it first.

Nicole raced back into her office just in time to get it before it went to voicemail. "Essere Equine, this is Nicole. How can we help you?"

A deep voice came through the other end of the line. "I'm in need of some therapy. But not the equine kind. The kind I can only get from you."

Nicole laughed and lowered her voice so the kids couldn't hear. "Now you're Marvin Gaye, with the sexual healing?"

She and Ryan were happy living in his tiny cottage on the ranch. Breakfasts and dinners with Cathy and Cal bookended their days. Ryan went off to the Dallas office while Nicole worked at Essere Equine.

Weekends were spent planning their wedding next summer on the ranch, or jumping in the jet and flying off to some romantic destination. Whatever they did, they always made sure they did it together.

∼

Nicole's eyes opened and looked at the clock on the nightstand. It read 2:35 am. "Oh come on, you have to be kidding me," Nicole said, as she turned to face Ryan in bed, grinning. "Again? You're insatiable."

Ryan pulled her close and kissed her, as his hand slipped under her nightgown. "I'm insatiable because I'm beguiled by you, my love."

BETROTHED TO YOU

CHAPTER ONE: DREAMS

Melissa was standing in the middle of a Japanese tea house when a blonde man... a handsome, sexy blonde man...walked up to her and silently handed her a branch from a cherry blossom tree. He pulled her to him and leaned down to kiss her lips ever so gently. Melissa closed her eyes and melted into his embrace. *It's been so long...* she thought as desire welled up from deep within.

As she was kissing the man, Melissa heard a voice. It was her daughter, calling her name. "Mama..."

Melissa tore herself away from the kiss and ran through the morning mist toward the voice. Nearby was a row of brightly dressed Geisha girls. One of them walked right up to her, and said, in Jenny's voice, "Mama!" Why was Jenny's voice coming out of a Geisha girl?

Melissa awakened to her semi-darkened bedroom, with her shoulder being shaken by eleven-year-old Jenny. "Mama, are you awake? It's Monday at 7:02 am. It's two minutes past the time we are supposed to go over my schedule for the week."

Blinking out of her bizarre dream, Melissa Tomson sat up

in bed and looked at her phone. Jenny was right. It was 7:02 am on Monday, and they did usually go through Jenny's schedule at 7:00. *Why didn't my alarm go off?* she wondered.

"Mama, come on. Get dressed. We are now three minutes late." Jenny's straight blonde hair was already brushed, and she'd put it in a barrette. Although she was homeschooled, Jenny was dressed for her school day in a pair of blue jeans and a red long-sleeved top with flowers all over it.

"Okay, okay, honey. Mommy's getting up now. I'm sorry my alarm didn't go off." Melissa stepped out onto the plush white rug near her bed and shrugged on a fluffy bathrobe. "You go on downstairs and work on your flower sketchbook and I'll be down in a few minutes."

Jenny didn't look too happy about this but did as her mother asked. Giving her mother a peck on the cheek, Jenny smiled, "Okay, Mama. I will see you in three minutes."

Melissa chuckled at her daughter, remembering the conversation they'd had a couple of weeks ago about the difference between "two" and "a few." "A few means three or more," Melissa had said.

As she heard her daughter counting the steps as she went down them, Melissa was filled with gratitude at how well Jenny was doing. She'd been diagnosed as being on the autism spectrum when she was three years old. The diagnosis came as a shock to Jenny's Dad Rick, who took it as a personal stigma that he had an "imperfect" daughter. Melissa, on the other hand, had suspected that something was different about Jenny from early on. She'd not developed as quickly as other kids her age and seemed very sensitive to things like sounds, bright lights and her clothing. Frankly, the diagnosis was a relief to Melissa, because Rick had belittled Melissa whenever she'd tried to talk to him about Jenny. "You're just looking to find trouble where there is none, Melissa."

Melissa had immediately enrolled Jenny in a program for autistic pre-schoolers. While it definitely helped, the real progress didn't happen until just last year. Jenny had been gifted a scholarship to an equine therapy program, and that had made all the difference. Jenny truly blossomed, and for the first time, Melissa began to have hope that Jenny would be able to live independently one day.

Looking at the clock, Melissa hurried as she pulled on a pair of jeans and a black t-shirt. Springtime in Dallas was still pretty chilly in the mornings, so she also threw on a gray cable-knit sweater. Since she wasn't planning on going out right away, Melissa figured the horsey-slippers that Jenny had gotten her for Christmas would work as foot attire.

As she headed to the top of the stairs, Melissa heard Jenny calling her again. "Mama! It's 7:08. It's been a few minutes. Are you coming?"

∼

Seated at the small table in their kitchen, Melissa and Jenny were side by side as they looked at the printed weekly calendar. "Okay, Jellybean," Melissa said, as she sipped a steaming cup of coffee. "What is on your calendar today?"

Jenny pointed to each item as she said it. "Wake up 6:45. Make my bed. Get dressed. Brush hair and teeth. Come downstairs, and go over calendar with Mama." She looked at Melissa.

"Good. I know we are a few minutes late, but we have extra time built in. We are still on schedule." Melissa was always amazed at how Jenny's internal clock operated with mathematical precision.

"I will eat cereal and milk for breakfast and then put the bowl in the sink. Since it is Monday, I have my horse riding lesson at Essere at 9:00."

The Essere Equine Therapy Center was where Jenny had her therapy and where Melissa worked as the center's marketing advisor. She took photographs and videos of the clients and ran the center's YouTube channel.

"Yes, and Emily is out this week, remember? You'll be working with Jason." Melissa could see a shadow of discomfort move over Jenny's face. But it quickly passed. This was huge progress from just a year ago when a change like this would have been enough to trigger a meltdown. Melissa had Ryan Cummings to thank for that!

Ryan and his fiancée Nicole had founded the Essere Equestrian Center and had become dear friends of Melissa's. They'd met when Ryan was embroiled in a lawsuit with Rick. Rick had left Melissa and Jenny right after the diagnosis and had refused most contact with Jenny throughout her childhood. *It's just as well,* she thought. *He was a liar and a crook, and I'm glad I gave Ryan the information that led him to being imprisoned.*

"After I ride with Emily... I mean Jason... then Carrie will bring me back here and we will do my school for the day. I have math and science..."

As Melissa listened to her daughter her heart warmed. *It's just you and me, kid. We're a team. I don't need a husband, and you don't need a Dad. We are doing just great on our own.* She never let herself dream for more...

CHAPTER TWO: THE BEST LAID PLANS

"Is it take your dog to work day or something?" Michael Davis was sitting at his reclaimed wood desk that sat in the "power position" of his home office. His secretary, Brad had insisted on using the ancient Asian design art of Feng Shui when they were deciding where to put the desk.

Brad's Chihuahua was sticking her head out of the satchel she was being carried in. The red bow on her head matched the red sweater she was wearing. "Very funny. Pepper has a vet appointment at 10. Besides..." he said, nodding to the Shiba Inu sleeping on a plush dog bed by the window, "Every day is 'take your dog to work day' around here."

Laughing, Michael replied, "This is my home office. It's more like doggy daycare with Sam around here." Sam lifted her head at the sound of her name, and then went back to sleep.

"I've got the research you wanted on the hotel idea. I'm no billionaire investor like you are, but it looks like building a boutique high-end hotel near the Portland Japanese Garden is a winning bet." Brad laid the folder on Michael's desk.

"Thanks for gathering the information for me. I really appreciate it." He spied the coffee in Brad's hand. "Is that coffee for me?"

"You know it is. Single-origin from Ecuador. Just the way you like it."

"You are the best, you know that?" Michael took a big sip as he opened the folder.

"That's what Pepper tells me all the time, don't you Pepper?" Brad kissed the dog's nose as he headed out the door.

∼

"So, how is life in Portland? Do you have chickens yet?" Ryan Cummings loved to tease Michael. They'd been best friends since college, along with the other two members of the informally titled "BBC 2." Andrew Atherton was the Vice President of Atherton Diamonds, one of the largest manufacturers, distributors and retail sellers of diamonds and other gems in the world. Cole Bennett was an investor in Atherton, as well as in tech stocks. Michael had just moved to Portland a few months ago to be near his parents, having founded a software company in Silicon Valley that he then sold for 1.2 billion dollars to Microsoft. Ryan was the head of the Hotel and Leisure division and Executive Vice President of Cummings Construction

"You're teasing me about chickens, Mr. I Live on a Ranch? For your information, I travel too much to have farm animals." Michael could envision the smile on Ryan's face as he teased him.

"So what's the deal on the hotel? Are you going to do it?" Ryan's voice changed to business. "I know we are having a huge development boom here in Dallas."

"Actually, that's why I called." Michael leaned back in his chair to look out the picture window. He loved springtime in Portland. "The numbers look good. Even though there are a ton of hotels going up, this is going to be a very small, expensive hotel that caters to Japanese tourists who come to town to see the Japanese Garden, among other things."

"Good. I'm glad you're going boutique. The market is really saturated for the big chain hotels right now."

"Do you still have the plans you drew up for the one near the Dallas Cowboys Training Camp?"

"You mean the one that Rick Tomson sued me over and I never built? I sure do still have them. Why?"

"Well, I figure it would be easier to modify existing plans than to draw up completely new ones. I was really impressed with what you'd planned."

"Thank you," Ryan said. "It wasn't going to be Asian-themed, but you're right that it wouldn't take much to convert the plans to suit your build."

"That's exactly what I was thinking. Can you send them over?"

"I can, but I have a better idea. Why don't you fly out for the Grand Opening of the Essere Equestrian Therapy Center? Cole is coming."

The idea of seeing both Cole and Ryan was too much to pass up. "That sounds great. Is Andrew making it in from Botswana?"

"I don't think so. Janet is pregnant again, and he doesn't want to be that far away."

"Pregnant again! That makes three kids! One of the rest of us better step it up, man."

"Not me, man. I have a wedding to plan," said Ryan.

Michael chuckled. "And by 'plan' you mean show up on the day wearing a tux?"

"Something like that..." Ryan's mischievous grin could practically be heard over the phone.

Michael turned back to his computer and opened his calendar. "Okay, so when is this Grand Opening?"

CHAPTER THREE: A LITTLE YELP FROM OUR FRIENDS

"Nicole, have you seen our latest Yelp ratings?" Melissa had her reading glasses on as she pointed to the computer. "We have two-hundred-and-fifty-seven five-star ratings!"

Nicole was passing through on her way to the break room and looked over Melissa's shoulder. "That's because we have a killer marketing advisor." She smiled and patted Melissa on the back.

"Well, the job would be a lot harder if we didn't have such a great leadership team." Melissa smiled at Nicole. Melissa had been acting as a marketing advisor for the Essere Equestrian Therapy Center since its soft opening four months ago.

Nicole had spent her career in publishing but made a shift to become the Director of the center when her fiancé Ryan surprised her with it. Nicole had branched out into documentary producing when she created the Academy Award-nominated "Amazing Grace", about an orphanage for AIDS-stricken families that was run by her best friend Janet. But, because Nicole didn't know that the Essere center was being built, she wasn't involved in documenting its construction, and that's how Melissa got involved.

Melissa had been acting informally as the marketing advisor since many of the photographs she took during construction were being used for marketing materials. A photographer by trade, Melissa also took keepsake photos of each of the kids as they interacted with the horses.

Now, with the Grand Opening just two weeks away, both Nicole and Melissa were swamped with details. The event was being held at the Center, which was located on C & C Ranch in Parker, Texas. But since Nicole and Ryan knew so many people, folks were flying in from all over the world. Melissa was spending hours a day juggling hotel reservations and flight times, in addition to managing the social media accounts and review sites. It was a pretty demanding job, but Melissa loved being able to work where Jenny was getting therapy, and she felt a huge debt of gratitude to Ryan for gifting them with a full scholarship.

"Hey Nic, did the delivery guy come yet?" Ryan asked as he walked in the front door of the Center.

Nicole popped her head out of the break room, holding a bottle of water and said, "Not that I saw."

"It's getting late and we are low on hay. I'll call the guy again." Even when he was irritated, Ryan kept a cool demeanor.

"Before you go, Ryan, since you're both here, can we take a minute and go through the last minute additions to the guest list?" Melissa pulled up the spreadsheet.

"Sure." They both gathered around Melissa.

"So, since Blake Shelton is on tour, his people said he couldn't make it this time. But we did reach out to Jason Aldean, and his manager said he would get back to us."

"He's a perfect choice. After what happened in Las Vegas,

he's become a symbol for resilience," Nicole said. "I hope he can make it."

"Also, Ryan, you mentioned that you were going to invite your friend Andrew?"

"Yeah, I talked to him but his wife is pregnant and he doesn't want to be that far away from her. They live in Botswana."

Melissa answered wistfully. "He sounds like a nice guy. When I was pregnant with Jenny, Rick spent six weeks in Germany on a real estate deal. I later found out that the foundation wasn't the only thing he was laying…"

Ryan couldn't help but laugh at that. "I'm sorry, Melissa. I didn't mean to laugh."

"No, no. Don't be. I meant it to be funny. Besides. It was a long time ago and I am so over that man."

"You've got new friends now," Nicole said.

"You got that right. Better friends than I ever had when I was married to him!" Melissa smiled happily.

"Speaking of friends, I did invite Michael Davis to come."

Nicole's face lit up. "Oh cool! I haven't met him!" Nicole had met Ryan at different events a few times prior to them becoming involved romantically, but Michael had been working on a project in Tokyo and wasn't at any of those. "Is he flying in from Japan?"

"No, he lives in Portland now." Ryan sat down on an office chair, straddling it backward like a horse.

"Portland! That's where I grew up," said Melissa. "Small world!" She typed his name on the guest list.

"Yeah, his parents live there. He made a ton of money when he sold a company to Microsoft, and then he ditched the California life for Oregon."

"Can't say I blame him," Melissa said. "I'd love to see my Portland friends again. There's no place like it on earth."

"Oh, I'll just hand you a cup of coffee and turn the hose

on you. Coffee and getting wet, that's pretty much Oregon in a nutshell, right?" Ryan quipped as he stood up and headed for the door to call the hay delivery guy.

"My fiancé is a very strange man," Nicole joked, as she strolled into her office.

Shaking her head fondly at how cute Ryan and Nicole were together, Melissa couldn't help feeling wistful. *I wonder if I'll ever fall in love again...*

CHAPTER FOUR: THE LOVE OF A GOOD WOMAN

"Mr. Davis, we'll be taking off soon. You might want to buckle up." The pilot stuck his head through the door of the flight deck on Michael's private jet. There were definite perks to being a billionaire, and not having to fly commercial was surely at the top of the list.

"Thank you, Richard." Michael fastened his seat belt and pulled out his phone to check his e-mails before the flight. Even though his plane was equipped with wi-fi, it was still insanely slow.

"We should be arriving in Dallas in about three and a half hours," Richard added. "We have a good tailwind."

As the jet began to accelerate to take off, Michael closed his eyes and tried to visualize the hotel. He was glad Ryan was going to give him the plans, as Ryan was the best architect he knew. Plus, this was a great excuse to see both him and Cole. Although they had monthly calls on Google Hangout to stay in touch, they didn't often get together in person. The last time they had all gotten together was in London when Ryan was in that car accident. *Even though*

Andrew can't make it, it will be a BBC 2 reunion anyway, he thought.

"Michael!" Ryan's deep voice echoed through the airport terminal.

Spying his friend, Michael broke out into a big grin. "Ryan, it's good to see you." They hugged briefly and headed for Ryan's truck.

"How was the flight?"

"Uneventful. Richard is a great pilot."

"Uh, yeah, I know. You stole him from me, remember?"

Michael laughed. "Oh yeah, I forgot about that. I think it was more that he wanted to be based in California and not here in Texas…"

"Do you want to grab a coffee on the way to the ranch, or are you still drinking tea?"

"Haha, no. That was only in Tokyo. I'm good, though. I had some espresso on the plane." The men chatted amiably as they walked to the parking lot. "How's life in Texas?"

"It's good! I love getting to spend so much time with Uncle Cal and Aunt Cathy."

"Are they still having the family dinners at five sharp? Those dinners were the stuff of legend in that family!"

Ryan laughed. "Yes, indeed. And God forbid someone should be late! Aunt Cathy gives ya' the stinkeye."

"I assume they're coming to the Grand Opening? It will be great to see everyone again. And I'll finally get to meet Nicole."

"It's about time. We're getting married this summer, and I'd hate for you not to meet her until the wedding!"

"Yeah, I was disappointed I couldn't make it out for Janet and Andrew's wedding. But you guys weren't even involved then, right?"

"Right. But you know how women are. They get all sappy at weddings. Speaking of weddings, you're next."

"Uhhh I'm not tracking you there, pal." Michael blinked in confusion. "I'm not even dating anyone."

"Exactly. The rest of us are all either married or about to be. You're the only one who's still single. We're starting to wonder what's wrong with you." Ryan playfully punched Michael in the arm.

"The only thing wrong with me is I work too much. It's a little hard to keep a relationship going when you're flying all over the world for weeks at a time."

"True, true. I'm just saying. There's a lot to be said for the love of a good woman." Ryan put his truck into gear and headed it toward home.

Michael grinned and winked as he said, "And even more to be said for the love of a bad one…"

CHAPTER FIVE: PLAYERS GOTTA PLAY

The Grand Opening was in full swing. The handlers were helping kids on and off the horses in the arena. They had set up a tent outside the office area, and there were enticing aromas coming from the food trucks that filled the parking lot. Jason Aldean was singing for a small group of folks and would be hosting a full concert after the sun went down. Guests were sampling Texas BBQ, Korean food, pizza, and there was even an old fashioned ice cream truck for the kids.

Because so many of the kids were autistic like Jenny, there was also a "sensory sensitive" tent set up for parents to take their children if they started to get overstimulated. This tent had soothing lights and was set far enough away from the festivities that it was calming and quiet. This tent also had carefully chosen foods for kids with allergies and food sensitivities. No attention to detail had been missed.

Melissa was feeling a little anxious about the showing of her video. She'd taken hundreds of photos during the construction of the center, and they'd pieced them all together into a video slideshow. Although she was an accomplished photographer, she also knew how important this event was to Ryan and Nicole and wanted everything to go perfectly.

Speaking of whom, Melissa saw Ryan standing near the door to the office with two men. She assumed they must be Cole and Michael; Ryan's college friends. She could see the one man's face, and he looked like Cole, from the description Nicole had given him. Dark hair. The other guy - the blond one - had his back to her. Not wanting to interrupt, Melissa figured she'd grab an iced tea from the bartender and head over to the horse arena.

"Me! What about you!" Melissa could hear Ryan's booming voice. "Those women were only being nice to me so they could get to you."

The other man agreed. "He's right, Michael. You were the one that all the ladies wanted. We were just sloppy seconds."

"Now, that's not fair. It wasn't *all* the ladies." He paused in false modesty. "Just most of them."

The friends all laughed. "Remember that weekend when we all flew to Monte Carlo?"

"You mean the one with the twins? God, we spent so much money that weekend…"

"I haven't been able to drink Dom Perignon since. How many bottles did we go through?"

Melissa just shook her head as she walked past them. This was a side of Ryan she hadn't seen before and didn't particularly like. It reminded her too much of Rick and his cavalier attitude toward women. These were the kinds of people she despised. Never had to work for the good things in life. Private jets and money to burn. Melissa had been a single mother for far too long to value those kinds of shenanigans.

Needless to say, so far, she wasn't too impressed with

Ryan's college friends. Granted she hadn't even seen the face of that Michael guy. But she didn't need to see him to know he was a total player. *I can spot the type a mile away*, she thought.

∾

Standing in line for her iced tea, Melissa saw Jenny approaching with another girl. It was Andi, the daughter of the ranch manager, Steve and his wife Lucy. She was also a student at the Center, as she'd been paralyzed in a car accident as a young child.

"Mama. Can Andi spend the night tonight?" Melissa was still amazed at the emotional progress Jenny had made since starting at the Center. Six months ago, she would never have been able to have a friend spend the night. But since equine therapy and meeting Andi, they'd had several sleepovers. Lucy had shown Melissa how to help Andi in and out of her chair, and from that point on the girls had become inseparable.

"Absolutely, sweetheart. We can bake some cookies, and you can give them to Aunt Cathy and Uncle Cal."

"We love baking cookies!" The girls cheered and went off to get some pizza from the food truck. Her heart warmed as she heard Jenny say to Andi, "This is the best day ever."

As Melissa walked over to the arena to check on the horses, she could see Ryan and his friends from a distance. Nicole was there along with a dark-haired woman that Melissa assumed was Cole's wife, Claudia. The five of them stood there laughing and having a good time, and it gave Melissa a serious case of the blues. *What would it be like to be part of a group of friends like that, instead of always being the outsider?* But, Melissa had different priorities than they did.

Their lives were about jetting around the world and a lavish lifestyle. Melissa was a single Mom whose sole focus was providing a good life for Jenny. *And that's enough for me,* Melissa thought.

CHAPTER SIX: SMALL WORLD

"Can I get you anything else?" Ryan's secretary Nina had just handed him and Michael cups of coffee as they settled into the conference room at Cummings Construction. "Anything else at all," she said, looking directly at Michael.

"No thanks, Nina. Just send Melissa back when she arrives."

"No problem, Ryan." Nina closed the glass door behind her.

"Does it ever get old?" Ryan grinned.

"What's that?"

"Women flirting with you nonstop. It's been going on as long as I've known you."

"You're funny. I have no idea what you're talking about." Michael felt a blush rise to his cheeks.

Shaking his head with a smile, Ryan changed the subject. "Anyway, here are the plans for the hotel." Handing Michael the file, he continued. "As you can see, it was to be a high-end boutique hotel with the ultimate in luxury. This is not your mega-hotel. Before each guest arrives, the staff is briefed on the guest's personal preferences and the room is set up accordingly. The rooms are actually designed to be adaptable to different styles. So, if one guest prefers a clean, contemporary look, the furniture and decor will be swapped out before the guest arrives. If the next guest in that room prefers Art Deco, the room will be redecorated in that style."

Michael nodded. "And, of course, they are charged accordingly."

"Exactly. These are the discerning guests for whom money is no object. Each experience will be completely unique."

"I love it. As you know, the exterior and common areas of the hotel are going to be Japanese-inspired. But, not the usual things one thinks of when you think of a Japanese hotel. I'm looking to bring in the flavor of actual Japanese homes. Luxurious homes, yes. But a sense of home, not a hotel."

"I think it's a great idea." Ryan added. "More home-like guest experiences are in now."

"That's why I asked you to invite Melissa Tomson today." Michael took a big sip of coffee. "This is really good, by the way." He got up to look out the office window, as it overlooked downtown Dallas.

Smiling, Ryan said, "I'll be sure and tell Nina you said that. She'll be thrilled." Pausing a moment, he added, "I did wonder why you wanted Melissa here."

As if on cue, Ryan could see Nina and Melissa approaching the door, and he rose to open it. "Come on in, Melissa. Thanks, Nina."

Melissa hadn't been back to Ryan's office since the day they met and she offered to give him the information that ultimately led to her ex-husband's imprisonment. That's probably why she looked a bit nervous as she walked in the door.

Ryan spoke as Michael turned around to greet Melissa. "I don't know if you two met at the Grand Opening or not, but Michael Davis, this is Melissa Tomson. Melissa, Michael."

There was an overly long silence as they each stared at each other for a moment. Ryan looked back and forth between them.

"Mel?"

"Oh my god, it's you." Melissa stood there with her mouth agape.

"But, your name is Mel McConnell. Not Melissa Tomson." Michael was completely confused.

"Mel is my nickname, and Tomson is my married name. I got married after we…" Melissa shook her head as if to shake off the vision of what she was seeing. "After you never called."

Ryan cleared his throat, to remind them that he was still in the room. "Could somebody please explain to me what's going?"

At the same time, they spoke. "It was New York."

"Before I met Rick."

"I was working on a project with Cole."

"I lived there before I moved to Texas."

"It was one night…"

Melissa's face went pale. "Is there a ladies' room I could use?" Before waiting for an answer, she burst out the door toward Nina's desk.

Blinking in shock, Ryan said, "What the hell happened between you two?"

Michael wiped his hand over his face nervously. "It was a one-night thing. I was staying at The Peninsula going over the Wilson deal with Cole. She was there on a business dinner, but the guy's flight got canceled. We met, had dinner, and one thing led to another. You know."

Ryan was still confused. "Melissa? That is so out of character for her. The woman I know isn't the kind of person to have one-night-stands."

"This was a long time ago. I'm not the same guy I was then either." Michael looked out of the window, pondering. "She left her number, but I never called. I had the sense she was... different... from the other girls I'd dated. I figured it was best to end it before it began. I never planned on seeing her again... especially like this!"

"It's definitely a small world..." They stopped talking as they could see Melissa walking back toward the conference room.

Almost imperceptibly, Michael commented, "God, she is more gorgeous than ever."

∽

Melissa had a steely expression on her face as she walked back in the door. Professionally extending her hand toward Michael, she said, "It's good to see you again, Michael. Please forgive my outburst before. I was just taken by surprise." She smiled courteously and sat down.

Relieved that she didn't appear mad, Michael sat opposite her. "Thank you for coming to meet today. I'm sorry that we didn't get a chance to meet... well, meet again... at the Grand Opening. But I was most impressed with the photographs you took during the construction of the Center. I've seen your work online, actually. You have a keen eye for photographing architecture."

"Thank you."

"The reason I wanted to talk to you is that I am building a

boutique hotel in Portland, and Ryan here gave me the plans for the hotel he'd been planning to build here before he built the equine therapy center." Michael handed Melissa the folder.

"I see?" Melissa was looking at the drawings. "What does this have to do with me?"

"Well, I was hoping that you might accompany me to Japan to take source photographs that will serve as inspiration for the hotel."

Melissa's face contorted into a mixture of shock and indignation. "Excuse me? You want me to *go with you* to Japan?"

Ryan smiled and laughed softly as he witnessed the awkward scene. "Very smooth, Mike."

"No, not like that. Business. Strictly business." Michael leaned back in his chair. "Honestly."

Melissa inhaled sharply. "Surely there is someone else who is better-suited to this. Someone, I don't know... Japanese?"

"No, that's just it. I want this to be different. I want this to be traditional Japanese but with an American flair. Specifically Portland. Ryan said you grew up there?"

Melissa pursed her lips and shook her head. "I did. But, surely you can't expect me to just drop everything and go to Japan with you. Not after..."

Ryan sat silently as if to make himself invisible. Michael leaned forward and said, "Look, I am really sorry. It was wrong of me not to call, and I have no excuse other than to say I'm not that guy anymore. And, this really is just a business trip. I was going to offer you five thousand dollars before I knew that we knew each other. Separate rooms and everything. Please? I know that you are exactly the right person for this job."

Melissa sighed as she stood up. "I can't answer you now. I

need some time. To think." As she opened the glass doors to the conference room, she blurted out, "I'll let you know my answer tomorrow, Michael. I'll text you."

As the men watched her leave, Michael thought, *What a small world, indeed.*

CHAPTER SEVEN: GIRL TALK

Melissa couldn't get away from the office of Cummings Construction fast enough. She'd practically run out the door. Her mind was in a daze as she repeatedly hit the elevator button to take her to the parking garage.

Okay, okay, calm down. Breathe. Melissa started the Volvo and pulled out of the underground parking lot. *What the hell just happened?*

Melissa literally could not believe that Michael Davis was the same Michael Davis she'd had that fling with in New York. It was the only time in her life she'd had a one-night-stand, and if it had been up to her, it would have been much more than one night. *God, he was hot. That was the best sex I ever had in my life.* Noticing that she was speeding on the highway, she took her foot off the accelerator.

But, just as she'd suspected at the Grand Opening when she overheard their conversation, Michael was nothing more than a rich playboy. How many other women had he said he would call, and then didn't? She was nothing more than a notch on the pretty boy's belt.

Melissa was grateful she was going to lunch with Cathy, Nicole, and Lucy. She needed a glass of wine and some good old-fashioned girl talk. *What am I going to do about the Japan thing?* she wondered. *I can't just pack up and leave Jenny. I have responsibilities now.*

As her car cruised down the highway, Melissa's mind wandered to what it would be like to take the trip. Just the two of them. Dinners. Photo shoots. Going over the previous day's shots. Breakfasts…Those blue eyes and soft blonde hair… *Stop it, Melissa*, she thought. *You're not doing this.*

As she pulled in to the parking lot of the Cheesecake Factory, she'd made up her mind. She was not that young, naive girl anymore. She was a mother now. She needed to stay as far away from a dangerously handsome playboy as possible. It was decided. Melissa was going to text Ryan the next day and tell him that Michael was going to need to find someone else.

∾

"I can't believe it." Nicole was shocked. "I'd never met Michael before the Grand Opening, and it never occurred to me that you guys might know each other."

Cathy was the senior of the women, and she poked her fork in her salad as she wisely commented, "The Lord works in mysterious ways, Sugar."

Lucy took a sip of wine and asked the question they were all thinking. "So, Mel, are you going to go to Japan?"

Melissa shook her head. "There's no way I can. I have Jenny and my work at the Center."

Nicole asked, "Didn't you say your Mom has been asking Jenny to come see her? Spring break is coming up." Nicole raised her eyebrows. "You could do this if you wanted to, Melissa."

"I have to work!" Melissa took a big bite of her club sandwich.

"This *is* work, not a vacation, Mel." Lucy added, "And now that the Grand Opening is over, you can take a break from the Center to focus on other work. We can handle your work for a few weeks."

Melissa shook her head. "I just think it's a bad idea. I mean, I have a history with the man. And even if I did send Jenny to visit with my Mom in Portland, which she would love by the way, and you guys did handle my work, I just think it sends the wrong message."

"To whom?" Cathy raised an eyebrow. "As far as anyone around here goes, you're just a single Mama takin' on work to support her family."

Nicole added, "Think about it, Melissa. If only for the money. Think of what you could do for Jenny if you had five thousand extra dollars."

Melissa sighed. "Jenny does need braces.... I just don't know. I've never been to Japan and it does seem like a good career opportunity. But I can see a million ways from sundown for this to go wrong. What if he hooks up with some Japanese Geisha girl while I'm there or something? You never know with these types."

"Then you just ignore it, Facetime with Jenny or us, and earn your fee." Nicole always was the practical one.

"Besides. People change, Mel. You changed." Lucy looked at her pointedly.

Cathy set her wine glass down and leaned into Melissa. "Honey, if there is one thing I have learned in my somethin' somethin' years on this earth, it's this. When your most trusted girlfriends are all tellin ya' that it's a good idea to do a thing, it's usually a good idea to do the thing. Your girlfriends won't steer you wrong."

Lucy raised her glass in a toast, "Aunt Cathy is right. Here's to girlfriends. And to Melissa going to Japan…"

CHAPTER EIGHT: ANCIENT HISTORY

Michael was already seated in the office in his private jet when the car containing Melissa arrived. He could see out the window as she emerged from the black limousine and as the driver retrieved her bags from the trunk. Spying her high-end luggage and the ease with which she communicated with both the driver and the pilot, Michael was reminded that although Melissa's life had changed and become far more simple, she clearly was accustomed to wealth and privilege. *I cannot imagine how any man could leave a woman like her*, he thought. *She has it all... looks, intelligence, and compassion. Plus she's a damn good photographer.* Of course, he'd had his chance years ago and had blown it himself. So, he really wasn't in a place to judge.

Walking to the door to greet her as she boarded his plane, there was a noticeable professional distance in her eyes. "Welcome aboard, Melissa..."

"Thank you, Michael." Looking around, she admitted, "It's been a few years since I've been on a private jet. Yours is lovely."

Richard stuck his head out of the cockpit and said to them both, "We're about ten minutes from departure, so if you'd like to get something to drink, now's the time to do it."

Michael escorted Melissa back to the large leather recliners and gestured to one of them. "Is this okay?"

"Looks great."

"Would you like something to drink? Coffee? Tea? Water? A glass of wine?"

"Water would be great."

Nodding to the flight attendant, "Two sparkling waters, please, Kathleen."

An awkward silence fell between them until Kathleen returned with the waters. As they sipped from the crystal glasses, they both spoke at once.

"How is your daughter?" he asked.

"So you're living in Portland now," she said.

Laughing, that broke the ice.

"Ladies first," Michael said. 'Your daughter is named Jenny, right? I think I saw her at the Grand Opening with Andi."

"Yes, they are great friends now. I am so thrilled with the progress I am seeing in Jenny since we started at Essere. We spent ten years struggling to overcome her social awkwardness, and it only took a few months working with the horses and therapists there for her to find a best friend."

"It must have been very hard for you, handling everything on your own."

"It was, at times. But Jenny is such an easy kid that it made it all worthwhile."

Another silence followed, but this one was a little less awkward.

"So, how do you like Portland?" Melissa asked. But before Michael could answer, Richard came on the loudspeaker and announced that the plane would be taking off and instructed everyone in the cabin to fasten their seatbelts.

Answering her earlier question, Michael said, "I love Portland. It's so different from Silicon Valley. It's got the same Pacific Northwest flavor to it, but everyone there is so much more down-to-earth. I'm very glad my parents moved there."

"You moved to be closer to them?"

"Yes. My Dad, Mike made his living as a general contractor, and my Mom Carol was a stay at home Mom. Dad is getting up there in years, and I wanted to make a move before I needed to if you know what I mean."

"I do. My Mom, Diane, raised me all alone. My Dad ran off with his secretary when I was nine. I kind of took her for granted when I was a teenager, but gained a lot of respect for her when Jenny was born and her father did the same thing - ran off with his secretary." She quickly added, "But, it's all good. My Mom, Jenny, and I... we're a family."

"Was she okay with this trip?"

Melissa smiled and said, "Oh yes. My Mom flew out last weekend, and then she and Jenny flew home yesterday. We wanted to give Jenny time to get comfortable with the idea of spending a few weeks in Portland while I was out of the country. Jenny is going to miss Andi and the horses, but she is really looking forward to spending time with Grandma. My Mom spoils her."

"That's what grandparents are for, I guess." Just then, the plane started to move.

"I love flying," Melissa said as the plane began to taxi. "There's something about being above the clouds that gives you perspective in life."

To that, Michael raised his water glass and said, "Exactly. Here's to seeing things from a different perspective."

∼

Six hours later, Michael was drinking coffee in his airborne office and Melissa was napping in the bedroom at the back of the plane. They still had about five hours to go before they landed in Tokyo and he was attempting to get some work done. He kept trying to focus on the itinerary for their trip and the e-mails he was trying to write, but all he could think about was Melissa sleeping in his bed. He kept replaying the one night they'd spent together over and over again. The hot, passionate kisses. Hands tugging and exploring every inch of each other's bodies. Moving together in unison, in every imaginable position… He was getting hard just thinking about it. And, to think that she was literally on the other side of that door. He could just get up, walk over there, and… *And what, Michael? Things didn't exactly end well between you two. You had every opportunity to pursue her and you didn't. Just let it go. This is a business trip. Stay focused on your work.*

∼

"Michael?" Melissa emerged from the plane's bedroom, with her blonde hair slightly messy and blinking from just waking up. "How long did I sleep?"

"A few hours. Did you sleep well?"

"I really did. That mattress is so comfortable." Melissa smoothed her hair and sat in her leather recliner, fastening her seatbelt. "How long until we land?"

"Richard says about an hour. Kathleen has a light meal prepared for us before we land. It'll be about five pm when we pull in to the gate."

Gazing out the window, Melissa appeared lost in thought. "I've never been this far away from Jenny. It feels weird."

"I bet it does. Thank you for coming with me."

She looked at him pointedly. "A single Mom's got to do what a single Mom's got to do. The fee you're paying me will cover braces for Jenny. I couldn't exactly turn that down."

"I'm happy to help."

"I just want to reiterate something, Michael. This is strictly a business trip. What happened before..." she paused..."won't happen again." My sole focus is on providing for Jenny. I don't have the time or inclination for distractions."

"I get it, Melissa. I really do. And for what it's worth, I'm really sorry about before."

"No need to be. It's ancient history. It all worked out for the best."

Despite her assurances, as the plane began to descend, Michael's mood went down with it. *I'm not so sure about that,* he thought. *It doesn't seem like it worked out for the best at all.*

CHAPTER NINE: UNFORGETTABLE

As Michael's plane approached the Narita airport, Melissa looked down at the expansive ocean. Tiny white clouds dotted the horizon as the green mountains and trees began to take shape over the island. gray smoke was billowing from the smokestacks next to the shore, as the plane dropped lower and lower. Huge cargo ships looked like tiny toy boats headed into port. Then, as if magically, the plane turned and the skyline of Tokyo appeared, just as they were touching down.

"Nihon e yōkoso," Michael said. When Melissa just grinned and shook her head cluelessly, he repeated in English, "Welcome to Japan."

Melissa had never been to Japan and wasn't quite sure what to expect. She was very glad to have gotten some sleep, as the fifteen hour time difference would be very rough, otherwise.

"Welcome to Tokyo, guys," Richard's voice said over the speaker. "Current time is 4:52 pm. We made good time due to that tailwind. We are just waiting for the gate to free up."

Melissa checked her phone to see if she'd gotten any

messages from her Mom or Jenny. There were four text messages, one with a photo of Jenny and Diane eating donuts with powdered sugar all over their faces, laughing, and the message "Let the spoiling begin!" Melissa felt an intense pang of homesickness, and tears stung her eyes. *What am I doing here? I'm thousands of miles away from home, on a trip with some man. I should never have come here.*

Her inner voice then changed tone and said, *Melissa, this isn't "a trip with some man". This is a business trip, and you're doing it for Jenny. Stay professional, do your job, and you'll be home before you know it, five thousand dollars richer.*

"Is everything okay?" Michael was looking at her with concern.

"Yes, thank you. Jenny is eating so much sugar already I'm going to have send her to detox when I get home."

∽

"Hello, Mr. Michael and Miss Melissa. My name is Sakura, and I am your assistant for this trip." Sakura appeared to be in her mid-twenties and wore her glossy black hair in bangs that hung evenly across her round face and straight next to her jaw. Her makeup was simple, with a light trace of eyeliner and a slight cherry colored gloss on her lips. She was wearing a dress with a floral print, and a brown knit sweater to accommodate the chilly spring weather.

"Nice to meet you," Melissa said as Richard guided her down off the steps.

"Hello, Sakura. Nice to see you again." Michael slung his computer bag over his shoulder as he stepped onto the tarmac. How is your daughter Daisy? She is five years old now, right?"

Sakura blushed at the attention of her handsome boss and demurely said, "She is doing well, thank you." Gesturing to the car waiting nearby, she said, "This is the car that will take you to your hotel. I will follow behind and meet you there. All of the arrangements have been taken care of and you are both already checked in."

Melissa felt Michael's hand on the small of her back as they walked toward the car. "Thank you, Sakura," he said. *Why does his hand feel so good there?* she couldn't help but wonder as she climbed into the limousine.

∽

The car pulled up to the Palace Hotel, and Melissa felt a few butterflies of excitement. She'd traveled, of course, and her ex-husband was in the hotel development business. But, they always reserved the best accommodations for clients and prospects. She never got to experience this side of the business before.

Sakura was already there, and she emerged from the glass doors with an iPad in hand. *How did she get here so fast?* Melissa wondered.

The driver pulled their luggage out of the trunk and gave it to the waiting bellman, as another one opened the door for Melissa.

Walking in between Melissa and Michael, Sakura went over their itinerary. "Welcome to the Palace Hotel. Miss Melissa, you are staying in the Palace Suite, and Mr. Michael, you are in the Terrace Suite. Your luggage is being taken to your rooms. Please place your handprint here on the iPad screen so that the room will recognize you. This is instead of hotel keys."

Melissa did as she was told, but was in awe of the beauty of her surroundings. Floor to ceiling windows revealed cherry blossom trees in full bloom. Modern lamps hung down, illuminating gray marble tiles. Soft music played and the hushed tone of refined elegance permeated the air.

"Please take one hour to refresh, and then the car will meet you here to take you to meet with Mr. Akiro." She then said, quietly to Melissa, "The dress code is business evening attire. Do you have a dress with you, or do you need me to send one up to your suite?"

Melissa flushed a bit at hearing this. She'd brought a few dresses that still fit from before she'd had Jenny. Hopefully, they would be appropriate. "I believe I can find something suitable to wear, Sakura. I appreciate the offer, though." The last thing she wanted was for Michael to be buying her clothes.

As they approached the elevators, Sakura pushed the button and then stepped back. "I will not join you for your meeting with Mr. Akiro, but I will be here at the hotel when you return." She gave a slight bow and then backed away.

The doors slid open and Michael and Melissa were alone for a brief moment before they got to their floor. The last time they were in a hotel elevator they'd had their first kiss. This fact was quite obvious to both of them, and Melissa was trying to push the memories from her mind.

Michael, on the other hand, was not. "This is a lot nicer than the last elevator we were in, isn't it?"

"I don't really remember," Melissa said, looking at her shoes.

"True. We weren't exactly checking out the scenery." He was leaning against the wall, looking at her *that* way, and smiling.

Melissa cleared her throat and said, "Look, Michael. The only way this is going to work is if we put what happened in the past and stop talking about it. I'm uncomfortable enough as it is..." Her voice trailed off, as he just grinned and looked her up and down.

Taking a step toward her, he said, in a husky voice: "You're uncomfortable, are you? Mmmm. What could be making you feel that way?" He leaned in, close enough for her to smell the fruity aroma of his cologne. "All right, Melissa. We'll do it your way. No more mention of that night. But, trust me. It's not a night I will ever forget."

The elevator door thankfully slid open, and Melissa practically tumbled out the door.

∽

CHAPTER TEN: THE TRUTH ABOUT MONEY

Michael walked Melissa to her suite. He'd obviously given her the larger one, as he was trying to overcome the image of The Schmuck Who Never Called. Not that a twenty-four-hundred square-foot suite with enough room for ten people would make up for his behavior, but it was a start.

She was absolutely astonished when she pressed her hand on the doorpad and the doors opened to reveal the opulent accommodations. "Michael, this is too much. I don't need this much room!" But he could see that she was thrilled.

He'd been tempted to book the adjoining Club Deluxe room but thought that might send the wrong signal. So, he chose a much smaller suite that was actually two floors higher.

"I'm glad you like it, Melissa. Get settled, rest a bit and I'll come get you in an hour."

"That's okay. I'll meet you in the lobby." She still seemed a little shaken at what had transpired in the elevator.

I probably shouldn't have gotten that close, but damn she is one sexy woman.

~

Pressing the elevator button for the 20th floor, Michael grinned as he thought, *This is going to be a helluva trip.*

~

An hour later, Michael was having a Sapporo beer at the bar when he had the urge to turn around. Walking toward him, across the marble floors of the lobby, was Melissa. Michael literally lost his breath at how stunning she looked. A sapphire blue satin dress hugged her voluptuous curves. Her golden hair cascaded in loose curls over her shoulders. And silver high heels with a matching purse completed the outfit. He couldn't believe she was with him.

Clearly, the other patrons of the hotel were taken aback as well. Virtually every head turned as she crossed the room. He could practically hear them wondering, "Who is that? An American actress? A model?"

She was scanning the room, looking for him, so he stood to catch her eye. A smile crossed her lips as soon as she saw him, but she tucked it away almost as soon as it emerged.

~

"My god, Melissa. You look beautiful."

~

"Thank you, Michael." She sounded professional, but he could tell she was secretly pleased. Every woman loves to be told she is beautiful, but the truly beautiful ones usually aren't aware of their beauty and so it means more to them.

Just then, a uniformed man came up to them. "Mr.

Michael. Miss Melissa. Would you follow me this way, please?"

∽

Michael and Melissa were in the back of the limo on their way to meet Akiro. Michael wanted to explain the nature of the meeting and his relationship with Akiro.

"Akiro Nishiyama and I were business associates many years ago. As you know, I started a company several years back, and sold it to Microsoft."

Melissa took a sip from her water bottle and nodded.

"I was living in Tokyo when I wrote the code for the software platform, and Akiro lived in the same building as me. We went out for a few beers and I realized that he was a whiz at getting funding. We were thinking of going public, but we needed to source a certain amount in investment money before we did it. Akiro lined up some serious money through his Japanese connections, and that's when Microsoft took notice and came in and bought the company."

"Makes sense," Melissa said.

"Part of the Microsoft deal was a five-year non-compete clause, which meant that no one in the company could get involved in a similar business for five years. That was fine with me, because, frankly we made a boatload of money and I didn't want to be writing code anymore, anyway. But Akiro was not happy about it and almost cost us the deal by refusing to sign the non-compete. In the end, he did, but he was still pretty pissed about it. We had a bit of a falling out, and I haven't actually seen him since."

Melissa seemed surprised at this. "Really? Wow. Five years is a long time."

"It really is. I guess I'm telling you this because I don't really know much about what we are walking in to. I contacted him when I knew we were coming to town because I wanted to talk to him about potential investors for the hotel project."

"So you don't know if he's still mad or what?"

"Exactly. The arrangements for tonight were made over e-mail, and I'm not even sure where we're going for dinner. It was a 'have my people contact your people' kind of thing."

"I see."

"And the thing is, Akiro was kind of a jerk when we first started working together. But he was really good at what he did, so I overlooked it. I'm curious to see what's happened to him over the years."

"What do you mean?"

"Well, Akiro made several million dollars - well, the equivalent in Yen, and that kind of money can change a person."

Melissa sighed and said, "Don't I know it. Rick sure changed when he made his first million." She then gazed out the window and added, "But then, maybe the truth is that money just brings out who you really are."

As she said that, the car made a turn, and both Michael and Melissa could see their destination looming nearby.

"You have got to be kidding me," Michael muttered under his breath.

Melissa, on the other hand, was too stunned to speak.

The partition between the driver and his passengers came down, and the driver said, "We have arrived at your destination, sir. I will be parked nearby and will pick you up when your meeting is complete."

∼

Michael and Melissa both craned their necks upward as they exited the black limousine. The outside of the shiny gold building was lit up with sparkling crystal letters that said "Club Chick Roppongo." It was the kind of building that made Las Vegas look like Beverly Hills - ornate to the point of gaudy was the best description.

Well-dressed businessmen stepped between the monstrous marble columns and onto the red carpet that blanketed the lobby.

Although Michael had never been here before, he was well aware of the type of establishment. It was a traditional Japanese "hostess club," where for an extraordinarily high price (at least one hundred US Dollars for one hour), men could socialize with attractive female staff members. This wasn't a brothel, as there was no touching allowed and the men did not leave with the women. Instead, the ladies would engage in flirtatious conversation, share a drink or two, sing some karaoke, and otherwise make the men feel attractive and attended to.

Why on earth would Akiro want to meet here? Michael wondered.

Before he could explain the situation to a very stunned-looking Melissa, Akiro came walking out of one of the private rooms.

"Kon'nichiwa, kyūyū!" Akiro said as he approached them.

"Hello to you too!" The two men bowed slightly and then went in for an American-style "bro' hug."

"And who is this gorgeous lady?" Akiro said, eyeing Melissa. His black hair was slicked back, and he wore a shiny blue suit, with a bright red shirt. Glittering onyx cufflinks adorned his wrists, and there was a thick gold necklace around his neck. Although the man was a multimillionaire, the look suggested more sleaze than sophistication. He lunged toward Melissa in an attempt to hug her.

Michael stepped between them, gracefully diverting contact between Akiro and Melissa. "This is my business associate, Melissa Tomson. She is with me to take source photographs for a project I'm working on."

Akiro licked his lips and then smiled, revealing a row of small white teeth. "Business associate? Michael, my friend, you have lost your touch. This woman is too beautiful to keep for business and no pleasure…"

Michael's stomach lurched at his former friend's behavior. One glance at Melissa and he could see she was horrified at what was transpiring. Clearly, the years had not taught the man any manners.

Michael put his arm protectively around Melissa and escorted her into Club Chick. *Let's get this over with as quickly as possible,* he thought.

CHAPTER ELEVEN: ASSUMPTIONS

"Here is your wine, Miss." The woman placed a jeweled crystal glass on the table in front of Melissa. She also set down a platter of Nigiri that probably cost more than Melissa's rent back home.

Michael and Akiro were drinking whiskey and reminiscing about when Michael lived in Tokyo. Most of the conversation was in Japanese, but occasionally Michael would try to bring Melissa into the conversation by saying something in English. But, it was fine with Melissa. She didn't much care for Akiro Nishiyama or the way he kept leering at her. She really had no interest in socializing with him.

At one point, Michael pulled out his phone and started showing Akiro some photos of the hotel renderings. The jet lag was starting to kick in, and combined with the wine, Melissa was struggling to keep awake. "Excuse me, where is the restroom? she asked the hostess as she set down their third round of drinks.

Walking in the direction the woman pointed, Melissa took notice of her surroundings. The inside of the club was as elaborately decorated as the outside. Small cocktail tables filled red velvet-lined booths, and there were paintings of semi-nude women lining the walls. Melissa was struck at two things. One, all of the women were extremely beautiful, and two, the men all stared at her shamelessly. *I guess they don't see a lot of blonde women here,* she wondered.

After splashing some cold water on her face in the restroom, Melissa steeled herself to return to the table. Walking back, she began to notice the oddest thing. The men at the tables were different from when she'd first gotten there, but the women were the same.

Where am I? Did Michael take me to a Japanese brothel? She couldn't be sure, but there was definitely something strange about this place.

Approaching the table, she saw Michael and Akiro laughing heartily at something, and two women had joined them. Suddenly, Melissa wanted nothing more than to leave and go back to the hotel and call Jenny and her Mom. *I don't know what Michael's deal is here, but if this is the life he lives, I want no part of it.*

Melissa walked up to the table, grabbed her purse, and whispered to Michael, "I'm going to have the driver take me back to the hotel. I'm really tired and need to call Jenny before I go to sleep."

Michael started to stand up, and said, "I'll go with you."

Melissa said, perhaps a bit too forcefully, "No. You stay here and finish your business. I'll see you for breakfast tomorrow."

Michael looked back and forth between Melissa and Akiro. The two women were fawning over Akiro, and Michael said, "Okay, if you're sure that's what you want. Text me and let me know you got back okay, alright?"

"Sure thing," she said, as she marched out of that horrid place.

The car pulled up to the hotel at midnight, and Melissa could never remember being so drained and tired in her life. Sakura was there waiting, as promised, but the women didn't say much to each other as Melissa was anxious to get up to her room and call Jenny. As she waited for the elevator, she noticed Sakura sit back down in the lobby and resume typing on her laptop. *That poor woman has to sit here and wait for Michael to get back.*

As she pressed her hand on the doorpad, the doors opened and Melissa sighed as she walked in. But everything looked different to her. What had once seemed a generous gesture now seemed ostentatious. "Why would he give me a room that's bigger than my apartment? Is he showing off his wealth? Trying to buy my affections?" Feeling irritated and thirsty, Melissa went into the kitchen to grab a bottle of water before settling down on the plush couch to call home.

The Facetime ring had never sounded more soothing to Melissa, and when the faces of Diane and Jenny appeared on the screen, Melissa wanted to crawl through cyberspace and hug them.

"Hi, Mama!"

"Hi, Jellybean!" Melissa felt tears sting her eyes.

"Are you having fun in Japan? Have you seen any panda bears?"

Laughing a bit, she said, "No honey, panda bears are from China."

"Oh. Well, my Hello Kitty panda is from Japan."

"She sure is honey. What are you and grandma going to do today?

Jenny pulled out her calendar and showed Melissa. "I woke up at 6:45 and made my bed. I got dressed, brushed my hair and teeth. I came downstairs, and am going over the calendar with Grandma."

Diane stuck her head in the frame, "We're sticking pretty close to the schedule you said she keeps at home. I figured it was best to do that."

"Thank you, Mom. I can't tell you how much I miss you guys."

Diane's eyes squinted as she observed her daughter. "Is everything okay, sweetheart?" She sounded concerned but also had a false cheer to her voice as to not alarm Jenny.

"I'm fine, Mom. Just really tired."

"Grandma is taking me to the Japanese Garden today to see the cherry blossoms. Can you see cherry blossoms where you are?"

Smiling, Melissa said, "That's great! Yes, I can. There are trees all over the hotel. I'll take a picture tomorrow and send it to you."

"Is your room nice?"

"It is! It's bigger than our apartment back in Dallas. Let me give you a tour." Melissa turned the camera around and showed her Mom and daughter the luxurious accommodations.

"My god, Melissa. That place is incredible," Diane commented after Jenny ran off to get her sketchbook. "This Michael must be some guy."

You have no idea, Mom. No idea...

∽

At 8:00 am, Melissa was downstairs enjoying a cup of coffee and a pastry at the Sweets & Deli inside the hotel. They normally wouldn't open until 10:00 am, but when the staff saw her looking in the window, they opened early just for her. "You accompany Mr. Michael Davis, yes?" *There are defi-*

nite advantages to traveling with a billionaire, she thought, as she took a bite of the flaky Mini Coco De Crema pastry.

"Miss Melissa, Ohayōgozaimasu." Sakura approached Melissa wearing another floral print dress and her sensible shoes.

"Good morning to you too. Would you like some pastry?"

"No, thank you very much." Looking around, she asked, "Is Mr. Michael here yet?"

I doubt he's going to be feeling very well this morning, Melissa thought with attitude. But she simply answered, "I haven't seen him yet."

The women walked companionably over to the lobby chairs. Taking seats next to each other, Sakura asked, "Was your evening pleasant?"

Melissa was one of those people who is horrible at hiding her emotions, and she was sure she must have made a face before she answered, "It was... different."

"I have not been to a hostess club before," Sakura said. "My colleagues cannot afford such places."

Surprised, Melissa asked, "Would they want to go to them if they could afford to?" *Was prostitution something that was acceptable in Tokyo?* she wondered.

"Well, yes. Hostess clubs are very popular with wealthy businessmen. Only the most beautiful women can become cast members."

"Cast members? Like Disneyland?"

"Why, yes. It is all a very good act. The women act for the men, and the men give them tips and drinks." She leaned in and whispered, "The women have drinks that do not contain alcohol. They get money to encourage the patrons to order expensive drinks. But it is only an act because the men are not allowed to touch the women. A hostess club is not the same as in the United States."

Melissa took another sip of her coffee and sat back,

stunned. She'd been wrong in assuming that the club was a brothel. *What else could I have been wrong about?* she wondered,

Just then, Michael emerged from the elevator. His long legs strode across the marble floors, and she thought, *He looks better than he has a right to, this morning...*

CHAPTER TWELVE: CLEARING THE AIR

Michael always prided himself on being able to read a room when he walked in, but he had no idea what to expect as he approached Melissa. She'd seemed pretty irritated last night, and he'd learned with women that it was best to just let them be when they got like that. But, he couldn't help wonder if he'd made the right choice. He certainly didn't want to make another mistake with her.

He couldn't really read her expression as he walked up to Melissa and Sakura in the lobby. Sakura stood immediately, while Melissa gathered her things.

"Mr. Michael. Ohayōgozaimasu."

"Good morning, ladies." Michael smiled, but Melissa wouldn't meet his gaze.

"I promised Jenny I'd get some pictures of the cherry blossom trees before we leave. Let me go do that now." Melissa grabbed her phone and coffee and headed over to the picture window.

Sakura pulled out her iPad and handed him two paper tickets. "These are your Green Car passes for the Nozomi

Shinkansen. I will be traveling on the same train, but in general class."

"Sakura, you could have traveled the bullet train in first class with us," he said, taking the tickets. "You are always welcome to join us."

"No, sir. I would not be comfortable with that." Sakura looked down at her shoes. The Japanese were sticklers for formalities at times.

Watching as Melissa walked back toward them, Michael still couldn't get a feel for how she felt this morning. *Ah well, time will tell.*

∽

The Nozomi is the fastest transportation between Tokyo and Kyoto. What would normally be a 5 ½ hour ride by car only took less than 2 ½ hours on the bullet train. Pretty impressive to be able to span 450 km, or 270 miles in that time. But, when you're in the middle of an argument with someone, two hours can feel like ten.

Fortunately for Michael, Melissa was back to her "professional distance" mode. She was friendly enough, cordial, and smiled at times. But he could still sense a hesitation in her.

That club last night didn't do a lot to improve her image of me, he thought. *I'll have to work harder to show her that I'm not the playboy I once was.*

Michael and Melissa were seated in the Green Car of the bullet train, and she seemed lost in thought as the scenery whizzed by. Figuring he'd better address the elephant in the room, he said, "Hey, look. I'm sorry about last night."

Melissa looked at him and smiled wanly. "No problem, Michael. I understand."

"The thing is, Akiro has really changed over the years. He always had kind of a slimy element to his personality, but when we were working together he kept it in check. I've never seen him treat anyone as poorly as he treated you last night."

Her eyes softened a bit.

"After you left, I actually confronted him about it. I told him that he gets a one-time pass for bringing us to a place like that because he didn't really know you were coming. I have no desire to go to places like that anyway, but it is a fact that a lot of business is conducted in hostess clubs like that. But, to bring you there was just over the line. I told him that if he ever treated you, or anyone else like that in my presence again, it would be the end of our business relationship."

Melissa sighed, and said, "Thank you, Michael. I appreciate that. I guess I am a little jumpy because of the way Rick treated me during our marriage. I was nothing more than a pretty face and body to him. And then once we had Jenny, and she was diagnosed, we were no longer the 'perfect little family' in the eyes of his clients. So, he left us and completely dumped his daughter. I can't tell you how many times I overheard her saying her nightly prayers asking God to 'please bring Daddy back home'. It broke my heart. So when I met Akiro, it was like he was the same person with a different face."

Michael had tears in his eyes and put his hand over Melissa's. "I am so incredibly sorry he did that to you. You didn't deserve any of it. And, my god, Jenny... that beautiful girl. Rick doesn't deserve to be her father."

Melissa smiled wryly. "Well, he's in prison now. He was more interested in paying off judges than in spending time with his daughter. So, he's getting what he deserves. The good news is that Jenny is over it. Does she miss having a Dad? Probably not. Ryan or Steve take her to father/daughter things at school. She has Uncle Cal. We have a good life now, and that's all anyone can ask for."

"I'm glad it all worked out for you, Melissa." Pulling out his laptop, he asked, "So, how about we go over the Kyoto shot list? I have a few ideas for some great photos."

Melissa slipped on her reading glasses and turned to face him. Michael was relieved that they'd gotten everything out in the open. He was just praying there would be no more problems for the rest of the trip.

∽

Sakura was already waiting for them as the doors to the train slid open. *How did she get out of her train car so fast?* Michael wondered.

"The cars should be waiting for us outside the terminal. The two of you will be in the limousine with Mr. Ricky Ito, and I will be driving behind you in a rented car."

"Ricky Ito! That's quite a name." Melissa grinned, as she and Sakura walked next to Michael. The station was crowded with commuters, but Melissa's blonde hair stood out like a beacon.

"That is his music name. He is trying to become a music superstar, and he drives to pay the bills until he gets famous," Sakura informed them with a little smile.

"Everyone has a story, right?" Michael tried once again to convince Sakura to travel with them. "You are welcome to join us in our car if you like."

"No, thank you. I prefer to travel alone. Your car is waiting out that door, and my rental station is over there. I will meet you at the hotel. We are staying at the Kurama Onsen." She looked at Melissa and explained, "It is a traditional Japanese hot spring hotel."

Melissa involuntarily rubbed her neck and said, "That sounds divine."

Thirty minutes later, Ricky Ito pulled the car up to the Kurama Onsen hotel. Nestled in the verdant mountains of Kyoto, the hotel looked more like a private home than a hotel.

"Thank you for sharing your music with us, Ricky," Michael said, grinning at Melissa.

"It is my pleasure, sir. I am thankful to you for listening." He opened Melissa's door, and as Michael scooted out, Ricky went to the trunk to get their luggage.

Walking out from the lobby was Sakura, holding her ever-present iPad. "Mr. Michael and Miss Melissa, there has been a slight problem. When the reservation was made, we requested three guest rooms. But, the person who took the reservation did not understand the request, and he reserved one room that will fit three people." Sakura looked really upset. "I am so very sorry. I am waiting on a return call from another hotel that has different rooms."

Michael felt awful. "That was probably Brad's fault. His Japanese leaves quite a bit to be desired." Shaking his head, Michael could almost imagine his secretary, holding his dog Pepper in one hand and his cellphone in the other, saying "We need reservations for three people."

Melissa was staring at Michael intently, with one hand on her neck and the other rubbing her chin. She took a deep breath and said, "Look. It's getting late. We've been traveling all day. I don't mind staying in the same room if you don't."

Michael was taken aback. "Uhhh. That's fine with me…"

Sakura looked back and forth between the two of them. "I can get a room for myself at the hotel down the street. It does not have the onsen - the hot springs - but that does not matter to me. If you are sure, Miss Melissa, I will make a phone call to reserve a room there for myself."

Melissa smiled, winked at him, and said, "Sure. No reason not to trust you, right Michael?" Was she flirting with him?

"Absolutely. Scout's honor." He held his fingers up in the Boy Scout sign.

She headed toward the entrance to the hotel. "All right then. Mr Ricky Ito, bring our suitcases this way."

CHAPTER THIRTEEN: HOT WATER

Melissa stood in the women's locker room looking at the blue and white kimono that was wrapped around her. "Are you sure this is right?" The locker room attendant had shown her how to wrap it.

"Yes. You are to be nude under the kimono, and then you remove it once you enter the onsen. There is a woman side and a man side."

"So the men and women have different onsen?"

"Hai." She leaned in to say softly, "But there is an opening at the end, and if you wish to go over to the man side, is okay."

Looking at the murky hydrogen sulfide mineral water, Melissa realized that no one would be able to see below the surface.

"Do not get the water in your hair," she said, handing Melissa a hair tie. "The minerals will be very hard to remove from your hair."

Okay, let's do this. Melissa slipped off the kimono and out of her slippers and stepped cautiously into the warm pool.

The water was illuminated from within, and Melissa felt as if she were wading into a giant pool of milk. The minerals smelled a bit like rotten eggs, but not in a bad way.

Putting her curls in a loose bun on top of her head, she headed toward the part of the onsen that was outside the building.

Feeling her muscles relax, Melissa took in the serenity and beauty of the onsen. She understood why people had been coming here for hundreds of years. The natural minerals that came from the depths of the earth were healing on a physical and spiritual level. *My Mom would love this place,* she thought as she approached the opening to the men's side of the pool.

Am I crazy to have agreed to share a room with Michael? she wondered. This could either be a huge mistake or a grand adventure.

Peeking her head around the corner to the men's side of the onsen, the first thing Melissa noticed was how much bigger it was than the women's side. It was twice as big!

The milky water steamed as it hit the cool spring air, giving the feeling that they were in a huge bowl of milk tea. Golden lights were strung over the top, from tree to tree. The men's locker room was surrounded by tall bamboo trees that rustled in the breeze. She could see the shadows of jagged rocks covered in dark moss that surrounded the pool. It was like something out of a travel brochure.

Melissa was starting to break a sweat, and her eyes stung a little from the steam. She could barely see and reached for an icy cold hand towel from a basket by the edge of the pool. Wiping her face, she heard the distinctive deep-throated laugh that could only be Michael's. He was on the other side of the onsen, laughing with some men who were headed into the men's locker room.

Michael saw her and began to wade over in her direction.

Melissa was incredibly glad that the water was so murky that he wouldn't be able to see that she was nude.

"Hi." His face was flushed from the heat, adding a glow to his handsome features.

"Hi." Melissa found herself having trouble thinking of anything other than the fact that he was naked and about seven inches away from her.

"I'm glad you came over. I was just talking to some guys and they said that their girlfriends were too shy to come to this side."

Melissa grinned and said, "Well, no one has ever accused me of being shy." Wiping her neck with the iced towel, she added, "This is really beautiful Michael. Thank you."

Moving closer to her, Michael looked her straight in the eyes, and almost whispered, "It's getting hot in here, isn't it?"

Melissa felt an electric shock travel from between her legs up to her belly. Her head felt light. Michael was a few inches away, naked. The look in his eyes told her that he was aroused. All she would need to do would be to reach her hand out, under the water, and touch him. He was tantalizingly close.

Just then, a voice called out. "Mr. Michael. Your dinner reservations are in thirty minutes. Would you like me to call and move the time?"

Imperceptibly stepping back in the murky water, Michael answered, "No. That's okay. We'll be right there. Tell Ricky Ito that we will be dressed and at the car in fifteen minutes." He added softly, "Does that work for you?"

Melissa took a deep breath and nodded yes. "That will work." The combination of the hot mineral water, the long day, and proximity to Michael made her feel like a giddy schoolgirl. *Get a hold of yourself, Melissa. You're a grown woman.* And yet, as she made her way back to the women's side of the onsen, she couldn't help but smile.

Ricky Ito pulled the car up to the curb at the historic Ichiriki Ochaya tea house. "I've never been inside this place," he said to Michael and Melissa as he opened the car door. The black and red walls created a dramatic backdrop for the traditionally dressed Geishas that were walking in. Black cars pulled up in front and behind them, as well-dressed people emerged and went in. Crowds of tourists snapped photos, as if it were Angelina Jolie on the red carpet.

"This is incredible," Melissa said, with wonder.

Michael told them both, "We are having a private meeting and dinner with a Geisha, where we will learn more about the history of the art."

"Is it okay to ask questions, do you think?" Melissa asked as she stepped out of the car.

"Absolutely. I'm sure there will be a translator there, but I am looking forward to learning more myself."

"How did you even get invited?" Ricky Ito asked. "Not only do you need a lot of money, but you need to have a relationship with management. I know people who have been trying to get reservations here for years."

Michael smiled as Ricky closed the car door behind him. "It's a long story, but I had a business associate when I lived in Tokyo whose daughter was training to be a Geisha. At first I was shocked, because I thought they were prostitutes. But he told me a little bit about the history and what they represent. When I knew we were coming to Kyoto, I made a couple calls."

As they made their way in the traditional building, Melissa looked at Michael and realized that her attraction to him was growing by the hour. What an amazing adventure this trip was turning out to be.

~

An hour later, Melissa and Michael were enjoying a delectable meal and they were learning about the rich and varied history of the Geisha. It was explained that a girl starts out as an apprentice. First, she is called a "Minerai" and is one who only watches. Once she observes the Geisha for a while, her own training begins, and she is called a "Maiko." This stage can last up to five years. Then, around the age of 20, the Maiko is promoted to a full-fledged Geisha.

~

As the Maiko showed them the traditional dances, Melissa asked the female owner of the establishment, through the translator, "In my culture, dancing and performing for men would be considered demeaning. A lower class than men. But in Japan, it seems to be different. I see there is pride in the Geisha. Why is this?"

The translator answered. "The Geisha hold very high status in our culture. It is a woman-run society, and is a way for a woman to have power, status and money without having to be a wife." She continued, "Just as in the Middle East, women wear burkas out of choice to honor their tradition, Maiko and Geisha are able to choose this as a way to be independent and still honor history and tradition."

As the Maiko poured Michael a cup of tea, the Geisha leaned in close to the translator and said something softly to her. The translator then whispered to Melissa, "It would be our honor to dress you as a Maiko."

Melissa didn't know what to say. She wasn't particularly keen on the idea. On the other hand, she understood that this was a great honor and didn't want to offend the women by saying no. *What the heck,* she thought. *This is an adventure, right?*

"The honor would be mine," Melissa said, as she stood to follow the women out of the room. Michael's eyes showed confusion until Melissa assured him, "We'll be right back. We have a surprise for you."

CHAPTER FOURTEEN: PHOTO FINISH

※

Michael was alone at the table, drinking his tea and trying not to check his cell phone. Melissa had been gone for more than twenty minutes, and he had no idea where she was or what she was doing.

Taking another bite of crab, his mind wandered back to the onsen. Melissa looked so enticing, with her flushed cheeks and those golden curls piled atop her head. When he was standing so close to her in the water, he had been fully aroused. One step closer, and he would have touched her.

Knowing that she had been naked, right next to him, there for the touching was almost too much. Even now, as he sat here waiting for her, he felt himself stirring again.

Enough, Michael. Think of something unsexy. Just then, his phone buzzed. It was his mother.

"Michael. It's your mother."

That worked. "Hi Mom," he said softly. "I know it's you."

"Why are you whispering?"

"I'm in a restaurant."

"Oh, well, I can barely hear you."

Rolling his eyes, he asked, "What can I do for you, Mom? Is everything okay at home?"

"Everything is fine. I just wanted to know if you'll be home in time for your father's birthday. We're having a thing and I wanted to let the caterer know the final count."

"We'll be home in two days."

"We?"

"Yes, I am traveling with a business associate."

"Business associate? What business associate? It's not that Akito fellow is it?"

"Akiro. And, no, Mom. Her name is Melissa Tomson."

"Her? You are traveling with a woman and you didn't tell me?"

Hearing the women walking down the hall, Michael lowered his voice to a true whisper and said, "Look, Mom, I don't have time to get into this. I'll be home in a few days and we can talk then. Bye."

∽

The door to the room slid open, and the Geisha, Maiko and translator walked in. Where was Melissa? Just as he was about to ask, the women parted to either side of the doorway, and Melissa walked in, dressed in full Maiko attire!

Her golden curls had been sprayed black and pinned up elegantly with a flowered hairpin, that trailed down one side. Her face was covered in white makeup, and elaborate dark makeup adorned her eyes and eyebrows, making her look Japanese. The only thing he recognized were her lips. They were filled in with bright red lipstick, but he would know those lips anywhere.

She'd changed into traditional attire, with a sapphire blue kimono that reminded him of the dress she wore last night (was it only last night?) to the club. Her shoes resembled platform shoes.

Taking her cue from the other women, Melissa walked over to Michael, and kneeled by his side. "You are the most beautiful Maiko I have ever seen," Michael said in a low voice.

Smiling, she said, "Thank you. May I pour you some tea?"

The sight of her, kneeling before him, pouring his tea, made Michael's heart expand. This strong, independent, single Mom had transformed herself like this. She was not subservient in any way, but instead radiated a feminine power that attracted him like a moth to a flame.

As she stood to dance for him, following the guidance of the other women, Michael realized one thing. He was falling in love with Melissa Tomson.

~

Two hours later, they were on their way back to the Kurama Onsen hotel. Ricky Ito was singing along to his own music, and Melissa was back to her natural blonde state. They were talking about the evening, when Melissa's phone rang.

"It's my daughter. She wants to Facetime. Do you mind? She is very particular about keeping to a schedule."

"No problem at all. I have some friends who have an autistic son, and I know how important familiar routines are. Go ahead, take the call."

Melissa tapped the button on her phone, and a girl came on screen that was the spitting image of Melissa. It's as if Michael were looking back in time at Melissa as a child.

"Hi Mama."

"Hi Jellybean. How's my girl?"

"I am doing good. Where are you?"

"I am in a limousine!"

"What's a lemozone?"

"A limousine..." Melissa sounded out the word carefully "is a big pretty car with a driver. I am coming back from a fun dinner where I got dressed up in pretty Japanese clothes. I'll show you the pictures and tell you all about it when I see you."

"Oh, cool. Grandma and I went to the Japanese Garden yesterday. I made a sketch of it. Do you want to see?"

"Of course, honey. Show me your drawings."

Michael could see mini-Melissa flipping through a thick sketchbook.

"This is the strolling pond garden." Jenny pointed to an astonishingly accurate sketch. "The pond doesn't stroll, though. The people do." Melissa laughed at the unintentional joke.

She then flipped a page. The next image looked almost as if he were looking at a photograph. White sand was raked in circles around a circular grass area. Next to it was a perfect rendition of a weeping cherry blossom tree. "She's amazing," Michael whispered to Melissa.

"That is at the flat garden. This is the last one..." she said as she flipped the page, "and is the reflecting pool." Michael could see a still, green pond surrounded by well manicured bushes, the pink flowers of the weeping cherry reflecting off the water's surface.

"That is beautiful, honey. You did all that last night?"

Melissa's mother appeared on screen, and Michael once again felt as if he were looking into a time machine - this time going into the future. Diane looked exactly like he imagined Melissa would look in about twenty five years. Her gold hair had a bit of gray at the temple, but she had the same dimples and straight nose that Melissa and Jenny had. Clearly the genes were strong in this family.

"Yes, she worked feverishly from the time we got home

from the garden until I made her go to bed. Then, right after breakfast, she did the last one. I had no idea she had such talent!"

Melissa warmed at her mother's compliment. "Jenny's counselor told us that sometimes people who are on the spectrum have an extraordinary talent for something like math, or music, or art. Jenny is able to recreate places that she's been to with mathematically precise accuracy."

Jenny came back on screen. "We have to go, Mama. It's 9:03, and we are three minutes late to go to the market. Grandma said we can bake cookies this afternoon."

"All right, Jellybean. I'll talk to you tomorrow."

"You are coming home in two days, right?"

"Yes. I am going to take some photographs tomorrow and then the next day we will fly home. I can't wait to see you."

"I love you, Mama."

"I love you too, Jellybean."

∼

As the car came to a stop, and Ricky Ito got out to open their doors, Michael couldn't stop thinking about Jenny and her drawings. *There has to be some way to capture her incredible talent. I will figure out something...* he thought.

CHAPTER FIFTEEN: CHERRIES AREN'T THE ONLY THINGS THAT BLOSSOM IN JAPAN

Michael and Melissa walked into their room at the Hotel Kurama Onsen, and although it was late, the table was set with a light meal. As they kneeled on the tatami mat, sipping tea and cherry wine, and drinking miso soup, they reflected on the day and how the dynamics between men and women were so different here than at home.

"Always before when I thought of gender relations in Eastern cultures, I thought of them as sexist," Melissa said as she sipped her wine. "But in the time I've been here, I have grown to see a grace and beauty in the difference between men and women."

"I know what you mean. I grew up in California, and although my mother was a stay at home Mom, she was always a feminist. I was raised to see women as equal to men. So, when I came here, I wasn't sure how to take the differences between men and women. Like you, I saw it as sexist."

"But there is a difference between something being different and being unequal," Melissa added. "Jenny is different because she is autistic. But does that make her 'less than' other people? I don't think so."

"Right. Just as we learned that many Geishas are placed on that path as young girls, Jenny didn't choose her path. It's a bit arrogant of people to think that just because someone is different than they are, that there is anything wrong with them."

"Exactly!" Melissa said passionately. "Geishas have more power than many other women in this society. Many people in our culture don't see that people on the autism spectrum have value and, yes, power. They are seen as 'disabled'."

Taking a deep breath, Melissa could tell that the wine and fatigue were going to her head. Between the train ride, the onsen, the dinner with the Geishas and now this deep conversation with Michael, Melissa's head was spinning.

"I will be right back. I need to use the little girls' room." She giggled a bit at the use of the diminutive term when they were just talking about female empowerment.

∾

Melissa took a little longer than usual in the restroom, as she was experimenting with the bidet feature on the unusual toilet. The warm spray felt good, and she couldn't help but think of the handsome man sitting there wearing, probably, nothing under his robe.

"This is moving pretty fast, Melissa," she said to herself in the mirror. "You better slow this bullet train down, or somebody's going to get hurt."

"What did you say?" Michael called from the other room.

"Nothing," she smiled. "But I am really tired, and I want to be fresh for our photo shoot tomorrow. Sakura and Ricky Ito are going to be here really early. I think I'm going to hit the mat." She giggled again at her own joke.

Michael stood up and walked to her. "Okay."

Melissa looked up at him, and their eyes locked. They stood there, facing each other, in their matching hotel robes, looking into each other's eyes, as time stopped. She took a deep breath as if to steel herself from the passion that was rising.

"I had an incredible day with you today, Melissa. You're an extraordinary woman." He reached out and touched her hair.

"I…" She wanted to tell him that she had enjoyed the day too. But the words wouldn't form.

He leaned down, slowly moving his face toward hers. She closed her eyes and could sense his lips right near hers. He was waiting. Waiting for her to give him a sign that it was okay.

Her eyes fluttered open, and she smiled slightly. That was all the sign he needed, and his lips gently touched hers, as softly as a butterfly landing on a branch. A second kiss, just as gentle as the first, and then he pulled back. "Oyasumi utsukushī."

She didn't know what he said, but she didn't need to understand. His kiss had told her everything she needed to know.

∼

"Good morning." Sakura was standing next to Ricky Ito outside the car. He leaped to get their luggage. "Again, I am sorry about the misunderstanding with the rooms. I hope there was not a problem." Sakura looked sincerely upset.

Melissa smiled and gave the woman a small hug. "It was actually great. Michael and I stayed up very late talking about Japanese culture."

"Speaking of culture, we'd better get going. We have quite a few stops today on our photo tour," Ricky Ito said.

Melissa had her digital camera bag, along with her tripod and various other items to capture the beauty and drama of the city of Kyoto. Although the photos were only intended to be used as source images for the design of the hotel, it was likely that the images would adorn the walls of the hotel once completed. This was a once in a lifetime chance to get these shots, and she was eager for the challenge.

∽

The day went by in a blur. Their first stop was the Arashiyama Bamboo Forest, with trees that seemed to reach to the sky. She captured the Golden Pavilion as reflected by the koi pond that surrounded it. They lingered on the Path of Philosophy and placed wishes on the Yasui Kompira-gu Shrine. They then stopped at several temples, where Melissa got incredible photos that would be easy to recreate in Michael's hotel.

The whole day had also been filled with a delicious sexual tension between Melissa and Michael. Lingering looks, "accidental" touches, and sitting in the back of the car with their thighs pressed together added an enhanced sense of delight to the sights they shared together.

As they headed back to the train station to take the bullet train back to Tokyo, Melissa kept stealing glances at Michael. *I don't know where this whole thing is going, but I haven't felt like this in years...*

CHAPTER SIXTEEN: KANPAI

It was their last night in Tokyo, and while Michael was eager to get back home and see his dog Sam and his parents, part of him didn't want the trip to end. He felt so close to Melissa, and this trip had far surpassed his wildest dreams. Memories of her storming out of Club Chick, serving him tea as a Maiko, looking so sensuous with her flushed cheeks in the onsen, and that kiss... Oh man, that kiss.

Michael had refrained from kissing her during their Kyoto photoshoot. As much as he'd wanted to taste more of her, he also wanted to honor the fact that he'd invited her here on business. Allowing her to focus on her work was a mark of respect. Keeping his hands off her had been a challenge, to say the least, but it was something he felt was very important.

His cellphone rang, and the caller ID told him it was Sakura. "Mr. Michael, all of tonight's arrangements are in place. I have 'phoned your associates and they will be meeting you at the Shinjuku Golden-Gai at 8:00."

Before they boarded his plane tomorrow to head home,

Michael wanted to show Melissa some traditional Japanese nightlife. So, he'd had Sakura call some of his friends from when he lived in Tokyo to meet them for a night of drinking and karaoke at the "golden quarter" of the most popular nightlife district in town.

"You did not call Mr. Akiro, is that correct?" He didn't want to risk any problems with Melissa, and so he'd told Sakura not to invite him.

"That is right, sir. He was not called."

"Thank you very much, Sakura. One other thing. Since this is our last night in Tokyo, may I invite you to join us?"

"I would appreciate that very much, Mr. Michael. I will see you both at 8:00."

∽

Michael had texted Melissa that he would meet her in the lobby bar unless she wanted him to come by her room on the way down. She'd responded that she was Facetiming her Mom and Jenny and would be down shortly.

As Michael sipped on his Sapporo, he reflected that he hadn't been this excited for an evening out in years. His life had become a revolving door of work projects, and he was finding truth in the adage that "all work and no play makes Jack a very dull boy".

Lost in thought, he was startled by a delicate hand on his shoulder. Turning around, he was once again taken aback by Melissa's beauty.

"Hey," she said with a smile.

"Oh hey!" He swiveled and got off the bar stool to give her a quick embrace. "If it isn't Mel Tomson - the beautiful woman with a man's name. You look amazing."

Fluffing her golden curls and smiling, she said, "Why, thank you!"

She was dressed perfectly for a night on the town. Dark blue jeans were tucked into knee-high chocolate brown boots. She was wearing a Hard Rock Cafe Tokyo shirt, and a denim jacket.

Pulling the shirt out for him to see, "You like my shirt? I got it at the gift shop when I was getting some things for my Mom and Jenny. I doubt we're going to such a touristy place, but I really liked the shirt."

"It looks perfect on you." *She fills it out perfectly, is more like it*, he thought.

"Do you want a drink here, or…?" he asked, as he lifted his bottle.

"No, we can go. I have to keep an eye on how much I drink these days. I'm a responsible mother, now!"

Michael smiled at her. "Yes, you are. But for tonight, you can let your hair down a bit. So to speak. I will take care of you and make sure nothing happens. You can trust me."

Grinning flirtatiously at him, she winked and said, "I'm not so sure about that, Mr. Davis. I suspect you might be another thing I need to keep an eye on."

∼

Their Uber dropped them off at the Golden Gai district. Although the whole thing spanned just a couple of blocks, it was the best place to get away from the more touristy establishments in Tokyo. Melissa seemed curious to see the long alleyways with tiny doors that led to small bars that could only hold between five and thirty people. Most of the signs were in Japanese, and many of the places only welcomed regulars.

They had a few minutes before the others showed up, so the first place Michael took Melissa was Albatross. Grabbing a couple of beers at the bar, they headed up to the rooftop terrace so that Melissa could see the city lights of Tokyo.

Standing there, with his arm around her, sipping the frosty liquid, and looking out at the twinkling lights of one of the busiest cities on earth, Michael couldn't remember ever feeling more "at home". It wasn't the city, per se. It was Melissa. He knew in his heart that wherever she was, was where he would feel at home.

∽

"A yen for your thoughts," she said, grinning up at him.

Not wanting to betray his thoughts, he said, "Just admiring the city lights."

"This has been an amazing trip, Michael. I can't thank you enough."

"I'm just glad you agreed to come." At that moment, his phone buzzed. "The others are here. Let's finish these drinks and head down to meet them."

Draining their glasses and setting them on the bar, the duo headed back out to the street.

Waiting for them were four people. Michael introduced everyone.

"Mel Tomson. These are my friends, Emiko and Tomo. We lived in the same building when I first moved to Tokyo."

"You mean you lived in the apartment below us and had to hear our stomping around," Tomo said, as he embraced his friend. "I swear he must have thought we were river dancers."

Emiko bowed slightly to Melissa. "Nice to meet you, Mel."

"And this here is my friend Kenji. He was another expat like myself. Originally from Australia, his Japanese Dad brought Kenji and his sister here when they were, what, teenagers?

"I was seventeen. And none too happy about leaving my

mates. But a couple of years later I met old Michael here, and suddenly I wasn't as homesick anymore."

"Good to meet you, Kenji." Melissa nodded.

"And this is Kenji's wife, Liz."

Liz hadn't lost one bit of her thick Cockney accent, despite having left England almost ten years ago. "Nice o' mee' ya."

Kenji laughed as he said, "I was up a gum tree when I brought an Englishwoman home to mi parents."

Liz playfully punched her husband, "Give ova'. Your muvva loves me."

"Where is Sakura?" Melissa asked, looking around. "She's usually the first one anywhere."

"I am here, Miss Melissa." Sakura stepped out from a shadow, as a car drove off.

Michael couldn't believe his eyes. Gone were the sensible shoes and the iPad. The floral dress had been replaced with leather pants and stiletto shoes. Her normally straight glossy hair was curled, and her dramatic makeup made her look like a completely different person.

Even Melissa had a shocked expression on her face. "Sakura? Wow. You look… wow."

Michael gave her a courteous embrace and said, "Since we are out as friends tonight, please call us Michael and Melissa."

"Okay, I will." Gesturing to a very nervous looking man at her side, "This is my husband, Nobo."

"Nice to meet you, sir." He bowed.

"Now, now. None of this sir or miss business tonight. Let's get this party started!"

The six companions walked down the narrow, lantern-lined street, arm in arm. The street glistened from an earlier Spring shower, and the night was comfortable.

Three hours and many, many beers later, Michael and Melissa found themselves standing on a narrow stage in front of a red and black patterned curtain. They were each holding a microphone, as their friends cheered them on.

The music began, and Michael leaned over to her and shouted over the crowd. "This is my Dad's favorite song. He played it all the time when I was growing up."

"Seriously?? Sweet Melissa by the Allman Brothers is your Dad's favorite song? My Mom told me that the reason they named me that was because I was conceived to that song!"

Looking over at Melissa, glowing and happy, and singing horribly off-key, Michael wished he could just freeze time. It might have been the alcohol or the company of his friends. More likely it was the way he felt about Melissa. But whatever it was, Michael was happier than he might have ever been in his life.

As the song ended, Michael spun Melissa around, and she landed in his arms, facing him. Kissing her in front of the cheering crowd, Michael whispered, "You are my Sweet Melissa…"

CHAPTER SEVENTEEN: MILE HIGH

"Nice to see you again, Ma'am." Richard took Melissa's carry-on bag as she climbed the steps into the jet.

"Thank you."

Melissa felt horrible. They had stayed out far too late last night and drank far, far too much alcohol. What started out as beers became whiskey straight up, and then…if memory served her correctly, sake-bombs.

After they'd gotten hoarse from karaoke, the group headed over to a pachinko parlor. These loud, smoke-filled establishments looked as if a kid's party had a baby with a Vegas casino. Rows of machines, sort of like pinball, were decorated with bright pastel colors and cartoon characters. But the gambling was very real and rather addictive. Michael lived up to his promise to take care of her, by pulling her away from the machines when she started to take out her debit card to keep playing after they'd lost five thousand yen.

This morning, she was grateful he'd stopped her, as fifty dollars is a sufficient amount to lose in a drunken parlor game. Her cracking headache and queasy stomach were a reminder of both the drink and the fact that they'd stayed out past 5 am. This was largely because she'd insisted that they get some ramen. It was the stuff of drunk people around the world, she reasoned. And so they found themselves slurping the salty noodles at a time when most reasonable people were getting ready for work and having cereal.

Now, with only about two hours of sleep behind her, they were boarding Michael's plane to go to Portland. Her plan was to get some shuteye so that she could be fresh when she saw Jenny and her Mom.

"How are you feeling this morning, my dear?" Michael looked bright-eyed as he grinned at her. *Why does he look so good this morning,* she wondered?

"I feel like a college student the last night of spring break."

"I'm glad you had fun. You needed to let loose, a little, I think."

"Thanks for getting me back to the hotel. After the ramen, everything is a little blurry. Did we say goodbye to Sakura and her husband?"

Laughing, he said, "Yes, she said that she will send you a friend request on We Chat."

Richard's voice came over the loudspeaker, just a little too loudly for Melissa's comfort. "Okay guys, buckle up. We're headed back to the States."

∾

Seven hours later, the plane was somewhere over the Pacific Ocean. For a moment, Melissa forgot where she was as she lay there on a comfortable mattress, eyes closed, waking up to the white noise sound of the airplane engine. Slowly, memories of the trip bubbled into consciousness. Interwoven with every experience she'd had was a dawning realization that Michael was not the man she'd thought he was when she first met him. At every turn, he had shown himself to be a man of character. He defended her when needed, complimented her, supported her and protected her. There was not one hint of the spoiled playboy that he seemed to be after that one-night-stand where he never called.

One thing that Melissa had learned in her life was that, for her, a man's character was his sexiest trait. It didn't matter if a guy looked like he should be on a shirtless calendar. If he was a jerk, he was unattractive to her. What mattered to her more was what kind of a person he was. Michael Davis had shown himself to be a man of character. And, Melissa found herself wondering if the feelings she had for him were deeper than physical attraction.

Not that there is anything wrong with him physically, she thought, still laying in his bed with her eyes closed. Those hands… and lips… and long legs. His eyes and they way they clouded over with desire for her. Melissa began to feel warmth between her legs as she thought of his body.

As if he read her thoughts, the door to the airplane's bedroom opened. Melissa's eyes fluttered open, and she saw Michael just leaning up against the doorway, looking at her.

"Mmmm… hi." Melissa stretched like a cat. "Where are we?"

"A couple of hours out from Portland." His voice sounded deeper than usual. Husky.

"I see."

Michael took a few steps toward the bed. Their eyes met, and she could see in his eyes the one thing she needed to see. She could see that he loved her. Melissa took a deep breath, and exhaled, releasing the last remnants of doubt, and said, "Come here."

A slight smile curved his lips, and his long legs only needed a few steps before he was at the edge of the bed. Melissa was still laying down, so she moved over to make room for him. Laying beside him, she was glad that they were both clear-headed. She wanted to experience every moment of their union, and not waste it with hazy, alcohol-induced rushing.

Wordlessly, Michael reached out and stroked her hair. Tucking her curls behind her ear, his finger traced her jawline. His touch felt electric, and she felt energy travel through her entire body with just this one gesture.

Moving closer, he leaned in to kiss her. Gently, at first. Their lips touched, softly. Then, as the passion built, the kisses became more fervent. The tip of his tongue darted into her mouth, and she opened her lips in an invitation for him to go farther.

His wide palm traced its way down to her breast, and he cupped and lifted it. When his thumb traced her nipple through her lacy bra, her nipple stood erect, as if it wanted every ounce of his attention.

Suddenly, he swung his body over, straddling her lower legs, as he towered over her. Tugging his shirt over his head, Melissa took a sharp breath at the sight of his muscular chest, arms and an enviable six-pack of abs trailing down to the waistband of his jeans.

Leaning over her, Michael kissed Melissa again, deeply. She arched her back, and he expertly unclasped her bra, and her shirt was off before she knew it.

Bowing his head reverently to cup each breast, Michael kissed them. Flicking each nipple with his tongue before closing his mouth around it, Melissa began to writhe in pleasure.

"Oh, you like that, do you?" he said softly.

His hand found its way to her waistband and unbuttoned

her pants. She knew that he would soon discover how much she wanted him.

"Oh... you *do* like that," he noted as his finger slipped into the wetness of her. Rubbing her secret spot with one finger as the others slipped inside, Michael didn't even need to ask, "How about this?"

Melissa lost all sense of anything other than Michael's hand as it moved rhythmically. Her hips began to move with him, and she could feel her climax rising. Then, his hand stopped moving.

Melissa opened her eyes to see Michael grinning. Slowly, he swung off of her and stood by the bed. *Where is he going?* she wondered.

Michael unbuttoned his jeans and lowered them. Melissa felt a spasm of pleasure as she saw what awaited her. He was fully aroused. *I am going to come all over him*, she thought with pleasure.

Removing the last of her own clothing, Melissa lay back, wet and wanting him. Michael came back on top, between her legs, and kissed her.

She was so ready for him that, despite his impressive size, he slid right in. He filled her completely, and the sensation turned her on so much that she involuntarily began thrusting her hips to bring him deeper. "Oh! Oh, Michael!"

Michael barely needed to move. His strength and presence met her as she moved beneath him, to her own pleasure.

The white heat began between her legs and curled up through her abdomen as she began to climax. It rose through her chest and expanded out through every cell in her body. Raising her knees to bring him deep into her core, and grabbing his back to press him against her, Melissa screamed in pleasure as her climax overtook them both.

Just when she thought it was over, Michael began thrusting with his own passion, and he threw his head back, flooding her with his warmth, causing her own pleasure to crest again.

For a few moments, they stayed like that - locked in a lover's embrace. Neither of them wanted the feeling to end. It was powerful.

CHAPTER EIGHTEEN: PUN AND GAMES

Melissa was grinning at him and sipping from a water bottle. They were about to land in Portland, and neither of them could stop smiling. She kept making silly puns.

"Now, that's what I call 'coming in for a landing.'"

He smiled and shook his head.

"It gives the term 'up in the air' in a whole new meaning."

He was about to break out laughing when she added, "I guess we're a member of the Mile High Club now. Do you think we get membership points if we do it again?"

Michael roared. "Good lord. Is this what you're like?" He could not be happier. "You must be looking forward to seeing Jenny."

"I am," she said. "This is the longest we have ever been apart."

"That reminds me, I was thinking and had an idea I wanted to run by you."

Eyeing him with surprise, she said, "Okay, shoot."

"I was thinking about Jenny and her incredible talent for drawing. I thought it might be cool to ask Jenny to draw a terrace for the hotel, and I'll get Ryan to draw up the architectural plans, and we'll build it."

Melissa looked taken aback. "Wow."

"Think about it. Not only would it be a beautiful space, but it would help to dispel some of the stereotypes about people on the spectrum.

Melissa had tears in her eyes. "That would be... I can't even find the words... thank you. Yes. Jenny will love the idea."

"You, speechless? Somebody better call Houston, because we definitely have a problem."

The goodbye at the airport was difficult but made easier by the fact that he would be seeing her the next day at his parents' house for Mike Sr.'s birthday. "I would love for you and Jenny to come," he'd said. After convincing her that it would be fine with his family, he sent her off in his car with a kiss and a promise to call ("no, really, I will"), and then he walked back to where his Tesla was parked.

∽

Even though his car was practically silent as it rolled into the driveway, Michael's dog Sam must have sensed that her owner was home, because he could hear her barking as he turned the car off. She practically danced out the front door, as Brad opened it to greet his boss.

"Welcome back. Somebody missed you," he said, nodding at the dog as she was running in circles around Michael.

"Hey, girl. How's my Sammie?" Michael reached down to pet her, as she was sniffing him to find out where he'd been. "I have returned from the land of your people. Let's go inside. I brought you a present."

"Did you bring one for me?" Brad said, playfully.

"Yes. I brought your boss back home so you can go back

BETROTHED TO YOU

to your own house." Michael smiled as he slung his bag over his shoulder and headed in the frosted glass front door.

The men walked in, and Michael gave Sam a bone he'd brought back from a Japanese market. "Here you are, Sammie girl."

As Sam ran off with her meaty treat, Brad followed Michael into his office. "Your mail is in the usual place," he said, gesturing to the bookshelf. "Your Mom called me several times when she couldn't get hold of you." Michael rolled his eyes at that.

"Also, somebody named Takeo Nizuma called on the office line several times. He wouldn't say what it was about. Just that he was with the Mizuki Financial Group."

Michael frowned. "Don't know who that is. I'll call him back tomorrow."

"The only other thing is that you got a voicemail from Andrew. He tried to call you when you were on the plane, but your voicemail is full. Janet had the baby last night. It's a girl. You won't believe what they named her."

Grinning, Michael could only wonder what his friends would name their baby. "What?"

"Bebe."

"Bebe?"

"Yes. Bebe Situ."

Michael burst out laughing. Andrew and Janet had named their daughter after the name that group of friends had taken on - the BBC 2.

"Wow. Well, let's send some flowers to Janet and a toy basket to little Bebe." Shaking his head as he went upstairs to unpack, Michael wondered, "What's next? A son named Bill Yunaire?"

CHAPTER NINETEEN: SURPRISE PARTY

"Mama!" Jenny ran out to the limousine as soon as it pulled in the driveway of Diane's townhome.

"Jellybean!" Melissa's eyes spiked with tears as she embraced her daughter. Smelling her hair, and wrapping her arms tightly around Jenny, she whispered, "I missed you *so* much."

Looking at the long black car, Jenny said, "Is this a lemonzine?"

"Yes, honey. This is a *limousine*."

The driver was setting Melissa's luggage down on the porch, and said, "I'll be back for you tomorrow at five?"

"Thank you, Edward."

Diane had been standing at the door and gave her daughter a warm hug as they walked into the kitchen. "You look amazing, honey. You're practically glowing. Did you have a seaweed treatment or something?"

Blushing a little, Melissa answered, "Uh, it was probably the hot springs. Those minerals are good for your skin."

With a knowing smile, Diane just smiled and opened the fridge to get them all waters. "If you say so."

"Mama, do you want to see my sketches? I made some more of the gardens."

"I do, but I also wanted to talk to you about something. Let's go sit down on the couch."

"Okay, let me get my sketchbook." Jenny ran upstairs to grab it, and Diane and Melissa headed for the living room.

"Is everything okay?" Diane looked a bit concerned.

"Oh, yeah, Mom. This is good news, I promise."

Jenny came down the stairs with the leather-bound sketchbook in hand. She sat down on the couch between her mother and grandmother.

"I have a friend whose name is Michael. He is the one I went on this business trip with," Melissa began. "He is building a hotel right near the Japanese Garden that you and grandma went to. He saw some of your drawings when you were showing them to me on Facetime."

Diane looked surprised.

"Anyway, he thought they were really good and was wondering if you would like to draw a picture of a terrace that he would build into the hotel."

"What's a terrace?"

"A terrace is like a patio garden. Where people go to sit and relax and enjoy the outdoors."

"Can we make it an indoor terrace, so that people can still use it when it's raining? Grandma says it rains a lot here."

" I think you can draw any kind of terrace you want and we can ask Michael about how to build it."

Diane's hands flew to her mouth in happy surprise. "Melissa! Are you serious? That is incredible."

Melissa flushed. "Isn't it?"

Jenny was so excited, she squealed. "Yes! I will start drawing right now." She grabbed her sketchbook and started toward the stairs. "I will show you my other drawings later, Mama. I have a *terrace* to design now."

∼

At 5:00 pm sharp the next day, the limousine pulled up outside of Diane's townhome. "He's here" she called upstairs to Melissa and Jenny.

The two females came downstairs, carrying raincoats and umbrellas, but dressed for a party. "Are you sure you don't want to come, Mom? Michael specifically invited you, too."

Walking them to the door, sipping on a cup of coffee, Diane said, "No, honey. I just want to sit by the fire and read some more of the latest romance novel I'm working on."

Realizing that her mother probably needed some peace and quiet after entertaining her granddaughter for a week, Melissa kissed her on the cheek and said, "Okay, no worries. Just stay away from delivery boys named Fabio."

"Romance novels aren't like that anymore, my dear." The women embraced, and Melissa and Jenny climbed through the car door that Edward was holding open for them.

Fifteen minutes later, the car turned onto Champlaign drive in the swanky neighborhood of Arlington Heights. Rows of million-dollar homes lined the street, and as they approached Michael's parents' house, there were all kinds of cars gathered around a two-story contemporary home. The garage door looked like a window in an Asian hotel, with opaque glass panels surrounded by black wood frames.The pattern was continued to the front door, which had slate tiles leading up to it.

"We have arrived, Ma'am," Edward said, as he went to open the door for them.

"This is a pretty house, Mama. Will I get to meet your friend Michael?"

"Yes, sweetheart, this is a birthday party for his father, Mike."

"Did we bring a present?"

Pulling a silver wrapped box out of her purse, Melissa showed Jenny and said, "We sure did. It's a framed picture of Michael that I took of him in Japan."

"He will like that very much, Mama."

They were both a little nervous walking into a house full of strangers. The house was as stunning on the inside as it was on the outside, with pale maple floors and white cabinets. Modern art adorned the walls, and over the glass stone fireplace was a huge painting of a woman with long raven-colored hair, piercing black eyes who was wearing a crimson gown and posing on a settee.

"Mama, look at the woman in that painting," Jenny whispered. "Her eyes follow us around the room."

Over by a sleek marble bar, Melissa spied Michael talking with some people their age. Her heart fluttered a bit, as he turned and saw her. He was wearing a pale blue collared shirt that matched his eye color exactly, and his muscular legs filled out the denim jeans he wore. Michael's face lit up, and he excused himself from the group and went over to them.

"You must be Jenny." He extended his hand for a formal handshake. "It is very nice to meet you."

Jenny giggled a bit as she shook his hand. "It is very nice to meet you, too, Mr. Davis."

Michael leaned over and whispered to her, "Please call me Michael. Every time I hear the name Mr. Davis I look around for my Dad."

"Where is the birthday boy?" Melissa asked, looking around.

Kissing her cheek, Michael whispered in her ear, "You look ravishing. How about we take a little plane ride?"

Just then, a voice that sounded just like Michael's boomed from the other side of the room. "There you are!" A tall man, with slightly thinning blonde hair that was white around his temples strode over to them. His legs were as long as his son's, and Melissa could see from his trim build that he had once been muscular and athletic. His eyes were the same piercing blue as Michael's.

"You must be this Melissa I have been hearing about." He gave her a quick hug. "I hope my son kept you out of trouble in Tokyo. That can be a pretty wild city."

"Nice to meet you, sir."

"Sir? Please. Call me Mike."

She smiled broadly and said, "Well, then, it's nice to meet you, Mike. This is my daughter Jenny."

Kneeling down to her level, Mike said, "So, you're the artist, are you?"

Blushing at the attention, Jenny answered, "Well, I'm not a *professional* artist. I'm only eleven years old."

"Well, Jenny, from what I've heard, you have a bright future ahead of you." Mike stood up and turned to Melissa. "Michael told me about Jenny and the terrace. I think it's a great idea!"

Melissa warmed at the compliment to her daughter and looked at Michael. "It's really so thoughtful of him." She then remembered the gift in her purse. "Oh, before I forget, I have something for you." Handing him the silver-wrapped gift, she said, "Happy birthday."

Tearing into the paper like an excited boy, his face lit up with delight when he saw the contents. The silver frame surrounded a photo she had taken of Michael in the middle of the bamboo forest. The photo was black and white, and the sunlight dappled through the trees adding a dramatic effect.

"Melissa, this is gorgeous. I see where Jenny gets her artistic eye from."

"Mama, can I go look at the fish tank?"

"Sure honey, but come right back."

Just then, a woman approached them who was the spitting image of the painting over the fireplace. Except this woman was about twenty years older and not quite as pretty.

"Mother. I'm glad you're here. This is my friend Melissa." Gesturing to the woman, he said. "Melissa, this is my mother, Carol Davis."

Mike held out the photo he'd just been given and said, "Look what Melissa just gave me. Isn't it extraordinary?"

But Carol never took her gaze off of Melissa. After what felt like an eternity, staring at her with those coal black eyes, she finally spoke.

"How was your paid vacation with my son?"

Taken aback, Melissa said, "It was a business trip, and it was lovely, thank you."

Michael interjected. "Melissa is my business associate, Mother."

Carol made a "harumph" sound under her breath and looked Melissa up and down haughtily. "In my day, women who were paid to travel with wealthy men as companions had a very different name than 'business associate'."

"Now, Carol," Mike said, frowning. "This is a party. Let's not start anything."

Glaring at Melissa for another moment, and looking from her to Michael, Carol's face contorted into a fake smile. "Of course, darling. What was I thinking? Let's go see if our *invited* guests need anything."

Michael's eyes were dark with fury as he watched his parents walk into the kitchen. Looking back at Melissa, he said, "I am so sorry. She isn't usually like this."

"What on earth was that about? Did I do something wrong?" Melissa was stunned. She couldn't believe someone could have such an instantly bad opinion of her, let alone Michael's mother.

Michael sighed and rubbed his forehead. "No. She just gets really...protective."

"Whatever it was, it was sure strange." Looking around at the other partygoers, Melissa felt really uncomfortable. "I hope you don't mind, but I think that Jenny and I are going to take off. I don't really want to be here anymore. I'm going to call an Uber and take it home."

Michael's eyes clouded over and his mouth formed an angry grimace. "I am so sorry, Melissa. But I won't ask you to stay where you aren't comfortable. How about I give you guys a ride home, and we can stop for dessert on the way? I'm sure Jenny was really looking forward to cake and ice cream."

Softening a little, Melissa said, "I don't want you to leave your Dad's party on account of me."

Leaning in close to her, Michael whispered, "I don't want to be anywhere other than with you and Jenny. My Dad will understand. We both know how she is."

And, with that, the three of them walked out the front door, piled into Michael's white Tesla, and headed out. "Who wants to go to Farrell's Ice Cream Parlor?" Michael asked. In unison, Melissa and Jenny said, "Meeeeee!"

CHAPTER TWENTY: SUCKER PUNCHED

Michael was sitting at his desk. Sam was sleeping as usual in her bed next to the window, stretching out in a patch of sun that was streaming in. Every time his mind wandered back to the party and how his mother had treated Melissa, a ball of rage began to form in his belly. She'd had a history of being rude to his girlfriends, but it had gone to a new level once the Microsoft deal had gone through and his net worth rose. She treated everyone - especially females - as if they were out to steal his money.

"You must be thinking about your mother. You look like you just drank some spoiled milk." Brad walked into Michael's office, carrying coffee.

Shaking his head and the dark thoughts away, Michael replied, "You know, you don't have to bring me coffee every day."

Nearly setting the cup down on Michael's desk, and then taking it away, Brad said with a flourish, "Oh, okay. Well, if you don't *want* it…"

Michael grinned, and said, "I never said that." Taking the

cup from his friend, he added, "I just don't want to be some sexist boss whose secretary has to make the coffee every day. I know how to make coffee, too."

Plopping himself on the chair next to the bookcase, Brad said dramatically, "Darling, I've had your coffee, and let's just say that if the whole billionaire thing doesn't work out for you, you won't be getting a job at Starbucks. Maybe gas station coffee, though. Besides, it's not sexist if I'm a male secretary."

Michael got out his notepad and picked up his phone to start returning calls. The first was to that Takeo Nizuma person. Dialing the number, he answered on the third ring.

"Kon'nichiwa."

"Yes, hello. This is Michael Davis. You called me while I was away on business?" Michael spoke in Japanese.

"Ah yes, I am calling on behalf of Akiro Nishiyama. This is in reference to the hotel that you and Mr. Nishiyama are building."

"Excuse me? I don't know what you are talking about. Hotel?" Michael was confused. "Akiro Nishiyama is not a partner in the property I am investing in."

"I have loan application here from Mr. Nishiyama in the amount of five-hundred-and-fifty million yen. In it, he states that you are his business partner and that you will be putting up collateral to secure his loan."

"What?" Michael was enraged. "I know nothing about this."

Mr. Nizuma cleared his throat. "I am afraid to say that we are not the first bank that Mr. Nishiyama approached. He was turned down by several other banks before coming to us."

Michael felt as if he had been punched in the gut. His so-called friend was running all over Tokyo lying on loan applications, saying that he and Michael were still business associates and that Michael would provide collateral on a loan that was the equivalent of five million dollars.

"Mr. Nizuma, I am afraid there has been a mistake. Mr. Nishiyama and I are no longer business partners, and I will not be providing collateral security on his loan. Thank you for calling me and alerting me to this matter."

Brad sat there with huge eyes. "Did I hear right? Your friend is trying to use you to get a five million dollar loan?"

Standing up, and angrily stuffing his papers into his satchel, Michael growled, "You definitely heard right. Can you call Richard and see if the jet is fueled up? I need to go back to Tokyo and straighten this out."

∽

"I'm going with you."

Michael was in the Tesla on his way to the airport, talking to his Dad. "Dad, I'm a grown man. I don't need my Daddy to come with me to fight my battles anymore. This isn't Timmy Simpson in the fifth grade."

Chuckling at the memory of the elementary school bully, Mike said, "Good lord. I had completely forgotten about Timmy Simpson. Look, son. I know you don't *need* me to come with you, and that you are perfectly capable of handling your own affairs. But here's the thing. We both know that Japan is a very family-oriented culture. Respect for elders, loyalty and honor are a way of life there; far more than here in the US. It's not that you need your Daddy to protect you. It's about sending a unified message that you don't mess with the Davis family."

Michael paused for a moment, considering what his father was saying.

"Besides. Your mother is gearing up for her annual D.A.R. silent auction, and I want to be as far away as possible. I'm thinking the opposite side of the world might do the trick."

Michael very well remembered his mother and her Daughters of the Revolution activities. She and a whole group of other women who could trace their lineage to the American Revolution organized a silent auction every year to support charities that preserved American history. It was a worthy cause, of course, but Carol took it far too seriously and wouldn't let her husband or son relax until it was over.

"All right, all right. Grab your passport and I'll swing by on my way to the airport. But we have to get going. Richard says there's a storm coming in over the Pacific and we want to avoid it."

"Sounds good, son. I'll meet you outside in fifteen minutes. Oh, and one other thing."

"Yeah, Dad?"

"Let's go show Akiro that you don't mess with a Davis."

CHAPTER TWENTY-ONE: A KEEPER

"Mama, is it time to go yet?"

Melissa was sleeping and she could tell from the darkness in her eyelids that it was most definitely not time to go yet. Moaning and rolling over, burying her head in her pillow she mumbled, "Not yet, Jellybean."

"But, Mama. The clock says 6:17 am. My Hello Kitty alarm went off seventeen minutes ago. That means we need to leave."

Removing the pillow from her head, Melissa turned to look at the clock on her nightstand. It did, indeed, say 6:17 am. "Maybe your Hello Kitty alarm is still set for Texas time. Either way, we don't need to leave for the Oaks Amusement Park for two more hours. Come on in bed next to me, and let's snuggle for a while before we have to get up."

As Jenny crawled in bed next to her, Melissa made room under the covers for her fully-dressed-to-shoes daughter. It was understandable. Jenny had never been to an amusement park before, and she had been talking about this for weeks.

In a whisper, Jenny asked, "Will we go roller skating today?"

"If you want."

"I don't know how to skate."

"That's okay. I haven't been skating in a very, very long time. We can hang on to each other."

"Will there be a lot of strangers there?"

"Yes, I think so. Amusement parks are full of people you don't know. But, there is no reason to be anxious, Jellybean. Everyone is having their own good time. We'll just stay with our friends from the Portland Autism Center and go on rides and no one will bother us."

Ever since Jenny's diagnosis as a toddler, Diane had become involved with the Portland Autism Center. She volunteered there and had become great friends with another woman who had an autistic grandchild. When they realized that Jenny would be in town, Diane and Fern had arranged a field trip to a small amusement park that had been operating since 1905. Melissa had such great memories of going there as a child and was really thankful that her Mom had arranged the trip.

"Will there be lots of noises and sounds?" Jenny was still spooning with Melissa, as they snuggled under the warm comforter.

"Yes, there will be. This will be a good chance to practice some of the calming techniques you learned at Essere. What will you do if you start feeling overwhelmed?"

"I will close my eyes and take five breaths, and imagine that I am riding a horse."

"Very good, honey. I know we will have a great time today. And, if you need to take a break for a while, just come to me and use our family code phrase."

"Okay, Mama. I will come to you and say, 'Elsa is frozen' and we will go someplace quiet.

"Perfect. Now, let's try and close our eyes for a little while until my alarm goes off."

In a soft whisper, Jenny said, "It is 6:24 am. Your alarm will be going off in 36 minutes. Let's close our eyes for 36 minutes."

∼

Melissa, Diane and a very excited Jenny pulled into the parking lot of the Oaks Amusement park at exactly 12:00 pm. Although they had gotten up at 7:00 am, they met with Fern and her grandson Aiden at Denny's for breakfast, and then went to the Portland Autism Center to meet up with the others who were going on the field trip. Everyone was wearing matching t-shirts with the Center logo on it.

"Why is the parking lot so empty? Diane wondered aloud as they pulled her SUV right up next to the front entrance. "I know they are open because I called to confirm weeks ago."

Some of the other families from the field trip were arriving, and the white-shirted people were making their way up to the ticket window.

As they approached, they could see a large white sign on the window that said, "Closed for Private Event."

Melissa's heart sank to her stomach. Jenny and the other kids would be absolutely devastated. For kids on the spectrum, a simple change of plans can trigger some very strong emotions. The idea of thirty disappointed children with autism... definitely not good.

She went up to the window to talk to the girl. "What's going on? We called and asked about this specific date and no one said anything about a private event."

The girl looked at Melissa blankly, and said, with no emotion, "Let me call my supervisor."

The tension level in the group was beginning to rise, as

people were starting to realize the park was closed. *This is about to go very badly*, she thought. *We better come up with a backup plan, and soon.*

"Are you Melissa Tomson?" A middle-aged woman walked through the gated entrance to the park."

"Yes?"

"My name is Vera Vaughn, and I am the Group Ticket Sales manager here at Oaks Amusement Park."

Blinking in confusion, Melissa responded. "It's nice to meet you, Ms. Vaughn. But how did you know my name?"

"A gentleman by the name of Michael Davis called two days ago and reserved the entire park for your group. We didn't know that you weren't aware of this."

Melissa was stunned. "What? Michael rented out the *whole park*? For us?"

"Yes. I'm so sorry for any inconvenience this misunderstanding might have caused," she said, nodding to some very unhappy children. "I hope you will accept our apology, and allow us to offer each child a ten dollar credit in the gift shop."

Diane had overheard the conversation and stepped forward. "Oh, that's not really necessary."

"Mr. Davis was very generous in his rental fee, and it's the least we can do," Vera said.

Melissa was almost too overwhelmed to speak. She couldn't believe Michael would do such an amazing thing for these kids. First, letting Jenny design the terrace, and now this.

As Diane started to head over to Fern to tell her the good news, she put her arm around her daughter and whispered, "That Michael seems like a keeper, if you ask me."

Watching the excited children stream into their very own amusement park, Melissa couldn't help agree. *He is definitely a keeper.*

CHAPTER TWENTY-TWO: FAMILY HONOR

"I can barely hear you." Michael was on his cellphone, and Mike and Richard were talking about last night's Trailblazers game while they were waiting to leave.

"I said, I can't believe you. Renting out the whole park for those kids... I've never seen anything so generous in my life." Melissa's voice was almost drowned out by the happy screams of kids on roller coasters.

With a smile, Michael pressed the phone closer to his ear. "I am so glad everyone is happy and having a good time."

"Oh, they are. Jenny is eating her first corn dog. Actually, she is on her third.."

"Uh oh. Watch out. Next thing you know she'll be entering a corn dog eating contest!"

"Where are you? It sounds like the airport."

"Actually, Dad and I are on the jet."

"The jet?" Melissa sounded shocked. "Where are you going?"

"Tokyo. I was just about to text you when you called."

"Tokyo! We just got back."

"I know. But I got a call from a banker telling me that

Akiro is running all over Tokyo trying to use my name to borrow money."

"How can he do that? Wouldn't you need to cosign?" Melissa was indignant on Michael's behalf.

"Yes, but Japan is a culture of 'handshake business.' Before the actual business is conducted, verbal agreements based on respect and honor are often made. When Akiro tells people that we are business partners, they are more likely to agree to do business with him before the actual contracts are drawn up. Then, it becomes dishonorable to withdraw from the agreement, and so Akiro can slip in that way. That's what he is counting on, anyway."

"But how can he just walk into a bank and lie and say you are business partners?"

"When we were at Club Chick, I showed him the renderings of the hotel. I didn't realize it at the time, but when I was talking with you, he AirDropped them from my phone into his. So he was showing them to bankers as so-called evidence that we are partners. How else would he have the architectural renderings of my hotel?"

"That is despicable."

"It really is. So, Dad and I are flying over to, well, have a word with him. Then, we'll fly right back."

"I'm sorry he did this to you, Michael. You guys were friends at one point."

"Yeah, well, money can turn friends into enemies. I've learned that lesson the hard way."

~

Nine hours later, the plane was approaching Narita airport. Richard announced over the loudspeaker, "Okay everyone, we'll be on the ground in about ten minutes." The plan was for Richard to refuel, grab a few hours of sleep while Michael and Mike were in the city, and then they'd head right back out before the storm moved in.

"How come there's no co-pilot?" Mike wondered as he was gathering his things. "It seems like it would be easier on trips like this to be able to share the flying duties. Plus, what happens in case of emergency?'

"This kind of plane is designed to be flown by one pilot. And, I don't normally make back to back trips like this. Plus, as you remember, I got my pilot's license when I first started the company because I was flying back and forth from California to Colorado. Technically, I could fly the plane in an emergency."

"I'm not sure I tell you this enough, son, but I am really proud of you. You've gone so far beyond what I accomplished in my own life."

"Thanks, Dad. Let's see if you still feel proud of me after we have our little chat with Akiro."

∼

As they stepped out onto the tarmac, Sakura was there, in front of a waiting car. Her floral dress and sensible shoes were back, along with the ever-present iPad. "Nice to see you again so soon, sir," she said.

"You too, Sakura. This is my father, Mike."

She bowed slightly in greeting. "Nice to meet you, Davis-San."

Sliding into the limo, Michael said to Sakura, "We will only be a few hours. You don't need to wait for us. I'm sure you have other business to attend to."

"No, sir. You are my business. I will be here when you return. Let me know if you need anything for your return flight."

Michael's mood grew darker as the car wound its way through the streets of downtown Tokyo. Looking at his watch, he noted that it was nearly 2:00 pm. Stealing a glance at his Dad, he could see the older man's eyes drooping a bit, despite the nap he'd taken on the plane. A feeling of gratitude washed over him as he thought about all the times his Dad had been there for him. This really was a matter of family honor.

"We have arrived, sir." The car pulled up outside a medium-rise modern building. They could see their reflections in the mirrored windows as the two men emerged from the long black car. Both had changed clothes on the plane and were wearing tailored navy blue suits. Michael had a conservative gray tie, whereas Mike's tie was red. "I want to wear the colors of the good old USA," he'd said.

"I'll pull the car over there, and wait for you," Richard said.

"Thank you," Michael said to the driver. Then, patting his Dad on the shoulder, he said, "Let's do this."

They walked into the building like two characters out of the movie "Men in Black". Brushing by the receptionist, on the way to the elevator, the woman jumped up from behind the desk and scurried behind them. "Excuse me. You must check in at the Welcome Desk."

Ignoring her, Michael pressed the elevator button. The doors slid open as the woman continued, panicked. "Please, sirs. You cannot go there. All visitors must check in at the Welcome Desk."

As the doors closed, they could see her rushing back to her desk, ostensibly to call security. They would be at Akiro's office before she had a chance to make the call.

Their expensive shoes hitting the marble tiles were the

only sounds as the two men strode from the elevator to Akiro Nishiyama's office. Bursting through the glass doors, they had a repeat of what had happened downstairs. "You can't go in there." "Stop!"

But, the men weren't stopping. Walking down the familiar hallways. Michael suspected that Akiro would be in the conference room, having his monthly meeting with his corporate shareholders. "It's right over here, Dad."

Sure enough, he could see his former friend at the head of the glass conference table. Black hair slicked back, Michael wondered how he had ever trusted Akiro. Right now, the sight of him made Michael sick.

Before the women who were following them could catch up, Michael and Mike shoved the conference room doors open.

To say that Akiro was surprised was an understatement. The color drained from his face as he looked from Michael to the businessmen seated around the room. These men were some of the most influential investors in the world. If Akiro lost face in front of them, his business would be effectively over.

Pushing his chair back, Akiro plastered a smile on his face as he said, in English, "Michael! What a wonderful surprise. I didn't know you were still in town."

The men around the table seemed confused as they spoke to each other in low whispers. "What brings you here?" Then, realizing he might not want to hear the answer, he added, "Actually, let's go into my office and we can talk business. I'm sure you gentlemen would be alright if we took a short break?"

Akiro started to head toward the door, but Mike stepped in front, blocking his way.

"I think your business associates should hear this,"

Michael said, as he made his way further in the room. "Akiro, sit down."

Addressing the room, Michael began. "You are all in this room because you are investors in Akiro's company." The men looked at him, some nodding in agreement. "Mr. Nishiyama and I were once business associates as well. However, it has come to my attention that he has been misrepresenting our business partnership to several banks around town in an attempt to obtain a rather significant loan."

Akiro laughed uncomfortably. "Now, Michael. Why would I need to do that? The men in this room represent billions of dollars of assets, and they are investors in this business. What you are saying makes no sense."

"You are right that it would make no sense if your company were doing as well as you have been reporting. But we have come upon some documents that indicate your business is not as profitable as you are claiming." Michael pulled some papers out of his satchel and plopped them on the table.

Akiro began to sputter. "What? Where did you... No, that is not possible."

Michael leaned forward, facing Akiro, with both palms on the glass table, opposite the stack of documents.

"Akiro, you are not the only one who can be underhanded. And you have tried to dishonor me and my family by lying and saying that we are business associates."

Standing to face the room, Michael continued. "These papers show that Akiro has been reporting false profits in this business." The room broke out in shocked murmurs. "Mr. Nishiyama was trying to fraudulently obtain a personal loan using my family name to cover the losses." Every person in the room was looking at Akiro with a mixture of shock and disgust.

Just then, a small older man slowly rose from the back of the room. His voice was as wobbly as his legs, as he said in Japanese, "I have been suspecting this for several months. Thank you, Mr. Davis, for finding the proof." Looking directly at Michael with eyes that watered from age, he said, "My name is Hiroshi Toyoda and I do not want our names to be tarnished from a scandal."

Speaking then to Mike, he said, " I understand the value that honor brings to a family. My family name, Toyoda, has been important in Japan since we started the Toyota auto company. I am disappointed that this company has brought dishonor to the Davis name."

Mike nodded his head solemnly, patriarch to patriarch.

Hiroshi gestured to the room and continued. "I am willing to personally cover the business loss, in exchange for the resignation of our CEO, Akiro Nishiyama." The room broke out in talk.

Michael looked at his Dad and nodded. Leaning close to his former friend so that only he could hear the whisper, he said, "If I ever hear that you have so much as mentioned that you know me, I will make sure you end up in prison for the rest of your life. You got lucky today, Akiro. Take the message, and turn your life around."

CHAPTER TWENTY-THREE: THE FAMILY TREE

"Do you think we should call it a day and head home?" Diane was holding her purse over her head in an unsuccessful attempt to shield herself from the rain.

Melissa was soaking wet herself, as she looked at the small figures running around the Oaks Amusement Park, safely tucked into plastic raincoats offered by the staff. They were having a blast.

Looking up at the menacing skies and increasing wind gusting through the trees, she said, "Let's give it a little while more." Then, looking at her drenched mother, Melissa said, "Actually, Mom, why don't you head home. You don't need to be out here getting wet like this. Jenny and I can take an Uber home."

"No, no, I'm alright."

"Seriously, Mom. Remember what happened last summer when you caught a cold that turned into pneumonia? It's really not necessary for you to stay. Jenny won't mind."

Diane looked unsure. "Well. A cup of tea and a nice fire does sound pretty good right now. And I don't want to be driving if this gets much worse. Okay, honey. I'll take you up on it." Kissing her daughter on the cheek, she said. "Stay safe and don't be long. We don't want you getting sick either."

∽

It was only another hour or so before the winds picked up, and the manager of the park told them that they would need to close. It wasn't safe for the kids to be riding the rides. "Looks like a pretty strong storm," the woman had said. "Get yourselves home and be safe."

Melissa and Jenny were drenched as they stood under the shelter in the parking lot. Melissa had her phone out and was ordering the Uber when she had an idea. All day long, she had been thinking about Michael and their future together. Literally everything was perfect except for one thing. Carol. Melissa couldn't understand why the woman had such an instant dislike of her.

Maybe if I went over there to talk to her, mother to mother, I could change her mind about me. If she could just see that I love her son... Melissa smiled as she heard herself think that. *Yes. I love him. I am in love with Michael Davis.*

Leaning down to Jenny, she said, "Jellybean, we are going to make a quick stop before we go to Grandma's house. I want to talk with Michael's Mom Carol.

"Okay, Mama. How many minutes will we be there?"

"I don't know, honey. Maybe ten?"

"Okay, so we are going to Mrs. Davis' house for ten minutes before we go to Grandma's house?"

"Yes, I think that's all it should take."

∽

"Stay safe in this storm," Melissa said to the Uber driver as she got out of the car. The rain was really coming down and the winds were blowing debris all over the streets. She'd never been in a hurricane, and while this wasn't as strong as one, she shuddered to imagine how much stronger hurricane-force winds would be.

Racing up to the frosted glass front door, Melissa and Jenny rang the bell. In an ideal scenario, Melissa would have left Jenny with Diane. But that wasn't possible today. Melissa just wanted to get in, say her piece and leave.

The door opened and a very confused looking Carol looked at the two drenched females standing on her porch and said, "Melissa, is it? Can I help you?"

Not really wanting to have this conversation while standing in the driving rain on a porch, Melissa asked, "May we come in?"

Not budging from the door, Carol asked, "May I ask what this is about?"

Sighing, Melissa's shoulders slumped. This woman wasn't going to give her an inch. "It's about Michael."

"Michael and his father are on a business trip. I'm not surprised that he didn't tell you."

"He did tell me. Please, can we just come in for a moment?" She gestured at Jenny, whose teeth were chattering from the cold wind.

"All right. But stay off my rugs." Carol led them over to a large picture window that looked out at a garden that was being battered by the wind. Large trees were bent over, flexing in the storm. Not offering them a seat, Carol demanded, "What is this about?"

Jenny was looking up, her eyes going from woman to woman, watching. Melissa realized she needed to be careful as she spoke.

"Mrs. Davis. I think we may have gotten off on the wrong foot."

Carol sneered at Melissa. "No, dear, I don't think we did at all. I know your kind."

Melissa implored, "What do you mean? We just met. How can you know anything about me?"

"Honey, do you think you're the first woman to come sniffing around my son? He has everything a woman could want for a husband. He's a billionaire. He's handsome, like his father. And, he has a heart of gold. That's like shark bait to women like you. He doesn't even see it. His whole life, women have been throwing themselves at him. But I see it. I know what you want." Then, looking at Jenny she added, "Although I will say that the whole 'I have an autistic child' thing is a new twist.

Melissa's blood began to boil. Using her most professional voice, she answered, "Mrs. Davis. I am afraid you are mistaken about me. Jenny's father is - was - a multimillionaire real estate tycoon Rick Tomson. If I wanted money, I could have had millions. I am not interested in your son for his money."

Carol, for once, was rendered speechless.

Melissa continued. "Look. I get it. I'm a mother too. I would do anything to protect my child from harm. But you don't need to protect Michael from me."

"Rick Tomson is your ex-husband?" Carol was still fixated on that.

"Yes. And he left us when Jenny was just a toddler."

"But he's in prison."

"Yes! Because of information I gave the prosecutor. Like I said, I am not the kind of woman you think I am."

"Mama..." Jenny was tugging on Melissa's shirt.

"Just a minute, sweetheart." Melissa knew that the ten minutes were up. "We'll go soon. Look, Mrs. Davis, I love your son. I would never hurt him."

"Mama!" Jenny was tugging harder. "Look!" Jenny was

pointing at the window.

"Jenny! Just a minute!" Looking back at Carol, Melissa continued. "You don't have to believe me or trust what I am saying. But, please at least give me a chance."

Before Carol could respond, there was a loud CRACK and the sound of shattering glass. The first thing Melissa felt was a blast of cold air and rain hitting her face. *What is happening?* she thought in a panic.

Looking around, Melissa realized that a huge tree branch had come crashing through the picture window, shattering glass everywhere.

Rain began to pour in, and Jenny was screaming. But Melissa realized it wasn't Jenny screaming. It was Carol. Her legs were pinned under the tree as she lay on the floor of her dining room. She was laying on her side, grasping for the white rug she'd been so concerned about before.

"Help me! I'm stuck!"

Jenny was standing there frozen in fear, and Melissa said to her, "Jenny, honey, come over here. Let's move the branch together." Jenny looked at her like a deer in headlights. "Jenny, come on. We need to help her."

With that, Jenny sprang into action.

"Okay, Jenny, you grab that end and I'll grab this end and we'll lift the branch up. Then, Carol, you roll out from under it."

"Okay," Carol gasped.

Rain was stinging her face as she said, "One...two...three... PULL."

The best they could do was lift the branch one inch off of Carol's leg.

Panicked, Carol shrieked, "It's not working!"

"Okay, I'll call 911." Grabbing her phone, Melissa hit the button to call 911. "There's no cell service. Where's your landline?"

Carol was beginning to get very pale. "We don't have one. My cell is in the kitchen. See if that works."

Melissa ran to the kitchen and yanked the phone from its charger. *Dammit,* she thought. *Nothing. What do I do?*

Running back to Carol, Melissa could see Jenny sitting in a corner rocking and breathing and counting, her eyes squeezed shut. Carol was struggling to get free.

Going over to Jenny, Melissa kneeled in front of her daughter. "Jellybean. Honey. Look at me. Open your eyes."

Jenny's eyes peeked open.

"Honey, everything is okay. You are okay. You are not going to be hurt. But I need you to do something for me, okay?"

Jenny's eyes were teary and full of fear, but she nodded her head.

Melissa could see Carol watching her, and they made eye contact for a moment. She turned back to Jenny.

"I am going to go find some help for Mrs. Davis. I want you to stay here. I am going to the next door neighbor's house." She looked at Carol for confirmation.

"The Harrisons are the closest. The blue house." Carol's breathing was getting shallow and she was starting to shiver.

"I am going to go call for help and then I will come right back. I need you to be really brave and stay with Mrs. Davis. Can you do that for me?"

"Yes, Mama. I think I can."

Grabbing a blanket from the couch, Melissa made a makeshift shelter for Carol with chairs. "Okay. The Harrisons. Blue house. I'll be right back, Carol. Try and stay calm."

Looking back at her daughter and the mother of the man she loved, seeing the shattered glass and the huge tree limb pinning Carol, Melissa thought, *I can do this. Blue house. Call for help.*

CHAPTER TWENTY-FOUR:
TURBULENCE

Michael and Mike were strapped in their leather seats, having a beer and talking about what had happened with Akiro.

"I never suspected that Toyoda would stand up and offer to pay off the debt," Mike chuckled as he took a swig from his bottle. "Just goes to show you never know."

Richard's voice came over the loudspeaker. "Guys, make sure you're buckled up. We are going to hit some turbulence. There's a pretty intense storm pounding the Portland area right now. We're going to try and go around it, but it's gonna be bumpy for a bit."

Both men tightened their seatbelts and then pulled out their phones to text home.

"Hey, Melissa. I hope you guys made it home from the park before the storm hit. Text me back and let me know you're okay." Michael envisioned Melissa, Jenny, and Diane warming up by the fire.

Leaving a message for his wife, Mike said, "Hey Carol, we're on our way back. Trying to get into Portland but we're diverted due to the storm. I hope you're safe and sound."

Carol may be a pain in the butt, but she was his pain in the butt and he loved her.

The cabin lights flickered as the tiny plane bounced around in the wind currents. Michael was glad that their flight attendant Kathleen had missed this trip. It was starting to feel like one of the roller coasters Melissa had sent him a picture of.

"How are you doing, Dad?"

"I'm good. I've been married to your mother a long time, son. A little hot air doesn't faze me."

Michael laughed. "Speaking of that, I wanted to talk to you."

Mike looked pointedly at his son. "What's up?"

"It's about Mom. She was so rude to Melissa at your party."

Mike frowned a bit and leaned back in his chair. "That she was."

"I really care for Melissa, Dad. I love her."

Mike narrowed his eyes and looked at Michael. "Whoa. I've never heard you say that before."

"I've never felt this way before."

"I see."

"But, I don't know what to do about Mom. She's so overprotective that it scares off every girl who comes around me. I don't want her to chase Melissa away."

"Look, Michael. I don't know if I ever told you this. Grandma Bea was the same way with your Mom at first."

Shocked, Michael said, "She was? But they got along so well!"

"Not at first, they didn't. After my brother - your uncle Bob - was killed in the war, my mother got scared and overprotective of me. She didn't handle it well. And when I started dating your Mom, she did and said all kinds of awful things to chase her off. Remind me to tell you about the time she put an egg in your mother's purse so it would smell and go rotten."

"Grandma Bea did that?" It seemed incomprehensible to Michael that his sweet white-haired grandmother could have ever done something like that.

"She did. But the thing is, your mother didn't react. She just ignored it, kept doing nice things for my mother. Eventually, my Mom just dropped the whole thing. She realized that Carol wasn't going anywhere, that we were in love, and that if she wanted to be a part of her future grandchildren's lives - your life - she better get in line."

"So, you're saying that Mom will come around if we just give it time."

"I'm saying that if this Melissa is the woman you say she is, and if you two love each other, it will work out. I guarantee it."

Michael sighed and looked out the window at the dark clouds. In the distance, he saw a break in the clouds, and a tiny ray of sunlight peered through. *I hope you're right. Dad.*

∾

A few minutes later, Richard came over the loudspeaker again. "Looks like we're through the worst of it. We should be landing in about half an hour."

Mike's phone made a sound, and he took it out to check the text message that had come in. "Shit." He said.

"What's wrong?"

"My next door neighbor Dwayne just texted me. There's been an accident at the house. Your Mom is hurt and they're taking her to the hospital."

∾

It seemed like an eternity until the plane taxied into the gate. Michael and Mike bolted from the plane and raced to the Tesla. "Which hospital?" Michael asked as he buckled himself in.

"St. Vincent's."

Speeding through the streets, swerving to avoid downed trees and branches, the two men were silent, each focusing on their own thoughts. Dwayne hadn't said much in his text, and cell service was still spotty from the storm.

Screeching up to the Emergency Room, Michael parked, and both men ran into the hospital. They hadn't noticed that the rain had stopped.

Mike ran up to the front desk. "Carol Davis. She was brought in here by ambulance?"

The woman behind the glass was moving at a glacial pace. "David?"

"No, Davis."

"Carol Davis?"

"Yes."

"Is that Carol with a C?"

"No, it's Carol with an F." Mike was getting exasperated, so Michael stepped in.

"Carol Davis. C A R O L D A V I S."

"Oh, why didn't you say so? Can I see some ID?"

After showing her their passports, she printed out Visitor Passes. "They are in room 28A"

Pounding on the metal plate that opened the doors, Mike was losing what little patience he had.

∽

Putting his hand on his Dad's shoulder, Michael said. "Dad. Look at me."

The older man paused and looked at his son.

"Whatever is going on in there, Mom needs us to be strong. Calm. Okay? Take a breath before we go in."

Nodding, Mike did as he was told. "Thank you. It's just... your Mom... she's my world." His eyes teared up. "I don't know what I would do if..."

"Let's not think about that now."

∽

Opening the door to room 28A, Michael and Mike were stunned. Carol had her leg up in traction, and who was sitting on the bed with her but Jenny! Carol was holding Jenny's hand and they were looking at Jenny's sketchbook. Melissa was standing next to them, and as soon as she saw Michael she ran into his arms.

"Mike! Michael. You're here!" Carol looked calm and comfortable. "Jenny was just showing me the sketches she was telling me about at the house."

Jenny added in, "Yes. When Mama told me that she was going to go get help and that I needed to help take care of Mrs. Davis, I didn't know what to do, so I started telling her about Essere and the equine therapy center. I showed her how to do the breathing exercises, and how counting can take your mind off of worrying."

Carol hugged Jenny. "This little lady hasn't left my side for one minute, have you?"

"We rode in the ambulance and everything. When they took her in the room to examine her leg, Mama and I sat in the waiting room. But now we are here, and I am showing her my sketches of Essere and the terrace."

"That is really amazing, Jenny. You were so brave." Mike said as he came around to hug Jenny.

"Thank you so much for taking care of my Mom, Jenny."

Carol turned to Mike and said, "I don't know if Michael

told you, but Jenny is some kind of art prodigy. Those sketches... some of them look like photographs. I've never seen anything like it in my life." Handing the book to Mike, she said, "Look at this one."

While Mike was flipping through the pages, Carol said, "Now that everyone is together, I have something I need to say."

All eyes turned to her, as she continued. "As I was in the ambulance on the way here, I realized something. Melissa, I had been doing to you what my mother-in-law Bea did to me. I made assumptions about you and who you were without getting to know you."

She teared up a bit and went on. "I love my son so very much and want him to have a happy life. I want him to have a marriage like Mike and I have." She looked softly at her husband before turning to Melissa.

"Any woman who can raise such an extraordinary child... all by herself... that speaks well of your character, Melissa. I misjudged you, and I hope you can accept my apology."

With tears in her eyes and a throat choked with emotion, Melissa responded. "Thank you so much, Mrs. Davis. I love your son so much. I really do."

∼

Maybe it was the pain medication, or maybe some miracle had occurred. But as he stood there holding Melissa, looking at his mother and Jenny, as Mike was kissing the top of Carol's head, Michael realized his Dad was right. Everything would be okay.

Melissa looked up at Michael. Her hair was a mess and her makeup had been washed off by the rain. She'd never looked more beautiful. "I love you, Michael."

"I love you too, my Sweet Melissa."

EPILOGUE

Ryan Cummings and his new wife Nicole stood in the lobby of the Kazoku Hotel and Garden. "Are you sure you don't want champagne?" Nicole asked him, teasing. "I heard you especially like Dom Perignon." Their wedding had been a simple affair at the ranch in Texas a few months back, and their schedules had been so busy that they hadn't seen Michael or Melissa since.

Cole Bennett and his wife Claudia were munching on the hors-d'oeuvres that were being passed around by tuxedo-uniformed servers. "Mmmm. This shrimp tempura is incredible," Cole said, holding it up for Claudia to taste.

"You like anything that's fried, Cole. It could be fried shoelaces and you'd eat it." Biting into it, her eyes lit up, and she said, "Oh my gosh, you're right." She then took off to find the server and get another sample.

It was the day they had all been waiting for - the grand opening of the hotel. There were probably fifty people mingling in the lobby and garden areas. Some were eating and drinking, others were taking photos of the garden.

In the hotel bar, on stage, was a man singing American

tunes, under a banner that said, "Ricky Ito, Famous Japanese Singer." There were several young, well-dressed females singing along with him, and asking for his autograph.

Beer, whiskey and sake were all flowing, and everyone was having a great time at the Grand Opening.

Just then, a screeching noise echoed across the lobby. "It's mine!" A little redheaded girl was chasing an older boy. "Oba, let me have it!" A woman, holding a baby, announced sternly, "Gouta. Don't run. Oba, give your sister back her doll."

"Is that Bebe?" Claudia and Nicole practically ran up to Janet. "She is so cute!"

Andrew strode up behind his wife, holding a diaper bag. Ryan and Cole just stared at him grinning. "What's in the bag, buddy?"

"Is that where you carry your diamonds?" His friends teased him mercilessly.

"Good on you. No one would ever think to look for them there."

Smacking his friend Ryan upside the head, Andrew brushed past them. "Just you wait. You'll see how cool fatherhood is."

Ryan and Cole looked at each other as if wondering, "Does he know something about our wives that we don't?"

"It's good to be together again, guys." Looking around, Ryan asked, "But, where's Michael? This is his party!"

"Good question. I haven't seen him since I flew in." Ditching the diaper bag behind the bar, the three men went in search of the missing member of the BBC 2.

Mike and Carol (who had recovered from surgery on her leg) were talking to some Japanese businessmen. "Mr. Toyoda, we are so glad you could make it. This is my wife Carol." Mr. Toyoda bowed, and Carol returned the honor.

Seated in the plush couches by the koi pond, Uncle Cal, Aunt Cathy, along with their friends Lucy and Steve were laughing with Diane over something. "And, wouldn't you know, she fell face first into horseshit," Cal said.

"Oh, Sugar, don't be crude," his wife admonished.

"All right, Darlin'. She fell into horse crap. Is that better?"

Lucy and Steve's daughter Andi sat in her wheelchair looking at the colored fountains as the water shot up and came down like a rainforest. She kept looking around the room for her friend, Jenny. Although Jenny and Melissa had moved to Portland after Spring Break, they had come to Texas several times for a visit. Plus, they Facetimed all the time. But Andi was excited to see her best friend in person!

At the front desk, showing the general manager an app on her Ipad, Sakura was gesturing animatedly. Her husband stood next to her, munching on shrimp tempura.

And, Richard, the pilot, stood alone, looking at the photographs Melissa had taken during that day in Kyoto. Their influence on the hotel was evident in every room.

∾

"Where's Michael?" Ryan walked up to Nicole, who was making faces at Bebe.

"I don't know. I haven't seen Melissa either."

Just then, Andi wheeled up and asked, "Is Jenny going to get here soon? I want to show her a picture I took of Essere."

Soon, everyone was looking around for the guests of honor.

"Excuse me." A small, nervous voice spoke over the microphone that Ricky Ito had been singing into. "Excuse me?"

People stopped talking and walked over to listen.

Some microphone feedback squealed through the air. "Um. My name is Jenny Tomson." She was reading from a piece of paper, and her hands were shaking. "I drew the design for the garden terrace." People began to gently applaud.

"It took one-hundred and ninety-two days for this hotel to be built. But today it is open. The name of the hotel, Kazoko, means 'family' in Japanese."

Clearing her throat, she continued. "We would like to invite everyone to the garden terrace now. Follow that hallway," she said pointing to the left, "and at the end, you will see a door that says, 'Zerībīn Garden.'" She smiled and said, "That means 'Jellybean Garden.' That's me. Jellybean. Okay. That's all. Let's go."

∽

Everyone began filing down the hallway toward Zerībīn Garden. As they approached the doors to the garden, the sounds of harp music began to waft out.

The bamboo trees were decorated with lanterns, and there were exotic flowers everywhere. But the most unexpected thing was that there were rows and rows of chairs, facing the huge picture window.

Instinctively, the guests sat in the chairs and waited.

"What the hell's goin' on?" Uncle Cal whispered loudly. "Looks like a damn church."

"Last time I saw this many flowers was when you were in the hospital, Ryan." Andrew elbowed his friend.

As soon as everyone was seated, Richard the pilot, of all people, came to the front of the room. The crowd quieted.

Nodding his head, music began to fill the room. It was a familiar song. One that everyone could recognize.

Wait, they all realized at once. *Isn't that...? Yes, it is. That's the Wedding March! This is a wedding!*

Looks of shock and joy registered on the faces of the

people in the room. Everyone turned as the doors to the garden opened.

Jenny came in first, dropping cherry blossom petals on the ground.

Then, arm in arm, Melissa and Michael entered. He was wearing a black tuxedo and she was wearing a floor length off-white satin gown. Her bouquet was made of red roses. Together, they walked to the front of the room.

Diane and Carol were sitting together and both women were in tears.

Richard spoke. "Surprise!" Everyone laughed. "It's a little-known fact that I am actually an ordained minister. So, let me say what is now probably glaringly obvious to you. We are gathered here today to witness the union of this couple, Michael Davis and Melissa Tomson, as they become man and wife. Jenny, will you join your parents, as you read your family vows?"

Jenny walked up to the front of the room and stood in between Michael and Melissa, holding their hands.

Melissa turned to face Michael, as he took her hand in his. Michael spoke first.

"Ever since the first day I met you, I knew you were special. Very different from anyone I'd ever met before. You are beautiful, of course.."

She looked down humbly and smiled.

"But more than that, you are a woman of substance. You have character and integrity. You're a great Mom and a talented artist."

"Awww.. go on," she said, laughing. "No, really. Go on." The crowd laughed.

"Not to mention silly and funny. Ever since you agreed to be my betrothed, my life has become complete. I am so happy to say these words." He wiped tears from his eyes, as he said, "I, Michael, take you, Melissa as my wife."

Turning to look at the teary, smiling faces of her friends and family, she then began her vow. "Michael, I came into this relationship with a scarred heart. My only experiences with men had been heartbreak from them leaving." She squeezed Jenny's hand. But you showed me what a real man is. What a real partnership is like. You've become a Dad to my daughter, and have filled a hole in my soul that I thought could never be filled. But I stand here today, with you, and all of our friends and family, and say these vows… I, Melissa, take you, Michael to be my husband, to love and to cherish…"

As the happy family walked back down the aisle to the clapping and joyful greetings of their friends and family, the sounds of the song, "Sweet Melissa" began to play.

ABOUT THE AUTHOR

Molly Sloan is a second-generation Irish American who traded her early modeling career for public relations. After 10 years developing business strategy, branding and crisis communication for some of the world's largest companies, she is living her dream of being a writer. "I love the psychological motivation behind the characters and exploring the emotional and intimate sides of relationships," says Molly, "my books are an escape, I hope readers think so too. Every book is a standalone story with a happy ever after ending." Molly lives in Oregon with her hot husband of 20 years and her little black kitty.
Follow her on Facebook at www.facebook.com/mollysloanauthor

and Molly's Amazon Author Central Page